FRIENDS WITH THE MONSTER

ALBANY WALKER

FRIENDS WITH THE MONSTERS

Cover Art By Pixie Cover

Edited By Elemental Editing & Proofreading

Proofread By Tabitha Finch

❀ Created with Vellum

INTRODUCTION

I accepted the monster inside me long ago, kept her fed on the lies that pass your luscious lips, feasted on your gluttony. But my favorite meal is that of wrath. That soul-deep vengeance makes me quiver with anticipation.

I'm a Sin Eater. If there are others like me, I've never met them, but I've met many other monsters—monsters that make you fear the dark, that make what you *think* you know about the obscure shadows lingering under your bed seem like a children's fantasy.

CHAPTER 1

Do you ever lie on your back, gazing up at the stars, wishing you were someone other than who you are? Yeah, me neither.

NIGHT HAS FALLEN. It's my favorite time of the day, when the evening is filled with endless possibilities. I drag the heavy curtain back and open my bedroom to the sky. Tracing my fingers over the mottled glass, I feel the cool air outside pressing in.

I peer out into the darkness and take a deep breath. The heavy, yellow glow of the moon is just beginning to peek out over the top of the tall pine trees in the distance, illuminating the miles between me and civilization. Who, if anyone, will visit me tonight? I brush my palm over the silk fabric covering my abdomen, acknowledging the ache building behind it. If I don't get any company tonight, I'll need to head into town tomorrow to hunt my own meal.

I make quick work of pulling back all of the curtains throughout the rest of the house, making sure to leave off all the lights as I go, since many of my friends prefer the shadows. I closed everything up early this morning—as I do every morning—to block the sun from entering my home.

In the kitchen, I light a few candles and carry them with me to the west parlor, where I begin most of my evenings.

A floorboard creaks, and I freeze. Anticipation makes my breath catch, but it's just the settling of my old house, crooning its worn-out song.

Disappointed, I curl up in a large chair with my candle flickering on the table beside me, casting an eerie glimmer on the walls.

I smile wistfully, remembering the first time a Will-o'-the-wisp visited me. I couldn't have been more than a few years old. I was lying awake in my crib, staring at the shine of a small nightlight my mother had placed in my room.

The first Will-o'-the-wisp was a deep purple, almost dark enough to fool my eyes into believing it was only the nightlight or my imagination creating the dancing ball of light.

But the presence that came with the Will-o'-the-wisp could never have concealed itself from me. Heat uncoiled in my stomach at the acceptance I felt from the tiny creature.

I still remember knowing, at such an early age, I wasn't like my family. I always felt a gnawing hunger aching in my stomach, yet no matter how many bottles of milk or jars of food my mother tried to feed me, I could not eat.

A breeze stirs my long, pale hair, pulling me back to the present. I turn my head to see the source of the chilled air and find nothing but empty space behind me.

A forlorn sigh falls from my lips just as I feel a caress from a rough hand skate over my cheek.

I swallow, and the steady thrum of my heart picks up as I inhale. He's here.

The scent hits me first. It doesn't smell of roasted meats or sweet desserts, but my mouth waters nonetheless.

I can already taste the heady flavor of rage swirling into my center as I drag in a deep breath. A low, appreciative moan unfurls from my chest as the ache in my belly subsides.

"You must eat." My eyes snap open at the demand. He's never spoken to me before. I always know when he's here, but he never allows me to see him.

I spin in my chair, eager to catch a glimpse of the monster that makes me feel full, sated.

Only his presence lingers. "Why won't you stay and visit with me?" I sink back into the chair. My eyes are heavy. I rarely, if ever, sleep at night, but I've just had my first decent meal in what feels like weeks. I may have been pushing myself too long, but I wanted to see my savior, wanted to taste the sins he carries.

Sometimes, I think I feel him watching me, but it's like he's only a ghost of himself, like he's not fully corporeal. Only peering in at me through a window or door, but not any window or door I can open.

"I wish you would stay," I mumble. He's not my only mysterious visitor. I have other companions who hide themselves from me, too, one of whom only comes when I truly am sleeping. He sneaks into my house, leaving me little trinkets to tell me he's been here.

I feel another caress on my cheek. "Soon," he vows, but my eyes are too heavy to open.

I NARROW my gaze at the creature in front of me. My glare should be enough to scare anyone, but the long-limbed shadow in front of me just holds my stare. "Uncle Skinny Legs," I warn.

A rusty, rasping sound comes from him: a laugh, but no words.

"Fine." I toss my cards on the table. "I'm out." His long fingers trail forward and snag the marbles off the tabletop—his winnings. He slowly lifts the baubles up near his face and a grin splits his lips. His razor-sharp teeth are dripping with thick saliva.

"You don't need to gloat." I tuck my arms over my chest and pout.

Uncle clicks his tongue, giving me a censuring look that, even though I can scarcely make out his eyes, I know is there.

I drop my arms and the glower. "Fine, but I'm going to

win next time," I tell him confidently. He pockets the marbles into his chest. I have no idea if he has a coat, or if he absorbs the treasures some other way.

A thump upstairs has me looking at the ceiling. "Who do you think it is?" I ask, almost too eagerly.

Uncle stands. "You're not leaving, are you?" I stand, too, and crane my head back to look up at his considerable height. He's all long limbs. If he turned to the side, he'd barely be visible.

I already know my answer. He never stays long. He's been visiting me almost as long as the Will-o'-the-Wisp have. Skinny Legs isn't really my uncle. I only call him that because I feel a familial bond with him that was always lacking with my family.

Uncle pats his chest over where he placed the marbles and gives me a slight bow before turning and disappearing wherever he came from.

Another thump from upstairs draws my attention. I grab a copper chamberstick that holds a taper candle and move into the long hall so I can go greet my next guest. When I reach the bottom of the stairs, a thrill of awareness skates down my spine. I can taste an essence in the air—agony. It smells of ripe strawberries, delicious and new.

I slink up the wide staircase, making sure to stay quiet as I do. It brings that sweet taste even closer, and my mouth waters. Damn, I must be hungry again. You'd think it would be easy being a Sin Eater, but I devour little lies like licks of a lollipop, yummy, but not at all filling. I don't even really know if that's what I am. With all the monsters I've met, none are like me, and none are sharing if they know others of my kind.

I open my mouth and pull in the tiniest bit of essence to taste. I roll the flavor over my tongue but can't place it, other than the soul-shattering agony. It announces itself like it has its own billboard. There's something achingly familiar yet also unknown to me, about whoever is up here.

Not everyone who visits me is eager to be my friend, so I stand here, as still as a virgin at her first lay, and as silent as a corpse. Well, most corpses anyway. Sometimes they'll talk your ears off.

When another sound alerts me that whoever is here hasn't left, I creep closer to my room, since that's where the noise is coming from.

"Shit," a masculine voice curses. I peer around the door, gauging if the entity will stay. Sometimes I scare the monsters, which is kind of scary if you think about it.

So, I don't think about it.

The sight on my bedroom floor frightens me more than Uncle Skinny Legs or any of the other monsters ever have.

There's a *man* sprawled out on my rug, half leaning against the footboard of my bed, holding his middle like it might spill out if he lets go. If the blood covering his hands and pooling beneath him is any indication, it just might.

Forgetting I have no idea who he is, I rush over to his side, setting the candle beside him and kneeling. "What happened to you?" I ask, pulling the throw off the end of my bed and balling it up to press it against his wounds. I take a second to look him over. His clothes are dark: black pants and what looks like a bulletproof vest over a long-sleeved, black shirt.

"Nothing too serious," he slurs, as he stares at me. I glance down, noticing there's something strange about the way he's looking at me. He's observing me like he knows me.

"It looks pretty serious if you ask me," I scold him and push against his belly. His eyes close on a wince, but he jerks them back open. "Should I call a doctor? How did you even get out here?"

He lets out a shallow cough, covering his mouth. His hand was already bathed with blood, but the crimson liquid on his lips is new when he pulls his hand back, and I don't think it transferred from his fingers.

I move back so I can stand, but he reaches for my wrist, his grip surprisingly firm. "I'm fine. No doctor." He's staring up at me. "I didn't mean to come here. I'm sorry…" His words trail off as his grip loosens on my arm, and his eyes fall closed as he slumps to the side—passed out or dead.

A frantic panic fills me. I have no idea who this man is, but something inside me is rebelling at the thought of anything happening to him.

I brush his long dark hair away from his face, revealing several scars marring his features. He's rugged, but achingly masculine. There's a thick white line through both of his lips, disfiguring his mouth a bit, but it doesn't detract from how handsome he is. He's battle worn, and his scars show just how many conflicts he's survived.

I palm his cheek and his face turns into my hand—not

dead, then. A heavy sigh leaves his parted lips. "I'm still not sure that you don't need a doctor." I worry my bottom lip with my teeth.

With the edge of the blanket, I wipe the blood from his mouth, being careful not to scrape too hard since the scarring there seems almost fresh. No new blood leaks out of his mouth, so I take that as a good sign.

He makes a low groaning sound when I stand up. "I'll be right back," I promise, even though I don't think he can hear me.

Rushing into my bathroom, I flip on the tap for hot water and grab a few towels and washcloths from the closet. I pause when I reach for the bucket in which I usually keep my decorative hand towels. Should I be worried about infection? *I* never get infected or sick, but this man…I shake my head and dump the towels out. I don't have time to worry about that now—I need to stop the bleeding first. He can get antibiotics like a normal human being later.

I cautiously carry the water-filled bucket back to the room with the cloths gripped under my arm. He looks exactly like he did when I left him: his head lolling to the side, his chin slumped on his chest.

Kneeling beside him again, I pull back the throw over his abdomen. It's too dark to see how mangled his stomach is, so I jump up and flick on the lights. My friends won't come with them on, but I'm not sure they would with his presence, anyway.

"Damn," I mutter, my knees slamming into the hardwood

floor as I get my first real glimpse of the damage that's been done to him.

There's bruising forming along his jaw and cheek, and cuts and scrapes on every inch of him I can see, but the three thick slashes across his stomach seem to be the most urgent injuries. Reaching for his heavy black vest, I look at his face even though he's out cold. "I'm going to clean you up. Don't wake up swinging." Under my breath, I add, "I'll bite back if you do."

He makes another sound, but I can't tell if he's trying to argue or if it's just a pained moan. "Okay, here I go." I unclip the first latch on his side and he doesn't stir, so I undo the next and the next, until both sides are open. Now I just need to get it over his head. I hem and haw for a few seconds before deciding the garment has most likely seen its last war, then I run back to the bathroom to grab a pair of scissors. However, the black fabric over his shoulders won't snip. No matter how hard I squeeze the scissors, the fabric just keeps sliding down the blade.

"Damn it." I plant my hands on my hips and glare. "This might hurt," I warn. Cradling his head with one hand, I drag the vest up and pull it over his head. He's putting too much weight against his back, so it takes a little maneuvering to get it out from behind him.

I'm panting with exhaustion when I'm done. The dude is solid and heavy. I wipe my inner arm over my forehead. "You did a good job, buddy. Now we just need to clean you up and stop the bleeding. Sound good?" I know I'm talking to myself, but I'm kind of freaked out.

I reach for the hem of his thin black shirt. When I pull it free from his skin, the blood soaking it makes a slurping sound. "Ewww," slips from my lips when I drag it away.

I shudder but force myself to continue. I reach a roadblock again when the shirt won't stay raised above his chest so I can get to the wounds. "Hope you weren't attached to this—not like it wasn't ruined before anyway," I comment, as I cut the shirt up the middle.

His torso is crisscrossed with scars, old and new, when the fabric splits open. "You must be a busy boy," I mutter, finally grabbing a washcloth and dipping it into the cooling bucket of water.

The water is rusty red when I'm finished. I plop myself on my rear and wipe my brow with the back of my hand, taking in the form before me. Each cleansing stroke of the cloth revealed hard planes of muscle and tawny skin that looks like it sees lots of sun—and possibly even more battles. I glance down at my arms, which are pale in comparison. I rarely venture out in the day, choosing to sleep the daylight hours away. Plus, the evenings are much more suited to my appetites anyway.

Standing, I grab some pillows off the head of my bed after wiping my hands on my pajamas. I toss them on the floor next to the man and brace his body to the side, so he slumps to the floor, flat on his back. I check his wounds, happy to see only a tiny trickle of blood seeping from the bottom slash—the deepest.

Lifting his head, I place the pillow under him and stand back, gazing down. I wish there were more I could do to get him comfortable, but I'm not strong enough to lift him onto the bed. Strength isn't one of my many gifts—neither is healing, which would have been useful tonight.

After a short break which I use to change into clean jammies, I watch his chest move up and down in a steady pattern. Eventually, I gather all the wet towels and cloths to place in the trash. There's no way I'm bothering to wash them. The blanket was a favorite, but I can buy another.

When I return to the room from downstairs, he's stretched his arm out toward the door, and his head is turned in the same direction, as if he's waiting for me. I dismiss those thoughts and lean in close, placing my palm over his chest to feel his heat and the thump of his heart against my hand. "I think you're going to be okay, big fella. I don't know how you ended up way out here, but you're lucky you found me."

He lets out a string of low words that I can't understand, then he's out cold again.

I should probably sleep in another room—hell, I should probably take myself downstairs—but I move over to one of my chairs. Dawn is coming soon, and this night has left me exhausted. I'm not really worried about him hurting me anyway, since he's in no shape to hurt anyone. Plus, I'm certainly not without…defenses.

CHAPTER 2

I swat at whatever is tickling my cheek. "Knock it off, Theius." I turn my face to the side, burying my cheek against the chair. My eyes bolt open. I had assumed it would be my furry little friend Theius, but then memories of last night hit me like a lightning strike, filling my veins.

I look over to the floor where the man should be, but he's not there. "Hello?" I call out, but my voice is coated with sleep, making it come out as a lazy drawl.

I squint at the windows. The drapes are still drawn, letting the late afternoon sunlight filter in. I never intended to sleep here last night—just meant to rest before closing up the house for the day and finding a more suitable bed to sleep in. I can't believe the glaring ball in the sky didn't keep me awake.

Sitting up, I wait for an answer. Don't tell me he was able

to get up and walk away after those injuries? "Without even a thank you," I splutter.

"Thank you," I hear a man grouse.

I jump up and look around, my eyes scanning the room—there, in the corner. He's propped himself up, his arms lifted in supplication. "I'm sorry to startle you." His voice is low-pitched.

"I thought you left." I skim my hands over my pajamas, feeling way underdressed in my soft sleep pants and cami. The remnants of his shirt are gone, leaving him bare from the waist up. I don't bother averting my eyes. I'm not a shy girl, but something about him makes me feel like he can see so much more of me than I'm willing to show.

Clearing my throat and feeling slightly awkward, I ramble, "How are you feeling? Should I call a doctor? You said no doctor last night."

"I'm healing, thank you. Sorry to drop in on your doorstep like this." His eyes scan over my body, taking me in from head to toe.

"My bedroom, you mean, drop into my bedroom. How did you even get in here?" I tilt my head to the side and study him much the same way he's observing me.

"Your door wasn't locked. You should be more careful." He manages to sound like he's chastising me.

I lower myself back into the chair, placing each hand on an arm as if I were sitting on a throne. "I don't worry much about people stumbling on me way out here. But if an event should ever arise where I would need protection, rest assured,

I have it." I snap my teeth together on the last word and give him the smile that would always make my mother rush from the room.

One side of his lips tips up a tiny bit. "Good to know."

After a long stretch of silence, I tap a finger on the arm of the chair. "You never did say how you ended up out here."

"I didn't," he confirms, still leering at me.

I can't get a good read on him. Last night he tasted like a human, but now everything about him is closed off, almost as if he's shielding himself from me. I narrow my eyes. There's a reason the monsters fear me, a reason I never have to worry about someone hurting me. I may not know exactly what I am, but I know I could pull his last breath from his lungs clear across the room, without even moving a finger.

"I would never hurt you," he tells me in an almost-whisper.

I let a tiny laugh escape my lips. "I know. I'm not afraid of you—just curious." I shrug my shoulders. "I don't get many hum—" I stop myself before I can finish. "I don't get many visitors," I correct.

One of his eyebrows arches. "Really," he drawls out, elongating the word like he's challenging me.

"Who are you?" I blurt curiously. He's making me feel like he knows more than he should. I'm second-guessing the whole human assumption. A human wouldn't be sitting up, acting like he's fine. The bandage I taped over his wound last night is still there, keeping me from seeing his injuries.

"I'm Gunnar." I hear a slight accent in his voice when he

pronounces his name. He glances down, but peers up at me from under his brow quickly after.

"Nice to meet you. I'm Damiana." I lift my hand from the chair, I have to stop myself from giving him a wave and place it in my lap instead. That small grin slants his lip again.

"Evening, Damiana. I thank you for your hospitality." He pronounces my name right the very first time, like it's rolled off his tongue countless times before. That never happens.

I cast a sideways glance at him. "Do I know you?" That achingly familiar feeling comes back. Could he be one of the many men I've used over the past few years? I dismiss the thought almost immediately. I would have remembered that face, that body. I let my eyes travel over his features, very much enjoying what I see.

"We've never met before," he answers vaguely, but I don't see how.

"Strange," I counter, but I can't argue. I have no memory of meeting him either, just the uncanny feeling we do somehow know each other.

"Why is that strange?"

"The sun has set," I announce without answering his question.

Gunnar glances to the left, looking out into the darkness through the window. "It seems it has." His reply is soft, almost like it makes him sad.

I rise from my chair again, this time with a slow grace. "Would you care to shower? I would offer you some clothing, but I fear I don't have anything that would fit." A grin tugs at my lips when I think of him in one of my silky robes or trying to wear one of my shirts.

Gunnar looks up at me without moving more than his neck. "So, no man of the house then?"

Another laugh tinkles from my throat. "Goodness, no." I shake my head. "Troublesome creatures, aren't they? Always spilling blood and grime." I poke a little fun at him about the mess he left on my floor. "And needy, too. They want to be fed and kept warm." I shudder as if the idea were abhorrent.

In truth, none could handle me for more than a day or two. I'm too blunt, too set in my ways to have only one man warming my bed. But mostly, I'm not willing to give up the only friends I've ever had.

I can't imagine any man being comfortable with Crabby or Samson stopping by for a late-night visit. And don't even get me started on Uncle.

"I'm not always covered in my own blood." He somehow manages to stare up at me like he's the predator in the room, even though I don't feel threatened in any way. "It's usually someone else's."

I smile again. Even though his words would terrify most people, I'm not most people. "I bet you're the life of the party." I sigh wistfully before moving a little closer, asking, "Do you need help getting up?"

Gunnar pushes up off the floor in a single fluid movement. I take a step back, surprised he can move that easily after such a serious injury. Now that he's standing, I lower my eyes to his abdomen. “You seem to be quite the fast healer, Gunnar.” My voice lilts when I say his name.

“Must have looked worse than it was,” he counters, not offering any other explanation. “Does the offer to shower still stand?”

“Oh, of course.” I pull my eyes from his lower body. “Right through there.” I point at the door to my bathroom.

Gunnar tilts his head down in a slow, single nod. “My lady.”

His tone actually makes me blush. I’ve never been called a lady, not in the way he’s saying it. “I’ll be downstairs if you need anything. Take your time.” I leave him alone in my bedroom before I decide his wounds definitely don’t look that bad and ask him if he would like help washing his back.

Distracted, I find my way to the kitchen. I don’t eat, but many of my friends do. I should have something for him, even if I don’t exactly know what he is.

I hear the sound of a few boxes being shifted in the pantry. “Dare, is that you?” I whisper, with my hand on the doorknob. I get a small, delicate squeak in response.

“I have company,” I mutter, cracking the door just enough to peer through the opening. Dare is raised up on her hind legs, her little hands poised over her rounded belly. Excitement blossoms in my stomach that I have someone to talk to. Bringing my hands up close to my chin, I clap them together softly. “I have a real visitor,” I announce.

The spikes all over Dare’s back and around her neck droop a little. “Not that you and all the others aren’t real visitors.

You're like my family—you know that," I assure her, recovering quickly. "But this is a man." I lean in even closer, so I can see her beady red eyes. "I think he might be human, but I'm not sure."

Dare's spikes immediately lift, responding to the perceived threat. I reach out and stroke her soft fur and the razor-sharp spikes dotted all over her body. "No, it's okay. He won't even know you're here, and I would never let him hurt you," I coo, tickling her under her chin. The tiny barbs there are like needles. I don't know anyone else who would dare touch her there. Dare's mouth lolls open a bit, showing off the rows of teeth she keeps hidden behind her lips as she leans into my caress.

"I'm going to get him a snack. Help yourself to whatever you would like." I marvel at the way none of her defenses affect me. I could slam my hand over any of her thorns, and they wouldn't penetrate my skin. "Just don't come running out to attack if you smell or hear him," I warn. "If you bump into anyone else, warn them, too." I give her tiny, rat-like face a little smooch. "See you in a bit, Dare."

I look over my offerings on the counter, wondering if I have enough. There are cookies, Pop-Tarts, candy bars, and chips. I tap my chin, thinking I need more. Rushing over to the fridge, I grab a couple cans of soda and set them off to the side. "Ice cream," I blurt. "I can't believe I forgot the ice cream." Satisfied, I climb onto the island, letting my legs dangle down.

I don't have too long of a wait before Gunnar comes into

the kitchen. If I didn't have extra senses, I never would have heard him coming down the stairs. He's still shirtless, but I don't mind the view.

He stops mid-step when he sees me and the buffet of goodness I laid out for him. "That's a lot of sugar." He winces a little.

Offended by his tone, I hop down from the counter and narrow my eyes at him. "None of it is for you," I sneer up at him.

He blinks at me, almost owlishly. "Oh, okay." I push past him, bumping my shoulder into his arm as I do. Gunnar clears his throat. "Sorry I assumed." I turn to look at him over my shoulder. He sounds contrite.

I roll my eyes. "It is for you—it's all I have." I shrug my shoulders. I guess it's safe to assume his diet is different from my monsters'. I'm not even sure why I was so bothered by his comment. I suppose it has to do with the fact that I wanted to impress him.

"Forgive me for sticking my foot in my mouth?" Gunnar looks a little sheepish as he gazes at me.

I flatten my lips, realizing I'm being silly. "It's fine. You're welcome to have anything else you would like, but…uh, it's all pretty much the same," I warn him. I'll need to make sure Dare is either gone or hidden if he goes into the pantry.

"This is perfect, more than enough," he assures me.

"So," I drawl, while Gunnar shovels the last bite of ice cream into his mouth.

He pauses, then pushes the empty bowl away. "That was delicious." He sounds almost surprised.

"You act like you've never had ice cream." I beam, happy that he really did seem to enjoy the treats.

"It's been a long time." He wipes his mouth with the napkin he held in his hand the entire time he was eating.

"I have more," I offer, already standing.

"No, no I couldn't." He waves his hand and grabs the bowl before I can. He stands and takes it over to the sink, rinsing it before opening the dishwasher and loading it into a slot. I tilt my head, considering him. He knew right where the dishwasher was—he didn't even have to look when he reached down to open the door.

I need to know more about this man. "So, Gunnar, we're old friends now, right? You've bled all over my bedroom, slept on my floor, showered in my bathroom, and eaten my food." I tick the items off on my fingers. "How about you tell me how you ended up on my floor with your guts falling out, and how you seem to be doing just fine now?"

Gunnar settles his ass against my sink, crossing his arms over his chest. "You don't have a guess?" He raises one brow, studying me.

"Oh, I have loads of ideas. You don't even want to know what's going on up here." I point to the side of my head.

He bites the corner of his bottom lip, but it doesn't hide the smile forming on his scarred mouth. "I'm dying to know exactly what you're thinking."

I shrug my shoulders, "You asked for it," I caution. I inspect him again. "A vampire…no." I shake my head knowing that's not right. "Werewolf." My eyes bug out. "I've never met a werewolf." I shimmy a bit, excited by the thought.

His eyes crinkle. "Sorry to disappoint you, but no. I'm not a werewolf."

"Darn…are you a demon?" I inquire skeptically. "A succubus, maybe?"

Gunnar stands up straight, his eyes going wide in the process. "No." He stresses the word. "That's a new one," he adds under his breath.

"What, why? You've got this allure thing going on for you." I wave my hands in his direction. "You're like a big ole bear. You look like you could rip someone's head off, but you also seem kind of sweet, too." I tilt my head and study him, finding my assessment a very appropriate description of him.

"A bear, huh?"

"You're a shifter, aren't you?" I don't give him a chance to respond. "I knew they were real," I mutter to myself.

"Sorry to burst your bubble, but I'm not a shifter," he declares.

"Really?" I deflate, and Gunnar chuckles. "Well, I know you're some kind of soldier or something." I tap my finger on my lip. "Are you a government experiment gone wrong? Just escaped their mind control and gained your freedom?"

He throws his head back to let out a belly laugh, and it's

deep and hardy. He's wheezing by the time he gets himself under control. "I don't know where you're coming up with this stuff," his eyes are dancing as he gazes at me with his hand over his abdomen, "but you've got to stop. I don't think my body can handle another round of that."

His hand over his stomach takes on a whole new meaning. He's taped on a new bandage. I'd already forgotten he was hurt. "Do you need to sit down?" I offer, pulling out a stool from the island.

"No, I'm fine," he replies, dismissing me easily, still wearing a grin.

"If you're sure." He's a big boy, a very big boy. I think he knows his limits and can take care of himself.

Leaning forward, Gunnar picks up a palm sized stone that I found sitting on my nightstand one day. He examines the rough rock, turning it left and right. The shimmery stone almost glows as he does. "This is nice. Where did you get it?" His tone is a little too interested.

I hold out my palm, letting him know I want it back. "It was a gift from a friend." He places the jagged stone in my hand, and I put it back in the small dish of stones I keep on the counter. A new one shows up every now and then.

After a very short stretch of silence, he takes a deep breath and his smile disappears, a more serious expression covering his face. "I need to get going."

"You do?" I surprise myself by how disappointed I sound. "I can give you a ride," I add, almost too eagerly.

He starts to shake his head as if he's going to deny the

need for a ride, but thinks better of it, and says, “Yeah, that would be great.” He reaches up, grabs the back of his neck, and gazes down. He almost looks shy—if a two-hundred-fifty-pound wall of scarred muscle could look shy.

“Let me go get changed, and I’ll take you wherever you need to go.” I wrinkle my nose and tighten my lips. Shit, I sounded too eager. I hold up a finger, indicating I need a minute, and scamper out of the kitchen.

“Come on, Dami, quit acting like you’ve never talked to a real boy,” I grit through my teeth, as I drag my hand over shirt after shirt in my closet. “Just pick something.”

“The green one looks nice with your hair.” I spin and find Aeson perched on my vanity.

I raise my finger up to my lips, warning her to be quiet. “I have a visitor. I don’t think he’s human, but I’m not really sure,” I whisper to her, grabbing the emerald green sweater she suggested.

She kicks her little legs and leans back against her palms. “What’s he look like?” Her voice goes all soft and sugary sweet.

“Too big for you,” I blurt harshly.

She slowly turns her head and her eyes find mine. “Is he now?” she drawls, one of her tiny, perfectly arched brows raised in a challenge.

“Yes.” I narrow my eyes at her.

Aeson lets out a tinkling laugh. She raises her fingers to cover her mouth, and her eyes go a little wide. “I’m sorry,” she splutters out an apology, still giggling a bit.

"Why are you laughing?" I drag my hair out of the back of the sweater and look in the mirror. Aeson is right, this color does look good on me. If I were going out hunting, I wouldn't even bother with pants. I twist to get a look at my ass. "Pretty nice."

"You know you can't talk to yourself when you're around normal people," Aeson warns me.

I face her. "Why were you laughing at me?" I demand again.

She stands up and walks to the edge of the vanity. "I wasn't sure you even liked men, let alone liked one enough to warn me away from him." Aeson is beautiful. Tiny and deadly, but still beautiful. I can't believe I'm actually feeling a little jealous right now.

"I don't like him." I avert my eyes from her and grab a pair of black leggings that look like well-worn leather.

"It's not a bad thing, Dami." Her voice is soft. I glare over my shoulder at her. "It's not. There's nothing wrong with letting people in, even if they are human."

"I have to go. I'm giving him a ride home." I ignore her comment and rush to the door. Right before I grab the handle, I pause. "Humans never stick around, Aeson. I'll be back soon." I hustle out the door, leaving it cracked for her.

CHAPTER 3

"Sorry that took me so long," I apologize, huffing a little from racing down the stairs. Once I left my bedroom, I had this irrational fear he was going to disappear if I didn't get down here fast enough.

Gunnar rakes his eyes over me, starting on my black painted toes, up my legs, and pausing on the way my chest fills out the sweater. Good call, Aeson. I'll thank her later.

When his eyes finally meet mine, I tilt my head and cock my hip, letting him know I caught him looking.

He swallows. "I'm ready when you are." His voice is a little raspy—I like it.

I turn and motion for him to follow. "Let me just grab my shoes and keys. The garage is this way." I don't need to check to make sure he's following me. My senses are keenly aware of him.

Gunnar runs his hand over the rounded top of my car. "This is Betty," I say, introducing him to the beauty.

He blinks at me a few times. "You named your car?" he questions slowly.

"This isn't just a car." I narrow my eyes on him and stroke Betty in apology for his blunder.

Gunnar raises his hands and takes a step or two backwards. "Sorry. I won't make that mistake again." His brows dip, like he's trying hard to control his facial expression.

"Just get in," I grouse.

"I don't think I even know how." He peers at the door, looking left and right, then traces his fingers over the flat door handle.

I push past him and tip the handle so it pops out. "My lady." I motion for him to climb in the open door. Gunnar's jaw tics twice. I like poking fun at him.

I make my way around to the driver's side and slide in. The seat is low, but it cradles me more comfortably than any other car I've ever owned.

"I wasn't sure I was going to fit, but it's surprisingly roomy."

"That's what he said." I chuckle at my own lame joke and tap the button to open the garage. The engine purrs to life with a throaty growl. Gunnar looks at me with raised brows. "You didn't just think she was a pretty face, did you?" I caress Betty's wheel. "So, where to?"

"You can just take me to town, if you don't mind. I'm

meeting someone there." Gunnar makes himself comfortable, shifting in the seat.

Just someone, huh? I don't think I like the sound of that. It sounds like it might be a woman. "Where are you meeting your *friend*?" It'll take me a good twenty minutes to get to town—more if I drive the speed limit. Plenty of time to find out a few more details about Gunnar and, hopefully, discover exactly what he is.

"Not my friend." Gunnar's voice goes a little dark. "Do you know Rumors?" He casts me a sideways glance. Definitely a woman then. Rumors is one of the local clubs that caters to a darker clientele. I've even found a few monsters there.

"I know it," I confirm lightly. "I've never seen you there." I keep my eyes on the two-lane road that leads into town. It's pretty empty, but I keep my speed under seventy, even though it's hard. Betty likes to stretch her legs.

"I'm not in the club often. How about you?" He's fishing.

"Maybe a few times a month. I like to dance." And eat, but I don't say that part out loud. One night at Rumors and I'm good for a week, longer if I can find someone who's cheating or being deceitful, which is pretty much everyone there.

Plus, I have other needs that need to be addressed. I never bring anyone home, but the men and women at Rumors know the score. No one goes there looking for a long-term commitment. It can be hard to find someone who's not full of sins and suitable for my more essential hunger, but I don't like mixing necessity with pleasure. Something about feeding off someone while I fuck them turns me off.

Gunnar makes a harrumph sound and crosses his arms over his chest. “You might know the person I’m meeting there.”

“Oh yeah, who’s that?” I keep my voice light, pretending I’m not dying to know.

“Vanessa.” He turns his head and watches me for a reaction. I force myself not to sneer. I know Vanessa. Who doesn’t know Vanessa? She owns the fucking club and she’s a fucking gorgeous, sexy-as-hell redhead with a killer body.

“Oh yeah, I’ve met her a few times.” She’s also full of sins. I fed off her once, but she left a bad taste in my mouth, so I’ve stayed away from her ever since. “Do you know her well?” I merge onto the highway. The traffic here is still light, but we’re getting closer to town, so it will only get heavier now.

“I’ve known her for a long time,” he answers, evading the question. I tap my fingers on the top of the steering wheel. I’m tired of his avoidance.

“How did you end up at my house, *in* my house?” I decide to just ask him outright. I hear him suck his tongue against his teeth. “Let’s drop the bullshit, shall we? I’m pretty sure you’re not just a human.”

“I was,” he says softly. “A very long time ago.” Gunnar looks down at his large hands, his palms facing up.

“And now?” I’m almost breathless with the knowledge that he’s different, like me.

"And now I'm not." He settles his hands on his legs and stares straight forward. His body language is telling me he's done talking about it.

I almost press him, almost demand he tell me more, but I don't. I have a strange desire for him to want to tell me about himself without me prodding.

"I'm not human either," I tell him, even though I'm pretty sure he already knew that. "I don't even know what I am, really," I add blandly. It doesn't bother me as much as it used to, but I'd still like to know where I came from, and if there's anyone else out there like me.

I pull into a dark parking structure adjacent to the club. The growl of the engine echoes off the cement walls and ceiling as I find a parking spot on the first level.

"You're coming in?" Gunnar actually sounds a little panicked.

"Might as well, I don't get into town all that often." I cut the car off and open the door. "Don't worry, I won't cramp your style." I give him a tight smile.

"I don't want people seeing us together."

My head jerks back, but I let out a bitter laugh. "Harsh much?" I turn and walk away from my car, leaving him standing in the parking garage. Over my shoulder, I wave at him with a single finger salute. "Fuck you, too, Gunnar. I should have let your guts fall out."

Even my stomping footsteps don't hide the sound of his shoes eating up the distance between us. He grabs my arm, but I tug free from his grip and slowly turn to face him. "Don't.

Touch. Me." I let a little of my power seep into my voice. I've never had to fight anyone physically, but I feel like I could rip his head off right now if I wanted to.

"That's not what I meant. You took what I said wrong." Gunnar pulls his hand back and drops his arms to his sides.

"So, it meant something other than you don't want people to see us together? Maybe I need to get my ears checked, 'cause that's what I heard." I cross my arms over my chest. I'm offended. I've never had a man say they didn't want to be seen with me. I'm fucking beautiful—I don't even need a dash of makeup. My skin is flawless, my lashes are long and dark even though I'm a natural blonde, and I have lips that make men dream of blow jobs. I could give Vanessa and her fake, fat-filled ass a run for her money any day of the week.

What the hell is wrong with me? Until I met this man, I could count how many times I've been insecure on one hand, but between the shitshow with Aeson earlier and now, I'm about to surpass my old totals.

"Most people don't like me, Damiana. If people saw us together, they might hurt you because of me."

I skeptically peer sideways at him. "I'm not sure if I should believe you, or if you're trying to cover your own ass."

"When I said I didn't want to be seen together, it had nothing to do with you, and everything to do with me."

I unfold my arms and smooth down the front of my sweater. "Okay, but you should work on your delivery."

"I will," he promises.

"I'm still going in there." I motion over my shoulder in the direction of the club. “I’m really not worried about what people think, or if people see us together, but if it makes you feel better, you can ignore me.” I walk away from him then, even though something inside of me is rebelling at the idea.

Sauntering over to one of the many exits of the parking structure, I take note of the city around me. It’s Thursday night: not the best night for hunting, but doable. The sidewalks are teeming with people walking to and from bars and restaurants.

“Cindy knows I’m not coming home. I told her I’m tired of her thinking she can run my life.” I slurp up the little lie like an hors d’oeuvre. The man talking to his buddy gets a small smudge on his soul for his sin. I squint my eyes and notice all the spots starting to pool together. If he keeps it up, there will be consequences.

Big lies, little lies they all leave a mark, even the ones we tell ourselves.

“Hey, beautiful, not your usual night,” Mick the bouncer drawls as I approach.

“I was in the neighborhood,” I reply, letting my eyes scan past the smallish line of people waiting to get in. “Busy?” I raise my brow, a little surprised.

“Usual crowd for a Thursday.” He steps to the side and sends his arm out in a slight wave, indicating I’m good to go right in.

I never have to wait, but I never presume that will be the case every time, either. “Thanks, Mick.” I give him a kind smile as I pass. His cheeks actually tinge a slight pink as I do.

"Anytime, beautiful," he mutters almost wistfully.

The hall is dark, lit with only blue, cone-shaped lights directed at the high ceiling. I'm not sure I would want to see what's staining the wall below the lights anyway. After a short walk, I meet another bouncer, but this one is newer. I don't know his name yet.

He opens the door with a slight bow, tipping his head to me. It almost feels purposeful, not just a standard greeting. I open myself up to see if he tastes human, but this close to the club my senses always get muddled. The only way I could be sure about him would be to touch him, and I don't want to invite that kind of familiarity. I keep my eyes on him as I pass, but he directs his gaze to the floor.

The rush of energy from the club doesn't wait for me to enter. Instead, it pours out the door and slams into me like a physical wall, distracting me from the strangeness of the security guy's behavior.

I let my head fall back loose on my shoulders and accept the waves of sin tingeing the air. My stomach aches a little with a hunger pang as I step through the door and into the club proper.

I glance over my shoulder, wondering if I'll catch sight of Gunnar. He'll probably wait another few minutes before even coming in. If he knows Vanessa, I'm sure the security knows him, too, so he probably won't have to wait in the line either.

A man passes me, near enough to touch. He's leaning in close to a cute girl with blue dyed hair, chopped into pixie cut, her eyes are all soft and glassy. She's either already a little drunk, or she's buying into every line he's cooing into her ear. There's no major deceit, just the little things people say to one another when they want to get laid. I guess it's probably something like 'you're the most beautiful girl I've ever seen,' or 'I've never wanted anyone like I want you.' Bullshit, utter bullshit, but it's what she wants to hear, and he's more than happy to oblige if it means she'll let him fuck her against the wall later tonight.

I take in the tiny lies and move deeper into the club. The dance floor is filled with girls dancing alone and in groups. Most of them have their arms raised in the air and are rolling their bodies seductively. I take note of several men on the outskirts watching the show, most of them with lust in their eyes and hearts.

One couple catches my eye. She's a pretty blonde, with her hair pulled back into a messy bun, letting a few soft tendrils fall around her face. She's tugging on the hem of her short skirt as if she's completely uncomfortable, while her eyes are trained on the man next to her—probably her boyfriend, if the anger seething off the blonde is any indication. She's absolutely enraged at the way he's watching the other girls and ignoring her. His eyes are bouncing over the dancing crowd, until he finds a dark-haired girl. Her skirt is so short you can see the bottom of her ass cheeks as she hops around.

Her arms are thrown in the air, and she's dancing like she doesn't care who's watching. She's not being overly sensual, but something about her screams confidence, and *that* is sexy. She doesn't have to try.

I make my way over to the bar, keeping my eye on the three of them. My bet, and I'm usually right since I have a knack for these things, is that before the night's over, I'll have a fat meal from whatever is brewing between them.

"Hey, what can I get ya?" Nat's tits are almost spilling out of her tight cut-off shirt as she grins at me, leaning over the bar.

"The usual," I tell her, and give her a wink to let her know her efforts aren't wasted. Nat and I had a night of fun a few years ago, and since then we've played the flirting game. She knows I don't double dip—I'm a one-and-done kind of girl—and she knew that before taking me back to her place.

"You got it. Anything else?" Nat traces her fingers between her cleavage in an offer.

I meet her eyes. "Just the usual." I make sure that my voice is kind, but that she also knows not to ask again.

"Nothing ventured, nothing gained." She shrugs her shoulders and cracks open a silver bottle of water that promises it's from the rainforest. It's probably bottled in New Jersey, but I don't care as long as it's sealed.

Nat pushes the bottle with a small napkin under it over to me. I already have a twenty-dollar bill on the bar to slide over to her. She drags the bill back and tucks it into the front pocket of her cut-off shorts, knowing it is hers to keep.

I turn and face the dance floor again. My blonde friend is trying desperately to get the man's attention, but he can't be bothered because he's too worried about the guy who's dancing really close to the dark-haired girl.

I see a short exchange between the man and the blonde. He jerks his hand in the other woman's direction. The blonde lays her palm over his chest and gives a small shake of her head. I move a little closer, the drama of the moment pulling me in.

"She's fine, Craig. She does this every weekend," she tells him, and it's not a lie.

"Look at that guy—he's a creep—and she's been drinking," he spouts back.

"So, let her have fun. I thought that was what we were here for. You said you wanted to dance, but you haven't danced with me once." I can hear a little anger seeping into the blonde's voice, but Craig ignores it.

He flings her hand off his chest. "If you want to dance, go dance. Nothing is stopping you." He's angry, too, but not at the blonde. He's pissed at the guy who has his hands wrapped around the friend's waist.

"You don't give a shit about what I do, but you're worried about Carissa," the blonde spits. He spares her a glance as she storms into the middle of the dance floor.

I'm close enough to him now to hear him mutter, "Yeah, 'cause no one wants to fuck you." It's a tiny lie, one he tells himself, because he doesn't want to be with her anymore. If I've seen this once, I've seen it a hundred times. The blonde is safe. She's sweet, she's the one his parents expect him to marry because she's loyal to a fault, but he can barely stand looking at her any longer.

With the blonde gone, Craig makes his way over to the friend. "Hey, Carissa, you doing okay?" he asks the question to the girl, but stares down the guy that's been dancing with her. Carissa giggles and leans into Craig's chest.

"I'm so glad you guys are here. Where's Lindsey?" She peers over Craig's shoulder.

Craig uses the closeness to wrap his arm around Carissa's back and pulls her in close, creating distance between her and the other man.

Without answering the question about where his girlfriend is, he starts swaying to the music, still holding Carissa tightly against him.

It doesn't take her more than a handful of seconds before Carissa is moving right along with Craig.

The low simmer of rage tickles my senses, and my eyes are immediately drawn to Lindsey, the blonde. She's standing a few feet back into the crowd and her hands are balled up into tiny fist. I'm pulled to her and the vengeful wrath she's feeling. I glance over my shoulder once to see Craig dip his head close to Carissa's neck as his hand slides down to cup her ass.

The hurt and anger from Lindsey mixes together, forming a potent feast. I open myself up to the sins from Carissa and Craig, making my way over to Lindsey for the real meal.

Her emotions are justified, so the smudge left on her soul for the searing hate she's feeling doesn't so much as leave a mark, but more of a scar. This is something that will shape the rest of her future.

Many things can happen from this point on. She could act on the rage building inside of her, but doing so would make the smudge Carissa and Craig are getting for their deceit look like a tiny stain in comparison.

Lindsey's feelings aren't going to get her in trouble, but acting on them will. Delivering her vengeance, as deserved as it is, would earn a mark that would eventually sully her soul.

I taste Lindsey's heart-searing pain when I take in the essence of her sin. She loves Craig. Even when she knew he never loved her as much as she loved him, she thought she was enough, thought if she could be everything he wanted, then he would come to need her the way she needed him.

I shiver as a true desire to hurt Craig and Carissa overcomes Lindsey, but it dissipates just as quickly as it came. I watch as inky black spots bleed together over Lindsey's heart, changing the person she is. I almost feel sad for her. If I could see my own soul, I bet I would have a black shield over my chest, much like the one she's forming now. But I'm not sure if I even have a soul.

I stay close to Lindsey, no longer hungry for sins—her trio has provided a meal that will last weeks—but still curious about how this will all play out. Call it the train wreck syndrome: I can't look away. She makes her way over to the bar, pushing herself to the front a little roughly. "Give me a shot." She shouts to be heard over the noise.

"Of what?" Nat leans in a little closer.

"Anything—something strong," Lindsey demands. Nat gives a slight twist of her head. I bet she can figure out what's going on, just like I could. You can't be a bartender for years and not pick up on all the drama.

I scan my eyes over the crowd to find Craig again, but I spot Gunnar, still shirtless. He's stomping across the ground like a man on a mission. People move out of his way without any prompting. Forgetting about Lindsey and Craig, I move parallel to Gunnar, making sure to keep a good distance between us, which isn't hard. It seems like people move into my way in the same way they move out of his.

I should have guessed he'd be going to the VIP section. His steps eat up the flight of stairs, and he bangs on the glass door separating the portioned-off section from the rest of the club. The wall is glass, letting everyone below know what they're missing, but not allowing them entrance. I know it creates quite a bit of jealousy in the lower tier. I've partaken of that particular sin of envy a few times when the night is slow of a more filling fare.

Sean, another one of the bouncers I know, opens the door and immediately steps back to allow Gunnar entrance. Something about the man I shared a ride here with seems different. Earlier this evening at the house, I never mistook him for someone that was weak, even with his injury, but watching him shove past Sean, and the few other security men working the VIP section, is showing me that I might have misjudged him a little.

I settle myself on a stool about midway between the bar and the VIP area. It gives me a good view of the raised portion of the club without looking like I'm staring in that direction. As soon as I nab the empty table, a nice-looking guy comes into my line of sight. He dips his head to the open stool across from me in question.

I mull over the idea. Sitting here alone invites its own attention. If I let him sit, it might keep others from trying, plus it will provide a little cover for me so I can keep watching Gunnar.

"Be my guest." I wave my hand over the table.

"Are you here alone?" is his first question. Creep.

"I have a few friends here." Not a lie. I do. I actually try not to lie, ever. I don't know if it comes with the same consequences as it does for others, but it does leave a bad taste in my mouth, literally.

"I'm Noah," he lies, but I don't tell him I know that.

"So, what brings you to my table?" I pretend to scan the bar, but I'm really just watching to see what Gunnar is doing.

"You looked lonely." Another lie. I take a second to actually look at the guy. He's good looking, and his hair is a light shade of brown, almost blond. He fills out his fitted, black dress shirt nicely, but Not Noah's hands look soft, like he's never known a hard day's work. Huge turn off.

"So, are you?" Not Noah asks.

"Am I what, lonely?" I chuckle a little. "You mean am I looking for a hookup? Not tonight." I make my final response hard, so he knows I'm not just playing hard to get.

"You sure?" he offers, like I'm passing up the offer of a lifetime. "I promise I'm better than whoever you're waiting for."

I give him my full attention then, letting him see just how

disinterested I really am. “Not on your best day,” I tell him, while leaning over the table a little.

I feel someone approach my side. I look up to find Sean staring daggers at the man across from me.

“This guy bothering you?” I glance up to the VIP section to see another bouncer now working the door. Gunnar is standing with his back to me, his arms down at his sides. I can see how rigid his posture is from all the way down here. I can’t see who’s in front of him, but judging from what he said, I can assume it’s Vanessa.

“No, Sean,” I reply, dismissing his worries. “He was just leaving,” I address the man across from me. Not Noah lifts his hands and stands with no comment.

Once he’s gone, Sean places his hand on the back of my stool. “Why don’t you go up? You know we can keep a better eye on you up there.”

It’s so sweet that he thinks he needs to keep an eye on me, but tonight it just might serve its purpose. It will get me closer to Gunnar, and maybe I’ll learn why he’s here, meeting with Vanessa.

CHAPTER 4

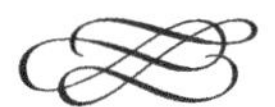

"Walk me up?" I peer up at Sean from under my lashes. The tattoo near his temple scrunches up when his eyes crinkle.

"For you, anytime." Sean pulls out the back of my stool as I stand, giving me more room to get around the table. He places his hand on the small of my back and guides me to the flight of metal stairs. "I'm surprised you're going up. You always say no."

"What can I say? You made me an offer I couldn't refuse." I reach for the door, but Sean beats me to it. His hands are rough from use and hard work as he closes his fingers over mine. "Thanks." I give him a grateful smile over my shoulder, thinking he's going to head back down, but he follows me into the glass walled section.

Sean places his palm on my lower back again and guides

me over to a small grouping of furniture. "Have a seat. Can I get you a drink?" I have the distinct feeling I've been herded instead of being rescued like I thought.

I narrow my eyes on Sean, not feeling nearly as happy with myself as I had. Sean doesn't meet my gaze this time. I lean in and snag his wrist so he can't escape. "Did someone send you for me?"

"What do you mean?" he inquiries, evading my question.

"Did someone send you down to bring me up here?" I focus on his face, so he can't avoid me by giving me another half answer. It's easy to lie with your words, but facial expressions and body language are harder to hide.

"It looked like that guy was bothering you." Not a lie, but not the full truth either. What bothers me more is the fact that Sean knows not to lie to me. He knows I would know if he did.

I release his arm and look around, feeling much more exposed than I ever have. No one but my monsters know what I can do. I don't see anyone I know other than Vanessa, even Gunnar has disappeared.

I unleash my senses, even though I'm full with Lindsey's restrained vengeance. There are too many people, too many emotions, and too many beings to sort through to find any one person or distinguish between them.

"I think I'm going to go. I'm not liking the vibe here tonight," I tell Sean, my eyes narrowed. I haven't made it this long without being smart. And a smart girl knows when to retreat, especially when she doesn't know what she could be up against.

Maybe Gunnar showing up at my house wasn't an accident. Maybe he lured me here. Sean takes a step back, his brows pinched. "You sure you don't want a drink?" He's trying to keep me here.

"No." I put some force into my word.

He dips his head and nods once. "Whatever you like, my lady."

"What did you just say?" I seethe. Gunnar said the exact same thing to me. Now I *know* he has something to do with this.

Sean tries to recover. "Whatever you like." He licks his lips in an almost nervous fashion.

"Why did you call me that?" I step a little closer into him.

He runs his palm over the back of his head—definitely nervous. "It was just a slip." The truth.

I deflate a little, since he's not lying. I take one last look around the room before heading back toward the door I just came through a few moments ago. I don't rush, I would never want to give anyone the satisfaction of thinking they could run me away from some place.

I focus on putting one foot in front of the other until I reach the main entrance. No one tries to stop me or keep me here like I'd been worried about.

There's a different guy on the door to the club, but Mick is still manning the outdoor entrance. "Leaving so soon?" he asks when I pass.

"Yeah." I give him a wave over my shoulder without an explanation. The line to get in is even longer than when I arrived, so I know he's too busy to press me for more. I doubt he even would anyway.

Betty is waiting for me when I round the corner of the parking garage, but she's not the only one. Gunnar is leaning on the pole I parked next to. My steps might falter, but I recover quickly. "Did you forget something in my car?" I take note of the dark t-shirt he's wearing. Wonder where he got that.

"No, I just wanted to make sure you made it out here okay," he answers, as he pushes off the pole.

I plant my hands on my hips. "I think I told you I can take care of myself."

"You did, and I know you can." He's not lying. "But I wanted to be sure."

"Why did you come to my house?" I should have known there was more to him showing up on my bedroom floor. Of course I did, I just didn't really worry about what it was.

"I didn't intend to. It just happened." His big shoulders move in a shrug. Again, it seems as if he's telling the truth.

"But why?" I urge him.

"I can't answer that." Gunnar opens his hands.

"Can't or won't?" I demand.

"Can't." He rolls his lips in like he's already said too much.

"Well, that's not at all cryptic." I throw my hands in the air and head toward my car. When I move to pass Gunnar, he reaches out like he might grab me, but I freeze and glare up at him. He pulls his hand back slowly and gives me another one of those stupid head nods, like the security guys at the club gave me.

"Have a nice life, Gunnar," I say with a whole lot of snark. I don't wait around to see if he would have responded.

Betty greets me like an old friend when I climb inside and slam the door shut. I give her dash a quick rub in apology then fire her up. When I check my mirrors to make sure it's safe to back out, Gunnar is gone. "Good riddance," I mutter, and speed out of the parking garage.

I don't bother worrying about the speed limit on the way home. I'm still borderline pissed off and a little out of sorts from what happened at the club.

Sean was acting strange. I bet it all goes back to Gunnar. He's the only common denominator. He seemed to be pretty familiar with the security from the club. I bet he was the one that sent Sean after me.

"Dumbass. I told him I could take care of myself." I glance at the clock, it's still early enough that Aeson may still be at the house, maybe even Dare. I push the gas pedal a little harder, ready to put this night and all the strange shit behind me.

"WHAT DO YOU MEAN, you're leaving for a while?" I toss the hand towel near the sink. Radmon lingers near the door, floating a few inches off the ground. Her grayish dress is all torn near the hem, letting you see the way her ankles are in an unnatural pointed position, allowing her toes to almost drag against the floor.

"There's always a time for us, and mine has passed, for now." Her voice is saccharine sweet, which is at total odds with her appearance.

"So, what—another monster is going to take your place?" I'm confused, I've had friends come and go, and sometimes I go months without seeing a particular person, but this is the first time any of them has come to me and told me they were leaving. "And what is a while?" I cross my arms over my chest.

"I'm not sure, Dami, but I'll be back. I always come back." She tilts her head to the side and examines me.

"Well, that's bullshit!" I spit.

"It's how it works," she cajoles. "We can't all be here at once. There are others that have been waiting their turn."

I drop my arms, my curiosity piqued. "Where do you go when you're waiting?"

Radmon glitches, her shape flickering in and out of focus. "I can't tell you that." She smiles at me ruefully.

"Why not?" I scoff, indignant that I'm being denied information for the second time in a week. First, it was Gunnar, saying there was something he couldn't tell me, and now her.

"I really must go, Damiana. I just wanted to say goodbye for now, dear friend." With those words, she disappears for the last time, her sweet voice still lingering in the air.

"Well, that fucking sucks." I look around at my empty kitchen. A glow from the window catches my eye—it's nearly dawn. With shuffling steps, I make my way over to the window, and close the heavy curtain, continuing through the rest of the house until I reach my bedroom upstairs. My thoughts are still lingering on Radmon. I hope she's not too lonely wherever she's going.

The sun is just cresting the horizon when I reach for the last set of drapes in my room. I gaze over my property as the shadows are chased away in the morning light. Movement near the dense tree line catches my eye.

An animal, much too large to be a dog or wolf, slinks between the trees. I shake my head, thinking the light is playing tricks on me. I couldn't have just seen a lion walking into my woods. I press my hand to the glass and peer out, hoping for another glimpse. "What the hell was that?" I look around like someone else might have seen it, but I'm alone, as usual.

"I should probably go check it out," I tell myself.

Hustling downstairs, I hop on one foot, jumping into my boots. Cracking the door, I shiver a little when the wind slices right through my sleep pants.

I tiptoe over the porch and down the steps, heading in the direction I noticed the animal. I click my tongue and make kissy noises. "Anyone out here?" I peer into the trees, waiting for any sign that I'm not losing my mind—a rustling tree, a twig snapping, anything.

After a good five minutes of making a fool of myself,

calling the animal like it was a lost puppy, I make my way through the damp grass and back to the house.

"Well, that was a waste." I close the door and lock it, slipping my boots off. "Yuk." I slide my pants down when the wet hem from the morning dew touches my bare feet.

Using my toe, I kick the pants up and snatch them out of the air, tossing them on the laundry room floor as I pass by on my way back up to my room.

My drapes are still open when I enter. Heaving a sigh, I walk across the room to pull the curtain closed. "I'll be damned. You shit!" There, just where I was standing outside only minutes ago, is a lion. Not just any lion: a huge fucking lion, with a mane that looks like it's made from shimmering strands of gold swaying in the breeze.

I drag the fabric back and crank the window open. "What the hell?" I grate through my teeth. The lion—and it is a fucking lion—lifts his head and opens his maw in a lazy yawn. His tail curls up, and a small tuft of fur on the tip catches the light, making it look like a flame before it flips back down, disappearing out of sight. "I hope you catch your ass on fire," I tell him, leaning against the window.

Even up here, I can hear the chuffing sound he makes before turning around to head back into the woods. I jerk upright. "Wait, I was just kidding. You don't have to go."

The lion looks up at me again for a long second, then slinks into the forest. I give him a few seconds before deciding he's really gone for good this time and crank the window closed.

I pull back the covers, still amazed at the sight of the animal. His mane was almost unreal. He was more like a mythical beast than any monster I've ever met. Maybe I'll ask Aeson or Uncle about him.

I wonder why he was here. The images of him near the tree line and thoughts of him prowling the forest leaves me with a contented feeling. Something about knowing he might be around makes me feel happy. Maybe it's just the thought of knowing who and what he is, possibly having a new friend. That thought spurs me into thinking about another friend.

The memory of Radmon flickering out of existence in the kitchen fills my mind. I'm going to miss her, even if she's only gone for a short time, but I have a feeling it won't be. I have a lot I need to talk to Uncle about—like why she had to go, and if he knows when she'll be back. Getting him to answer me might be an entirely different story, though.

It feels as if I lie in bed for hours trying to sleep when my racing thoughts finally slow enough to allow slumber to take me.

CHAPTER 5

He's been here again. I can taste him in the air the moment I step out of the bathroom, and he's rife with rage. I drag the towel over the ends of my hair and call out, "Hello."

A robed figure steps into my room as if he's coming from a portal. I blink at him several times, surprised he's actually letting me see him. Well, part of him. I can't really see anything but the long, billowy, black cloak.

Once he's in the room, all the essence of rage and anger dies as if it were coming from the same place he did.

"Hi." My voice comes out like a chirp, so I clear my throat.

"Hello, Damiana," he greets, saying my name like we're old friends.

"Are you here for a visit, or…" I let the sentence dangle. I mean, he looks like every image of the Grim Reaper I've ever seen.

"Or did I come to take your soul?" His voice is smooth, not at all like I would have imagined it being.

I narrow my eyes, trying to peer past his cloak. "I was just wondering the other day if I even had a soul," I answer, sounding disinterested in knowing if he really is here for me.

"You do," he informs me.

"Huh, good to know." I nod a little at the information. "So, thanks for always feeding me." I drag my toe across the carpet a little awkwardly.

"Someone had to do it." His robes shift and I go up on my toes, trying to get a better look at him.

"What some hot cocoa?" I toss the towel I was using on my hair over on my vanity chair.

The robes shift again. "You're asking Death if he wants hot cocoa?" He sounds almost mystified.

"What, you don't like it?" I ask suspiciously. Even I like hot chocolate, and I can barely stomach food.

His hood tilts. "I don't know. I've never had it."

"Well…you don't know what you've been missing." I walk past him to the bedroom door. When I turn, he's standing in the same spot. "Are you coming? I can't rectify your lack of chocolatey experience if you don't." I raise my brows.

When he still doesn't move, I give him a small wave over my shoulder. "Your loss. The offer still stands anytime." My heart is beating faster than usual. I want him to follow me, but I don't want to pressure him either.

I open the few windows I pass on my way down to the kitchen, letting some of the cool evening air filter into the house. Someone has a fire going. I can sense the burnt cedar and ash even though it's probably a mile away. It smells like fall.

I light a few candles and grab a small saucepan from the cupboard. I can feel him before I can see him. I go about getting the sugar, milk, and chocolate as if I expected him to follow me all along. I break off a few big chunks of the chocolate and set it aside while I heat up the milk and sugar.

"I haven't seen many of my friends lately." I pause and look over at him. "Do you know Uncle Skinny Legs? He always comes by a couple times a week, but I haven't seen him in days."

"I'm not the reason you haven't seen them." He sounds almost defensive.

"I didn't think you were." I give him the side-eye. "I think he knows I want to know where Radmon went, so he's avoiding me." I start chopping up the chocolate. "What can I call you?" I jump topics.

"Grim is fine." He moves a little closer, still obscured behind the heavy cloak.

"Really? Grim? Isn't that kind of cliché?" I inquire, before thinking about how it might sound.

"It's my name," he tells me slowly.

"So, you really are the Grim Reaper?" I drop the knife and examine him.

"Last I checked."

"That's so fucking cool. Are there more than one of you? Do you know how everyone is going to die? When they'll die?" I scrape the small bits of chocolate into a glass bowl and pop it in the microwave for twenty second intervals, stirring it in between.

"I know when I need to collect someone's soul." He comes even closer and pulls out the chair to sit. I pretend not to notice, I don't want to spook him. Instead, I check to make sure the milk isn't heating too fast. I don't know how to cook a lot, but I love hot chocolate, so I made it my mission to find the best recipe I could, and to learn how to make it.

"It's almost ready," I chirp, with just a little too much excitement in my tone. "Do you think there's weird shit going on lately?" I tilt my head, wishing I could see his face…I wonder if he's a skeleton.

"You ask a lot of questions." Grim puts his arms on the counter, and one sleeve pulls back enough so I can see some of his human looking hand.

"Not a skeleton then," I comment more to myself. He pulls his hand back into his robe. "I haven't had anyone to talk to in a few days—sue me," I mutter, completely unapologetic. "The lion was the last person…whatever…that I talked to, and he wouldn't even respond to me. He hid in the trees when I tried to go down to introduce myself." I roll my eyes and grab two mugs.

"A lion, you say?" Grim actually sounds interested.

"Not just a lion." I smirk. "He was rocking a golden mane. It was hard to tell from my window, but he looked really big, too. Not that I've seen many real lions. So, I don't really have a comparison," I ramble. Damn, I need to get out more if I'm this excited for someone to stop by.

After pouring half the liquid deliciousness in his mug and the other half in mine, I turn the handle so he can reach for his own cup. "It's hot," I warn him, probably uselessly since he just watched me cook it.

"Wait, you can eat and drink, right? I don't really eat. I can, but most stuff makes me yak."

"Yak?" he repeats slowly. I think I hear a smile in his voice.

"Yeah. Puke, vomit, throw up," I answer, like he might be confused.

"I won't *yak* in your kitchen," he tells me, and I'm certain I can hear his smile this time.

"So, there must be more of you then, if you're hanging out here. I mean, people are dying like every millisecond," I conclude, bringing the mug up and taking my first sip. Yummy.

"There are others," he answers, all cryptic and creepy like. I wonder if he's a wrinkled-up old man under there.

"Are all of you named Grim?" I watch him as he stares down at the mug in front of him. "How will I know it's you and not another Grim when I see you again?" I ask before he can answer.

"It would only ever be me, and I'm the only one they call Grim." His hood lifts up like he's now looking at me.

"The OG," I tease.

"OG?" he questions.

I wish I could see his face. "Original gangster, or old gangster. I was just teasing." I wave my hand. "Are you going to try it?" I motion to the cup.

"I'm thinking about it."

"Fair enough." I lean over the counter. "Back to my question—"

"Which one?" he interrupts me.

"About the weird shit." I take another sip.

"What kind of weird shit?" Grim reaches for the mug, his hand covered by the robe.

"Well, let me see. It all started a few days ago. I found a bleeding guy in my bedroom."

"That happen often?" His voice is light, like he's teasing me.

"Not as often as you'd think," I muse. "I'm pretty sure he wasn't a human, but I'm not positive. Scratch that, he wasn't human," I amend, waving my hand and dismissing my words. "He healed way too fast to be human."

Grim brings the mug near where his face should be. I hold my breath, waiting for him to pull back the hood.

I make a raspberry with my lips when the mug disappears into the darkness of his hood. "You're no fun," I accuse jokingly.

He ignores my comment. "You said it started with the bleeding guy. What else happened?"

"Oh yeah, well, I gave him a ride to a club I hunt at—

Rumors. Do you know it?" I round the island and pull out the stool next to him, but leave a little space between us.

"I do," he confirms, without giving me any other information.

"The security there was acting weird. I think it had something to do with Gunnar. He was the bleeding guy. Then the lion showed up. None of my friends have been to visit since, and then there's you." It's a really quick summary, but ever since Gunnar showed up it feels like something is changing.

The hood nods. "What's weird about me?" He sounds offended.

"You're not weird." I lay my hand over where I think his forearm would be. "It's weird that you're sitting here talking to me. I've asked you to stay tons of times, and you never do, so why now?" I can feel his arm shift under my hand, and he doesn't feel like a frail old man. I pull my fingers back and tuck them into my lap.

"I wasn't supposed to before," he replies.

"Why not?" My back goes ramrod straight.

"I can't tell you." I can't tell if he's lying or not. Strange.

"Can't or won't?" I find myself asking again this week.

"It's…complicated," he offers.

I let out a dark chuckle. "That's a vague book status, not a real answer."

"What is vague book?" The hood tilts.

"It's not a real thing, I was making a joke about Face… never mind." I roll my eyes, a little irritated.

"I can visit you now, though," he volunteers. I let out a

sigh, feeling like I'm being left out, but it's always been that way. I accept the monsters—accept I'm one, too—but they still treat me like I'm different.

"Fine." I huff, standing and snatching my mug. I'm regretting the hot chocolate. It isn't sitting right in my stomach tonight.

"I don't think anything you said is necessarily weird," Grim tells me as I rinse out my mug and place it in the dishwasher. The way he worded his statement once again leaves me unable to read if he's telling the truth or not.

I look up at the ceiling. "It's more a vibe than anything else. I feel like something has shifted. It's hard to explain." I can think of a few, more-subtle details, such as the way Gunnar knew right where my dishwasher was. How something about him felt familiar. There was even something about the lion that called to me, but I don't know how to put it into words. I'm probably overthinking this whole thing.

"You should always listen to your instincts," Grim advises, bringing his mug over to the sink. I take it from him and rinse it, placing it in the washer next to mine.

"I feel like that should have been said with more dramatic flair, and maybe some ominous music." I turn to look at him. "You should lose the robe."

He smooths his hand over his chest and stomach. "You don't think this look works for me?"

"Depends on what you've got going on underneath there." I fold my arms over my stomach and squint my eyes. "Most images depict you as a skeleton, but I saw your hand," I remind him.

"You did," he confirms. I stare over at him. I think he's staring back, but he could be looking out the window for all I know. I give him a shrug, if he wants to wear the robe, so be it.

"Want to play a game or watch a movie?"

Grim shakes his head a little. "I wish I could, but I need to go. Duty calls." Truth.

I deflate. "Really? But you just got here." I sound needy, but I don't care. I'm lonely.

Before he can answer, I feel the awareness of the rage seeping into the room. Looking behind him, I see a slight shimmer in the air.

"You don't carry the sins," I observe, looking back at him. It's the first time I've actually thought about the sins he usually brings to feed me, and how I haven't felt them since he first arrived.

"No, they are attached to souls on the other side." He takes a step back, getting closer to the shimmer.

"I really am grateful. Thank you," I murmur with complete sincerity. He's been coming to me since I was far too young to find more sustainable meals on my own. He doesn't respond.

"Don't be a stranger." I wave as he takes another step back, disappearing along with the mouthwatering essence that came the same time the shimmer appeared. I just ate, but my stomach grumbles at the missed opportunity.

I glance around the empty room, it's still early. Maybe

Theius or Samson will stop by. I sure don't feel like going back to the club tonight.

Instead of watching a movie, I throw on a sweater to head outside. Living way out here makes it easy for my friends to visit, but the isolation gets to me sometimes. I slide my feet into my boots and decide to go find Forea, the heart of the forest. She's always in the woods. Maybe she'll even know about the lion.

CHAPTER 6

I trudge through the woods, my boots growing heavier with every step. The ground is sodden with recent rain. I find myself walking next to the narrow path, rather than walking on it, to avoid the deeper mud.

The calls of frogs and crickets keep me company as I move deeper into the forest. I hear and feel the thump of a fast-moving animal before I can see it. Within seconds, I spot a large buck leaping over fallen trees and brush about fifty feet to my left. I must have spooked him, even though I'm trying to be quiet. "Well, at least I know the lion didn't eat you." I continue walking once he's disappeared, being mindful of how much noise I'm making as I go.

A clearing eventually comes into view, one that always seems to be bathed in moonlight no matter how cloudy or overcast the night might be.

Forea has her head bent low, drinking from a crystal clear pond. She's a magnificent sight to behold. Not all my friends are what you would call scary. I'm sure many people have stumbled upon her and confused her for a very large male caribou. She lifts her head at my approach, not at all skittish, with water still dripping from her face.

"Hi, Forea," I call, while leaning against a large bolder bordering the pond. I'm more tired than I have the right to be after a thirty-minute walk. Maybe I need to come out here more often.

Evening, child, she answers, but it's not out loud. I can hear her in my head. Her voice is feminine, but deep, almost sultry. Her huge antlers are bowed wide up behind her with small strings of moss dripping between the points, resembling jewelry.

How are you faring?

I use my hands and lift my butt up onto the rock. "I'm okay. I thought I'd come for a visit since it's been a while."

Time passes, child, with or without us. Forea turns so I can see her broad chest and the red patch that sits right in the center, as if her heart is exposed. Sometimes, I think she talks in riddles.

A small bunny hops into the clearing, moving right to the pond to drink while standing in the huge reindeer's shadow. There are other animals also: some bedded down, others munching on the grass and weeds.

What's bothering you? Your heart is heavy.

I bring my knees up to my chest and plant my chin on them. The rock is so cold under me that I shiver, but my feet need a break from standing. "Are there any new animals in the forest?"

Forea makes a grunting sound. *There are always new beings—sixteen moths are taking flight right now.* She lifts her nose in the air and I can see a tiny blast of steam as she puffs out an exhale.

"What about a lion with a golden mane?" I wrap my arms around my legs.

Ah, the Nemean. It's like I can hear her smile, but nothing on her physical face shifts.

"You know it then?"

I know him, child, just as I know you.

"I'd never seen him before yesterday. Has he been here long?" I take comfort in the fact that Forea knows him.

He comes and goes, just like the seasons, along with many others.

I nearly jump out of my skin when a bird screeches in the distance. I hadn't even realized how quiet and calm the night has gotten. "Damn bird," I mutter, readjusting my legs. "What about Gunnar? He was the injured male that made it to the house."

He did not pass through the woods, my dear.

"Are you sure? How would he have gotten to the house?" I know not to doubt Forea, even without my senses telling me she's being truthful, but I still ask the questions.

There are many ways one could travel and not venture into the woods. That statement confirms that he isn't human, but what could he be?

I lean back on my palms and look up at the clear sky. The frigidness of the rock finally warms under me, or maybe my body is growing used to the cold; either way, I'm more comfortable now. The small animals continue scurrying about, while Forea dips her face back into the pool for another drink.

I sit in the quiet of her and her animals' company for a long while. My legs are stiff when I slide off the rock. "You know you're welcome at the house anytime." I break the silence. Forea only dips her head a bit to acknowledge me.

My walk back is just as sluggish as my outward journey. The mud on my boots had dried, but they're caked over with even more by the time I make it to the tree line bordering the clearing of my house. The sound of someone's rapid breathing freezes me in my tracks.

"She's not here," he grumbles into a cell phone near his ear. I take cover behind a thick oak tree, but keep him in my sights. A shot of adrenaline courses through my veins. I'm not scared—quite the opposite in fact. I can't see the man's face, but I know he's human.

"I don't know. Her car is in the garage, but there's no one in the house." The man winces and pulls the phone away from his ear. "I know I'm not supposed to go in the house. I only checked because I hadn't seen any movement in hours."

"Well, shit," the man mumbles, pulling the phone away

from his ear again. In the next second, another man appears right next to him out of thin air. The newcomer grabs the other man by the throat and lifts.

"I didn't go in," he croaks, holding on to the arm that's lifting him in the air.

"Then how the fuck do you know she's not in there?" I tilt my head, his voice sounds familiar.

The man being choked makes some gurgling sounds before the other man releases him, and he falls to a heap on the ground, immediately grabbing at his neck.

"Footprints," the man gasps. "She went into the woods." It takes him several attempts, but he finally gets the words out.

"Fucking idiot." I know that voice. Gunnar? No, it couldn't be him, he sounds completely different. "She probably just went for a walk. Get back to the truck and get the fuck out of here before she comes back," he orders, stomping away from the man still crumpled on the ground. When he turns, the moonlight shines on his face, and I see it is, in fact, Gunnar.

"What the hell are you doing here, and why do you have someone watching me?" I mutter under my breath. Damn, I do talk to myself way too much.

His head snaps in my direction and I slip farther behind the tree. I want to know what he's up to before I decide what to do about it. Too bad, I actually kind of liked him.

I close my eyes and control my breathing. I can't do much about how fast my heart is beating other than force myself to stay calm. After several long moments without hearing a sound, I peer out from behind the oak to find the clearing empty, with no evidence that Gunnar or his little minion were ever here.

I give it several more minutes before coming out from the tree line, making sure he's not lying in wait for me. I skirt the house, moving around the back of the property, and when my back door is in sight, I dash from the cover of the trees and run up the stairs. The door opens freely—I hardly ever lock them, but it might be time to start now.

The house feels empty when I enter. I send out my senses to every corner just in case, but no one has been in the house. I think I'll be making a trip back to Rumors tomorrow—twice in one week, a new record for me.

"Yeah, nothing necessarily weird going on," I mock Grim, and kick off my boots, sending them sailing into the backyard. "You should really stop talking to yourself. Someone is going to think you're crazy." I slam the door hard and flip the lock for good measure.

I make my way through the house and yank my curtains closed as I do. How many times has that guy, or someone like him, been peeking in my windows without my knowledge? I've become too complacent. He should have never even gotten that close to me without alerting me.

Over the years, I've learned to dull my senses and only use them when I need to feed, but I think it's time I hone those impressions I get and figure out exactly what I'm capable of.

~

"WHERE ARE YOU GOING?" Aeson chirps from my vanity. I glance over my shoulder.

"Where have you been?" I turn to fully face her.

"Whoa, va-va-va-voom!" The tiny dark slashes over her equally dark eyes wiggle in my direction. "Hot date? Is it the bleeder?"

I run my palms over my short, bodycon dress. "You like?" I ask, spinning to give her the full effect.

"I do. If you could spare a few inches of fabric, I could make one for myself." She angles her head from left to right. "But it doesn't look like you can. The bleeder is one lucky SOB."

"It's not for the bleeder—not the way you're thinking, anyway. And his name is Gunnar," I confess, and drop onto the edge of my bed. "I think he has someone watching me."

"Kinky. Don't knock it until you've tried it." Aeson shrugs.

I roll my eyes. "I have tried it, and—again—not what I meant. He was here last night with a human." I pause. "He had the human watching the house. I caught him when I came out of the woods." I haven't had anyone to talk to about this. I barely slept all day thinking about what I was going to do tonight.

"Intriguing." Aeson rubs her tiny palms together. "Are you going to eat his face off?"

"No." I grab a pillow from the head of the bed and place it

over my lap. "That's just an Aeson thing. Most people don't eat off other people's faces."

She waves her hand at me like I'm the one being ridiculous. "It's a problem solver," she argues. "What's the plan then?"

"I haven't decided yet." I pull at the fabric of the pillow. "I want to know why he was here, and why he had someone watching me."

"Well, I only see two options." Aeson kicks up her little legs, showing off her spiky heels. "You could eat his face off, since everyone talks when you're munching on their eyelids." She peers at me like she's just offered the best possible advice.

She rolls her eyes when I don't immediately jump at the suggestion. "Or...you could play dumb, get close to him, seduce him, and find out what you want to know." She pauses for a brief second. "Then you can eat his face, or I'll do it for you."

"Taking one for the team, huh?" I toss the pillow off to the side of the bed. I kind of like the idea of not letting him know I knew he was here last night.

"You know me—I'm a giver." Aeson wiggles her shoulders in a shimmy.

I giggle despite the darkness of the conversation. I know for a fact Aeson hasn't chewed on anyone who didn't deserve it.

"Well, I'm going back to the club. Wish me luck." I smooth my hands down my dress again before heading to the closet for a pair of shoes.

"In that getup, you won't need luck: just a stiff breeze and you'll have everyone's attention." My fierce little friend winks at me as I head out the door. I poke my head back in just as Aeson moves to stand.

"Sorry I'm bailing on you again tonight." I can feel the frown on my face. I've been hoping for company the last few days, and now here she is, and I'm leaving.

"Don't worry about it. Go have fun. I'll see you soon," she replies, dismissing me easily.

"Feel free to raid the closet for anything you want," I tell her in consolation.

"Anything?" Her eyes are bright.

"Anything," I confirm.

"Woohoo!" She jumps down to the seat in front of the vanity, then slides down the leg of the chair. There's a smile on my face when I bounce down the stairs.

I'm cautious when I open the door connecting the garage to the house. This new feeling of apprehension has put me on edge, but I kind of like the intrigue of it all. I think I've gotten rather bored with the way things have been going.

I don't bother turning on a light; my eyes are already accustomed to the darkness. Betty is sitting in her usual spot. Even the dimness can't hide the glitter flecks in her paint.

After I'm seated, I hit the button to open the garage door, reaching out with my extra senses as it does. I spent the hours I couldn't sleep today pushing myself to see how far my ability to sense someone would stretch.

I struggled a bit at first. I've been training myself for a

long time to ignore and dull my extra senses. I didn't really feel like they had much purpose when I wasn't actively hunting. I let the awareness come over me now, dropping the walls I didn't even realize I had been erecting.

I can feel Aeson still up in my bedroom. She tastes like I would imagine a red wine would taste, heady with a sour aftertaste. Pushing further out, I feel a human, but not the same one from last night. He's about a mile from the house. I touch the edge of his soul. If he's sinned today, it's too small for me to sense, at least from this distance. But I do wonder what he's doing out here—another spy for Gunnar, perhaps?

A flicker of something dark appears near the human. I know without a doubt it's Grim, and my breath catches. Is he here to take the man's soul? Why else would both of them be here, now?

A sense of urgency comes over me, I need to know what Grim is doing here. Betty could cover the distance of a mile in a matter of seconds, but they would hear me coming before I could get close to them. I look down at my heels and dress. "Shit!" I slam my palms on the steering wheel. There's no way I could run in these shoes. I kick off my heels and climb out of Betty, feet be damned. I want to know what they're up to. Too bad my senses don't tell me anything other than if they're sinful or give me a gauge of their humanity, or lack thereof.

Cutting through the woods will offer me cover, and it's the quickest route, but I'll lose a little bit of speed running barefoot. I jog along my driveway, staying on the grass, but I still wince every time I step on a rock or almost trip over the uneven ground. Once I'm closer, I slow my trot and move behind the tree line.

My heart is racing and I'm panting. Yup, I definitely need to work out. But I'm also filled with excitement. Who knew what a thrill it would be to have someone stalking you?

CHAPTER 7

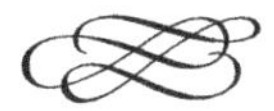

The human is leaning against his car, staring down at a cell phone in his hand, seemingly oblivious to the dark presence.

I look around for Grim. I can sense him, but he must be cloaking himself, because I can't see him anywhere. Making sure not to step on any twigs, I inch closer. The night is so quiet that I hear when the man's phone vibrates in his hand.

"Great, I was just about to win," he mumbles, then brings the phone up to his ear. "Yeah?" he answers.

I use his distraction to get even closer, but I pause, realizing that if I can feel Grim, he might be aware of me, too. Damn it. I pull back a little and focus on where I think he is—several feet on the other side of the road. His essence tastes smoky, like a campfire.

"No movement," the human says into the phone, not bothering to keep his voice down. Ha, I was right, he is here to watch the house. I wonder if it's Gunnar on the other end of the line.

Grim chooses that moment to step out of his shimmering portal. I tilt my head, realizing I can sense him when he's not really here. That's new. I wonder if it's because I've actually met him, or was it because I was actively looking?

I file those thoughts away to think about later and focus on what's happening in front of me now. The man drops the phone from his hand and takes a step back, the heel of his shoe scraping against the tire of his SUV.

"What the hell?" He looks at Grim, who's completely cloaked in his robe. The only new addition would be the gleaming scythe curved over his head. I slam my hand over my mouth to keep myself from speaking. That thing looks wicked. The dark wooden handle is worn smooth and bent crooked in places. It looks like it's been curved and honed into shape with years of use. The blade is outrageously large, and the arc of the knife edge catches the glow of the moon in an unnatural way. Runes and letters are etched along the top, giving it an even more terrifying appearance. It's strangely beautiful.

"Quiet," Grim orders. A chill skates down my spine when he speaks. His voice is layered, making it sound as if several people are speaking at once.

"Wha-what do y-you want?" the man stammers.

"I want you to tell the Berserker that I know the pact has

been broken. Without the covenant in place, all deals are off." Grim takes a step closer to the man. "He broke the decree, and now he will deal with the consequences."

"I'll tell him, I'll tell him," the man promises, arching back to get as far away from Grim as possible.

It takes everything inside of me to stay hidden behind the trees. I don't want to reveal how much I've heard, especially when I have no idea if any of this involves me. Grim disappears, dissolving back into the place he came from, and my awareness of him fades quickly.

The man collapses back against the car, a curse falling from his lips. Seconds later, he scrambles for the fallen phone on the ground.

"Are you there?" he asks, panting into the phone. "Holy fuck! I think that was the Grim-fucking-Reaper!" He reaches into his pocket and pulls out a small set of keys. The SUV chirps, unlocking. He fumbles with the door handle, trying to get in, while still holding the phone to his ear with his shoulder.

"I didn't sign up for this shit. Did you hear what he said?" He slams the door behind him, and I hear the lock engage. I don't really think that would keep anyone out, but if it makes him feel better… The engine turns over and he screeches off without another glance in the direction of my house.

Once he's fled, I step out onto the grassy strip near the side of the road. My feet are a little achy now that all the excitement is over. I wince, thinking about how much it's going to suck putting my heels back on.

On the walk back to Betty, my mind spins with the different ideas of what pact Grim could be talking about, and who the Berserker is. Gunnar comes to mind. The plot thickens.

Now, I don't just have to figure out what Gunnar is up to —I need to add Grim to that list as well.

It's Saturday night, and the line to get in is wrapped around the corner. Girls in skimpy dresses are huddled close, trying to keep warm in the evening chill, while guys have their hands shoved into their pockets, attempting to look unaffected.

I saunter up to the entrance, and Reggie's eyes scan me from head to toe. "Looking good," he purrs. I don't recognize the man with him.

"Hey, Reggie, busy night?" I cock out my hip a little to exaggerate my curves.

"Full house, but we always have room for you." His dark eyes scan me again.

"You're so sweet." I give him a seductive smile and step a little closer. The new guy unclips the red rope he's standing behind and steps to the side, allowing me to pass.

I look over my shoulder and notice the expression on Reggie's face has shifted. The flirty smirk is gone, and it's been replaced with a look of concentration as he brings his fingers up to his ear. I watch his lips move in a mumble, but I can't hear what he's saying.

The new guy jabs Reggie in the arm with his elbow when he sees me watching. Reggie pulls his hand down and tightens his lips into what I think he's hoping is a smile, but the effort is wasted. It's easy to see how forced it is, which makes me super suspicious.

I enter the dark hall where the once-blue lights are now a deep purple. The music is loud enough so that I can already hear and feel the bass hitting with each beat of the song through the floor and walls. Another security guy reaches for the door handle of the club as I approach. "Welcome to Rumors," he greets me.

He pulls the handle before I can respond, and the noise drowns out any reply I could have given him, so I nod my head while passing him.

Instead of heading to the bar like usual, I skirt the edge of the club. It's so packed tonight that I can't even see the dance floor through all the bodies clustered around the edges. I need a better vantage point if I want to look for Gunnar. With my luck, he won't even be here.

The veritable buffet of sins wafting my way is distracting me, though. Every person I walk past seems to be riddled with misdeeds, tempting me to stop and taste them.

A heaviness settles over me, almost like someone is pushing against me. I shove against the sludge-like oppression and find myself in a nearly empty section of the club. Several heads turn in my direction.

Vanessa is seated among a group of people. They look

human, but the darkness seeping from them tells me they're far from it.

"Sorry to crash your party." I wave my hand, noticing Gunnar emerging from a hallway. I let my eyes skip over him quickly, as if I don't recognize him. "Private event?" I purse my lips patronizingly.

"How are you even over here?" Vanessa stands up slowly and two beefy men rise with her.

"Pretty sure I just walked." I look over my shoulder to see if there's anything there that should have stopped me, but don't see anything.

"Are the wards not working?" She glares at a woman next to her.

"They're in place. I checked them myself," the girl replies quickly, looking at me closely with her head tilted to the side. The wards must have been the sludge I felt.

Vanessa focuses on me again. "You're Deanna, right?" She bars her arm across the man next to her as if she's holding him back. She knows exactly who I am. She's lying about not knowing my proper name.

"Close enough." I don't bother correcting her. "I can see this is an invite-only kind of thing." I give her a condescending wink, telling her exactly what I think of her and her friends. "I have other plans this evening. If you'll excuse me." I glance over at Gunnar for a brief second, then give Vanessa and her men a small wave, before I walk right through the middle of their group. I end up on the opposite side I entered from, pushing past the wards like I'm walking through water, and making sure they see I didn't feel an ounce of resistance.

"Who was that?" a masculine voice inquires.

"No one. Finish your business," Gunnar spits, abruptly ending any questions.

As soon as I clear the bubble Vanessa called a ward, that section of the club is obscured again. However, it only takes a scant bit of concentration before the whole group of them come back into focus. I make a point of looking around as if I'm looking for someone. "Hey!" I wave my hand and move a little farther into the crowd like I'm greeting someone. Once the bodies fill in around me, I turn to watch the warded section.

Gunnar marches up to Vanessa. I can see his jaw ticking as he grinds his teeth. I watch his mouth to see if I can make out the words he's saying, but I'm not able to read his lips. He delivers a fierce glare to the small group around Vanessa, before storming back toward the hall he came through.

"Somebody's in trouble," I singsong, looking around to find a place from which I can watch them without being detected, until I'm ready to find Gunnar again.

"Excuse me, sorry." I shimmy past a group of guys sitting across from the bar. They have two tables, but most of them are standing and drinking anyway, as they holler over the loud music to hear each other.

"Mind if I borrow a chair?" I blink up at a handsome man with a glass bottle in his hand. His narrowed eyes scan me. I study him back in the same way.

His hair is too short to be called long, but too long to be called short, either. He has a fine scruff covering his jaw. It's a shade or two darker than his light hair, but I notice how the very ends of his hair are tipped dark like the stubble on his jaw. Interesting.

I take a second to appreciate the width of his shoulders and neck. He's dressed pretty casually—dark jeans and a loose, long-sleeved t-shirt. It's not doing much to show off what's underneath, but it shows his confidence. He doesn't need to go all out to be noticed. He looks exceptionally comfortable in his own skin. I wish I could make out the true color of his light eyes, but the club is rather dark.

Nothing about him seems deceitful. If anything, he almost feels too pure. It's not that he's never sinned—it's only that I can tell he doesn't make a habit of it.

It takes the physical attraction I'm feeling toward him and makes him damn near irresistible.

There's something about him that makes me want to get him all mussed up and dirty.

"Sure, can I get you a drink?" he offers eventually, unaware of my less-than-pure thoughts.

"No thanks, just needed a place to sit," I reply, recovering quickly, and lift my foot in the air, alluding to my heels like they're the reason I want to be off my feet.

He glances around as if he doesn't buy it, and he's looking for the real reason I'm here. When he doesn't find whatever he's looking for, he tips his bottle in my direction. "Let me know if you change your mind about the drink." Then he turns back to the group he's with, ignoring me.

Damn, if I weren't already busy tonight, I would have him. I look down at his ass. The shirt might be too baggy, but those jeans are hugging his ass in a way that makes me a little jealous.

I wonder if he's the DD, since he doesn't seem nearly as intoxicated as the other men of his group. They barely even noticed me. To be fair, they really seem to be having a good time among themselves. That's why I chose them—well, that and the hottie. I'll have to get his name and his number for another time.

I angle my chair so I can see Vanessa. She's resumed a seat among her clique. The two goons beside her are still standing, appearing as if they might be more alert than before I sauntered into their little playdate.

I snicker, remembering how shocked Vanessa was when I busted in on her soirée. She's deep in conversation now with the woman who promised the wards were working fine. Maybe they were—against someone else—but after I felt the initial resistance, it was only a matter of pushing a little harder, like I was walking up a hill instead of on flat ground.

And now that I know what to look or feel for, I don't think I'll ever be fooled by a similar ward again. I wonder how many times I've been near one and didn't know.

That thought sobers me a little. When did I become so unworried? I shake out my hair to hide the fact I was actually shaking my head at my ignorance.

Remembering this isn't just a game, I watch the hallway Gunnar disappeared into. If he doesn't come out soon, I'm going to need a reason to go back and get him, or give him reason to come out to me.

An idea starts to form. A devious smile lights up my face, enough that I look down to hide the grin. This might just be fun after all.

CHAPTER 8

"How are the feet?" The question takes me by surprise. I've been watching Vanessa's crew like a hawk.

"Good, yours?" I reply on instinct, before remembering I made my feet the excuse for needing to sit down.

"A little sore, actually. I've been up almost twenty-four hours at this point." The cutie glances down at a heavy watch on his right wrist. He's pushed up his sleeves, baring his forearms: the sexy man equivalent of exposed cleavage.

I reach for one of the other chairs and angle it out for him to take a seat. "Don't let me stop you from taking a load off."

I peek back toward Vanessa. I haven't seen Gunnar once since I've sat down, but I think her little meeting is about to wrap up. Two of the people already left the group a few minutes ago.

"You waiting for someone?" He takes a draw from his beer.

"Depends, what's your name?" I prop my chin up on my hand.

"Calix. Depends on what?" he responds, grabbing the back of the chair and spinning it on one leg swiftly, until it lands backwards, and then he takes a seat. He rests his forearms on the top of the chair, dangling his beer bottle from two fingertips.

I raise my brow in appreciation. He's quick and quite graceful.

"Is that your real name?" I avoid his question. Fortunately, he's taken the seat I offered, so I'm still able to see the area behind him and watch for Gunnar.

He nods his head and confirms, "Sadly, it is." He's being truthful.

"Why sadly? I think it's a great name—unusual, but I have a strange name, too."

"I bet you have a beautiful name." I watch Calix's mouth move as if he's licking his front teeth.

"Most everyone calls me Dami, because no one pronounces it correctly."

"Try me." He tips his chin.

"Damiana," I say slowly, and reach across the table to take the beer from his hands. With my eyes still on his, I bring it up to my mouth and take a long drink.

"I usually don't like to share, but I can't say I mind so

much right now." Calix leans forward so his arms are now resting on the table.

Just as I'm about to ask what else he'd be willing to give me, I see Gunnar stepping out of the hallway. My shoulders fall, I was actually liking where this was going. "Damn it," I curse.

"What's wrong?" Calix's voice changes, becoming harder as he looks over his shoulder like he knew I wasn't focused on just him.

"Just something I need to take care of." I meet his eyes. "You got a number?" I'm not one to beat around the bush when I find something I want. And I want Calix.

"How about we trade? I'll give you mine, you give me yours?" He watches me closely. Normally, I wouldn't, but there's something about him that makes me want to.

"I'll make an exception for you," I tell Calix, then peek over at Gunnar. He's watching me with his arms crossed over his chest. He knows I can see past the ward, oh well.

I wiggle my fingers, miming writing on a napkin, asking Calix if he has anything to write with. He pats his chest immediately, but he's already shaking his head in denial. "You don't have your phone with you?" He looks me over again, noting I don't have anything with me like a purse, and I sure don't have any pockets in this dress. "Hang on, I'll get something. Don't leave." He leans in even closer to me.

"I'll wait as long as I can," I tell him, and I will, but if Gunnar comes over here, I might need to go.

Calix looks around. "Shit, I'll be quick."

"Not what a girl likes to hear, Calix," I quip, leaning back and eyeing him over his beer bottle before I drink the last gulp.

His top lip curls back in what could be called a smile, but it's much more like he's baring his teeth at me. "Even when I'm quick, I'm effective," he promises.

Calix stands and taps one of the guys he was talking with earlier on the shoulder, asking for a pen.

While he's working through the group, I stand and look for someone who will help me with my plan to get Gunnar's attention. There's a drunk guy near the dance floor, he's all clumsy hands and searching fingers. I've had my eye on him for most of the night—he's seeping sins. He'll work.

"I need to go, Calix." I tap his shoulder.

He turns to face me. "No luck." He spreads his hands, his eyes are wide like he's telling me he really tried.

"Maybe next time," I offer, feeling pretty bummed too.

"I have *my* phone." He pulls it out of his front pocket and holds it out to me. "You can give me your number?" He licks over his lips like he's worried I might say no.

I take the cell from his hand and hit the phone icon. When the keypad pops up, I dial my own number before handing it back to him.

"Thanks for the seat, Calix." I lean up and press my lips to his. It's not long or deep, but I do drag my tongue over his bottom lip before pulling back.

I watch his mouth as his teeth scrape over the path my

tongue just took. "Sure you can't stay?" he questions, his voice a little deeper.

"Wish I could." It's not even a little bit of a lie.

"Is an hour long enough to wait before I call?"

I throw my head back and laugh, he's not any more patient than I am. "I'm not sure how long I'll be tied up tonight," I answer noncommittally.

I trail my fingers over his chest as I pass. I was right, the shirt didn't do the hard body beneath it any justice.

Once I clear his group, I stomp over toward the drunk guy. I don't have to pretend to be angry, I'm pissed at the missed opportunity with Calix. Probably angrier than I should be, considering I've never let a missed hookup bother me before.

I get as close to the drunk as I can without actually forcing myself between him and the current girl he's ogling. Taking a deep breath, I let the beat of the music settle me. I start to sway my hips slowly, imagining the feel of someone's hands on my waist. I ignore the fact that it's Calix's hands I'm imagining.

I lift my arms in the air, taking up some of my hair as I do. It falls back down over my back and shoulders in a pale wave.

I know the drunk is going to touch me before he does. I can feel the slime oozing off him as his thoughts turn nefarious. Even though I hate the thought, I let him put his nasty hand on the swell of my hip.

One touch, and I spin around and shove him backwards. He stumbles, but there are too many people standing around for him to fall on his ass like he should have. He gets bounced right back up. He's so unsteady on his feet, he almost goes down again trying to regain his balance.

"Hey," he slurs, his eyes are all glassy, but his lips are lifted in a sneer.

"Keep your fucking hands off me." I thought this would be a good idea to get Gunnar's attention, but I want to kick this guy in the balls so badly.

The crowd shifts before he has a chance to respond. I feel a hand on my upper arm, and when I look over, Gunnar is standing next to me, glaring down at the drunk, who now has a security guy holding his shoulder, only the grip doesn't seem nearly as gentle as the one Gunnar has on me.

"Time to go," Gunnar announces, and tugs on my arm a little. The anger is still simmering inside of me, and I want to tug my arm out of his hold, but this is exactly what I was hoping for.

"I didn't do shit," the man spews. "That bitch pushed me."

I glare over my shoulder at him. The man grabs his chest and starts coughing violently. Even though I don't want to, I release the hold I have on his soul. This man is riddled with sins so severe, he's going to be dead within a few years anyway, and those years won't be very pleasant. I can already feel the tar surrounding his organs.

The first time I ripped out someone's soul was by accident. I was young and hungry. There was a teacher at school whose aura was dirty, but not black, and I pulled too much from her. Before I realized it, she was on the floor, clutching her chest. The next day, the school announced she had a heart attack, and they even brought in grief counselors. But I knew what had really happened.

I had eaten her soul instead of her sins. It was a very effective lesson on meal planning.

"Shut up. I should have tossed you out an hour ago." The security guy holding the drunk jerks his arm, causing the man to stumble again. He's too busy trying to catch his breath to argue anymore, though. I made sure of that.

Gunnar leads me in the opposite direction of the exit where the drunk is headed, his grip still loose on my upper arm. "If you wanted my attention, all you had to do was ask. Not almost get some idiot killed to get it."

I do pull away from him then. "I wasn't even close to killing him," I counter.

"I didn't say *you* were." He leans down in my face. Gunnar's eyes are wild, and there's a thick vein pulsing at the side of his neck.

I roll my eyes. If he thinks that's going to intimidate me, he's mistaken. "I've been watching that guy harass women all night. I was doing you a favor."

"Next time, just tell someone," Gunnar grates out through his teeth.

"Sure, I'll do that." I brace my hands on my hips when we reach a door that has 'Authorized Personnel Only' painted in bright yellow across the top.

Gunnar waves a keycard in front of a square pad, and a small, green light blinks twice before he reaches for the door handle and yanks it open. He looks at me expectantly, waiting for me to go in ahead of him.

"Tossing me out the back?" I strut through the door, not at all worried that he might be.

"Last door on the left." He motions for me to go forward without answering my question. The hall is lined with doors on either side, but the one Gunnar directed me to has another square pad next to the door. He swipes the same keycard near the box, then enters a six-digit code into a keypad. His fingers go too fast for me to follow, but it's not like I plan to sneak back in here or anything.

I hear the lock disengage this time, since most of the music from the club is drowned out behind the walls. The room is dark until Gunnar slaps his hand against the wall. I cross my arms under my chest. I figured with all that security, there would be something notable behind the door—not a boring-as-hell office with an old, metal desk that looks as if it's been around for a decade, and a worn-out office chair that's leaning to the left behind it.

"Fancy," I drawl.

Gunnar tosses the keycard on the desk. "Wanna explain why you sauntered past Gina's wards tonight?"

"First of all, I don't need to explain shit to you." This isn't going quite how I expected. I'm still feeling on edge. It can't just be the Calix situation. I'm looking for a fight. The drunk didn't provide nearly enough of a distraction.

Gunnar pinches the bridge of his nose. In a much calmer

tone, he tries again. "Will you please tell me how you were able to get past the wards?"

That appeases the anger in me a little. I look around the office again. There's a ratty old couch to the left of the desk. It looks as if it were pulled out of a dumpster behind a thrift shop, but I walk over and sit as daintily as possible on the arm of the sofa anyway.

"It wasn't intentional. I didn't even know they were there until I was past them," I answer honestly.

"Y-You...What? You didn't know they were there?" he stammers, like he can't believe what I just said.

"True story." I peer at the desk. "Is this your office? Because I think you could do better."

"Wait, if you didn't know the wards were there, why did you even go through them? That's what the wards are designed to do: keep people away." Gunnar flips a deadbolt on the door.

I narrow my eyes on him and open my senses, but just like the day he woke up at my house, he's somehow blocking me. Interesting.

I lean my upper body toward him and whisper, "Do you really want to know?"

He takes a slow step in my direction and his eyes dilate. I know I have his attention. "Yes." He nods.

"Then tell me what you are," I demand in my normal tone, leaning back again.

"You can't tell yet?" He seems almost surprised. A small

grin lifts one side of his mouth before he smothers it with a frown.

"I thought you were human when you were all bloody." I shrug my shoulders as I remind him that I've seen him when he was vulnerable. "But it's obvious you're not. You healed too fast." I tap my finger on my chin thinking. "You don't taste like one of my baddies."

"One of your baddies," Gunnar repeats, dumbfounded. "What are your baddies, and how many do you have?" His voice is deeper.

"Oh, lots. Tons," I confirm.

"Tons?" He swallows.

"Well, not tons really." I roll my eyes. "But lots."

"And what do those baddies taste like?" Gunnar lifts his chin and crosses his arms over his chest.

"Like darkness and nightmares." I smile.

He blinks at me for several moments. Eventually, I frown. He seems really weirded out. "So…" I prompt, trying to encourage Gunnar to talk again.

He shakes his head like he was lost in thought. "What do I taste like?" He turns his head to the side and waits for my response like he's scared to hear it.

"I can't get a good read on you. When you were injured, you tasted like pain." I purse my lips. "You must be blocking me somehow now."

He stands up a little taller. "Oh, well, okay then." The middle of his forehead wrinkles over his nose. "And the baddies?" he asks again.

"I already told you about my friends."

"Your friends," he repeats slowly.

I throw my hands in the air. "Why are we talking about this? It's not like I go around tasting my friends for sins."

"You brought it up," he defends.

I glare over at Gunnar. Should I just ask him why he's having someone watch me? No, this is entertaining. "What are you?" I inquire again, reminding him if he wants me to talk, he has to give me information first.

"Human…mostly," he hedges.

"Liar," I singsong. Even if I don't know what he is, I still know a lie when I hear it.

"I was… a long time ago." Gunner opens and closes his fists several times.

"That explains a little, but what are you now?" I tilt my head, examining him.

"A Berserker," he grumbles out quickly.

CHAPTER 9

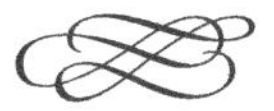

"A Berserker?" I roll the word over my tongue. I've only heard that name once before, when Grim was talking to the man outside my house. I'll have to ask Aeson for details, she'll probably know. I'm sure not going to ask him.

"Now, tell me more about your friends." Gunnar walks over to the desk and pulls out the chair.

"I thought you wanted to talk about the wards?" I remind him.

He waves his hand as he sits and the chair squeaks in response. "I'm more interested in these baddies."

"Why do you want to know about them?" I narrow my eyes on him.

"Just curious. I don't call my friends 'my baddies.'" Gunnar drags himself closer to the desk, his knees slamming into the underside. "Mother—" He tightens his mouth and adjusts his legs again. Not his desk then after all.

"Do you not believe I have friends?" I lift my chin in the air. I may not have any human friends, but my friends are better than humans anyway. Humans scare way too easily.

Gunnar holds his hands out defensively. "I was just curious. I was thinking they were your… never mind," he concedes. "I got off track." Gunnar makes a circle over his temple with his pointer finger.

I nod my head and agree. He has. If I want to get more information out of him, I should probably be a little more cooperative, too. "I really didn't know about the wards. I just felt a thickness in the air." I run my fingers over my thumbs and palms, thinking about another way to describe it, but come up empty. "It made me curious."

Gunnar makes a sound between a snort and a huff. "Considering the wards are designed to do the exact opposite of making people curious, it's no wonder they didn't deter you." He pinches the bridge of his nose.

"What's the big deal? I don't care about Vanessa and her miscreants." I eye the small sofa, this arm is starting to get uncomfortable, but I'll be damned if I sit on that nasty thing. I'd probably get mange or herpes from the cursed thing. "This place is nasty." I stand up.

"The big deal," Gunnar announces, while rising to his feet, "is you've made *other* people curious, and we both know what happens when people get curious." He crosses his arms over his chest and looks down his nose at me.

I plant my hands on my hips and glare back at him. "Maybe you didn't hear me, but I couldn't give two shits about Vanessa or her friends."

Gunnar's eyes travel up from my legs and linger on my breasts for a brief moment before he collects himself and focuses back on my face. Good to know the dress served its purpose. "You don't know anything about them or what they're capable of." His voice is harsh. I think he knows I caught him looking.

Lowering my arms, I saunter away from the sofa and closer to Gunnar. He licks his bottom lip in an almost predatory manner. My heart skips a beat. I think I would like to tame him. The earlier attraction I felt for him blooms.

I take my time giving him a once over, not shy at all to show him exactly what I'm doing. His black hair is cropped short, and his brow is a little too heavy for him to be classically handsome, but he exudes masculinity. The scar over his lips is distracting me. I want to bite it, see if it's as soft as his lips look.

I force my eyes to travel down to his chest. He's wearing a dark Henley, and there are a couple of buttons left open at the collar, exposing his neck. His shirt, unlike Calix's, is molded to him. I have no idea why I'm comparing the two of them, other than Calix is still on my mind.

Gunnar's hands tighten into fists at his sides. I don't let it deter me from checking out the front of his black tactical pants and deciding they're way too baggy.

"Do you know something about Vanessa or her friends that

you'd like to share with me?" My voice comes out a little husky, but I don't bother hiding the fact that I find him attractive.

"I know you should be more careful." Gunnar crosses his arms over his chest again, this time tucking his hands under his armpits.

I give him a curious look. He's definitely giving me mixed signals. "You seem to be warning me away every time we speak, Gunnar. I'm starting to wonder whether you know something I don't or you just don't want me around."

He blinks rapidly and drops his arms to his sides again. "I want you around," he answers quickly, then his lips thin. "I mean, I want you to be safe. People are willing to do stupid things for power."

It's my turn to cross my arms over my chest. "You're implying that I have power—how would you know that?"

"Anyone with any supernatural senses can tell you're powerful, Damiana," he tells me, speaking like he's talking to a child. "Why do you think your friends are drawn to you?"

"How long have you been watching me?" My back goes ramrod straight.

Gunnar curses under his breath. "Let's stop playing games, all right? You knew I was watching you. I felt you in the clearing last night when that idiot called me."

"You're the one playing games," I accuse petulantly. "I came here to figure out what you're up to and how you ended up at my house."

I spin as someone bangs loudly on the door. Gunnar stalks

past me and reaches for the door handle roughly. "What?" he barks, before it's even open.

"Sorry, boss. Vanessa is looking for you." The guy at the door doesn't meet Gunnar's stare, instead, he focuses right in the center of Gunnar's chest.

I watch Gunnar's back as it expands, and I can see a fine tremor work its way down from his head and chest. *What the hell is that?* I wonder, as I step around him and peer up at his face. The veins along the sides of his neck are standing out thickly, and his eyes seem to almost sink in deeper, making his brow even more pronounced.

"I didn't want to interrupt you, boss, but you told me to." The man at the door holds his ground, even as Gunnar stares at him with barely restrained rage. Strangely enough, I don't get the urge to feed like I usually do when such emotion presents itself. I watch Gunnar to see if his aura takes on any smudges, but I can't see that either.

"Hey." I kind of slap Gunnar's arm up near the shoulder. His head turns to the side slowly, and he examines me. The man at the door makes a quick gasping noise. Out of the corner of my eye, I watch as he leans his upper body the tiniest bit forward, as if he's about to intervene between Gunnar and me. "We're not done with this conversation," I announce.

The man at the door volleys his head back and forth, like he can't decide who to look at—me or Gunnar. I tap my toe, becoming impatient as Gunnar continues to stare at me.

"We will have to finish our conversation later, my lady."

Gunner barely opens his mouth when he speaks, but I do get a glimpse of sharper than normal teeth.

"Are you sure you're not a shifter?" I go up on my tippy toes to try to get a closer look at his face and mouth.

"Ho-ly fuck!" the man at the door mutters.

I spare him a glance. He's acting weird.

"No," comes Gunnar's single word response.

I roll my eyes. "Well, I'm not waiting here in this nasty-ass office while you go be Vanessa's errand boy," I spout, mad that he would leave me to go to her. I knew I didn't like that bitch.

"You will go where I think you'll be safest," Gunnar argues.

"Let's just see how that works out for you, shall we?" I cross my arms over my chest again and glare at him. I'm not at all intimidated by his bulking up, or the freaky teeth. Sometimes, I wish I had something on the outside that convayed what the inside feels like. A pair of scary-ass chompers might just do the trick.

"You will go home." Gunnar ignores my threat, and I deflate.

"Oh." I almost pout. "Fine, but don't think we're done. I'll be back here every night if necessary." I lean in a little closer. "And I have friends that will help me find you if you try to run or hide from me." I narrow my eyes at Gunnar, making sure he knows I'm telling the truth.

Out of the corner of my eye, I see the man at the door shift on his feet. Gunnar's top lip lifts in a sneer as he focuses back on the man. "Why are you still here?" he demands with a sharp bite to his words.

Without a word, the man about-faces and rushes down the hall. I hear the music grow louder when he opens the door to the club.

"Don't send people to watch my house anymore," I order, when the music dies down again. One of Gunnar's eyebrows rises, but he doesn't respond verbally. The look says, 'I'll do what the hell ever I want.'

I ignore him and his look, and stomp down the hall back toward the club. I don't like feeling like I'm being dismissed. My jealousy rears its head again. I jerk the door open and scan the club for the asshole owner. I don't spot her, but I do see Calix; his eyes were already on the door when I opened it.

Even better, I make it two steps before I feel a heavy palm on my shoulder. I don't have to look up to know who it is. "Gunnar, you better quit putting your hands on me without my permission." I scowl up at him. He yanks his hand back and lowers his head almost apologetically.

"Do you need me to escort you to the door?" Gunnar's features have softened a little, but not his voice.

"Nope." I pop the P sound. "You go deal with Vanessa. I have other things to keep me busy." I make sure to maintain eye contact when I tell him, but then look back across the club to find Calix.

"Fuck." I damn near stomp my foot. Twice in one night I was cockblocked by Gunnar. Calix is gone. I scan the area for him, but come up empty.

"Looking for someone?" Gunnar asks, impeding my view of the dance floor, his lips lifted into a sneer.

"I was, but he's gone now, thanks," I blurt, not at all thankful.

"Anytime, my lady."

I face Gunnar again. "Would you stop calling me that? I thought you had to run off. Go!" I shoo him with my hands. "Be a good boy and run along."

Gunnar shifts on his feet and encroaches into my space. Near my ear, he states, "Go home, Damiana. I'll come to you when I can."

"Don't do me any favors, Gunnar," I snarl, angry that his hot breath on my neck makes me want to turn around and kiss him. I walk away before he has a chance to respond, and before I have the chance to do something stupid like act on the urge to push him against the wall and kiss the shit out of him.

I'm not even paying very close attention when a man steps purposefully into my path, blocking me. "Move," I order, not bothering with niceties.

"What's your hurry? Want to dance?" He leers at me. Everything about him—from his black-stained aura to his over-slicked hair—is foul.

"Not on your life. Get out of my way." Something about him feels off, something that makes my gut twist just thinking about devouring his sins.

He lifts up his palms as if to say, 'your loss,' but there's something about the hardness of his jaw and the glint in his eye that's telling me something completely different. He backs away and lets me pass without incident. I take one quick look over my shoulder to find him still watching me.

I turn on my heel and march right back up to him, and his brow furrows. "Change your mind, sweetheart?" The closer I get, the oilier I feel. I examine his face, looking right into his eyes. He's human—there's no doubt about that—but something about him feels tainted.

He blinks several times, then reaches for a drink, bringing it up to his lips for a sip. Now that I know what to feel, I look around the club for others like him. I'm not surprised when I find them. Several of the corrupted humans are the same people I saw seated with Vanessa in the warded section. Could I really have closed myself off so much that I didn't notice something more was going on here, or is this something new?

Too much strange shit has been happening for it all to be just a coincidence. Gunnar's arrival, Grim letting me see him… I take a step back from the foul man. "Whatever you're doing to yourself," I move my hand around, indicating his feet where the sludge of blackness is the heaviest, "it's going to kill you. And I promise it won't be fun."

His face slips into a grin before he realizes I'm being serious. Then his mouth opens like he might ask me a question, but I turn back around and walk out of the club, happy to be away from the empty feeling coming from him.

CHAPTER 10

"What do you think it is?" I lay down a set of three sixes. Uncle Skinny Legs is folded into the chair across from me. His long, dark fingers are curled around a spread of seven cards. I can't see his eyes, but I know he's looking at his hand.

"Witches, I suppose," he drawls, his voice raspy with disuse. He rarely speaks to me. I didn't even realize he could until a few years ago. When he would visit, I would talk and talk, just to remind myself I wasn't alone. Then one day, he finally answered one of my silly questions—I can't even recall what I asked now. I was so surprised that I dropped my cards. He promptly looked them all over and made a deep rasping sound that I've come to know as his laugh.

"Witches?" I eye him over my hand, waiting for him to take his turn. "They're real?" I can hear how skeptical I sound.

Uncle lowers his hand and I note his blank face, I can just imagine the droll look he'd be giving me if he had more discernable features. It's only when he opens his mouth that you get to see what he really looks like.

"Okay, so I probably should have known that, but it's not like any of you guys are raring to answer my questions," I grouch, and pluck at my cards. "Why do they feel so bad?" I skeeve myself out—just remembering the oily tar coating the man's aura—and shiver.

"Dirty magic," Uncle announces slowly.

"Like Voodoo or some shit?"

Uncle shakes his head slowly in denial. He doesn't say it, but I know I'm not going to get any more answers from him. He picks up a card from the pile and slots it into his hand before laying them on the table between us. He has a run of four and a set of three nines.

"What about your discard?" I pipe up. I can't believe he's about to beat me again.

He laughs and waves his hand in my direction for me to go. I still have three cards in my hand, and I have to pick up another. The chance of me going out before him is nil. "Damn it, Uncle," I curse and drop a discard. I wasn't able to unload any of my cards.

Uncle ends up winning two rounds later, and he gathers his winnings of marbles and pockets them as usual.

"Will you at least tell me where Redmon went and how long she'll be gone?" I know he's leaving soon. He usually just sticks around for a game of cards, and then he's on his way to haunt parks and children's yards.

Instead of answering, Uncle lays his hand on my shoulder. He's a good two feet taller than I am. So, I crane my neck to look up at him.

"Ugh, why don't you guys just tell me? What's the big secret? Nobody tells me anything." I toss my hands in the air in frustration.

"We have rules, child." I look over my shoulder to see Theius crouched near the door to the kitchen. He rises to his full height of maybe three and a half feet, and shakes out his shaggy, grayish fur.

Uncle gives my shoulder a squeeze before he walks into the shadows, disappearing from view. I don't even really know how half of them get here, or why they come to me. Are they truly drawn to my power? I've been wondering about exactly that since Gunnar mentioned it at the club.

"Hey, Theius," I greet, heaving a sigh of relief. With the right bribe, I can get Theius to give me some answers.

I make my way to the kitchen with Theius close on my heels. He's one of the few baddies to visit me who's told me some of his tale. I drag out the stool from under the island so he can climb up. His claw-tipped fingers scrape the wooden seat, but I don't mind. It blends in with all the other scrapes and scratches from over the years.

"What'll it be tonight, Theius?" I open the fridge and peer in. I know he doesn't care for ice cream, or anything cold really. His legend says he was in a hunting party that got lost in a winter storm and he resorted to cannibalism to survive.

I don't know if it actually happened or if that's just the story told to frighten people, but I do know he's always hungry, achingly so. And I know what it feels like to suffer with that hollow feeling. "Only what you can spare, child," he replies, with a small drip of saliva already glinting off his gray lip.

"You can have it all, Theius." I wave my hand around the kitchen, hating that even after he eats, he'll still experience the same emptiness.

"May I have some bread?" He looks up at me with his dark, owlish eyes.

It takes everything inside me not to wrap my arms around him in a hug, but he would hate the pity.

"One loaf, coming up." I force some cheeriness into my tone. When I reach the pantry, I close my eyes and take a deep breath, grounding myself. I know there's nothing I can really do for him but offer what I have and hope one day he will find something that will sustain him the way sins nourish me.

I untwist the tie keeping the bread closed, and grab a plate from the cupboard, placing several slices on the dish before scooting it in front of Theius. Then I grab the large jar of peanut butter from the shelf and slide it over to him as well.

Theius's claws gouge into the soft bread as he carefully brings it up to his lips. "Thank you, child." He slowly savors the first bite.

I fold my elbows on the counter and lean forward, watching him closely. "Do you know much about witches, Theius?"

He pauses, making a hissing sound. "Nasty creatures. Don't go messing with that lot, Dami," Theius warns, before gathering another bite to eat.

"What makes them bad?" I round the island and take the stool next him, settling in to get comfortable.

"How they get the power. Witches aren't born with any magic. They have to take it from other beings, creatures like me and the one you call Uncle."

"How do they do that?" I nearly whisper. I don't think I want to know the answer.

"Rituals, murder, dark magic, very dark magic." Theius sets the piece of bread he was about to eat down and gazes at me. "Why are you asking about witches, Damiana?"

"I think I met one—at the bar where I go to feed," I answer, and scoop a large dollop of peanut butter onto his plate, leaving him with the spoon. "His aura was covered in this dark tar, and he felt wrong."

"Sounds like a witch. Be thankful it was just the one." Theius nods his head and uses his claw to scoop up half of the peanut butter I put on his plate.

"It wasn't just one. There were a few of them—and a Berserker."

Theius coughs and splutters at my announcement. I pat his furry back and reach for a napkin. He dabs his face, cleaning himself up before he blinks at me. "A Berserker, you say?" His voice is high-pitched.

"That's what he told me he was. Is he like a witch? He didn't feel like one." I recall how alluring he was instead. How attracted I was to him, how I couldn't really read him. Maybe that's his witch magic.

"No, no. Not a witch." Theius places his hand on the table and scoots back until his legs are dangling just above the floor.

"What are you doing? You've barely eaten." I look at his plate, he didn't even finish off half a loaf yet.

"I need to be going, child." He doesn't look at me when he tells me this, and I feel the faintest bite of a sin wafting over to me from his lie.

I suck in a breath. My friends never lie to me. They might not tell me everything, but they never lie.

Theius meets my eyes, and I don't bother masking the hurt I feel. His large, black owl eyes look down to the floor. "Goodbye, Damiana." Something about the way he utters the words feels final.

"Wait," I call in my desperation. Even though I'm upset he just lied to me, I still don't want him to go.

Theius, looks over his shoulder once before he scurries back toward the living room. I know I'd never catch him, even if I tried, so I let him go.

"Lesson learned: don't talk about witches and Berserkers to Theius." I look around the empty kitchen and sigh. There has to be someone willing to talk to me about it. Aeson is most likely my best bet. I've never seen her shy away from a topic. Now, I just need to wait until she shows up. It's too bad she doesn't have a cell phone.

"Cell phone." I snap my fingers and run up to my bedroom where I usually leave my phone. No one ever calls me. I use it mostly to play games.

But I did give my number out last night to a certain hottie named Calix. I was so freaked out by the witch that I never even thought to look at my phone when I got home.

I'm panting by the time I make it into my room. "Fuck, I need to exercise," I mumble, and reach for my phone. The moment I pick it up, I see it has a shadowed box that says, "Missed Call" with a number listed.

I hop up and down for a few seconds, before I tell myself to breathe and take a chill pill. I don't want to come off too eager, nor do I want him mistaking my need for a good fuck for more than that. I examine my fingernails.

If he's good, maybe I could use him more than once. He definitely got me all hot and bothered. And that was just from talking and looking at him—well, mostly looking at him. There's something to be said for instant attraction. I flip the phone over again. It's unlocked now, and I can see the number two near the little green phone icon.

A smile splits my face—he called me twice. I knew he wanted me just as badly. I touch the number listed in red and put the phone up to my ear. While it begins ringing, I turn to face the mirror. I pluck at my shirt, then the clock on the wall grabs my attention. I yank the phone away from my ear and hit the end button before smashing it against my forehead a few times. It's four o'clock in the morning: too late for the night owls and too early for the early birds.

I look back at the history to see that he called me around eight pm and then again at eleven pm. I toss the phone on the bed. I was probably still sleeping at eight, and downstairs at eleven.

"Damn it. Well, that was a bust."

I bite my lip and wander over to my dresser. Snagging open the top drawer, I peer in to see all of my more adventurous toys. Buzz, my go-to favorite, is in my nightstand, but I'm thinking I need more than just a quick wham-bam-thank-you-ma'am.

Just opening the drawer, and I'm already getting excited. I stand back and strip out of my shirt and yoga pants. My nipples are already hard, so I grab the little, pink, rubber nipple cups and pinch the tip until the suction grabs hold of my nipple and tugs pleasantly.

I place the other on and flick the tip. The pulling sensation tightens as it bounces around. Running my fingers over my labia, I let my middle finger slide between my lips. My clitoris is already a little swollen. I flick the nipple cup again, thinking about having that suction right over my clit.

I drag my hand up my stomach. If I get too excited, this isn't going to last, and I need a few good orgasms this morning before I go to sleep.

I move aside the black blindfold that came with one of the

kits I bought. I've never trusted anyone enough to use it. Besides, it's not like I ever bring anyone here, but the thought of Calix in my bed, with the blindfold over his eyes so he can't see what I'm about to do to him...

Yup, I want to keep that picture in my mind as I reach for my wand. Just as my fingers land on the pink tool, I have second thoughts. I do think I'll use it, but not just yet. Instead, I grab a plain ole dildo. It's soft and firm and has a big suction cup on the bottom which I can stick to the shower wall or the floor, so I can go to town on it. I toss the wand on the bed so I can make sure I end the night on a good note. A few minutes of that baby, and I'll be three Os in and sleeping soundly minutes later.

With every step, my breasts sway, and I can feel the tug on my nipples. I walk over to the window and take a quick look outside. I don't think anyone is around, but fuck 'em if they are. With my right hand, I slide two fingers into my pussy. I'm already a little wet, so they go in smoothly, but before I can get carried away, I pull my fingers out and glide them over the dildo. I open my legs far enough so I can push the dildo inside. I love how I'm not too wet yet, and I can feel every inch of it going in. With it held in place, I bend over so my ass is pointed right at the window and shove myself back. I groan at how much deeper it pushes in, and reach between my legs to make sure the section cup is adhered to the glass.

Doing it like this ensures it's at the perfect height every time. I spread my legs a little and lift myself off the dildo, working my hips just as I would if there were a man behind me. Bent over, the weight of my breasts makes the suction cups on my nipples feel even tighter. Without releasing the pressure, I jerk the cup off my left breast. It stings for a second then throbs with an ache that feels so damn good. I let that one smart for a bit, while I work myself against the dildo. I'm going to leave an ass print on the window, but I don't care.

When I feel like I'm too close to coming too soon, I push all the way back and don't move. My body is screaming at me to tighten my inner muscles, but I don't. I relax as much as I can and wait out the pressure of the orgasm. When I know one stroke isn't going to send me over the edge, I start to move again. Ever so slowly, I build the tension back up until I'm about ready to explode.

I tear off the other nipple cup and brush my palms over my breasts. The orgasm hits me hard and fast, and my legs want to crumple, but I keep my knees locked and ride out the pleasure for as long as I can.

I'm panting when I pull free from the dildo. I turn to see it still bobbing up and down, and a little laugh escapes me. "Thank you for your services, sir." I go to grab the shaft as I might if I were shaking a hand, but movement outside catches my eye. I see a small flicker of fluff as the lion's tail disappears into the tree line.

I crank open the window. "I hope you enjoyed the show!" I shout, not in the least bit concerned anyone else will hear me.

A loud roar has me jerking back. "Holy shit, that was loud," I mutter, then shout down, "Well, then, don't go peeping into my house!" I close the pane quickly. "Jerk, it's my window, and if I want to fuck it, I will!" I announce and look around. Spying the wand on the bed, I roll my eyes in irritation. Now I'm no longer in the mood for a couple of forced orgasms. "Jerk," I mutter again.

CHAPTER 11

I set my alarm for seven, just in case Calix called, but it's nearly eleven and I haven't heard anything. I toy with the phone. Should I call him again or is it too late already? I look at the time on the top of the screen. "It's now or never."

After hitting his number, which is now listed under his name, I bring the phone up to my ear.

"Hello?" a man growls through the phone.

"Uh, hello, is Calix there?" I slap my hand over my eyes. I haven't really called anyone since high school. I should have said, 'I would like to speak with Calix,' or some shit.

"Who is this?" the man barks at me.

"Who is this?" I counter.

"You called this number, girl," he states.

"And I'm looking for Calix—is he around or not?" I don't much like the snarling man on the phone.

"Hang on. Cal, one of your bitches is calling!" he shouts, not even bothering to take the phone away from his mouth.

"I'm not just any bitch, you asshole, but if you yell in my ear again, this bitch is going to kick your ass!" I growl right back at him.

A bark of laughter comes through the phone. "I like this one. When you're done with her, send her my way. Here." I hear some shifting sounds as the phone changes hands.

"Hey." Calix's smooth voice comes through the line.

I almost want to hang up. I'm a little pissed off at the asshole, and I'm used to being the one who gets tons of attention, with guys at my beck and call. I may not give them my number, but I don't really need to. Walking through the club, I can usually have anyone I'm interested in.

I don't think I like the fact that Calix is the exact same way, which is unusual for me. Hell, I have no problem sharing the person in my bed—another man, another woman. It all works for me, but there's something that bothers me when I think about that with Calix.

"Hello?" he calls again.

Shit, time to decide. "Hey, this is Dami. From the club." I wince. I can't believe I had to remind him of that, and I'm still talking to him.

"Hey, hey. I'm so glad you called me back." The background noise dies down a little.

"Yeah, seems like we missed each other." I flick my

fingers over my leggings.

"So, where are you? Are you going to Rumors tonight?" Calix asks.

"Nah, I was there twice this week, that's enough for me." I don't mention I'm avoiding the witches. Something about them and Theius's reaction to them kind of freaked me out. "You?"

"I would have if you were. Got any other plans, want to meet up?" Calix inquires, and I smile, feeling a little more confident. I guess I'm still not the only one who's a little eager.

"Your place?" I suggest, since I'm not sure I want him here. If he knows where I live, he could stop by anytime. And I'm just looking for a hookup, right?

"I don't really have my own place yet. I just got back into town a few nights ago. Yours?" he adds, sounding hopeful.

"Well…" I hedge, biting my lip.

"I'm not a serial killer," Calix offers, like it might sweeten the deal.

I chuckle. "Not really what I'm worried about."

"You got a man?" he questions boldly.

"No, but if I did?" I counter.

Calix doesn't respond for a few seconds. I hear him breathing down the line, so I know he hasn't hung up. "He could watch, but I'm not into men."

"Not a deal breaker then?" My voice goes a little soft. Few human men like to share with another man—a woman, sure, but not another man.

"No, not for you," Calix answers. "Plus, I don't mind an audience."

"How do you feel about ghosts? My house is haunted." It's an untruth that isn't really a lie. I came up with it years ago, in case I ever wanted to invite anyone over, but I never did. Still, it would explain the noises, and—hell's bells—if he saw one of my visitors, I could convince him that it was just a run of the mill ghost. They even have TV shows about the damn things.

Calix chuckles. "When should I come?"

"As often as possible," I reply without thinking.

"Sounds like a plan. I'll see you soon, bye."

"Wait!" I shout before he can hang up. "Don't you need my address?"

"Oh, yeah, sorry. I wasn't thinking," Calix drawls slowly.

"I'm kind of out of the way," I warn him.

"Do you mind just texting it to me?" he asks, as I hear a door slam closed.

"Sure, I can do that. To the same number?"

"Yeah, this is my cell. Rocky doesn't understand personal boundaries. He's the one who answered before."

"If I ever run into a Rocky, I might punch him just in case it's him." I retain the unusual name for the future, because I'm totally not lying.

"Don't do that. He'll just think it's foreplay." I can hear the smile in Calix's voice as a loud engine purrs to life. "Text me the address, and I'll see you soon," he promises, and the line goes dead.

"Eager beaver." I look at the phone then hit the little 'i' next to Calix's name, and different options for facetime and messaging pops up. I hesitate for just a second before pulling up the keypad and typing my address into the message. If he makes a pest of himself, I'll scare his ass away.

What's the worst that could happen?

SMOOTHING my hand over my hair, I look into the full-length mirror on my bedroom wall. After a quick shower, I put on a pair of yoga pants and a slouchy, boat-neck t-shirt that leaves my shoulder exposed. I don't want to look like I'm trying too hard, and we both know what he's coming here for. Finally, I unpin my hair, letting it fall down my back. I didn't bother washing it, so I wouldn't have to deal with it being wet.

Making my way downstairs, I turn on a few lights throughout the house. I usually don't bother, preferring the candlelight, but that might be a bit much for Calix. I snicker a little, thinking it might help with the haunted house feel.

Before curling up in the living room, I gather the universal remote that controls the TV and the surround sound. I click on the television, hoping to distract myself. I'm a little anxious; my friends stop by all the time, but this is the first time I've invited a man home with me.

I tickle my fingers over my collarbones and chest. As nervous as I am, I'm also excited. It might be fun to sleep with someone more than once, okay, well, more than for one night, or day. I might actually get to try out that blindfold or some of my other toys.

I look at the clock. It's been about forty minutes since our call ended. I don't know where Calix is coming from, but I probably should have asked him so I would have an idea of when he would get here.

I force myself to focus on the TV instead of grabbing my phone to check if he has called. I know he hasn't. After I missed his calls the other day, I made sure to turn my ringer on so it wouldn't happen again.

I hear the purr of a motor minutes later. I mute the television and send out my other senses. That same purity Calix exuded at the club washes over me. "It's him," I announce to no one, and unmute the TV.

Standing, I run my hands over my hips, smoothing my shirt, as I make my way over to the front door. The click of the lock disengaging is loud since the sound of his engine died moments before.

I leave the screen closed, but open the door and watch as Calix lifts his leg over a sleek, black motorcycle. I left the outdoor lights on so it wouldn't be too dark for him, and it's a good thing I did. I'm not sure the single headlight would have helped illuminate all the curves of my driveway.

I take a moment to examine Calix while he lifts a helmet off his head and shakes out his hair. His dark jeans are fitted just right and cuffed at the bottom, where I can see a pair of heavy boots. The black leather jacket he's wearing hides his shirt, but it makes a nice picture nonetheless.

Calix pulls a small set of keys from the bike and shoves them into his coat pocket, then turns to stare up at the house. His eyes lift to the upper floors.

"Hey," I call, giving him a short wave from the front door.

His eyes land on me and he gives me a slight smile in return. "Hey, you weren't kidding about being out of the way. Do you even have any neighbors?" His steps eat up the distance between his bike and the front porch.

I push open the screen, welcoming him inside. "Not for a few miles. You rethinking that whole serial killer thing?" I joke, stepping out of the way. "Come in."

Calix chuckles and lets out a low whistle once he gets a good look around my foyer. I glance around, too, imagining seeing it again for the first time. My old Victorian home was built in the late 1800's by a man for his new bride. Everything about it says Old-World excess, and I love every inch. From my unvisited conservatory to my echoing ballroom, every room has been restored to its former glory. The woodwork alone took months to rejuvenate back to the gleaming state it's in now, and that's only thanks to the small crew of workers that come by twice a week to clean the house.

Two things I hate: cooking and cleaning. I can't eat, so why should I cook? And cleaning just sucks. I have enough money to pay someone else to do it for me.

"You live here alone?" Calix is still holding on to his helmet, looking around.

"Pretty much. Let me take that." I reach forward, and he hands me the helmet. "Jacket?" I set the helmet on an ornate hall tree that has a large mirror and hat hooks, with a table and umbrella stand built right in. Both front corners are adorned with a large, wooden, lion head with its maw open wide, exposing fiercely sharp teeth.

Calix runs his hand over a wooden lion's mane, admiring it. Shaking his head, he unzips his jackets and loops it over one of the hooks next to the mirror. "This is amazing—the detail. I mean, I can't believe this is carved out of wood."

"Thanks. This is Leo and that's Savannah." I point to the one closest to Calix.

"But these are both males." He tilts his head.

"I know, but I didn't want Leo to be lonely, so I just pretend." I lean in a little closer, acting like the lions can hear me.

Calix shakes his head a little. "That's kind of adorable," he comments, like I've shocked him a bit.

It makes me uncomfortable, so I change the subject. "Do you want a drink?" I start walking toward the living room, which is really just one of the smaller parlors. I have a small bar set up in there, even though I don't really drink.

"Nah, I'm good." Calix follows me. When I glance over my shoulder, he's still looking around. "This place is huge. You ever get lost?"

"Not anymore." I throw myself into my overstuffed sofa.

Calix spins around once, taking everything in before his eyes land on me. Finally! I was thinking I should have gone with the candlelight, then maybe the house wouldn't be such a distraction.

"Your home is almost as beautiful as you are." Calix settles himself next to me on the sofa, draping his arm along the back and scooting close.

"Thank you." I preen under his compliment. I know I'm pretty, but it's always good to hear, especially when a man is looking at you the way Calix is looking at me.

I'm not sure what to do here. I'm used to frenzied hookups behind the club or in crappy apartments. Should I ask him if he wants to watch TV? Or just drag him up to my bedroom? Should I use my bedroom or one of the guestrooms?

The light offers me the first really good look I've had at Calix. His eyes are a striking shade of hazel, and when he tilts his head, examining me, they almost look green. I can see the contrast of the darker tips of his hair layered through his choppy haircut. The back nearly reaches his nape, but the sides aren't as long.

I lick my lips, thinking about his full mouth. His lips are almost root-beer colored, a much darker shade than my own, as is his skin tone. Calix's eyes track the movement of my tongue, and he licks his bottom lip in response.

I lean a little closer and beckon him with my finger. Calix dips his face close to mine, his nostrils flaring as he takes in a deep breath. I lower my lids, anticipating the moment his mouth will touch mine.

I feel the tip of his tongue lap over my bottom lip, then the top. My mouth parts as I let out a pleased sigh. His tongue is almost rough. Calix's lips land on mine almost immediately after. Using my hands, I crawl a little closer, pushing against him more firmly. Calix doesn't retreat; if anything, he gives back as good as I'm giving.

I slide my tongue into his mouth, feeling the smooth underside of his tongue as he licks into my mouth. There's not an ounce of awkward hesitation on either of our parts. Calix kisses me as if our mouths already know each other.

I brace my hand on his thigh in my bid to get even closer to him, and I can feel how tightly his muscles are coiled under my hand. He reaches for me, his hands going under my arms as he hauls me into his lap to straddle his hips.

Breaking the kiss, I stare down at him while I lower myself into his legs. Calix opens his mouth, and a heavy pant passes his lips. I grin when I feel just how much he's already affected by our sweet touches. A little bubble of excitement erupts in my stomach. I'm really hoping he knows what to do with the sizeable bulge under me.

Calix reaches up and palms my cheek, threading his fingers into my hair as he pulls me back down to his mouth. I run my palms over his shoulders, feeling the texture of his shirt under my hands and wishing it were his skin instead.

I nip at his bottom lip then pull it into my mouth, and his hand tightens in my hair, causing me to arch my back in response. Calix moves his tongue with slow, deliberate strokes as he kisses me. I'm so used to rushed, greedy hands that it takes me a moment to adjust to the way he's taking his time, causing liquid heat to pool in my lower stomach.

Calix places his hand on my lower back and glides it up under my shirt. His fingertips are a little rough—I can even feel the calluses on his palm skate over the smooth skin of my back.

I lower my hands from his shoulders and return the favor by sliding my them up and under his shirt. The short hairs covering his chest tickle my palms.

Knowing I'm enjoying the rough texture of his hands, I curl my fingertips a bit and drag my nails back down over his chest just enough to make sure he feels it. Calix lets out a low groan, his hand on my back dragging me closer as he bites my lip.

I grind down on his lap, happy I chose yoga pants instead of jeans. Now, I just need to get him out of his. I break the kiss and lean back as Calix's hand travels around my side and cups the underside of my breast. His thumb finds my nipple with uncanny accuracy.

Another wave of satisfaction hits me at my wardrobe choice. I hate bras, and this is the perfect reason not to wear one.

Calix's mouth and lips find their way to my neck as he kisses my throat and under my jaw. That tongue of his would be much better suited for working between my legs. I can just imagine how it would feel circling my clit.

I jerk upright and my eyes fly open when my doorbell rings with an eerily long trill of notes. Calix doesn't remove his hand from my breast—in fact, his palm tightens a bit. "Expecting company?" His brows are raised in question. I take note of his damp, swollen lips, and the way his pupils are dilated as he stares up at me.

The tones chime again. "Damn it, no. Who could that be?" I still don't bother getting up, and the bell rings for a third time.

"Whoever it is—they aren't going away," Calix offers.

I pull his hand off my tit and get my feet back under me. When I stand up, I can feel how damp my panties are when a chilled breeze hits me.

A growl of frustration rumbles within me. "I'm coming!" I shout, even though I'm much too far away from the door to be heard.

Calix hustles over to my side. "You would have been," he promises, his voice full of gravel.

"Ugh." I roll my eyes and cup my breast. My nipples are so hard, they're *aching*.

"What are you doing?" Calix asks, stifling a chuckle.

"My tits have blue balls. Give me a break." I'm not in a laughing mood. I reach the door in record time, just as the bell rings for the fourth time. "What?" I shout, ripping the door open after disengaging the deadbolt.

"Did I interrupt?" Gunnar pushes his way right past me, not even bothering to wait for an invitation.

"You sure as fuck did." I plant my hands on my hips and leave the door open. Hopefully, he'll be using it to leave really damn soon.

"That's regrettable," he purrs, but he means the exact opposite. I wouldn't even need to be a lie detector to know that. "Gunnar," he announces to Calix, his chin tipped up in the air.

"Calix," Calix responds in kind, then purposefully reaches down and adjusts his dick in his pants. I watch, transfixed, as his fingers make the material of his pants form around his erection. I want to stomp my feet and pout. I could be riding that damn thing.

Gunnar makes a deep sound in the back of his throat that has me taking my eyes off Calix's package and landing on him.

"What are you doing here?" I cross my arms over my chest and cock out my hip. Normally, I would be digging this back and forth banter between the two of them, maybe even playing into it to see which one I would fuck later tonight, but I'm horny as hell and with both of them standing here, I'm imagining fucking them both. Maybe even at the same time.

"You said you wanted to finish our conversation." Gunnar widens his arms. "I'm at your disposal." He gives me a barely perceivable bow.

"I'm busy," I snap back quickly.

"Well, send this animal home and get *unbusy*," Gunnar demands, eyeing Calix.

"Why don't you take your *crazy* ass back to wherever you came from," Calix retorts. That earns a glare from Gunnar.

"Knock it off." I wave my hand around. "The testosterone is getting thick, not to mention I'm already horny."

Both men turn to eye me. I feel the atmosphere shift as a bounty of sins fills the air. I toss my hands up. "You've got to be fucking kidding me."

CHAPTER 12

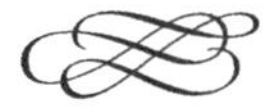

"What?" Calix and Gunnar say in unison.

"Nothing. Just wait right here, and don't kill each other, or fight or anything," I order, walking toward the kitchen where I felt the shift. "I'd want to watch that shit."

"Watch what?" Grim is standing next to my kitchen island, tall as hell, with his black robe billowing out around him.

"Two guys fighting. I'm trying to get laid," I answer.

"And you want the males to prove which is the superior?" Grim actually grows a little taller.

I wipe my brow and push my hair off my forehead. Having people over, real people, is kind of exhausting. "Nah, but they're both doing this macho bullshit right now. What's up?"

"You said I could come back." Grim sounds a little affronted that he needs to remind me.

"Of course, you can visit anytime you like." I wince.

"Except now?" he argues.

There are already two guys here, what's one more? "Can you lose the robe?" I eye Grim, wondering what he looks like under there. I'm a little surprised how much I want him to stay. I like hanging out with Grim, plus, I feel this connection with him. He's known me since I was young. "I'm pretty sure one of them is like us, but I'm not sure about the other."

"You're inviting me to say?" he asks, sounding strangely formal.

"Sure, absolutely. Why not?" Any hope I had of have a non-self-induced orgasm is waning by the second, but I'll get over it.

I'm never going to be able to focus like this though. I could always excuse myself up to my room, grab Buzz, and give myself a quick O. It would probably be a service to everyone here. I'm going to be a crabby bitch if I don't. I shift from left to right. My clit is still swollen. Damn it.

"Are you alright?" Grim inquires.

"Yup, peachy." I grimace. "So, are you going to lose the robes and stick around?" The hood nods.

"Okay, great. Awesome." I give him two thumbs up. "I just have to run upstairs." I purse my lips, debating whether or not to tell him why. Deciding discretion is the better part of valor, I just kind of give him an awkward wave before rushing toward the back staircase.

"Can't get anyone to hang out with me, then all of the sudden I'm super fucking pop—" I groan at my word choice. "Scratch that. I wish I was fucking."

"I've warned you about talking to yourself," Aeson chirps, as I'm rounding my bedroom door. I deflate. I can't have a ménage à moi with her in here.

"Hey, Aeson," I mutter slowly.

The little Brownie eyes me with suspicion. "You smell funny," she states, and wrinkles her nose.

I squeeze my thighs together. "I do not!" I snap back, peering down at her on my way to the bathroom.

As soon as the door closes, I cup my crotch. Don't tell me she can smell my horny ass. Sure as shit, I can feel how damp my yoga pants are. I bring my palm up to my nose and sniff. "I do not stink!" I shout through the door.

"I didn't say you stink, I said you smelled funny," she hollers right back. I poke my head out of the bathroom door. "I have company," I scold, admonishing her yelling, before slipping back into the bathroom.

"Is it the bleeder that smells like that?"

"Ugh." I can just imagine her wrinkled-up, little nose as she says it, while I'm pulling my pants off one foot at a time.

I clean up quickly with a wipe. Damn Brownie and her nose. I strut out of the bathroom, sans pants and panties, going to my closet with my head held high.

"What the hell are you doing?" Aeson asks.

"Getting some fresh clothes." I flip on the light switch and grab a pair of jeans. Maybe these will keep my greedy pussy from telling everyone in the house I need a stiffy.

I make my way over to my dresser, grab some panties, and step into them with Aeson watching me.

“Look at you,” Aeson coos at me. “You brought a man home, I’m so proud of you.”

“Three.” I pull my jeans up and go on to my toes to get them over my hips.

“Yes! I knew you were listening to me all these years.” She sighs wistfully, like a proud mother.

“There may be three, but I’m not fucking all of them.” I look in the mirror and fluff my already tousled hair.

“Don’t sell yourself short. You’re not fucking all three of them *yet*,” Aeson argues.

“At this point, I would be happy with one. Besides, one of them is the biggest cockblocker I’ve ever met, and the other one is, like, Death or something. I have to go,” I tell her, already walking to the door.

“Death?” I hear Aeson whisper on my way out of the room. Yeah, let that sink in.

I hear them before I can see them. “Where the hell did you come from?” It’s Calix’s voice, he sounds slightly incredulous.

“None of your damned business, you mangy beast,” Gunnar snarls.

“Hey, hey!” I have my hands up—trying to dispel the brewing fight—and accidently block my view so I don’t see Grim right away. But when I do, I stop dead in my tracks—no pun intended.

“Grim?” My hands fall out of the sky to slap the sides of my legs.

“Damiana.” My name rolls off his tongue, and I shiver

slightly. So much for the cold wipe making me forget how badly I want something between my legs.

"But…" I splutter. Every time I imagined Grim, it wasn't like this. I pictured a skeleton, or an old man, but never this. My eyes travel from his bare feet, up past his black pants, and over his loose black shirt, until they land on his achingly beautiful face.

He is sheer perfection. Every proportion is designed to draw you in. Hell, if people knew this is what Death looked like, they would probably run to him. His light eyes stare at the ground as he brushes his shirt over his stomach. Holy fucking shit, it's kind of sheer, and I can see his chiseled abdominals beneath the fabric.

I hold up a finger, then close my eyes while tapping the middle of my forehead with the same finger. I'm not going to get that image out of my head anytime soon. "Can I—" I clear my throat. "Can I talk to you for a minute?"

I open my eyes to find Gunnar sneering a smile at Grim, and Grim scowling back at Gunnar.

"Who, me?" Grim looks around.

"Yes, definitely you." I nod. "I'll just be another moment," I tell Gunnar and Calix, who seem to be getting along remarkably well since the Angel of Death appeared, and that's exactly what he looks like: a fucking angel.

"What is this?" I accuse, the moment we're out of the foyer.

"What?" Grim looks down at himself again.

"This is what's under the robe?" I whisper animatedly.

"Yes, do you find me off-putting?" Grim tilts his head away from me like he doesn't want to hear the answer.

"Off-putting? Are you fucking kidding me with this shit?" I look him up and down again.

"Tell me what you would prefer. I can change my visage for you." He doesn't meet my eyes.

I blink at him several times. He can't be serious. "Wait, is this what you really look like, or did you," I roll my wrists, "glamour this up?" I can't think of a better way to describe it.

"This is my true self." Grim tips his chin in the air a little, exposing the line of his neck to me, yum. But I think I've offended him.

"Well, good thing you wear the robe, buddy. I'm just saying." As soon as the words leave my mouth, I hear how horrible they sound. But that's not at all how I meant it.

Grim blinks his gray eyes at me several times, seemingly at a loss for words. I slap my palm to my forehead. "That came out wrong." I reach for his forearm. Remembering the day in the kitchen when I touched him just like this and he pulled back from me, I remove my arm before he can.

"You're seriously beautiful." I stare into his face, making sure he sees how truthful I'm being. "I was just taken by surprise, I mean…" I wave my hand up and down, encompassing his entire being. "Wow!" It's all I can say.

"Really?" Grim's lips lift in a slow grin before he smothers it. "Why did you ask to speak with me alone? Would you like me to tell the others to go?"

"No, no. They're fine," I say, dismissing the thought of

them leaving and asking Grim if he would like to finish where Calix and I left off. "I guess I don't know why I wanted to talk to you alone. Let's get back out there. They've been on their own for too long, and it's too quiet."

Grim holds out his elbow to me in an offer. I wrap my fingers over his arm, happy that he initiated the touch this time.

As we enter the foyer, Calix and Gunnar are separated by several feet, each ignoring the other's presence. "Hey, this is my friend Grim. Grim, this is Gunnar and Calix." I point to each of the men. "So…" I let the word trail off. I really don't know what to do with three strange men in my house. When Uncle and Theius come to visit, I don't want to tie them to chairs and have my way with them.

"Want to play cards?" I ask, sounding too hopeful.

"Cards?" Calix winces.

"I would be honored," Grim intones.

"We need to talk," Gunnar announces, crossing his arms over his chest.

"Not in mixed company," I grate through my teeth.

Gunnar looks around. "Is there someone else here?"

I tilt my head toward Calix, probably not nearly as stealthy as I thought it would be because all three of them look at me sideways.

"Him?" Gunnar points at Calix.

I widen my eyes. Gunnar tilts his head back and laughs. "You dirty cheat, she doesn't even know what you are!"

"Shut up, Berserker," Calix grinds out.

"Wait, so you guys know each other?" I step away from Grim and back away from all three of them in the process.

I never once sensed any deception from any of them. How could I have let a little attraction and sexual frustration distract me so much? I was supposed to be figuring out why Gunnar had someone watching my house; instead, I invited Calix here and he's already involved in this.

"You!" I seethe, while pointing my finger at Calix. "You're involved in this, too?"

Calix's eyes widen. "Involved in what?"

"And you," I sneer at Grim. "I thought you were my friend."

Grim looks around like he's completely confused. "I am your friend, Damiana. I've been taking care of you for years."

"You've been doing what?" Gunnar crosses his arms over his chest and glares at Grim.

The look Grim levels at Gunnar would stop most people from asking any more questions, but Gunnar doesn't look deterred.

"You've been watching her for years. You think I didn't sense either of you?" Grim includes Calix in the stare down.

"What the fuck is going on here?" I plant my hands on my hips. I hate that they're making me second-guess everything I thought I knew.

"I kept to the bargain." Calix steps closer to Grim, ignoring my question. His eyes catch the light, and they almost look like they're lit from within. How could I have thought he was a human? "I checked on her a handful of times. You've both been with her all along?" Calix accuses.

"I never exposed myself to her. Not until he broke the covenant." Grim points a finger at Gunnar.

"I didn't mean to come here," Gunnar defends himself with a shade of indignation. "I was ambushed by a coven. I thought I was finally fucking dying, so I jumped here. It wasn't even intentional."

I pinch my temples between my thumb and middle finger, trying to collect myself, but decide to say fuck it. "What are you guys talking about?" I shout so loudly, my voice echoes off the high ceiling of the foyer.

The sneer on Calix's face smooths as he moves as if he may take a step toward me. "Not a good idea, fuckface, I'm pissed at you. You lied to me," I challenge.

"I did not, never, Damiana. I may have omitted, but I've never lied to you, never will."

"It's the same. You're still responsible." I turn my face away from him.

A wave of anger crashes over me. I've been shunned by everyone who was supposed to love and take care of me. For what? They were scared of the little girl who could see auras and talk to monsters?

I thought I was past all the hurt I felt for being isolated, but to find out that these three knew something about me, even checked up on me and never once made themselves known, has me dragging all my defenses up.

Just like the wave of anger crashed into me, I use the same

wave to push them away. "Get out!" I demand, and I can see Calix's feet starts to slide backwards. Gunnar holds his ground for a second longer, but the door slams open and he loses traction. I don't feel guilty at all as I watch his large frame go sailing out the door and land on the driveway.

Calix's reflexes are a little better. He turns with a smooth grace and bounds out the door, but the wind still lifts him at the last second and he crashes next to Gunnar on the driveway, then rolls onto all fours.

Grim is the last one standing. His shirt is blown back, not leaving an ounce of doubt about his tight body beneath it. I focus on him and my long hair stirs. "I trusted you." The anger in my voice can't mask the hurt.

"You still can, Dami, none of us would ever hurt you. We're here to protect you." He argues, but I'm far too mad to hear anything he has to say.

"Leave, before I make you," I growl.

"I'm sorry, Damiana, we shouldn't have…I should have—"

"Get the fuck out of here now, before I rip open a portal and shove your ass through it," I interrupt before he can finish. I doubt I could do something like that, but he doesn't need to know.

I can taste the sins from the other side of the portal. I don't ask, I just take. Closing my eyes, I call the sins to me. There are so many I can't distinguish one from another, I just take my fill. When I'm sated, I open my eyes to see Grim stepping backwards into the portal. "I'm sorry," he manages to say before he disappears.

I look out the still open front door to find Calix brushing off his pants with his eyes locked on me, while Gunnar is still picking himself up off the ground. "Get lost." With the flick of my wrist, I slam my front door, sagging the moment they're out of sight.

"One thing at a time," I mutter to myself. I can figure out what's happening, one thing at a time.

CHAPTER 13

I didn't get much sleep today. I spent most of the morning tossing and turning, then beating myself up from not keeping the three of them here and demanding answers. When I did finally fall asleep, I dreamed of Calix and his stupid rough tongue in places he never got to explore last night.

"Stupid dreams," I grouse, kicking my leg out.

"What are you muttering about, and would you sit still?" the pale redhead across from me chides.

"Nothing, sorry." I force my leg to stop jerking.

"Boy troubles?" Bloody Mary inquires. The fresh, bloody tears leaking from her eyes are dripping onto her already stained white blouse.

I snort. "Maybe ten years ago, Mary. I'm thirty years old."

She waves her claw-like fingers at me, dismissing my words. "Men, boys, they're all the same."

"True," I concede.

"So, tell me what's bothering you." Mary picks up a delicate teacup and brings it to her gnarled lips.

I contemplate brushing the question off, but if I really want answers, I'm going to need to talk to someone. "Do you know Grim?"

"*The Grim.*" She lowers her teacup slowly, not meeting my eyes.

"Yeah. Big, black, showy cloak."

"I've heard of him, why do you ask?" Mary's voice goes a little tight and high-pitched.

"Well, he fed me when I was little, did you know that?" I don't bother waiting for her to answer, I just keep going. "He never let me see him, so I didn't know who he was until the other day, then he and two other people—" I wince, that doesn't sound right. "Beings," I amend, still not liking that term to describe them, "kind of let the cat out of the bag, saying they've been watching me. That there's some bargain or deal that has something to do with me."

"You don't say?" Mary fluffs the pristine, flowy white sleeves of her shirt, staring at her lap as she does.

"I got mad at them and kicked them out last night before I got any answers about what they've been up to." I start kicking my leg again. Mary is acting dodgy.

"Kicked him out, you say? You kicked Grim out?" Mary

says the words slowly, like she needs to taste them to see if they're true.

"Yup, I told him I was going to shove his ass through a portal."

Mary's eyes bulge. "Oh my," she gasps, and brings one claw-tipped hand up to her breast as if I've offended her delicate sensibilities.

I let out a little snicker. It's funny to watch a woman with blackened, sunken eyes that bleed and who has a slashed-up mouth look affronted. "That's just..." Mary shakes her head slowly, like she can't believe it. "And he just let you talk to him like that? *The Grim*?" She leans in a little closer when she says his name, as though she doesn't want to say it too loudly.

I chuckle at that. "I didn't give him much of a choice, Mary."

"Oh my," she says again, and looks around like he might pop out at any moment.

"So, got any info on this deal they were talking about?" I ask her point blank. It seems like everyone in my life has answers but me.

"I do not," she states firmly. I narrow my eyes at her. I don't think she's lying, but what if my senses don't work as well on my friends? I've always just trusted my instincts, but now I'm doubting myself, and I don't much like it.

"Another cup of tea, Mary?" I query, when she starts to fidget with her shirt sleeves again.

"I really shouldn't. I need to get going," she refuses.

"But..." I look at the clock, which shows me it's only a

little after midnight. "You usually stay longer." I stand as she does. Mary smooths down her blood-soaked bodice as if she's making sure it's presentable. How the stains never get anywhere but the front of her dress, I'll never know.

"You know what they say: it's three o'clock somewhere." Her smile is brittle.

"Yeah, sure." My voice comes out flat. If Mary notices, she doesn't let on. Instead, she excuses herself to the powder room and closes the door without bothering with the light. Mary travels through the mirror. I may not know how all my friends arrive at my home, but I know how she does.

"Well, she was in a hurry to get out of here," I mutter, picking up her teacup and saucer to take to the kitchen.

The doorbell chimes, and it startles me. I have to scramble to catch the cup from tipping off the saucer and crashing to the floor.

I place it back on the table and head toward the door. There are only a few people it could be, and I thought I scared them away yesterday. I expect the bell to chime again, but the person on the other side is much more patient than Gunnar was yesterday.

I can hear a shushed argument as I approach the door. "Ring it again," Gunnar demands.

"No, you fool, she's coming," Calix replies harshly.

"Shut up, the both of you," Grim intones.

I open the door and lean against it. "Back so soon?" I don't want them to know I'm actually happy they're here. Now I can demand some answers.

"May we come in?" Grim requests for the group.

I narrow my eyes. "You've never asked before," I remind him.

He meets my stare. Waiting. I huff, but step back from the door and roll my wrist out in an invitation for them to enter. "I'm warning you, you better have come prepared to tell me what's going on, or you'll end up on your keisters, just like last night."

Gunnar pushes his way to the front, shoving past Calix, and reaches the door first. "Of course, my lady," he croons at me.

"You can stop all that shit." I wave my hand at him, encompassing his whole body. "I'll be thinking and acting with more than just my lady bits, thank you." I make sure to give Calix a good glare too.

Grim makes a sound close to a choking cough. I'm tempted to slap him on the back a few times, but I don't want to touch him. He replaced the sheer black shirt with a fitted black tee, but I already know what he's hiding beneath it, and I did just promise not to let my vag lead the way.

I plant my hands on my hips when everyone makes it into the foyer. "So, what kind of conversation is this going to be?"

"What do you mean?" Grim looks at the others.

"I mean, is it a 'hey, I'm really your dad and I've come to collect you and take you back to the underworld, because some miscreant stole you from my loving arms' kind of a story?" Please don't let that be the case. If I find out I'm lusting after my dad, I might just hurl. That's a little twisted, even for me. "Or is this a 'you were supposed to be dead, and we've come to kill you' kind of thing? I'd like to know before I decide what room to take you guys to."

Calix blinks at me several times. "Are we sure this is the right time?" he eventually asks, but he's not talking to me, he's asking Gunnar and Grim.

"Don't be a pussy," Gunnar snaps, and takes a step in front of the group. His face softens a bit, reminding me of the man who woke up on my bedroom floor instead of the bossy jerk from the club.

"I told you to knock that off." I waggle my finger at him.

"What?" He looks around. "I'm not doing anything."

"Yes, you are, and you know it. Trying to be all cute and shit." I cross my arms over my chest and give him a disgusted sneer.

Gunnar's mouth opens and closes a few times. "I don't even know what to do with that comment. I've never been accused of trying to be *cute*." He sounds completely baffled.

"Any room of your choosing will do fine, Damiana," Grim supplies, ignoring Gunnar and his exasperation.

Calix nods his head. "This isn't bad news, Damiana." He looks to the others for confirmation, but no one else agrees with him.

"If I mess up my kitchen, I'm kicking your asses… I'll..." I look at them, coming up short for threats.

"Yes, yes. Anything you'd like," Grim agrees without me finishing. I give him the side-eye, but head down the hall toward the kitchen. I think I need some hot chocolate for this. And I'm not even going to offer them any. Ha!

"Ha, what?" Calix looks around like he missed the joke, and it's then I realize I must have said part of my thoughts out loud.

"I'm not going to make you any hot cocoa." I give him a sinister smile, as if it's the most horrible harm he could suffer.

"Ooookaaaay." He eyes me. "Is that code for something else?" he questions, not understanding what an amazing experience he's about to miss.

"No, you've just never had my hot chocolate." I strut into the kitchen, waving my hand at the bar stools lined up opposite the stove under the island. Funny how perfect all three of them look lined up there. Oh, how I do love a captive audience. I start to spin on my heel to grab my pot, but stop myself. I want to get them talking. In my experience, when I ask the hard questions, everyone suddenly has some other place they need to be.

"You guys are staying until all my questions are answered, right?" I regard the three of them.

"That could be a long—" Gunnar starts, but Calix reaches over and swats his arm.

"Yup, we'll stay until *all* the questions are answered," Calix offers instead.

"Unless one of us is called away," Grim adds. "We each have duties where our presence may be required, but if that should happen, the others would stay." Grim nods to the two other men.

"Agreed," Calix and Gunnar both declare at once.

"Spooky. It's almost as if you guys have done that before." I pick up my wooden spoon and pot to get started.

It doesn't take much focus to make the drink—I've done it countless times—but I wait until all I have to do is stir before urging them to begin.

"Who's going to start talking?" Each of them takes turns looking at the others. "Well, someone has to. How about you?" I point my chocolate covered spoon at Gunnar, then at the other two. "They said you broke the covenant, or whatever, by showing up here."

Gunnar makes a sour face and glares at Grim and Calix. "A long time ago—"

"When?" I demand interrupting him.

"About thirty-one years ago," he supplies, not sounding very happy, "it was decided that we would be your guardians." He opens his hands on the island like ta-da, that's all there is to the story.

I continue stirring my hot cocoa. "First, why would I need guardians, and second, where the hell were you?" I shout the last part of the question, letting the spoon go; it continues on the circular path for a few moments then stops.

Other than the sound of my breathing, the room is silent. Grim licks his lips. "We also decided that we would be your guardians from afar," he explains slowly, his voice just loud enough to be heard, as if he's worried that he's going to set me off.

"Which one of you assholes thought that was a good idea?" I accuse all three of them.

"It was a mutual decision, one that wasn't made easily," Grim continues, his voice calm.

I flick off the burner on the stove, no longer in the mood for hot chocolate. "So, let me get this straight. You three were charged to be my guardians and thought the best way to do that was to dis-a-fucking-ppear from my life. Only, this idiot almost gets himself killed and somehow ends up bleeding to death on my bedroom floor."

My statement doesn't really require an answer, but Gunnar gives me a resounding, "Yes," with a head nod included just in case I don't get the verbal reply.

"I wish I drank, 'cause I could use something right now." I glance up to the ceiling, asking for patience. "Okay, let's come back to that idiocy in a minute. Tell me why I need guardians." I plant my hands behind me on the counter.

"Well…" Calix looks at the others. "Well, you see, you could think of us like family." He winces as he says "family", and his palms flip up as if he's at a loss for words.

I pinch the bridge of my nose. "Fucking hell, so you guys are like my dads or brothers or some shit?" I can't even look at them. I'm going to have to accept the fact that I'm a twisted bitch.

Several noes resound through the room, some louder than others.

I peek up through my fingers. "I think I need to sit down." I walk away then, expecting them to follow.

I drop into my cushy sofa, ignoring the fact that Calix had his hand up my shirt in this room less than twenty-four hours ago.

"Has anyone ever told you that you guys suck at this? I mean, really, who put you in charge of being my guardians? Seems kind of irresponsible." I purse my lips to show my distaste.

"Guardians are appointed when a soul decides to be born on this plane," Grim states, trying to rein in the conversation.

"Wait, so you're saying I chose to be born here?"

"You did," Calix answers.

"Well, that was stupid," I scoff.

"No, it wasn't, but when you were born here, it changed some things," Grim supplies.

"Like what?" I tilt my head to the side and study him. He looks about the same age as I do. As a matter of fact, they all do. None of my monster friends age, so they probably don't either.

"Well, once you were born, things shifted. We're no longer *just* your guardians." Gunnar takes a seat in one of the chairs.

"So, you have other charges—people you watch out for?" Suddenly, maybe this isn't so bad, maybe they didn't abandon me like my family did. They had more than just me to worry about.

"No," Calix states, speaking up again.

My brow furrows. "Then what do you mean?" I'm getting angry again. "Just spit it out."

"Once you were born, the connection between us changed. We all felt it." Grim draws in a deep breath.

"And?" I prompt.

"Occasionally, the connection between a guardian and their ward can shift, forming a bond, if you will." Grim's face is almost blank. He's speaking as if he's reciting information from a textbook.

"So, what does that *mean*?" I question again, casting my eyes over all three of them.

"It's why we all agreed not to involve ourselves in your life," Calix adds, while prowling around the edge of the room. He throws a narrow-eyed glance at Gunnar, who completely ignores him.

"Well, that's just stupid." I snort.

"Just fucking tell her!" Gunnar barks. His eyes are a little wild, and his chest is expanding with every breath.

"Is this the whole Berserker thing?" I ask Grim, jerking my thumb in Gunnar's direction, indicating his outburst.

"Berserkers can be unstable," Grim agrees easily.

"I am not unstable, you asshole, and you know it," Gunnar spits.

"Listen, Kitten, we only have room for one drama queen, and that's me, thank you very much. So take it down a notch, will ya?" I pat the sofa next to me, indicating he should come over and take a seat. "Jeez, you're acting like you're the one who's been kept in the dark your entire life." I roll my eyes. "Continue," I order Grim, since he seems to be the only one actually providing information.

Gunnar stalks over and throws himself down on the sofa. I hear an audible sigh leave him once he's settled.

"While the bond does happen occasionally, it usually only happens between one of the guardians and the ward, typically after spending years together. However—"

"You use a lot of transitions. Are you stalling?" I interrupt Grim. "It kind of seems like you're stalling."

Grim lifts his chin in the air an infinitesimal bit. "I am trying to explain our situation to you. Neither of these two seem to be willing to help, and you are interrupting me." I watch as his light gray eyes swirl, until it looks as if he has tiny fissures of lava running through his irises.

I stand up and take two quick steps closer to get a better look. "Now that's what I'm talking about. This wouldn't scare anyone," I motion to his body, "unless they were afraid of dying of lust, but that," I point to his eyes, "is freaky as fuck, especially if you were still wearing the robe." I tilt my head, imagining those eyes glowing out from underneath the cowl.

I plop back on the sofa. "You were saying?"

Calix stops mid-stride and turns his head slowly to look at me. "She has no sense of self-preservation," he announces to the room.

I ignore him. I would only need self-preservation if I felt threatened, and I don't.

"Our bond formed the moment you were born," Grim continues, undeterred by my comment or Calix's.

"So, you and I are bonded?" I eye him dubiously. Sure, I

feel a connection to him; hell, he fed me for years. Not to mention he's gorgeous, with a body to die for—quite literally.

"Why are you smiling like that?" Gunnar scowls at me.

I pat his leg. "Don't worry, Kitten. I was just thinking."

"Stop calling me Kitten," Gunnar grouses.

"No," I chirp back.

"Yes, you and I are bonded, but…you are also bonded to the Nemean and the Berserker." Grim is acting as if he has the patience of a saint, dealing with all of us.

"Were you an angel?" I ask Grim.

"Can you focus for like five minutes?" Gunnar tilts his head back, groaning.

I glare at Gunnar. "I'm not sure if I even like you." That earns me a scowl. "What's a Nemean?" I purposefully turn my cheek to Gunnar.

"I'm a Nemean, but I do have a name, Death," Calix deadpans, calling out Grim.

"And a Nemean is?" I wonder if there's some book or something I was supposed to have.

"A lion." Calix stands a little taller, his chest puffs out a bit.

"You!" I accuse. "You're the lion from the woods? You ignored me."

Calix has the good sense to look contrite as his eyes bounce around the room. "I wasn't supposed to make contact with you."

Gunnar snorts.

"You watched me…" I cover my eyes with my hand, not

wanting to look at him or think about what he seen me doing. Not because I'm embarrassed, but because the thought of him watching me masturbate is kind of hot. Yup. Kinky bitch—party of one.

"Watched what?" Gunnar prods.

"Nothing, never mind," I rush out.

"Then why is he smiling like that?" Gunnar doesn't give up. I peek up at Calix from under my fingers, and he is, indeed, smiling. It's lecherous.

I groan. "Grim, what does the bond mean?" I try to focus on the important topic.

"Quite simply, it means we're all connected to you. Fated, if you will," he answers.

I drop my hand from my face and into my lap. "Fated for what?"

Calix takes a few steps closer to our group. "Fated mates," he announces.

CHAPTER 14

I burst out laughing. I can't help myself. When no one else joins in, my laughter starts to die. "Wait, you can't be serious." I'm still chuckling.

"Oh, he's very fucking serious. What the hell is so funny?" Gunnar gives me another scowl.

"I think I liked you better when you were eating ice cream, *Kitten*," I state, dismissing him and rolling my eyes.

"Yes, well, you can see why we decided it might be best to ignore the pull of the bond until a later time. We thought at some point you would seek us out and choose a mate." Grim is once again speaking calmly.

I look between all of them. "So, what? I'm supposed to choose between the three of you now?"

"That would be for the best." Grim nods slowly.

I puff out my cheeks and blow out a raspberry. "There are

a few issues with that." I hold up a finger. "One, I don't know what this mate thing really means. Two, I don't know any of you. Three, why should I have to choose only one? I mean, if you're all connected to me..." I shrug my shoulders. There's no point in beating around the bush.

If the mate thing means what I think it does, I wouldn't mind all three of them in my bed. But I don't know if I could ever really trust any of them, because they left me to fend for myself. Sure, Grim guaranteed I survived by feeding me, but that was only once in a while. And what did the other two do for me? Nothing, that's what.

I cross my arms over my chest and glare at them, once again mad that none of them stuck around to actually guide me and teach me who and what I am.

"She looks pissed again," Calix mutters, not answering my question about choosing.

"You know what? I am pissed. At what point did you decide only one of you having me as your mate was more important than actually teaching me about what and who I was?" Grim looks down first, the embers in his eyes all but distinguished now. Calix follows suit.

"Do you know what my first memory is?" When no one responds, I shout, "Well, do you?" I lurch to stand.

"Starving, that's what. Being so hungry all the time that all I did was wail and cry." I scrunch up my face, hating that I'm admitting this. "My mother got to the point where she just left me in my room for hours so she wouldn't have to listen to me," I seethe.

Focusing on Grim, I feel the air shift around me, and my hair lifts as a slight breeze surrounds me. "Do you know who came to me first?" I lower my tone and practice his calm demeanor.

"It was the Will-o'-the-Wisps, then Uncle Skinny Legs," I tell him, before he can answer. "Imagine being a child and longing for my mother to hold me, just so I could have some comfort while I was starving to death, and he comes slinking into my room." My words are met with silence.

I continue, "I didn't have any room for fear. I was too lonely for that, too desperate." I look down my nose at all three of them in a sneer.

"You think I mean something to any of you, that you're my mates? What a joke. Every one of you put yourselves before me." My chest is heaving; I'm filled with indignant rage. "I needed you then, but I don't need you now!"

I don't bother telling them to get out of my house. Instead, I walk out of the room with my head held high. I learned a long time ago that actions speak louder than words. Their actions prove that I don't mean anything to them.

I can thank my bitch of a mother for teaching me that lesson early on. In public, I was her beautiful little darling. She would dote on me and pretend to be the perfect mother. But the truth hid at home, where she constantly told me what a freak I was, threatened to lock me up if I didn't stop talking about all my *imaginary* friends, and made neglect an art form.

I slam my bedroom door so hard the pictures on the walls tremble. It was so satisfying, I'm almost tempted to do it again, but I don't. I pace around my room, angry and lonely, instead. I want to punch my own teeth in for letting self-pity and loneliness bubble to the surface. Being lonely is better than being abandoned. I repeat those words over and over in my head, until I feel like I can believe them.

"Everyone leaves, Dami. Better you leave them than they leave you." That's what I tell myself when I've finally exhausted enough energy so I feel like I can lie down without coming out of my own skin. I don't bother stripping out of my clothes. I don't have enough willpower to make the effort. I drag the comforter over my head and block out the world. Most people do this when they're scared of what's in the dark, but I find the light of day holds many more horrors.

A NOISE down the hall has me turning over and placing the pillow over my head. The rattling is familiar, but I'm not ready to get up. I lie in bed for a long time, wanting sleep to take me again. The brittle rattling comes once more, this time closer.

I toss the pillow off my head and smooth my hair away from my face. "Dami," the crooked man whispers, while his bones clink together as he makes his way across my room. I look over the side of the bed. He walks like a crab, his limbs all twisted and backwards.

"What's wrong?" My voice is smoky from sleep.

"Death has come," he announces in a whisper, his head twisting at an unnatural angle as he peers at my bedroom door.

"You mean Grim?" I scrub my hands over my face.

"Yes, and two others." Crooked man's fingers pop as if they're breaking when he moves closer.

I throw my legs over the side of the bed. "Why the fuck are they here again?"

"You knew?" He scurries away as I stand, making an ungodly racket as he does. Does he even notice the way it sounds when he moves, like breaking bones and grinding cartilage?

"I didn't know they were here now. I thought I sent them packing last night." I stretch and move my tongue around my mouth. I think something crawled in there and died last night —oh yeah, I just forgot to brush my teeth.

I make my way over to the bathroom, leaving the door open. It's not like I need privacy to pee or anything.

"Why were you warning me that they're here?" I inquire around a mouthful of toothpaste foam.

"Death doesn't make social calls." The crooked man clatters a little closer.

I let out an unladylike snort. "Yes, he does—he's been visiting me for years. I didn't know who he was until recently, but I assure you, he does make social calls." I rinse my mouth out with water and head back into my bedroom.

The crooked man hisses, "I just wanted you to know. I must go."

"Why? You just got here." I bounce back onto my bed. I

don't want him to go yet. With him here, I have an excuse not to go downstairs and find out what the hell Grim and the others are doing here—again.

"Be careful, Dami," he warns, while rattling out the door to disappear.

"Jeez, it's like everyone is scared of him or something."

"Because they are." Grim steps into the doorway that the crooked man just left through.

"Eavesdropping is rude," I chastise Grim.

He lowers his head with a slight nod. "Forgive me. I didn't know I was intruding."

"Why are you here?" I force myself to appear unaffected, but I'm not. Why does he have to be so damn beautiful and aloof? It's a recipe for the perfect Dami man candy—totally not fair.

"We had a bargain: no one would leave until all your questions are answered. May I?" Grim steps into the middle of the doorway, asking for entrance into my bedroom.

It's probably not the best idea, but I sigh and mutter, "Whatever."

Grim walks over to one of the chairs near the end of my bed, and I turn so I can keep an eye on him—not to notice how good he looks stalking into my bedroom. He's still wearing the black t-shirt and dark jeans from last night. Maybe they really did stay here all day.

"I'm pretty sure I said everything I needed to say yesterday." I look down at my nails.

"I think there's much that still needs to be discussed. I

understand you're upset, Damiana, but that doesn't make everything else irrelevant." I ball up my fists. Grim still has that über calm demeanor. I want to scream in his face.

"You understand *I'm* upset. How very magnanimous of you." Even though I'm trying to remain calm, my words are clipped, and my tone is harsh. He's making me feel as if someone else might have a different response, that maybe I'm being a brat.

"Would you like some hot cocoa? I've been practicing your recipe." I finally hear a note of something in Grim's voice, something other than his quiet calm.

I'm immediately on guard. Why would he practice my recipe? There must be something he wants from me. "Why, what else haven't you told me?" I ask skeptically.

"There is a lot we haven't discussed."

"I knew it! You wanted to butter me up," I accuse.

"Butter you up?" Grim looks at me with his head tilted to the side.

"Yeah, give me something in exchange for me giving you what you want." I cross my arms over my chest.

"The drink?" Grim's brow furrows as his eyes scan from left to right quickly. "I thought it would make you happy. Does it not?"

"I'm more concerned about what you'll want from me in exchange."

Grim's back goes ramrod straight. "And what did you expect in return when you offered it to me?"

"Nothing." I snort.

“Yet you made it, shared it with me—why?” Grim’s questions come quickly.

“Because I thought you were my friend,” I spit.

“Damiana, I want nothing from you other than for you to listen to me…and the others.” Grim’s lip lifts in a sneer when he says *the others*.

I focus on his words to see if I sense a lie, but he’s not easy to read. None of them are. “Why isn’t it obvious if you’re lying or telling the truth?”

“I could speculate, but I don’t know for certain,” Grim tells me.

I lift my hand in an invitation. “By all means, speculate away.”

“Would you care to join the others downstairs?” Grim’s face is sedate again. At least I know he’s capable of emotions.

“Fine, whatever, so long as it means you’ll answer me.” I rise, and Grim’s gaze tracks my movements, those tiny little lines of heat warming up his cold gray eyes. Interesting.

He lifts his hand and motions for me to go ahead of him. I put a little extra sway in my steps, nothing wrong with working with what you got.

I can hear the clang of pots and pans when I’m halfway down the stairs. “What the hell is going on down there?” I cast an accusatory glance at Grim behind me.

He lifts his hands in the air as if to deny involvement. “I was with you,” is all he says.

“My kitchen better not be a mess. Linda and her crew don’t come for another two days. I’m not cleaning up after them." I stomp down the rest of the stairs, coming to a halt when I reach the kitchen.

There are plastic bags all over the counters, each bulging with food. "Where did this all come from?" I note the name on the side of the bag isn't from my usual delivery service.

"I ordered it." Calix pops his head up from around the backside of the island. "You didn't have any real food, just a bunch of junk."

"And this is normal for you? You just go into someone's home, insult them, and then take over like you live there?"

Calix watches Grim. "I thought you were going to talk to her?"

"I did; now we are here." Grim comes up directly behind me. He's close enough that I feel my hair stir as he breathes.

Calix licks his lips. "So, she doesn't know we're not leaving?"

"She did not," Grim deadpans. "I thought we should ask her instead of tell her."

"What do you mean you're not leaving?" I step to the side and turn so I can see both of them.

"Well, it was your idea actually," Calix coaxes. "Yesterday, when we made the deal to stick around until all your questions were answered." He lifts his hands like that explains everything.

"And that translates into an invitation for you to move in how?" I look around at the messy state of my kitchen. "You're cleaning this up," I demand. "Is that a fucking roast?"

Gunnar comes out of the pantry. "Did you know you had a

Nettle Rat living in there?" He pokes his thumb back toward the pantry.

"That 'had' you just used, as in past tense, better not be your doing." I glower at him. If he did anything to Dare, I'll show him I can go fucking berserk on his ass.

"I just saw a nest near the back. I didn't touch it," Gunnar defends.

"You better not. That goes for all of you. If you do anything to my friends, I'll make sure you regret it." I walk over and slam the pantry door. Gunnar hops out of the way to avoid being hit by the door.

"You know Nettle Rats sting, right? They're venomous," Calix informs me, as if I'm a fool.

I turn to face him and give him a droll stare. "Dare couldn't hurt me if she tried—not that she ever would."

"Dare? You gave it a name?" Gunnar looks around like someone might be playing a prank on him.

"Her, and no, she told me her name."

"She talks to you?" Grim blinks several times, looking quite mystified.

"Yes," I answer slowly, thinking they might actually all be the slow ones.

Calix purses his lips and gives a humph. "Who knew." He turns around and starts putting the groceries away again.

"Back to the business of you not leaving…" I may be easily distracted, but I'm not that bad.

"Works out perfectly, really." Gunnar lifts his lips in a

mockery of a smile. "We can answer your questions, you can get to know us, and we can go from there."

Grim lets out a soft sigh.

Several thoughts collide in my head at once. On one hand, it's what I've always secretly longed for. Companions. On the other hand, I don't trust them, and what's to say they won't just leave me whenever they feel like it. Sure, they say they'll stay, but no one ever does. But that's not true either. Uncle has been returning to visit me since I was a child and, when I think about it, so has Grim.

I look over at him, searching past the perfect exterior of dark hair and the chiseled jaw, trying to see what's beneath. Grim sucks in a breath of air, it whistles past his lips and his chest expands. I watch as he holds it, not taking his gray eyes off me. "You'll answer my questions?"

Grim exhales slowly. "To the best of my ability, yes."

I narrow my eyes on him. "What does that mean?"

"It means we might not have all the answers, Damiana, but we'll do our best," Calix answers, before picking up a huge chunk of meat from the island, and holding it in his hands as if he's waiting for my response.

"Why should I trust you, any of you?" I don't meet Grim's eyes when I ask. It seems he may be the only one who ever really tried to help me.

"You can trust us," Gunnar announces, causing Calix to hang his head back on his shoulders and groan at the brute's tone. "You trusted me to stay in your house and to seek me out at the club." Gunnar makes an effort to soften his voice.

"That was before I knew you guys abandoned me," I argue, speaking the truth.

"None of us really abandoned you, Damiana." Calix sets the meat back down on the counter and holds up his hands to stop me when I open my mouth to argue. "I know if feels like that now, but we've all been around more than you know. We've all tried to help you along the way, even if it doesn't seem like it. Give me…give us," he amends begrudgingly, "a chance to prove that to you."

Could that be true, or is it just wishful thinking on my part? "You better not do anything to scare my friends away, and I'm still not cleaning up after you," I warn.

I'm smarter than this. I shouldn't be letting them stay, but there's some part of me that wants them to. Stupid loneliness.

Grim pulls out a stool from under the island, and he places his hand on my back, urging me forward to sit. I jerk away from him a little. I'm not ready for him, or any of the others for that matter, to touch me.

My hormones and head don't always agree on the order in which I should get what I want. I'm hoping my head will win this battle and hold out for answers, while my body just wants to jump any one of them right here in the kitchen.

I eye Gunnar while he starts helping Calix put away the groceries. Something about him puts me on edge more than the others. I've never been one for an angry fuck, but I feel like I could give it to him good.

Grim doesn't acknowledge the way I spurned his touch. He just pulls out the stool next to me and takes a seat. He inspires a different kind of lust. He's always so calm and in control, and I'd like to see him tied to my bed, with my black sheets under him and the black blindfold over his eyes. Nothing else. I bet I could make him squirm.

I put my elbows on the counter and cover my eyes with my fingers, while massaging my temples with my thumbs. "What were we talking about upstairs?" I blurt. I have to get these thoughts out of my head.

"You asked why you can't always sense the truth from us," Grim supplies without an ounce of hesitation.

"Right, right, and you said you had a theory," I murmur, recalling the beginnings of the conversation, and urging him to continue.

"Telling whether or not someone is lying to you is a defense mechanism. Maybe some part of you knows you don't need to use that awareness with me, us," Grim concludes, amending his slipup.

"*Or*, you could be blocking me somehow. I just learned about wards, there are a lot of things I'm sure I don't know about."

"Wards are cast by *witches*," Gunnar states, sneering the last word. "We aren't witches."

"You work for one," I reason.

"I don't work for her. We have the mutual displeasure of working together. Believe me, it's not something I enjoy."

I again try to tell if he's being truthful, but I can't. "Why work with her at all then?"

"The witches need to be kept in line, and I'm the one who has to do it, for now," Gunnar replies.

"Wait, didn't you say a coven ambushed you? That's how you ended up hurt here." I look at the others for confirmation. "A witch's coven?"

"Yes." Gunnar scowls and I hear a distinct snicker from Calix.

A loaf of bread goes sailing right over the spot Calix's head was moments earlier and splats into the wall. The bag explodes on contact, sending crumbs and slices of bread to the floor. Calix pops right back up and puts another roast into the freezer.

"Not all covens take kindly to being watched," Gunnar continues, as if uninterrupted. "I got a little lazy," he admits, while brushing is hands together. "But rest assured, I took care of that threat."

"A little lazy? Last I heard, you haven't even left the city in years. You've been sending your men out to keep an eye on the other covens," Calix challenges.

"Vanessa's coven is one of the largest in the country. Hers is the gauge which the others in the region use as a guide," Gunnar defends indignantly.

"And it had nothing to do with the fact that you didn't want to get too far away from Damiana?" Calix taunts.

Gunnar takes a step toward Calix. "Knock it off." I slap my hand on the top of the island. The sting on my palm is welcome.

Gunnar levels a nasty look at Calix but resumes putting away the groceries as if he's accustomed to the domestic task.

I feel the heat of Grim's arm as he lays it across the back of my stool. "While we were chosen to be your guardians, we also have other duties," he adds.

"I can pretty much guess yours." I give him a little snort. "What about you, Calix?"

"I keep the beasts in line." He leans his hip against the island. "The largest shifter population is in Russia, so that's where I spend most of my time."

"Lion: king of not just the jungle, huh?" I joke.

Calix preens under my gaze, straightening his back and licking his lips. "Yes, my queen."

"Give me a break," Gunnar barks.

I giggle. "So what sorts of shifters are there?"

Calix takes a deep breath and looks up at the ceiling in thought. "Wolves have the largest numbers, bears, hyenas, all kinds of cats." He shrugs. "There are more, but those are the most dangerous predators. Then there are the others, like me and the dragons, but we're not the same. We're born, not turned."

My mind is spinning with all this new information. Witches and shifters are real. How many other supernatural beings are there? "How come I don't know any of this? How is it I've seen Will-o'-the-Wisps and Wraiths, but I had no clue about Berserkers and Newmans like you?"

Gunnar snorts.

"Nemean lions," Calix corrects.

"You should have grown up without any of this knowledge," Grim states from beside me. "It's my fault the nightmares come to you." His eyes meet mine.

"What do you mean?" I turn in my seat so I can see him better.

"You called to me as a child, a babe." Grim's voice dips lower, as if he's divulging a secret. "Your soul called me. You were dying."

"What?" Calix gasps in disbelief.

"Why didn't you tell us this?" Gunnar snaps.

Grim ignores him and answers my silent questions. "You really were starving to death." He reaches out and slowly smooths his finger over my cheek. I'm too shocked to even try to stop him. "I couldn't let you die." The embers of fire begin to glow within Grim's eyes. "I tethered your soul to your body, making it impossible for anything to kill you. But there was a cost."

I search Grim's eyes for answers, and he licks his top lip. "I don't have an explanation for why you were starving, Damiana, but when I fed you, it turned you into a beacon for them. I didn't even realize it until I came back one night and found you playing with a Deep One."

"A Deep One?" I scan my thoughts for what he could be referring to.

"Little girl, white dress, comes from the bottom of the ocean," Grim explains, describing one of my childhood friends.

"You mean Cece," I correct him.

He closes his eyes on a long blink. "I observed you with her. You two played together for hours, and you smiled." Grim watches me intently.

"I haven't seen her in years," I muse. I'd almost forgotten about her. She did tell me she came from the sea, and as young as I was, I didn't understand, so I just started calling her Cece.

"I'm sorry I didn't protect you—"

"Protect me? From Cece?" I interrupt Grim. Reaching over, I grab hold of his arm. It's the first time I actually feel gratitude toward him since he told me they were supposed to be my guardians. "Don't ever apologize for that. Without her and Uncle, I would have gone insane."

Grim's mouth thins to a slash. "You shouldn't have needed me to feed you. That part of you should have been dormant until you were much older." He doesn't do as good of a job maintaining his calm demeanor now.

I drop my hand from his arm and let his words sink in. I should have been a normal child. The idea of what could have been—how different my life would have been—sends a pang to my chest, but then I wouldn't have Uncle, Redmon, or Aeson. I can't imagine a life without them. I never felt like I was part of my birth family anyway. I always secretly thought I was adopted.

"You should have told us she almost died," Gunnar insists, unaware of my thoughts.

Grim comes to his feet. "Why? Could *you* have done something to change it?" His voice booms with several layers at once, his calm exterior shattered.

Gunnar lets out a hissing breath. "No, yet you should have told us. She's not just yours!"

"Shut up," I mutter angrily.

The bickering continues. "It was a big deal. You should have told us," Calix agrees, taking Gunnar's side.

"See? Even the animal gets it." Gunnar throws his hand in Calix's direction.

"Shut up, shut up, shut up!" I slap my hands on the island again, while getting to my feet. "What the fuck is wrong with you people?" I trade a glance with each of them. Grim is the only one of them that meets my stare. Gunnar suddenly finds the floor very interesting, while Calix is pretending to examine the few boxes and bags still on the counter.

"Can you for, like, five fucking minutes, not think about yourselves?" I ask rather calmly. "Would that be okay? So maybe I could get some fucking answers?" The calm doesn't last, though. By the end of my statement, my sarcasm is on full display, and I'm shouting again.

CHAPTER 15

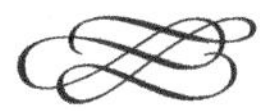

"Grim, please." I roll my wrist in an effort to tell him to continue. My hands are trembling, and my insides feel a little like Jello.

I'm still trying to wrap my head around the fact that I have Grim to thank for my entire existence. Without him, I wouldn't have survived infancy.

"I failed to keep you safe," Grim admits again without hesitation.

"No, you didn't, and that's not what I want to hear. Feel sorry for yourself later. I want to know why—if you saved me —you didn't show yourself to me. Why didn't you ever stick around long enough to give me an explanation?" I demand.

Grim takes a shallow breath. "I feared it would leave you even more open to other supernatural threats. I monitored the beings that visited you. I knew they had no intention of ever seeing you hurt: they were drawn to you, they protected you." Grim lifts his palms a little and his lips tighten into a thin line. "I didn't know what the consequence of my visits would be. I had no idea if your mind or your body would withstand all of this information. Humans aren't supposed to see into our world the way you do."

"I'm not human," I nearly spit, taking offense. Humans are weak and shallow.

"No, but when you were born, you should have been as fragile and naive as a human," Grim reasons with me. "Children are more open to the supernatural world around them, so I thought if I let you grow up, you would forget about the nightmares that visited you, until it was time for you to awaken. I was trying to protect you."

I plop back against the stool, not really sitting, but still needing it to lean against to stay on my feet. "I never forgot them, not any of them," I inform Grim. After a brief pause, I add, "Fine, whatever. I can almost understand your reasoning, even if I think it's stupid, but why wait so long?" I include the others in the conversation now. "I'm thirty years old, old enough to know the truth about myself, to have *awakened*, or whatever the hell you called it."

Calix takes a few steps closer until he's just opposite me on the other side of the island. "We really did think you would seek one of us out. We all agreed that three mates would be too much."

I let out an unladylike snort. "Speak for yourselves." I plant my hands on my hips.

Calix continues as if I didn't just challenge him and interrupt him in one sentence. "Have you ever felt like you were missing something, someone?"

I scrunch up my face and look around. "Is that a joke?" What the hell kind of question is that? Of course I've been missing something my entire life.

"Were you ever tempted to find it? Are you drawn to any of us?" Gunnar lifts his chin slightly in the air, waiting for my response.

I cross my arms over my chest. "So, that's what you're waiting for: me to just pick one of you. And then what—you think I'll become your property? Ain't happening, Kitten," I declare, sparing the others a glance after looking down my nose at Gunnar. "As to the question of whether I'm *drawn* to one of you, I wouldn't kick any of you out of bed for eating crackers, but that's just basic attraction. You're all fuckable, but I don't particularly like any one of you." I pause. "Well, maybe you, a little." I give Grim a wink, holding my fingers pinched close together.

Which is met with grouching from Gunnar. "You only like him because he fed you. I was around, too. I'm the one who brought you all the stones," he replies crossly.

I slowly turn to face the man-child who is about as close to a tantrum as an adult could get. "You were the one leaving the rocks?" I question.

"Not just rocks—they're gemstones." Gunnar folds his arms over his puffed-out chest.

"What happened to keeping our distance?" Calix fumes, his eyes narrowed at the other two men.

"I've already explained why that wasn't an option for me, nor could I stay away once I met her." Grim doesn't even bother to sound contrite.

"Maybe there's something wrong with you that you could, Calix." Gunnar alleges. "The desire was almost uncontrollable. Maybe the connection isn't so strong with you."

"Fuck off, Berserker. Some of us have control of ourselves, unlike your unstable ass," Calix snaps back, with just as much venom.

I take a good look at Calix, wondering if what Gunnar claimed might be true. Do I feel something different for him, from him?

I take in the lean lines of his body, the graceful way he moves, and all I feel at this moment is an undeniable attraction. That same pure feeling I had when I first met him at the club is still there, but it's tainted with mistrust.

I observe Gunnar next. My hackles rise just looking at him standing there, snarling at Calix. There's no denying I still find him alluring. All his scars stand as proof of his will to survive, to fight for what he wants, and I actually respect that. It doesn't hurt that he's built like a brick shit house—his biceps look like they could crush a coconut. I bet he could fuck for hours and not get tired. I flick my gaze away from him when he takes a step in my direction.

I force myself not to look at Grim, because if there is one

to whom I'm more pulled, it would be him, and I'm not ready to acknowledge that.

"If you think I'm going to pick one of you, and we'll live happily ever after or some shit, you're wrong. I'm not that girl. I like dick, in all varieties. I'm not picking just one."

"Is everything about sex with you?" Gunnar throws his arms in the air. "We're not just talking about dicking. We're talking about a connection, with feelings and shit." He ruins his flowery words with the curse and the disdain with which they were delivered.

I lean forward. "Fucking is all I know about any kind of mating, you ass-munch."

"I propose we do something about that," Calix interjects, before Gunnar and I can start arguing. "That's why we're all here, so you can get to know us, decide which of us you'd like to be with."

"You're assuming that my choosing one of you is a forgone conclusion. I've already told you: I'm not picking one of you. You want to stick around, let me get to know you?" I shrug as if it's no skin off my hide either way. "But you need to prepare yourself for the inevitability that I might not choose any of you, or maybe that I'll want all three of you." Another shrug, and this one is accompanied with a twist of my lips. Might as well scare them away before I really do find myself liking one of them.

Calix looks at Gunnar first. I bet he's gauging whether or not he'll stick around. I watch him too, but he doesn't open his mouth to argue—which surprises me—nor does he make a move to leave.

"I'm not going anywhere," Grim states, before I even have a chance to glance at him. "If having them around makes you happy, I can choose to *not* kill them. I've suffered their existence this long." He lowers his head an infinitesimal amount, like he's conceding to me.

"I'm not bowing out, either," Calix quickly adds.

I swear the width of Gunnar's shoulders expands, but he lets out a deep breath and calmly declares, "I am agreeable to your terms." He pauses, before adding, "For now."

I scratch my eyebrow. Well, that's not what I expected. I figured there would be a fight, and I would get rid of them all. I can't say I'm that upset. Why not have three hot guys around trying to get you to 'catch feelings for them?'

"No fighting," I demand, when I can't come up with anything else to say.

"There are bound to be…disagreements. How should we settle them?" Calix inquires, sounding all grown up and shit.

"Uh…" I look around the kitchen like it might provide an answer.

"We will discuss them," Grim replies. "Any grievances should be addressed while we're all together."

"What he said." I wave my hand in Grim's direction.

"I think we need rules of engagement," Gunnar announces, as if he's planning a strategic maneuver instead of tiptoeing into the—dare I think it—*dating game*. Is that even what we're about to do?

"What would you propose?" Grim settles himself with his ass leaning against my island. I find myself licking my lips. Damn, if he isn't gorgeous.

"Touching—there should be no touching," Gunnar responds quickly.

"Now, wait just a damn minute." I shake my head and focus on Gunnar instead of Grim's tight ass in his dark jeans. "I'm a tactile person. I happen to likey the touchy."

"I agree. Why should we hold ourselves back for you?" Calix sneers at Gunnar.

"How about because if I see you touch her, I'll rip your fucking arms off. Would that work as enough of a deterrent?" Gunnar takes a step toward Calix, who just stands his ground like he's not at all intimidated.

"You could try, Viking." Calix smiles darkly, and I see the tips of his very sharp, very inhuman teeth. Damn, that shouldn't be sexy.

"I said no fighting," I call out, even though there's some part of me that would like to watch these two go at it.

Gunnar drops his arms to his sides, but his fists are still balled up. "Then a schedule, perhaps," he suggests through his teeth.

I snicker, then cover my mouth when they all look at me. "You wanna schedule touch time?" I burst out laughing at the absurdity of it.

"We could schedule alone time." Grim tilts his head. "After all, there are times each of us must be away, when our duties can't be avoided."

Calix leans against the counter on his elbows with a wide grin on his lips. "Not me—I'm free and clear. I'll always be around." He winks at me and I get a little fluttery feeling in my stomach. My hand covers the spot—what was that? I scowl to cover how uncomfortable the feeling made me and spin on my heel, facing the opposite direction.

"How did you manage that?" Gunnar asks incredulously.

"You may have visited her and left rocks, but I've been preparing. I knew this day would come, and I wanted to make sure I could make up for lost time," Calix hedges, with a hint of cockiness in his tone.

"Well, that's bullshit. I can't get out of my commitment." Gunnar looks around as if there might be someone he could appeal to.

I settle myself back on the stool. Watching them interact is entertaining. I usually only have myself for company, and maybe one visitor a night if I'm lucky. This is like watching reality TV, but so much better.

"What commitment? To the witches?" I question, wishing I could eat popcorn. This would be the perfect time for popcorn.

Grim casts Calix a distrustful glance. "I, like the Berserker, have obligations. I must come and go," he admits.

"Don't worry, boys, I'll take real good care of her." Calix doesn't bother to hide the leer he's tossing in my direction.

"Hurry up and put the rest of this away so we can go back into the living room. Then you guys can tell me about your *commitments*." I give the word a little extra dark flare for emphasis.

"Give me two minutes, and I'll be done." Calix leans away and gets right back to work, shoving groceries into the fridge and freezer.

"I've warned you about bragging about your speediness." I waggle my finger at him jokingly.

Calix looks over his shoulder with a sultry, traffic-stopping grin. "If I would have moved a little faster the other night, we might already be rid of these two." I can tell by the gleam in his eye that he's joking. If anyone would be okay with sharing, I know it would be Calix. He's already said he likes an audience. I glance over at Gunnar and burst out laughing. He looks like he swallowed a lemon, and that just makes the mental picture of him watching Calix and me even more comical. Nobody asks why I'm laughing.

I pat Gunnar's firm bicep on the way to the hall. "Come on, I want to hear about the creepy witches, and why you work for them."

"With them," Gunnar immediately corrects me.

"With them." I roll my eyes, agreeing.

CHAPTER 16

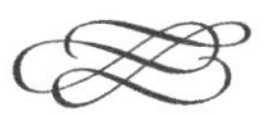

"So, you're some kind of watchdog." I settle back into the couch. Gunnar is next to me, making it hard to pay attention to his words, instead of the thickness of his thigh.

Gunnar purses his lips, thinking. "I make sure they don't get reckless or too power hungry."

"Uncle told me that witches steal their power from people like us. You let them do that?" I watch Gunnar for his reaction.

"No." He shakes his head vehemently. "That's exactly why I keep an eye on them: to make sure they aren't doing shit like that."

I look over at Grim, wondering if I should ask to talk to Gunnar alone. I don't want to embarrass him or get him in trouble. The blasé look on Grim's face doesn't give me any answer.

"You haven't been doing your job, Berserker," Grim states. I gape at him a little.

Gunnar turns his head slowly and examines Grim, who is seated in the chair directly across from me. "What did you say?"

I pinch the bridge of my nose. "Gunnar," I call his name before he can rail at Grim, who would probably be completely unaffected by Gunnar's outburst. "The witch I ran into at the club—the male witch? He was dirty. Tasted like death." I glance at Grim again. "No offense, because you don't taste like death; you always bring me yummy treats." Grim lets the tiniest grin slip over his mouth before he regains his stoic bearing.

"What the fuck are you talking about?" Gunnar snaps at Grim.

"I'm talking about the dead Kappa whose soul I carried last week, and the Lämpmen the week before. It's been happening for the last several months."

Gunnar looks down, and I can see his eyes tracking from left to right. "How could that be? Where did this happen?"

"Far from here, but getting closer," Grim divulges.

Calix comes strutting in through the door but slows once he assesses the mood of the room. "What did I miss?" He looks between us.

"I need to go," Gunnar announces, standing. He faces me, his hands already balled up into tight fists, his shoulders bunched with tension. "I'll be back as soon as I can. Can you tell me about the witch from the club: his name, what he looked like, anything?"

I search my mind, but he was just another face. "He wasn't one of the people Vanessa was having her meeting with or whatever. He was just a guy—nothing special about him except how he felt, and his aura, which was oily." I grimace, wishing I could give him more.

Gunnar nods his head jerkily. "I'll find out what's going on." With a swiftness I would expect from Calix, Gunnar leans down and steals a kiss from my lips. He's gone in the next second, literally disappearing right before my eyes.

I blink several times, wondering if I somehow missed something. "You broke the no-touching rule!" Calix shouts into the air as if Gunnar can still hear him.

"Seems like we have a mystery afoot, Watson." I rub my hands together, mostly to distract myself from wanting to touch my lips where Gunnar just planted one on me.

"Let's hope the Berserker doesn't get in over his head." Calix frowns. "How did you cross paths with the witches?"

I curl up on the couch. "I went to the club to find Gunnar and ran right through a witch's ward, apparently. I honestly never even knew they were real before that."

Calix takes a seat near me on the couch, and his arm goes to the back as he turns his body toward mine. I like the way he gets close to me without demanding it. It's almost subtle.

Grim is watching us from the chair, I can feel his eyes on me. "Would you recognize the witch if you saw him again, or the feeling he gave you?" Grim inquires.

"I would, now that I know what I'm looking for." A slow grin builds on my lips. "Why, did you want to go to Rumors and see if we can find him?"

"The Berserker would hate it—we should go." Calix doesn't bother to hide the delight he would get from pissing off Gunnar.

"You *have* been using a lot of energy," Grim comments.

I catch on immediately. "I am feeling rather peckish."

"A girl's gotta eat. Let's go." Calix pops up from the sofa and grabs my hand to bring me with him.

I look down at my yoga pants and slouchy t-shirt. "I need to change. I'll only be a few minutes." I take off upstairs to change, pulling my shirt off as I hit the third-floor landing. I want to look hot, but I don't have a lot of time. Scanning my closet, I get an idea when my eyes land on a pair of black, calfskin leather pants. "Too easy," I mutter, while unclipping them from the hanger.

Ten minutes later, I'm hopping down the stairs with a heavy pair of Doc Martens on my feet. "Ready!" I call out when I don't see Grim or Calix. "They better not have left me."

"Not a chance," Calix announces, as he comes around the corner with what looks like a chicken leg gripped in his hand. His eyes scan my bright teal bra which shows beneath my mesh shirt, then move down to my low-rise leather pants. "Pretty, pretty bird." He licks his lips before taking a huge bite out of the meat in his hand.

Grim walks in behind Calix and separates himself from the

other man by stepping a few feet to the left. "Would you like me to get you a cloak?" His eyes scan my body, too, the little rivers of ember bleeding into the sooty ash color of his eyes.

I do a little spin. "Are you worried I'll get cold?"

"Not especially," Grim deadpans. I love how he can look and sound so completely unaffected, but his eyes tell an entirely different story.

Calix wipes his mouth with the back of his hand. "It would be a sin to hide that beauty under a cloak, so keep the robes for yourself, Death." Calix extends his elbow to me after pitching what's left of the chicken leg into the trash bin. "I wanna show off my queen."

"I'm not anyone's queen, but I love giving a good show." I look up at Calix from under my eyelashes.

"You want to ride…or drive?" Calix pours as much innuendo into those six words as possible while he gazes down at me. I like how his reaction to me is so completely at odds with Grim's. With the three of them around, I'll never get bored.

"Driving…shit! I only have a two-seater." I pause and pull my hand from Calix's inner elbow.

"I can handle transportation." Grim comes up behind me, invading my space, but I certainly don't mind.

"For all of us?" I ask, a little surprised by the offer.

"If the Nemean is agreeable." Grim raises one brow, almost as if he's challenging Calix to accept.

In return, Calix's eyes narrow. "I'm restricted to the more human modes of transportation in this form, so I will accept your offer that we may arrive together," he answers, sounding strangely formal.

"Wait, you're going to portal us there?" I nearly bounce with giddy excitement.

"No, I can't take you to the other side." Grim eyes me like I might just be crazy.

"I was about to withdraw *my* consent," Calix mumbles.

"Then how?" I look around like he has a magic carpet tucked somewhere.

"I just need you to tell me where Rumors is and where within we should blink to," Grim tells me, as if I know what the hell blinking is.

"You probably pick up ODs from there often enough. Club over on Seventh and Wayne," Calix answers before I have the chance.

"I know it. I'll take you first." He nods to Calix.

"Shit. You can't take us both?" Calix rubs his hands together. "I hate spiritual travel."

"Just hold still," Grim warns, while placing his palm on Calix's shoulder. "I'll drop you in the bathroom. I trust you'll be able to find us?"

Calix's upper lip lifts in a small sneer. "Of course I can find her."

"I will return for you." Grim watches me as he and Calix disappear.

I take a step forward and wave my hand in the space they were just standing in. "Weird. I want to do that." I pout, disgruntled that I don't have some super-awesome way to get around like Gunnar's and Grim's disappearing.

Grim pops back in right where my hand is, so I end up with a palmful of his chest. "Well, hello." I tell my brain I should move my hand, but my damn fingers decide a slow walk down Grim's abdomen is a much better idea. "How did you pop up so fast?" My other hand finds its way to Grim's chest and demands the same scenic route down his stomach.

"Without the burden of the Nemean, I can travel much faster." Grim's voice is pitched low. His chest is rising and falling quickly. Instead of backing up from him, I take another step closer. "That's interesting," I say, even though I'm not even really paying attention to what he said. I'm much more engrossed in the way his breath keeps catching when my fingers travel over his chest and stomach.

I feel a sharp tug on the ends of my hair. My head jerks back and I gasp. Grim's mouth lands on mine as he devours me. There's no first-kiss awkwardness, no trying to figure out what I like, just him shoving his tongue into my mouth as he wraps his arms around my waist and drags me tightly up against his body.

Never once does the thought of resisting enter my mind. Why the hell would I want to? Grim is kissing me like a dying man searching for water. He jerks back when his tooth hits mine. His eyes are all fire as he looks down at me. "Sorry." He almost looks sheepish before he delves right back in, this time a little more careful not to knock his teeth into mine.

I'm the one to pull away this time. I'm panting for air, but

Grim just starts kissing his way up my neck. I let out a small groan when he bites the bottom of my earlobe. He freezes, my flesh still between his teeth, panting into my ear.

My hands cling to his shoulders as Grim's teeth slide off my earlobe, but he sucks it back into the warmth of his mouth. I feel his tongue slip up behind my lobe as he kisses his way up to the crest of my ear. Holy shit, I don't think anyone has ever kissed me there, and it fucking feels good, or maybe it just feels good because it's Grim, and that unshakable exterior has finally crumbled so I can see the beast beneath.

In two quick strides, Grim has my back against the wall. He's not at all gentle, and it stirs something inside me. He plasters his body to my front, leaving no doubt just how affected he is. I reach down between our bodies and grab his cock. Grim hisses out a breath and grinds into my hand.

"Well, hello, big boy," I purr, working my hand over his length. Grim bites my bottom lip roughly.

"Stop speaking," he growls and thrusts his hips. The wall behind me creaks in protest as my breath flees my lungs.

"Or what?" I gasp with a shallow pant.

Grim places his mouth right next to my ear, and I can feel his lips tremble as his hot breath teases my ear and neck. "Or I'll have you right here, right now, against this wall."

"Is that supposed to be a threat?" I squeeze my hand around his dick. I wish he didn't have these stupid jeans on, even if his ass does look amazing in them.

Grim bites the side of my neck, hard. My head hits the wall behind me with a loud thud as my entire body goes lax.

It's not that I'm worried he's going to hurt me; in fact, it's quite the opposite. It's like he hit the magical, do-whatever-you-like button, 'cause I'm here for it.

Grim releases his teeth from my neck slowly. The burn left behind has my knees feeling a little loose. "Damiana, I will only take you when I know you're mine. Are you mine?" He stares right into my eyes, the fiery embers tracing through his slate gray eyes, looking like rivers of lava.

I drag my fingers off of his erection. "I'm no one's pet." I hear myself saying the words, but it's not what I'm really thinking. I'm thinking he could have very easily made me his if he hadn't made it a demand, if he would have just shown me with his body how much he truly wanted me to be his. I push against Grim's chest, but he doesn't let up. He's still holding me against the wall.

I break eye contact. I don't need him to see how very much I would like to be his, and not just for the fucking. Stupid, lonely heart. It's going to be the death of me. I peer up at Grim and realize how accurate my thoughts really are.

Blinking to the club was anticlimactic, to say the least. I was standing in my kitchen one moment, then pinned between Grim and a nasty bathroom stall the next. There was no woozy feeling or even flashing lights in a tunnel or some shit. The only thing of note was the hard dick nudging my stomach.

I push open the stall door with a sultry smirk on my lips.

Good to know I'm still affecting him. A blonde, leaning in close to the mirror to reapply her lipstick, freezes when she catches sight of me—or it could be the Angel of Death who saunters out behind me that has her staring.

I give her finger guns and an over-the-top wink. She blinks several times, her eyes volleying between Grim and me through the mirror.

I leave her to catch her own tongue and push my way out of the VIP bathroom. If it had been the club-level bathroom, we probably wouldn't have found an empty stall. Calix is leaning against the wall with one foot lifted behind him, so his knee is jutted out, and his arms are crossed over his chest. He's wearing a scowl that would keep most men from approaching him, but it doesn't seem to be too much of a deterrent to the ladies, if the small group around him is any indication.

"Where the hell have you guys been?" Calix comes off the wall and stomps over to me as soon as I step out of the bathroom.

"Got held up." I meet his eyes. I'm definitely not lying. If Grim hadn't been holding me against that wall, I'm sure I would have fallen a few times. Calix glares over my head at Grim, whom I can feel way too close to my back.

"So, have you seen Gunnar?" I go up on my tippy toes to impede Calix's line of sight.

Calix studies me before answering, "No, but I've been standing here waiting for you guys for," he makes a big show of looking down at his wristwatch, "twenty minutes." He sends another glower at Grim.

"Let's see if we can find the *bitches*." I say the word dramatically slow and give Calix a wink, so he knows I'm really talking about the witches. I just don't want the people around us thinking I'm crazier than I really am.

Calix takes a step closer to me, sandwiching me between himself and Grim. Keeping his eyes locked on mine, he lowers his head and sniffs me. I straighten my back, feeling affronted. Do I stink? I lift my arm in the air and take a whiff of my armpit. I smell like deodorant. I did get a little hot and bothered with Grim, but I don't stink.

Calix's eyelids lower slowly, and a grin lifts one side of his lips. My heart starts beating a little faster. He sure doesn't look like he thinks I stink. I can feel Grim's heat on my back and Calix's against my chest. Well, if this isn't just any girl's fantasy. My nipples tighten in my bra. Grim didn't want to give me what I needed, but I bet Calix would be willing. I wonder if Grim would be up for watching. I mean, it's the least he could do, right? He's the one that got me all excited and then backed off.

"What the fuck are you doing here?" Gunnar shouts. I can feel his heavy footfalls as he nears us.

"Uh-oh, Kitten caught us," I mock whisper. A new idea begins to form in my mind, and this one has some merit. All three of them—hell, I don't even need any of them to touch me. If they all just stood around and watched me get myself off, that might be fun, too.

"Whatever you're thinking, knock it off," Gunnar snarls.

"Make me." I meet his gaze and say the words slowly.

Gunnar's face scrunches up and he drags in a deep inhale, his body expanding along with it. If he thinks this hulking out thing is scary, he better go peddle his wares elsewhere. I think it's kinda hot.

"You know I like the beast look, right? It really works for you." I step out from between Grim and Calix, not because Gunnar told me to, but because I am ready. I'm starting to realize that these boys are nothing but teases. Two, or rather four, can play at that game.

"I'm going hunting," I announce, and slip right past Gunnar while he's busy staring down Grim and Calix.

CHAPTER 17

I quickly lose myself in the crowd. I know I don't have a lot of time before one—or all three—comes to find me. I said I was going hunting, but I didn't mention what I was hunting. My intention *was* to find a suitable man or woman to show those guys I can scratch an itch anytime, but now that I'm away from them, I have no desire to look for another warm body. Stupid, stupid head: it seems as if it's decided I need one of them to satiate me.

I scan the crowd in the VIP lounge, looking for that icky feeling I got from the witch, but I just sense the run of the mill sins that always plague this place. I don't even have the desire to feed.

A flash of light catches my eye, and I see the door to the lounge open. Vanessa is leading a small group of people into the section. As soon as I spot them, I feel the stench of their magic.

A foul taste fills my mouth, but I work hard to keep my expression unbothered as I make my way over to the bar. I recognize the man holding the door so the group can enter. He was the guy who interrupted Gunnar and me in his office a few nights ago. He steps into the lounge as the last of the group comes through the door.

The space was packed before, but now it feels beyond overcrowded. Two men make their way over to a large conversation area with a couple of couches and chairs. One leans into the partiers already seated there and speaks. When the man leans back, the people look around, seeming a little bewildered, but they all start to rise and abandon their seats.

Vanessa and her group make their way over and the crowd parts for them. I face the bar. "May I have a bottle of water, please?"

"You got it," a good-looking guy behind the bar replies quickly. Before I can drag a twenty out of my bra—these pants don't leave room for pockets—Calix places a bill on the bar right next to my left elbow.

I know it's him by the way he feels. Everyone else in this place is tarnished, but somehow it makes his purity shine even brighter.

"Anything for you?" the bartender asks with a chin jerk.

"Nothing, just hers." Calix pushes the money closer to the man.

I lick my lips before cracking the lid on my drink. I know Grim is close, too. My stupid fucking body is somehow tuned in to his as well. I spin on the stool, using my boots on the bottom riser. Lifting the bottle to my lips, I whisper, "They feel like the oily guy," then take a sip, covering my mouth.

I watch the entire VIP lounge, but keep an eye on the group. Gunnar is speaking to the man that interrupted us, but he's not being very subtle about keeping an eye on our small group. Every time I glance past him, he's looking at us.

"He's not very stealthy," I mutter, making a big deal about looking over the crowd.

"We don't really need stealth, Damiana. What we need are answers." Calix leans his arm behind me on the bar.

"Well, if they're up to shady shit, and they realize we're on to them, it could foil our plans." I look up at him and smile like I'm really just flirting with Calix.

He grins down at me. "Foil our plans for what—world domination?" I can tell he's teasing me and my excitement.

"No, but if they're hurting my friends, I'm going to stop them." Who's to say they wouldn't go after Uncle or Theius the next time they need a boost of magic.

Grim bumps into my side. I look over and see a tall redhead sidled up a little too close to him for comfort. Without thinking, I reach across Grim's body, place my hand on her hip, and shove her away. "Mine."

The redhead gapes at me, her pretty mouth hanging open as if she can't believe my audacity. "Move along." I shoo her with my fingers and wrap my arm around Grim's back, tugging him closer. Grim turns so the front of his body is flush to my side. I give his butt a nice little pat as a reward. There's no way I'm going to let someone else touch him. They don't know it yet—hell, I'm not even sure when I decided it—but some part of me did choose all three of them as mine.

I wrap my other arm around Calix just for good measure. I don't need anyone getting any ideas.

"Comfortable, queenie?" Calix asks. I give his ass a pinch in response. "Don't distract me. I'm working." He bursts out laughing, attracting way more attention than we need. Vanessa even looks over at our group, and her brow furrows.

"Great." I scowl.

"What's wrong, bad blood?" Calix's hand goes to my shoulder near Grim.

"No. I've just never liked her. Now I know why," I theorize, but it's probably just an excuse. Even if she weren't a witch, I still wouldn't like her.

"She's the head of the coven," Grim comments, as if he's answering his own question.

"Shush," I warn, and look around. We're still drawing some attention. It would probably be hard not to, with two gorgeous guys and a woman between them. I bet they're wondering what we look like when we fuck, importing our faces into the countless pornos they watch. I know I'm doing a little imagining myself.

Grim would be under me, tied to the bed so he couldn't

escape. Calix would be behind me. A little double dipping sounds so damn good right now.

"Should we go over and introduce ourselves?" Calix interrupts my thoughts. I glower at him and the thought of speaking with her.

Not one to back down, I stand up, but I need to set some ground rules. I grab hold of Grim's chin and pull him down so I can see that he's looking in my eyes. His mouth parts just slightly, and I feel the breath of hot air that escapes. "You may not like it, but I *refuse* to share you." Grim licks his lips in response.

I turn to face Calix. "Same goes for you. Don't do anything that will piss me off," I warn him. He seems way flirtier than Grim, and watching him flirt might just send me over the edge. Not to mention, who knows what would happen to me if I ate a witch's soul, nasty thing that it is.

"Come on." I take a step and pause. Grim hits my back. I like that he's staying so close. I spin on my heel. "Are we pretending we don't know Gunnar? I don't know the plan."

"Let's let him decide." Calix places his hand on my back, urging me forward.

When I turn around, I suck in my already flat stomach and smooth my hand over my hair.

"Back again so soon?" Vanessa grates through a fake smile as we approach. "And you brought friends." She doesn't hide her lecherous stare as she gives Grim and Calix each a good once over. "And you are?" She leans forward just a bit, but it allows the low cut of her loose fitting top to dip even farther, exposing her nipple. If I can see it, I know the guys can, too. I grit my teeth.

Taking one step back so I'm between the two men she's asking about, I loop my arms through each of theirs.

"Cal," Calix says, his voice coming out flat and disinterested. Vanessa gives Grim a moment to respond, and when he doesn't, her nostrils flare a bit.

"I do hope you're enjoying my club. If there's anything you ever need…" She lets the sentence linger before turning her full focus on Grim.

Vanessa leans a little lower and winks. "Strong silent type. I like it."

"Don't," Grim tells her.

Vanessa's brow wrinkles, and after a few awkward seconds, she lets out a little giggle like it's some sort of joke. "Why don't you guys join us?" Vanessa offers, and with a wave of her hand, a small spot on one of the sofas opens up. I can't believe she's inviting us to sit with her, especially after Grim just gave her such an icy reception.

Grim steps forward, taking me with him. I let my arm slide out of Calix's elbow, so as not to drag him with us, too. Grim quickly releases my arm and takes hold of my waist, turning me so I'm standing directly in front of him, then he pulls me snugly against his body. Wrapping his arm around my stomach, he lowers us to the couch with me on his lap, as if he's done it a thousand times. I get a little thrill, liking the way he can so easily control my body.

Calix saunters over and sits on the arm of the sofa, before

reaching for my hand and laying it over his thigh. The visual is effective; Vanessa's eyebrows rise slightly.

Gunnar steps over, his stance wide as he peruses everyone. Is this the coven? It can't be all of them—the man from the other day isn't here.

"Have you met Drott?" Vanessa lifts her hand toward Gunnar but keeps her eyes on me.

"Drott?" I question, peering up at Gunnar.

"We're acquainted," Gunnar replies, ignoring the fact that she introduced him under a different name. Vanessa's eyes narrow, but she doesn't say anything. "I need to speak with you." Gunnar focuses on the bitchy witch.

"I'm entertaining. It can wait."

"No, it can't." Gunnar's voice raises a little at Vanessa's denial.

I lift my hand to cover the smile forming on my lips. She's about to get in trouble. "Surely, it can't be that important." Vanessa clicks her tongue at Gunnar.

"I would say a dead Troll in the alley is very fucking important." The veins in Gunnar's neck start to thicken and the sockets around his eyes darken.

The thin lines around Vanessa's mouth tighten until her lips are pulled back in a sneer. She lurches to a stand, her two beefy bodyguards rising with her. "What are you talking about?" Her words are just a little slower than her reaction. She isn't surprised. But she is madder than a wet cat. I squeeze Calix's thigh. He remains completely calm.

"A Troll?" I look at Gunnar, but he's watching Vanessa.

"He means one of the homeless who live under the bridge," one of the women near the back chimes in.

I look over my shoulder to find her. "You can't be serious," I say as a chuckle escapes me. The woman looks around for someone to back her up. I would know she was lying, even if I didn't sense it.

"They're Charmed, you idiot," Vanessa hisses.

The woman lowers her head and examines her hands. "I thought I was helping. I know we aren't supposed to talk about these things outside the wards."

The man next to her places his hand on her shoulder in comfort. "We were all new once," he soothes, while giving her a little shake. She musters up a small smile in gratitude, but looks down right away when he removes his hand.

I shift, and Grim tightens his hold on me, forcing my body to hold still. I examine the woman and her aura, the black smudges around her feet are faint. Quickly, before anyone can leave, I look at them all, gauging which of them is the dirtiest, since they're the ones who will have the answers.

Surprisingly, the man who comforted her has the most muck on his aura. It's condensed over his hands and chest, while heavy globs are littered around his feet. It looks like it would be weighing him down. He rises quickly, heading for Vanessa.

"Let me up," I mutter under my breath to Grim. His arm tightens for the briefest second before he releases me. I step right into the man's path. "Hey, that was really cool of you." I bat my eyelashes at him.

His brow furrows, and he looks around like he can't believe I'm talking to him, then he peers at Grim and Calix out of the corner of his eye. "Oh, yeah, well, like I said, everyone makes mistakes."

"You seem to know what you're doing." I bite the corner of my bottom lip. "What's your name?"

"Joe, Joe Bishop. You're Damiana." I preen a little, pretending to be happy he knows my name.

"That's me. See you around, Joe."

Joe's head goes up and down, then shakes from left to right. Poor dude doesn't know if he's coming or going. "Yeah, okay."

When I look away from Joe, Gunnar and Vanessa are having a hushed conversation, but it looks heated, if Gunnar's demeanor is any indication.

"What do you think will happen next?" I lean over near Calix, excited that I'm in on the drama. This is way more exciting than what I'm used to.

"I think we should head back." Calix is watching Gunnar.

"What? But it's just getting good. Vanessa is about to be in a shit-ton of trouble, I know it. I don't want to miss that." I can't believe he wants to leave now!

"Look around you, Damiana." This comes from Grim. I do as he asks and note all the witches around me and their sooty auras.

"Okay?" I prompt, I'm not sure what I'm missing, but it must be something. Grim locks his arm around my waist again and starts to move us backwards, like he's keeping me hostage. Kinky—I think I could do the whole Stockholm thing with him.

In my ear, he mutters, "None of them have any real power, but their souls are corrupted. There's something else going on here."

I watch Joe and the others like him. Grim is right. I sense the filth on them, but that's it. They just feel like humans, soul-sick humans, except Vanessa. Her aura isn't nearly as smudged as the others, yet something about her sets my teeth on edge. I want to knock her down a few pegs.

There's still too much that I don't know, that I don't understand. Before I realize it, we're back in the ladies' bathroom. Grim is towing me backwards into the small stall. "I could walk, you know. You don't have to kidnap me." Grim's arm loosens and I almost regret reminding him I'm a willing captive.

Calix stuffs himself into the tiny stall with us. "Oh my God. Work, girl!" I hear someone smack their lips together.

I can't resist the challenge. With the sweetest smile I can muster, I start to moan. "Oh wow, both of you? But I'm not that type of girl." Then I burst out laughing. "Just kidding! Who wants my ass?" Calix lets out a loud snort then covers his mouth with his hand. His eyes gleam down at me with a naughty twinkle.

Calix moans next, then smacks his hands together while he lets out a man whimper. "Do it again, mistress."

"Would you two shut up?" Grim demands, his voice dark, and it reminds me of when he told me to keep quiet. I fight to turn around, elbowing Calix and Grim in the process. When I'm done, I'm staring up at Grim. I expected to find his face placid, but his jaw is hard, and his eyes are narrowed on me. He's straddling the toilet so there's enough room in here for all three of us.

I run my fingers up the inside of his thigh, watching as he squirms the tiniest bit, and heat starts to build in his eyes. "Don't like to play?" I finally ask, when I reach the button on the top of Grim's jeans. I let the nail of my pointer finger drag over the skin of his lower stomach.

"I need to concentrate." I watch as Grim's face smooths out, and the tic in his jaw softens.

"Fine." I roll my eyes. The small cubical gets hot fast, and I'm not just talking about my body heating up because I'm pressed between two hot men like the cream in a doughnut. I blow my hair off my cheek. "Stop breathing so much. It's hot as balls in here."

"Hold on to her, Nemean," Grim orders, as his arms come up around me. I wrap my arms around Grim's back and lay my head on his chest, just so I have something to do with my hands. Calix fuses himself to my back and grabs a hold of my hips tightly.

"I thought you could only take one at a time?" Calix questions, as a cool waft of air circles around me.

"I never said that." Grim steps back as soon as we're in my kitchen. I miss his heat immediately.

"Asshole," Calix mutters without any real anger.

"Why did you want to leave?" I hop up on the counter and

let my feet dangle. My boots feel heavy, so I bend down and loosen the laces, letting them fall to the floor with a thump.

"I think that coven leader has found a way to siphon magic from her coven without taking the price on her soul. There's no way she could remain the leader of such a large group and not show the evidence of her magic use." Grim answers.

"What do you mean? How can you tell?" Calix makes his way to the fridge and grabs a carton of orange juice. He doesn't even bother with a glass. He chugs it directly from the jug.

"You're right," I tell Grim, thinking about all the times I've been close to Vanessa. Something about her always repelled me, but I was never really sure what it was. Almost everyone in the group today felt slimy but her. Yet there's something about her I don't like. I don't feel threatened by her, but I do feel something. "You can't see their souls, auras?" I focus on Calix.

"No, but I'm guessing you both can." He trades a glance between me and Grim.

"I bet Gunnar can't either." I tap my fingers on the counter. "Why put someone in charge of the witches who wouldn't be able to see something like that?" I ponder, not really expecting an answer.

"Berserkers were created by shamans, or witches," Calix explains. "They were short-sighted, as usual, when they created the beasts. When they cast the spell creating the warriors, they only gave them a single purpose, to defeat that current threat, which they did, but when there was no one left to fight, the warriors went mad."

I feel the portal pull open just as Grim heaves out a sigh. "I must go."

"Wait, when will you be back?" I hop off the counter. I don't want him to go. Stupid, stupid, lonely heart. I should rip the damn thing out. I would probably make better decisions. Actually, I probably need to place a little more blame on my pussy, she seems to be getting me into a lot of trouble lately too.

"As soon as I can. Stay away from the club while I'm gone," he tells me, then to Calix, he says, "It's not safe." Just as Grim goes to take a step backwards, he adds, "Stay with her."

"No place else I'd rather be." Calix gives Grim a mock salute.

Grim's black cloak swirls around him, he lifts his left hand and takes hold of the wicked scythe that appears at his side.

As soon as he's gone, I turn to Calix. "The robe and sickle are a smart play. He's too damn pretty to be scary."

"Are you kidding me? Don't ever tell him I said this, but he's one scary motherfucker, with or without the robe."

"Really? I don't see it." I shake my head. "Want something to eat? Then we need to get back to the Berserkers."

"I'm always down to eat." Calix lowers his head and leers at me. With that one look, I remember we have the whole place to ourselves.

"Anything in particular you're craving?" I lick my lips.

Calix's eyes roam over my body. "Crave is too small a word to describe what I'm thinking."

I take a step in his direction. All thoughts of the Berserker origins and how Gunnar came to watch over the witches flee from my mind. Right now, all I'm thinking about is how hungry Calix really is, and what that rough tongue of his will feel like between my legs.

Calix takes the hint and meets me halfway across the kitchen floor. I'm already turned on. Just being around him and the others lights me up enough that I may have to start carrying extra panties, so I don't go around in damp undies all the time.

Calix's hands are gentle but eager when he pulls me close. His lips land on mine quickly. I get the feeling he doesn't want to be interrupted again. That's okay, neither do I.

I'm pawing at his shirt the moment our mouths fuse. I want my hands on his skin. Calix pulls away just long enough to tug his shirt over his head and drop it to the floor, then his hands are back in my hair, holding me while he kisses the hell out of me.

Kissing has its place, but I've never been that into it. I've had a series of first kisses my entire life, and most of the time they're awkward and stunted. It didn't feel that way the first time I kissed Calix, and it sure doesn't feel that way now. His hands slide down over my shoulders and skim over my body. I can feel the heat of his touch through my mesh shirt as if I were not wearing anything, but I still want more. I fumble with the hem of my top, dragging it up, but my long hair gets caught in the clingy fabric. Calix stills my frenzied hands and slowly removes the shirt, not yanking out my hair in the process.

I wrap my arms around his neck and hop up, locking my ankles around his back. His hands go right under my ass and he holds me in his arms. "Table?" I question between kisses. I don't really care where we go at this point as long as he gets inside me.

"No, I want to be in your bed," Calix purrs, rolling his hips, but I'm too high on his waist to get any real benefit from it. I feel his tongue lap from the top of my breast and up my neck. It sends another shiver of excitement through me.

"Upstairs," I tell him, while tilting my head back.

"I know where your room is, Dami." Calix spins and puts my back against the wall. He loosens his hold so I slide a little lower on his body. I let out a tiny moan of protest. These leather pants are cute and all, but way too thick. I can't feel him against me the way I need to. After another round of kissing, I straighten my legs until my feet hit the floor. Calix leans down lower and follows my mouth as I do.

I reach for him, tugging the button on his jeans and pulling the zipper down at the same time. "Are you sure you're ready?" he whispers between drugging kisses.

His words give me pause. I pull back. "For sex? I've been ready for days." But it seems like he means more.

"This isn't just sex, Damiana. I won't give you up if I have you." His voice is pitched low, and he delivers the words like a warning. I get a twisting feeling in my stomach, one I don't know how to interpret. But is he really telling the truth? Guys say all kinds of shit when they want to get into your pants, I know this for a fact.

"Will it change something between us?" I pull back from Calix a little more, so I can see his eyes. I may not be able to sense lies from him, but I'm well versed in reading lies from people as they fall from their lips. I can't help but notice the way people act when they lie: a twitch, not meeting someone's stare. I watch Calix for any of those clues now.

He swallows. "Not like you're thinking." He brushes his hand over my hair. "But it will change something in me. You can't give me that and then take it away." He drops his forehead to mine and takes several long breaths.

Grim pulled this shit on me too. "I've told you from the beginning, I'm not choosing just one of you. If you can't handle that, then we shouldn't do this." I give his chest a slight push. I don't want him to back away, but I won't lie to him either.

Why would I choose one of them? How do they even know we're fated or whatever the fuck they called it? It sure didn't make them stick around when I was younger, why would it now? My mother and father didn't stay around long enough to even raise me; what would make me think these three would be any different?

I admit I do feel a pull to them—more than I've felt toward anyone else—but I've never really given anyone else a chance to get close to me, either. I've always been too worried about losing the only real family I've ever had, the ones who have actually stayed by my side.

"You don't have to choose just me. I'm just asking you to choose me *too*, Damiana." Calix shuffles his feet back a few inches to give me the perception that he's giving me some room, but it's not much.

"Why can't we just be..." I wave my hands around, looking for the right words, but I come up empty. "Why do we need to define any of this, can't we just—"

"Fuck?" Calix's nostrils flare as he barks out the word. "I already told you, it could never be just sex, not between us."

"You say that shit now, but I've heard all the same lies from a hundred different men. I'm just not stupid enough to fall for the bullshit." I cross my arms over my chest. "Every time I witness a woman falling for that garbage, I pity her. Do you want to know why?"

"I don't really care, because I'm not lying to get into your pants. If I wanted to just fuck you, I could bend you over the fucking chair." Calix's eyes do that glowing thing as he throws his arm behind his back, motioning to the living room.

I ignore his heated words. "I pity them because I know they don't believe the lies, but they tell themselves that they do, and *that's* the biggest lie."

Calix grabs a hold of my upper arms. "Are you even listening to me? I'm not asking you to choose one of us; they're idiots to even think you could. I just want you to know it will change something between us." Calix releases my arms and takes a few steps backwards. "But I don't think you're ready for that." He examines me for a brief moment before turning his back on me and walking away.

I get that ugly twisting feeling in my belly again. Only now, I think I know what it is—it's fear. I hate that watching him walk away from me instills that panic in me. I ball up my fists, determined to keep myself from reaching out to him.

CHAPTER 18

After giving myself a few minutes to calm down, I head up to my bedroom. I need time to decompress. Calix may not realize it, but something inside of me has already changed. Watching him walk away from me was fucking hard. I haven't felt the need to beg someone to stay in so very long. How could I give them that power over me?

My mind conjures up the last time I saw my parents. I was nine, and even though I knew my mother hated me, I begged her not to leave me when she dropped me off at boarding school. It was right after I accidently killed my teacher. I think she somehow knew I did it, or she suspected, at the very least.

She and my father never once promised to return for me. At least they did me the favor of not lying. They didn't even show up for my graduation. I had a meeting with their lawyer a few days prior, explaining how my trust worked. He made it perfectly clear I wasn't to contact them. Not that I ever would have anyway.

I dig my fingernails into my thighs to bring myself out of those thoughts. Thank goodness for the leather pants, or my nails probably would have cut the hell out of my legs.

"What a crock of shit," I spit. I'm angry at myself for even letting the thought of them sticking around soften me. I've been telling myself this entire time not to get attached, but look what I've fucking gone and done, and I didn't even realize it was happening. Now I'm sitting here, wondering if Gunnar is alright, where Grim has taken off to, and I can't even think about Calix right now. I know he's still here—my senses are even more aware of him after our make out session.

I need to get them to leave me alone before I do something really dumb and desperate, such as let them know how much power they have over me. I'm not able to control myself around them. Whether it's the bond or just my own idiocy, I can't really say, but I do know they're dangerous.

With jerky movements, I unlace my pants and roll them over my hips before kicking them off into the corner, my bra gets removed right after. I need a shower and a lobotomy—at the very least, I need to build my walls back up. I had no idea they had already begun to crumble.

I'm scrubbing my scalp, probably a little too hard, when I sense Grim's portal opening. He's not in the bathroom with me, but he's damn close. A wave of sins wafts through the air, but it's not even the least bit tempting. My stomach actually rebels at the thought of consuming anything.

I quickly finish up my shower, I need to have a very important conversation about boundaries while I still have some resolve.

I'm not trying to be quiet when I walk downstairs, but I think Gunnar and Calix are too deep in conversation to notice me, or should I say arguing too damn much to hear me.

"You think I'm going to accept your word? You're an animal, for Christ sake," Gunnar spits.

"I don't care what you think about me," Calix growls. "I'm telling you she's cut herself off from any emotion, and if we push her too hard, too fast, we'll lose her. Not one of us, all of us." I want to argue that I haven't, but I keep my mouth shut.

"And how did you come to this conclusion?" Grim inquires.

"Go upstairs and hug her, not kiss her, not try to have sex, but connect with her. Try talking to her about a relationship." I hold my breath at Calix's words. There is no way that's happening.

"I don't see what you're getting at," Gunnar declares. I can just imagine him standing there with his arms crossed over his chest and his face in a scowl, the scars making him look even more fierce.

"Because you have the emotional maturity of a thirteen-year-old," Calix snaps.

I hear one heavy footfall. "Don't move, Berserker," Grim threatens, his tone icy. "Damiana said no more fighting, you will listen." I hear some mumbled words, but Gunnar doesn't argue.

"Listen…" Calix forces some calmness into his voice. "She's more than willing to take us to bed, but nothing else."

"Did you fuck her?" Gunnar's voice is low and unruffled, but I sense a dark undertone.

"I could have, but I wanted her to know I want more from her, and she…" Calix curses under his breath. "She looked fucking terrified."

Gunnar snorts. "That's just her reaction to you, Nemean."

"You push her, you'll lose her, and both of you need to get over this shit with her picking one of us. If you think she could do it, then you should just go find someone else to bond to. It's not a fucking choice, you morons," Calix argues.

"I won't do it. She can pick," Gunnar states.

I step out from behind the wall. Calix is the first to see me, his lips tightening into a thin line. "He's right." Gunnar spins around when I speak, I can't believe I actually surprised him. "I don't have any issue picking. I don't want any of you."

I have no problem sensing the huge lie from my own lips. I wonder if it will leave a mark, and if it does, will Grim see it? I still have so many unanswered questions, but not one of them is worth having my black heart ripped out. I can't believe the cursed thing is still in there beating, but this is proof it can still work. I need to protect what's left of it before I really turn into a monster.

Grim is still cloaked in his robe. He makes an imposing figure, but I'm still not afraid of him, only what he could do to me. Gunnar takes a step forward as if he may reach out to me, but I cut my eyes to him and dare him to try. Berserker or not,

I'll rip his fucking arm off and beat him with it if he tries to touch me. He takes a step back.

I look at all three of them lined up before me. "I thought having you around might be fun, that I could learn some shit, but I've decided I don't care enough to be bothered with you. That's what you said, right, Calix? That I don't have any emotions?" I tilt my head and examine him.

Calix licks his lips and his eyes are a little wide. "I'm not going anywhere, Damiana. I've waited your entire life to be with you. You can be pissed at me all you want, but I'm still not leaving."

I narrow my eyes at him. I want to reach into his chest and grab a hold of his soul, pulling it until it's barely tethered to his body before releasing it. That would scare the hell out of him, probably get him to leave me alone for good, but I can't force myself to do it. What if I tugged too hard, did something wrong, and really hurt him? I could never live with myself, plus, deep down, I know I don't want him to leave me. I want him to fight for me, even if he has to fight *me*.

I wish I didn't have any emotions, because then I wouldn't be so worried about him—any of them—shredding what's left of them when they leave me.

Grim steps forward, his robes dissolving into smoke behind him. "I apologize, it seems we're all a little…" He balls up his fists and squeezes. "More raw than we're used to."

"I don't even get why you're here. What did you expect to happen? I'm really trying to wrap my head around this, but come on. None of it makes sense to me," I confess, telling them the truth about the bonded situation.

"Again, it seems we made a mistake." Grim dips his chin.

I knew they weren't going to stick around. This bond bullshit is stupid, and I'm an idiot for halfway believing it. "I knew it." I cross my arms over my chest to cover the ache from Grim's words. "I'm not bonded to anyone."

"Oh, yes you are," Gunnar interjects.

"He just said you made a mistake," I accuse, pointing at Grim.

"Not about that." Calix pinches the bridge of his nose. "Whatever you were going to say, Death, spit it out."

Grim sends Calix a glare, and his eyes even begin to glow a little with rivers of lava. I watch, fascinated. "I should have explained the situation to you better. I would like to do that now, if you will permit it?"

I turn just the slightest bit and study Grim. Of course, I want to hear what he has to say, but should I? Will it make it harder to send them away? Who am I kidding…I don't want them to leave. Why am I so confused? "I doubt it will change anything." I cross my arms over my chest defiantly.

"We are all linked to you, not just because we are your guardians, I felt it the moment you were born, and it has only become stronger. It was only our selfishness that wanted you to choose, but deep down I've always known it would never happen."

Gunnar steps forward. "How?"

Grim turns to face the man questioning him. While Grim is

an inch or two taller, Gunnar has a good forty pounds on him. "How have you felt for the past thirty years?" Grim questions, and Gunnar's brow furrows. "Like you were missing something?" Grim prompts.

Gunnar shifts on his feet, not meeting Grim's gaze. "You know what it's been like," he finally answers.

"Yet you would want that for Damiana?" Grim continues.

"What...no, she would have me," Gunnar stumbles, having a hard time getting out the words.

"But what about me and Death?" Calix inserts. "She would still yearn for us."

"How do you know?" Gunnar puffs out his chest. I'm watching all three of them with rapt attention.

"Because that's what I feel for her. Why would what she feels for us be any different?" Grim reasons plainly, as if Gunnar should understand this by now. Then he turns to face me. "Are you afraid of us?"

I blow a raspberry with my lips. "Not like you're thinking." I regret the words the moment they come from my mouth, but I can't take them back, so I try to backtrack. "I welcomed the monsters as my friends a long time ago. You guys just aren't that scary."

"I won't ask you to choose. I just ask that you give me a chance," Grim implores. Isn't that almost exactly what Calix said? I feel like I'm the butt of some joke I don't understand the punchline to.

"Why bother?" I ask slowly.

"Why bother what?" Calix eyes me.

"Any of this." I wave my hand in their direction and look down my nose at them. "Is it just the competition of it all?"

Calix lifts his arms wide and shakes his head. "I can't even fault you for thinking that. It's not like any of us have behaved as a mate should."

I open my mouth, but find I don't have any words. I didn't expect him to agree with me or validate my thoughts.

I look at the three of them standing before me. They couldn't be more different. Calix is somewhat relaxed, with his hands loose by his sides. Grim is stoic, I would need a hammer and chisel to break past his hard exterior, and then there's Gunnar. His arms are crossed over his puffed-out chest, and he's separated himself from the others by space and with his attitude.

"It would never work. You understand that, right? Not long-term. I'm just trying to make it easier for all of us," I confess. "What do you see happening with all of us living here like one big family?" I snort, even though I secretly would love something like that. I wouldn't have to give up my friends, wouldn't have to worry about one of them finding Uncle or Aeson visiting me.

"It might be a little early to discuss the future now, but eventually, something like that," Calix hedges.

"This is ridiculous." I let out a bitter laugh. "I don't even know why I'm listening to you."

Grim reaches for my arm when I turn to walk away from them. I look down at his hand, then up at him. He releases his hold immediately. "No one said it was going to be easy, but it's got to be better than not even trying." His eyes beseech me.

My forced resolve wavers, but then I look up at Gunnar and see his angry scowl. "Don't you see? This only ends in heartache. And I'm not sure I could survive it.

I do walk away then. I need to make building my proverbial walls my number one priority. They seem to crash through them like they're crumbling a sandcastle. "We're not going anywhere, Dami, so get used to it."

"Shut up," Gunnar growls at Calix. I sense a shift and I slow my steps. "You can put that away, Death, it doesn't scare me."

"It should, Berserker. I'm older than the sands of time, yet you try my patience." Grim's voice is layered with many others. "Make her doubt us again, and I will seek her forgiveness after slaying you, rather than ask her permission."

That shouldn't send a tingle of heat and excitement through me, but I'll be damned because it does. I don't want him to kill Gunnar; that would actually make me mad—sad? I'm not sure, but I like that Grim is willing to do it for me. Good thing I've accepted I'm a twisted bitch; otherwise, that thought might just bother me if I hadn't.

I've been moping in my room for the last hour, and I'm not sure how I can come out without looking like an asshole. They're still here, I can hear them moving around the house.

It's so stupid, but a big part of me is happy they didn't leave. Maybe I'm the one with the emotional maturity of a thirteen-year-old.

This is probably the first time in my life I wish I needed to take a shit. It's not like I have the excuse to go out there because I'm hungry. I stand up, but sit right back down on my bed again. If I go out there, I'll seem weak.

I stand up again. Sitting in here makes me seem like I'm hiding, and that seems weak, too. I'm no closer to a decision now than I was a half hour ago.

Pounding on my door interrupts my warring thoughts. "What?" I shout through the closed door, angry I was startled, and still kind of pissy from earlier.

A throat clears and Gunnar's smooth voice comes through the door clearly. "We're going to discuss the witches. Would you care to join us?"

Now there's an idea: a safe, neutral topic. I take a few steps closer to the door. "Shut up," Gunnar hisses to one of the other guys. "Damiana?" he calls louder.

I feel as if this is a trick to get me out of my room, but that's exactly what I want, too, so I'll pretend to fall for it.

"Yeah…I'll be down in a minute," I yell back.

"See, was that so hard?" Calix goads Gunnar.

"It would be a lot easier if you would leave me the hell alone," Gunnar grates. I snicker at their bickering. I wonder where Grim is and what happened after hearing him threaten Gunnar.

When I walk into the hall, I almost hiss like a cat. All the drapes are still open, and the sun is blaring through the windows. "Stupid ball of fire," I curse, covering my eyes with my hand and dragging the heavy curtains closed as I pass them.

I make my way to the TV room. The guys are so damn loud that they're easy enough to find. I plop down on one of the chairs, pretending we didn't have a heavy argument a little while ago. If I ignore it, maybe they will too.

Grim is on the couch, and he looks slightly out of place, as if he doesn't really know how to relax. He's holding his back stiffly instead of leaning into the cushion. Calix comes in from the kitchen with a big bowl of something in his hands. I take a whiff of the air, and yummy, buttery goodness hits my nose, except I never think that butter smells like yummy goodness.

"What have you got?" I push myself up in the chair, trying to see inside the bowl.

"Popcorn." Calix tips the bowl toward me, letting me see, and a fluffy, yellow kernel slips over the edge of the bowl. He reaches out with his other hand and snags it right out of the air before popping it into his mouth. I eye him and his catlike reflexes.

"Do you want some?" he asks, sounding curious. Popcorn has always been on my list of temptations, but just thinking about how violently ill I get when I eat has always been enough of a deterrent. Plus, I never kept it in the house.

"What's it taste like?" I lick my lips.

"You've never tried it?" I shake my head in denial. Why is my mouth watering?

"Do you want to?" Calix comes a little closer. He digs into the bowl, searching, and then he brings out one kernel, pinched between his fingers.

"I don't want to get sick." I eye him and the popcorn. One bite probably wouldn't hurt, right?

Calix pulls his hand back. "You would get sick?" His brow furrows.

I swallow and my stomach lets out a loud gurgle. "Let me try it."

"I don't want you to get sick." Calix looks around to see if anyone else has any input. Grim edges forward on his seat, his attention locked on me.

"I'll be fine—come on." I roll my wrist, eager for him to let me have it now that I've decided I'm going to try it.

Calix closes the distance between us, and he lifts his hand as if he's planning to feed it to me. I lean forward a bit and open my mouth. The moment it hits my tongue, the saltiness is almost overwhelming. The texture is a little strange too. It almost melts, but it's kind of crunchy at the same time.

"I can't tell from your face if you like it or not." Calix moves over a little, and I see Grim and Gunnar both watching me.

"I'm not sure…it's weird. Nothing like I expected. So salty." I scrunch up my face a little and stick out my tongue.

"Do you want to try some more?" Calix offers.

"I don't think I do," I mutter. I'm a little disappointed, to be honest. I feel like it was a big letdown after all these years of wanting it.

Calix slinks over to the couch and lounges into the opposite corner from Grim. I look over at Gunnar. He has one palm against the wall and is leaning forward, looking down at his phone in his hand.

"I thought we were supposed to be talking about what happened with the witches," I snap. I don't like that his phone has his attention, and that's just kind of fucked up. Gunnar jerks his head up and stands upright, his phone forgotten in his hand.

"Give me a breakdown of how the coven works," Calix orders, while crunching through a handful of popcorn. "Is there a hierarchy like with animals?"

Gunnar lumbers over and takes a seat in the remaining chair. "Vanessa has been the High Priestess for a little over twenty years. She runs the coven."

"Twenty years?" I question dubiously. "She barely looks older than twenty."

"I assure you, she is much older than twenty. Try closer to sixty." Gunnar leans back in the chair.

"I'd like to know her skin care routine." I think I hate her a little more now.

"I don't think you'd be willing to follow her procedure. Besides, it's not like you're aging anymore either," Gunnar supplies.

"Wait." I scoot forward in my chair. "Are you saying I'm not going to age?" I couldn't have heard him right.

"You haven't noticed?" Gunnar's eyes travel over me. I reach my hand up to my face and trail my fingers over my cheek. I look over at Grim and Calix to see their reaction to Gunnar's words.

"That can't be right," I whisper.

"Are you really that surprised?" Gunnar asks, his brow furrowed. "Have any of your baddies aged over the years? Why would you think you would be any different?"

"I don't know. I don't even really understand what I am." My voice grows shrill.

"Damiana, why are you upset?" Grim stands up and takes a few steps closer to me. "I told you I tethered your soul to your body."

"I not upset. I'm freaked the fuck out. I'm going to be stuck like this forever?"

"You would rather die slowly?" Grim crouches in front of me.

I think about his words. Would I? Why hadn't I thought about this before? I mean, I know that things like Dare's nettles never hurt me—nothing ever really has—so why didn't I already come to the same conclusion?

I know why: if I had to think about living like this forever, with only my monsters to keep me company when they had the time to stop and visit me, I would slowly go insane. I would rather age and die if that's all I had to look forward to.

Grim places his hand on my leg just above my knee. "How long are we talking about here, surely not forever?" I inquire, staring into Grim's eyes.

"Nothing is forever, Damiana. At some point, we will all cease to exist."

"Exactly how old are you?" I examine Grim's features. His gray eyes are calm, lacking the embers that sometimes burn there. I notice a slight bit of stubble beginning to darken his jaw, and it somehow makes him more human. His beauty is almost too ethereal at times.

"Old." Grim's voice sounds tired.

"How did you become my guardian?" I look up at Gunnar and Calix to include them. "How did all of you end up with me?"

Grim drags his hand off my leg and rises from his crouched position. It sets off little alarm bells inside of me. Calix is suddenly busy digging through his diminishing bowl of popcorn, while Gunnar shifts uncomfortably on the chair. "Well?" I prompt. "Anyone going to answer me?"

"I can answer, but I'm not sure you'll be satisfied," Grim reveals cryptically.

I turn my body toward his, giving him my full attention. When he doesn't begin speaking right away, I clear my throat, encouraging him to continue.

"I was drawn to you," Grim admits, though he sounds reluctant.

"Explain please," I demand.

"I'm not sure I can. I've never been a guardian before," Grim confesses.

"I have." Calix sighs. I watch as he sets the bowl aside, drops his elbows on his knees, and folds his hands together. "I'm a born shifter. There's not very many of us—a few dragons or a kitsune here and there. I've accepted the responsibility of guardianship over newly born shifters a few times over the years." He pauses and looks up at me.

I sense a 'but' coming. "It's always been pretty straight forward before. There's really not too much involved until the shifter reaches maturity. But it was different with you from the very beginning."

There's that 'but' I was expecting. I don't have time to ask why I was different before he continues, explaining, "With the others, I was just doing it to pass the time. I could have walked away and not thought twice about it. I did it to make sure my job was easier down the line, really. If I teach them from the beginning, I don't have to worry too much about them later in life." Calix relaxes against the sofa, his arms spread over the back. I nod my head, seeing the wisdom in that. "I couldn't have walked away from you, not even from the very beginning. I didn't realize how different you were, but I should have suspected something."

"I'd never accepted a guardianship before you," Gunnar admits.

"Who passes out these 'invitations' to be guardians?" I wrap the word in air quotes, trying to understand this whole process.

"A Cherub visited me." Grim watches me as if he's waiting for a reaction.

"A cherub, like a baby angel?"

"Not quite. A real Cherub isn't at all like man has portrayed them." Grim's lips curl into a tiny smile.

"Freaky-ass things, four faces." Calix gives off an exaggerated shudder.

"Right," Grim agrees. "I hadn't been visited by a Holy One in…ever, I don't think." He looks past me, into open space.

"You're making me think that's unusual. Was it the same for all of you?" I look around and watch Gunnar and Calix nod in agreement.

"I'd never been asked by an angel," Calix adds. "I knew there must have been an important reason I was asked. It was only after I accepted that I found out they had been asked and accepted the position as well." He lifts his hand and indicates the other guys.

"Same for me," Gunnar supplies.

This is the first time, I think, that we've all sat down and had a conversation that hasn't ended with yelling or one of us having a fit. Most of the time it's me, but whatever.

"As the Nemean mentioned before, we normally wouldn't have come into your life until you were much older. But I knew, the moment you were born, that my task had changed." Grim brings his attention back to me.

"Well, aren't I just special?" I mock slightly, feeling a little strange about the whole thing. Why did a freaking angel push me on them? And if angels are real, why the hell didn't any of them visit me? An angel might have been a tad more comforting than a Yowie when I was a child. But then again, from the way Calix reacted to the Cherub, maybe not.

I'm not really sure learning how they came into my life is helpful, but I did want to know.

A heavy silence falls over our group. It's not like any of them are usually talkative, except Calix occasionally, but it still feels too oppressive.

"Weren't we supposed to be talking about Vanessa?" I pretend like I'm not the one who brought this entire topic up.

CHAPTER 19

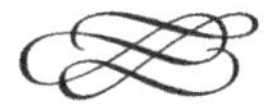

"She's been the High Priestess for the past twenty years," I remind Gunnar, so he knows where he left off, just in case he forgot.

"Yes, and I've been overseeing her coven in particular for the past ten years." Gunnar resettles himself into the chair.

"What exactly do you oversee, and how come I never saw you before if you've been around for ten years?" I ask a little skeptically.

"We had a deal, remember?" Gunnar's voice has an edge as he glares over at Grim and Calix on the sofa. "I wasn't allowed to be in contact with you."

Calix lets out a loud snort. "Yeah, you just sneaked into her house and left rocks all over the place."

"At least I didn't try to trick her into thinking I was just a human. And they're not just rocks," Gunnar mutters defensively.

"Stop," Grim orders. "There is no point in arguing about what was—we are here now." He levels a scowl at Gunnar. "We need to figure out what's happening with the witches. There's no way she should be as powerful as she is and not show the evidence of her magic."

Gunnar's nostrils flare as he takes a deep breath. "Over the last few years, the coven has doubled in size. I didn't only stay here because of Damiana." He pauses, as if to prove a point. "I also wanted to keep a closer eye on Vanessa and the club she's running. She's always had new seekers joining, but not at this rate."

"She must be siphoning the magic some way. Her followers weren't leaking magic the way she was, but they showed all the markers of magic usage, dark magic," Grim reasons.

"And you think it has something to do with the Charmed dead bodies you've found?"

Gunnar nods a little, his eyes going unfocused.

"I'm concerned about the number of bodies, and where the rest of the power is. Even the coven leader wasn't holding that much magic. She's either sharing it with someone else, or someone else is sharing it with her."

"Fuck!" Gunnar punches the top of the chair arm and I hear a crack.

"Hey, knock that shit off," I scold him. When Gunnar lifts his fist up from the chair, the arm has a huge dent, and a thick piece of wood is jutting out like a broken bone through the fabric. "Really?" I blink at him, expressionless.

"I'll fix it," he offers, trying to poke the wood back through the rip.

I roll my eyes. "Don't bother, you can replace it."

"I will." Gunnar is still trying to piece the arm back together.

"Why are you so upset anyway? If Vanessa is breaking the rules, just kill her and be done with it."

"I would be happy to, but if I kill her without evidence, then we would have a war with the witches on our hands." Gunnar gives up trying to fix the chair and a piece of wood crashes to the ground, but everyone pretends to ignore it.

"I don't really see a problem with that, either. If they're causing trouble, get rid of the whole lot of them. If they're killing monsters, they deserve it."

"If we did that, it would make all the other factions uneasy. They would think we were trying to take over, and I just don't want to deal with that headache." Gunnar circles his fingers over his temple.

"Well, what are we going to do about it then?" I look at all three of them.

"We need to figure out who the other players are. Berserker, do you have any ideas?" Grim examines Gunnar.

"I might. I have a few of my men watching Vanessa. She's not likely to do anything with me around. I'm hoping she'll lead them to whoever she's working with."

"So, we're just going to sit around waiting for her to do

something?" I can't keep the incredulous tone from my voice. "How do we know the guy isn't out killing a Kapa, or another Troll right now?"

"Someone did," Grim states. "The reason I was called away was for the death of a Mimic."

Calix whistles through his teeth.

"What's a Mimic?" I trade glances with all of them.

"A being that can take over another's shape. Some people call them Doppelgängers," Grim informs me.

Gunnar rises to his feet. "If they're strong enough to take out a Mimic…I need to put a stop to this now."

"We can help," Calix interjects, scooting forward on the sofa.

"Yeah, I want to help." I nod eagerly. One thing I've never had was a strong sense of purpose. I've never even had a job. The only thing I can claim my parents ever did for me was fill my bank account. But that money came with a price, one I was happy to pay because I knew I didn't want anything to do with them—ever.

Spending their money is the only thing I've ever worked hard at. It's probably why I bought such an old ass house that needed so much work. The more of their money I could squander, the better.

"You said a male witch tried to talk to you at the club, asked you to dance?" Calix watches me.

"He did," I confirm.

"Do you think he sensed her power? I mean, it would be hard not to, right?" Calix questions the others.

"Anyone with any abilities would be drawn to her," Gunnar acknowledges, nodding his head in agreement.

"So, I should be bait, right?" I wiggle in my seat a little, excited that I'm going to get in on the action.

"I don't know if that's a good idea," Calix says slowly.

"Why not?" I send a defiant glare his way.

"Well..." Calix looks around. I think he's hoping for some support, but Gunnar is focused on the broken chair. After a quick look at Grim, who's sitting as rigid and stoic as usual, Calix adds, "We don't know who the other witch is, or if it's even a witch. It could be dangerous."

"For who?" I snort disbelievingly.

"You, Dami, you're not invincible," Grim supplies.

"Neither are any of you," I argue quickly. I'm not sure if it's a relief or not, knowing that there is something that can kill me. "You guys aren't leaving me out." I cross my arms over my chest, my mind already made up.

Gunnar lets out a heavy sigh, mumbling, "I knew this was going to happen," as if I'm the biggest inconvenience ever.

"Suck it up, Kitten. I'm the best partner you'll ever get."

"Of that I have no doubt. It's dropping you into the wolf's den I don't like," Gunnar grouses back.

"No worries, Berserker, I'll take care of our little lamb." Calix smirks.

"The lion and the lamb," I muse out loud, while shaking my head. I guess I can't complain too much. I'm the one who started the animal references.

"I will be with you as well," Grim adds, as if he thinks I've somehow forgotten him.

I give him a wink, then inquire, "So, should we go back to the club tonight?"

"I suppose, if you're set on being there." Gunnar lets his head fall back on his shoulders. I rub my hands together, already making plans. I bet that guy Joe we met earlier at the club might know a little something. It probably wouldn't be hard to get him to tell me what he knows.

The heavy sound of breathing fills the room. Gunnar's head is all the way back, his neck fully exposed as he blows out another breath.

His face is completely soft, so different from how he usually looks. I think back to the last time I saw him sleeping, well, passed out really. He's even more relaxed now. I'm sure the fact that his guts aren't slipping out of his belly has a lot to do with it.

"We should all probably get some sleep. You guys are staying here?"

"I haven't slept in a few days; that would be good." Calix avoids answering me directly, and his voice is just this side of drowsy. He might have been close to falling asleep, too.

"I have no need for sleep." Grim is still sitting rigidly on the couch.

"You don't ever sleep?" I prop my head up on my elbow and watch him. I bet I could work him over good enough that he would be plum tuckered out and in need of a nap.

"I rest, but not in the way you do," Grim answers.

A smile spills over my lips. "Do you watch me sleep? I don't know if that's creepy or cute." I playfully narrow my eyes at him.

"It's not creepy," Grim deems it so, as if by just saying it's not, all is settled.

"Whatever you say." I lift my hands in the air. "I'm about to head up to bed now, care to watch?"

Grim stands up quickly. It's probably the fastest I've ever seen him move. "Yes, thank you. I find watching you sleep very...relaxing." He flounders for the word for a moment.

I chuckle, not at all expecting him to take me up on the offer, and if he did, I wasn't thinking we'd actually sleep.

Calix stands next. "If he can, so can I," he declares, like a child calling dibs on a toy.

I roll my eyes. "Suit yourselves." Of course, I would get three mates who are more interested in my *feelings* than getting between my legs.

WHEN I COME out of my bathroom, Calix is stretched out on my bed, with his arms folded behind his head and his feet crossed at the ankles. Grim is glowering at him from over near the wall.

I freeze. I've never had anyone in my bed. "Making yourself right at home, I see," I snark, hoping it will cover the awkward pause.

"This bed is big enough for a few of us." Calix pats the space next to his hip, inviting me into my own bed.

I glance over at Grim. This feels more intimate than I bargained for. I mean, it's my bed, my sheets. I thought I could get Grim up here and maybe fool around, but with both of them here, I know that's not happening. I shuffle my feet and Calix leans up on his elbows, tilting his head to the side as he studies me. "Everything okay?" he asks.

"Yeah, yeah," I murmur, dismissing him, and break eye contact while I climb into bed. The moment I lie down, I freeze again. I'm not even breathing.

"Damiana, would you like us to leave?" Grim pushes his shoulders off the wall, stepping closer to the bed.

Do I? "No, stay." My lips utter the refusal before my mind even settled on the answer. But it's the truth. I don't want them to go. I'm just not used to having anyone this close to me.

Grim surprises me when he takes a seat on the edge of the bed. His fingertip glides over my forehead and down over my eyes as he gently draws them closed. "Sleep, goddess." My eyes pop right back open and I give Grim an accusatory scowl. There's something about the Angel of Death calling me a goddess that freaks me out. I felt the same way when Gunnar kept saying that 'my lady' bullshit.

I don't really know what to say, so I just eyeball him for a few seconds then close my eyes again. I peek at him after a few seconds and warn, "Don't be creepy."

"I am not creepy," he intones.

Calix snorts and I let out a chortle. "You are, in fact, most people's definition of creepy—just saying." I turn on my side to get more comfortable, forcing myself to close my eyes and settle down, but this is weird. What if I talk in my sleep or drool? How do people do this every day? I feel more exposed now than I would if one of them were inside me.

Calix's breathing evens out quickly behind me. I'm just starting to relax when I feel him turn over and curl around my back. I lie completely still as he weaves his hand under my arm, draping it over my stomach. A sense of calm falls over me.

When I open my eyes, Grim is staring down at the hand over my belly with a heavy frown on his face. I reach out and touch his leg, his eyes jerk up to mine.

"Should I remove him?" he asks quickly, and licks his lips. The way he says it seems so final. He's so sweet.

"No, it's not so bad. Want to lie down and be the little spoon?" I whisper, half joking.

"Little spoon?" Grim tilts his head as his brow furrows.

"Like nesting spoons. Right now, I'm the little spoon and Calix is the big spoon," I explain.

"I want to be the big spoon." His chin lifts a little.

"Well then, you have to go lie behind Calix." I hook my thumb behind me.

"That's not acceptable. I will only nest spoons with you." Before I can even giggle at the way he responded, Grim lies down and gives me his back.

I swallow and lift my arm to accommodate him. "Scoot back a little," I breathe. Only a few moments ago, I was uncomfortable with him being here, now I'm telling him to cuddle closer. I think I might be insane after all.

Grim does scoot back then. I have to reach my arm up a little to get around him, but every drop of reservation I had about them being in here with me while I slept evaporates the moment he lets out a heavy breath. "Little spoon is nice." It's almost as if he's speaking to himself.

My last thought before I close my eyes is how absolutely shocked Aeson would be if she saw this. She's going to laugh her ass off when I tell her about it.

CHAPTER 20

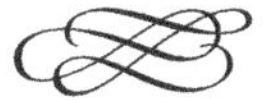

"I just want to make sure I'm clear on the plan." I look around and see Grim, Calix, and a still angry Gunnar watching me.

To say he was pissed about our little sleep over and he didn't get invited would be an understatement. More like he was madder than a wet kitten. I almost snicker at the imagery, but school my features.

Waking up to Gunnar bellowing at the top of his lungs was a new experience for me—and Grim, too, it seems. He was the one who said he only rests, but he had to be sleeping with the way he jumped up. He sure seemed like he was startled. I think his ass teleported to the door, blocking Gunnar's raging, psycho self from entering the room. Grim's scythe and cloak appeared as if summoned right along with him.

Calix just tightened his grip around my waist and let out a

soft sigh, as if waking up to screaming and hollering is an everyday occurrence for him.

"What are you unclear on?" Grim asks patiently.

I rake my eyes over his body. Damn, he can make a t-shirt and jeans look good. Does he just conjure that shit up, like his robe? "I'm still not sure where Kitten fits in. Is he with us, against us?"

"I'm with *you*." Gunnar accentuates the last word.

"So, no good guy, bad guy? I make a really good bad guy," I offer, while waggling my eyebrows.

"What do you know about being the bad guy?" Calix snickers.

"I'll have you know, a Brownie taught me her interrogation techniques." I smirk, full of pride. That gets Calix's and Grim's attention.

Gunnar actually cracks a smile. "No shit?"

"Aeson, she's one of my best friends," I brag.

"No, no. I really don't think that will be necessary." Calix darts his eyes to Grim. "Let's just go in, hang out, and see what we can learn."

"I think we should talk to that Joe guy. Something about him was iffy." I pull on a leather jacket and lift my hair out of the collar.

"If he's there, we'll talk to him," Grim concedes. "Tell me about this back office." He looks at Gunnar.

I groan. "Not that place! It's worse than the bathroom."

"You wouldn't think that if you knew half the shit that goes down in that bathroom," Gunnar mumbles dejectedly.

"I thought I was going to contract herpes from your couch," I counter.

"It's not that bad. Back of the club, ground level, last office on the left," Gunnar directs Grim. "If you need a quiet exit, the code to get back in the door is zero-five-two-zero."

"That's my birthday, May twentieth," I chirp.

"I know." Gunnar glances down at me.

"Oh…you did that…like, on purpose?" I stammer a little. I don't even really celebrate my birthday.

"Yes, it's a date I'll never forget," Gunnar admits, unabashed.

"I knew there was a reason I liked you, Kitten." I grab hold of Gunnar's shirt and drag him down to my lips, planting a quick, hard kiss on his mouth.

When I release him, Grim is watching me. "I knew it was your birthday too," he blurts.

A burst of laughter erupts from me. "If you want a kiss, all you have to do is ask." I set my hands on my hips and wait.

"I want a kiss." Calix raises his hand and responds quickly.

Grim pushes his way in front of me before I can step over to Calix. Grim scowls at the other man then turns his attention to me. "May I have a kiss, please?" Grim's voice is pitched low as he crowds into my space. He licks his bottom lip and waits. He has the patience of a saint.

I hear Gunnar's huff and a shuffling movement. I bet he's turning away so he doesn't have to see, and he should, because this isn't going to be just a peck. I mean, Grim asked so nicely.

I wonder how many more times I could get him to say please. I peer up at him from under my lashes and beckon him down to me with a crook of my finger.

He leans down, his eyes still locked on mine, and pauses with his lips a hairsbreadth away from mine. Without any more notice, I push my lips against Grim's and slide my tongue into his mouth. His hands wrap around my head, and he gives back just as much as I'm giving. I bite his bottom lip in response.

"Oh, okay. I think we need to get going," Calix singsongs. I ignore him and wrap my arms around Grim's torso. I've never really thought about my height, but right now, I wish I were a little taller, so he wouldn't have to bend down, and I could feel his entire body against mine.

Grim breaks the kiss, leaving me a little breathless. He doesn't pull away though. While staring right into my eyes, he announces, "I call big spoon." I take in how serious Grim's face is, and another surge of laughter escapes me.

"Ah, hell. Little spoon," Calix grumbles.

"There's no calling dibs!" Gunnar hollers. I look over my shoulder to find him across the room, his face contorted into an angry mask. I know from my small bit of past experience that he's close to losing what little control he maintains over his Berserker abilities. An evil grin spreads over my face. I wonder what will happen when he loses the battle. Fun stuff, I'm sure.

I clap my hands together before we dissolve into another argument. "Time to go. Chop, chop."

"That's bullshit, and you know it. You guys slept with her last night." I can already see Gunnar's features returning to normal. Maybe he's finally getting used to the other guys. I hope he doesn't ditch the attitude altogether, though. I like my kitten with claws.

"How else are we supposed to decide—draw straws?" Calix mutters jokingly.

"It's getting late." I tap my wrist as if I'm wearing a watch. This conversation is making me a little uncomfortable.

"You take the Nemean, and I'll bring Damiana." Grim wedges his way back closer to me, bumping Calix out of the way as he does.

"I can't transport others the way you can," Gunnar admits through his teeth.

"Fine. Hold on to her, Nemean," Grim orders over my head.

"No problem, thanks for the ride." Calix lines himself up against my back. It's a pretty nice position to be in under different circumstances, but right now it feels a little smothering when Grim pulls me in tight against his chest.

In a blink, we're in a dingy office, but the couch I remember has been replaced with a ratty looking cot. "You either picked the wrong room, or someone did some redecorating." I pull myself out from between the two men and push my hair back away from my face. I should have put it all up into a ponytail. The back of my neck is already starting to sweat.

I hear a door down the hall slam into a wall and a loud

bellow. “That would be my kitten.” I pinch the bridge of my nose.

Another door slams. “Damiana?” Gunnar shouts.

“Would someone open the door before he breaks it down?” I throw my arm in the direction of the door. “Good thing we decided not to be stealthy.”

Calix stomps over to the door and rips it open. “Would you shut up?”

Gunnar’s yell cuts off mid syllable. “Why the hell are you in there?” His tone is still abrasive, but not nearly as loud.

“You need to work on your inside voice, Kitten.” I push past Calix at the door and into the hallway.

Grim is tight on my heels. “Why do you call him kitten when the Nemean is the feline?”

I stop in my tracks. “You know, I hadn’t even thought about that.” I turn to gaze at Calix and Gunnar who are standing side by side. In theory, the name would be much more fitting for the lion, but it works so well for Gunnar. He’s like some feral kitty that just needs a little lovin’. I won’t tell them that though. “Well, it’s too late to change it now, he’s stuck with it.”

“You don’t have a special name for me,” Grim informs me.

“You want a nickname?” I blink several times. The Angel of Death is asking me to give him a nickname when he already knows I call the Berserker ‘Kitten’? Most men would more than likely feel emasculated by such a name.

“Do you like him more?” Grim’s brow furrows.

"I can't believe we're having this conversation." I look at the grimy walls of the club's back hallway. "And right now."

"Well?" Gunnar prompts, his chin lifted in the air a tiny bit.

"No," I reply with a sigh. "Giving him a nickname doesn't mean I like him more. It just came out in the moment and kind of stuck. I think it fits him really well." I open my hands after giving them the explanation. It's the truth, I don't like Gunnar more than the others, but the first time I met him, he was sweet and needy, then I got to see the other side of him. And yeah, the kitten name just works for me.

Gunnar gives Grim a scowl, probably for asking the question in the first place, but the subject is dropped after that.

"Are we going out?" I point over my shoulder, indicating the door to the club.

"Yeah." Gunnar shakes his head briefly and adds, "I'm going to check in with a few of my men. I'll meet up with you guys in a little bit." With his eyes boring into mine, he demands, "Stay out of trouble."

I roll my eyes. "I never get in trouble."

"We'll keep her out of trouble," Calix offers, as he poises his hand on the doorknob, ready to open it.

"You stay out of trouble," I grumble, and make my way over to the door. The magical residue hits me like a physical wave crashing over me. My senses feel like exposed nerves as every sin in the place bombards me. The entire club feels as if it's been tainted with the same dark magic I sensed from the bad witch.

"Wait." I lift my hand and I feel Grim's fingers curl over my shoulder as he drags me back. "The whole place is saturated," I grit out past a wheezing breath. I feel like I'm smothering in the magical ick and gore permeating the air.

"What's wrong?" Gunnar steps in front of me.

"You can't feel that?" I cringe.

"I don't know what you mean either." Calix looks at Gunnar for confirmation, his brow is drawn low as he opens and closes his fists.

"A Charmed one was killed here, and not long ago." Grim wraps both of his arms over my chest and curls around me.

"What?" Gunnar spins to look out at the heavy crowd in the club. People are dancing and laughing as if it's just another night.

"If you can't sense it, how do we know it hasn't happened here before? They could have been killing right under your nose." I let the disgust I feel drip from my words. It's not Gunnar I'm appalled with, but the situation itself.

"I have no fucking clue, but I'm about to find out." Gunnar smashes a glass box on the wall and pulls down a little red handle. His fist is coated in a thin layer of blood, but he doesn't seem to notice. A bright pulse of light flashes from the ceiling in regular intervals. The music cuts off next.

It only takes a breath before people realize the fire alarm has been triggered, and panic hits with the exhale.

Shouts and screams fill the air as the sound amplifies to a level even louder than the music was blaring moments ago. Pandemonium ensues.

There are a few stragglers who look around in a daze, unsure of what's happening. They're probably too drunk or high to catch the urgency of what's really going on. The others all flee for the exits: some caught up in the wave of people pushing toward the doors, others charging head-on with such determination that they don't care whom they trample in the process.

"Holy hell," I curse under my breath, as I take in the scene before me. A few of the patrons at the back of the mob look around for other possible exits, their eyes wild with fear, and then they land on us standing in the open door.

"Over here!" one guy shouts, and runs in our direction. Gunnar steps back, his arm out wide he pushes me and Grim, because he still hasn't released me from the wall. He flattens himself against the hall right along with us as a hoard of people swarm the corridor.

Grim is breathing hard as he changes his position. His face comes into focus above me and he squashes me to the wall.

"What the hell?" I gasp, as my breath leaves my lungs.

"Be still," Grim orders.

The flow of people only lasts a minute or two, but it feels like eons as we're jostled and battered from every side. I can't even see Calix. Gunnar still has his arm banded over Grim and me.

The moment the crush of bodies is gone, Grim places a gentle kiss on my temple and steps back. I draw a heavy breath in, placing my hands on my knees.

Seemingly unaffected, Grim steps over and grabs hold of

Gunnar's throat with him still pressed to the wall. Gunnar doesn't put up an ounce of fight as his heels leave the ground. I'm watching, but I'm too worried about my next breath to do anything about it.

"You are not on a battlefield, Berserker, with no thought of your consequences." Grim's mouth is close to Gunnar's ear as he speaks. "Put her in danger again with your thoughtlessness, and I will end you." Grim releases Gunnar's throat and steps back, giving him a little space, but he doesn't retreat far.

I'm waiting for the shitshow to start, but Gunnar doesn't even react to the threat. Instead, he gives Grim a nod of agreement and turns to face me. "I made a rash decision," he explains. No apology, not that I needed or expected one. He just states the facts. "It won't happen again."

I stand up straight and let my back and head relax against the wall. I eye Calix; he's a little ruffled, but seems to be okay, too. I nod also, not sure how to respond to Gunnar's words.

After we gather ourselves, we walk into the empty club. I note a few members of the security team rousing partiers who were too stupid or drunk to leave with everyone else.

Vanessa is standing at the top of the VIP staircase, her hands on her narrow hips. The air around her is smudged with oily magic. "Somebody better have a good fucking explanation." She eyes the club. The place is a mess: stools are turned over, their silver legs jutting into the air like spikes. Cups and glasses are littered among the rubble with napkins sprinkled like confetti everywhere.

Yet my eyes are drawn to the bar along the back wall.

There's a pentagram etched into the front, which is typically obscured by the countless number of bodies pressed up against it waiting for their drinks, mine included.

I take another look around with freshly searching eyes and see small runes and symbols dotted throughout the entire area. How could I have never noticed this? Some part of me had always been drawn to this bar in particular—could this be part of it? Did I sense the magic of this place without even realizing it?

Vanessa's stance shifts when she sees me: her brow furrows and her hands slide off her hips. "Seems you're coming around a lot more lately, Deanna. To what do I owe the honor?" Vanessa's eyes slip in Gunnar's direction after butchering my name. She gazes at him as if waiting for his explanation, as if he owes her something, or at least as if she thinks he does.

I take a step forward, not liking the way her eyes linger on him. "What can I say? This place draws me in like flies to a shithole. What the fuck have you been doing to stink this place up, *Vanessa*," I sneer, spitting her name.

Her eyebrows lift as her lips tighten. "I think it's the recent influx of desperate clientele that may be bringing the place down."

Calix moves up to my side. "You think so?" I tap my chin and kick out my hip to the side. "I'm not so convinced. I think it has more to do with whatever fucked up rituals you've been performing here, if you ask me."

Vanessa's eyes dart to Gunnar again, then back to me. "I

have no idea what you're blathering about. And it's obvious neither do you. Being born Charmed is wasted on someone like you," she hisses defensively.

"Is that so? Is that why you crave our magic so badly, because you were born without an ounce of power?" I know I'm ruffling her feathers by the way she's shooting daggers at me.

"I earned every lick of power I've ever gotten. Can you say the same?" Vanessa's voice is low, fused with indignant rage.

Everyone left in the club is watching us. There are several witches inching closer to her—even a few of the security team —while the others stand stock still, waiting to see what will happen next. You can feel the building tension for violence in the air. I drag in the essence and my body sings from it, like having fuel thrown on my fire.

"Want to know a secret?" I waggle my eyebrows at her as I take another step closer to the bottom of the stairs.

Vanessa puffs out a breath. "What could you possibly know that I don't already? You're nothing but an ignorant child compared to us."

She waves her hand like she's encompassing the entire room and everyone but me in it. Including my guys. That raises my hackles.

A slow, evil grin forms on my lips as I grab hold of the metal handrail for the staircase. "Maybe you do know my secrets," I lean my torso forward and lower my voice to a whisper, "but I know yours, too."

Vanessa licks her lips as commotion at the front door has most of the people positioned around us looking in that direction, but I don't break our stare.

"Fire Department! Clear the building!" is repeated a few times, as men and women in full firefighter gear stomp through the door, ready to put out the nonexistent fire—and the metaphorical one that was flaring between us.

"Be seeing ya," I announce to Vanessa with a cheerful lilt. Grim and Calix flank my sides, urging me to the door the firefighters came through. I look over my shoulder to see Vanessa and Gunnar in a similar standoff to the one we just shared.

"Don't open the club back up for business until I can perform a thorough investigation. If you do, it will be grounds for the immediate stripping of your title, with prejudice," Gunnar states, and it's clear he's not talking about the night club, he is speaking about Vanessa's coven.

Vanessa doesn't verbally respond, but her anger is written all over her face.

CHAPTER 21

I'm bouncing on my toes and throwing jabs in the air like a boxer after we clear the rescue personnel. "That was amazing! I want to kick her ass! I was like, you suck, and she was like…blah, blah, blah." I stick my tongue out and make an ugly face.

Calix lays his hand over mine and guides it down to my side. "Okay, simmer down, killer."

"We should go back in there and wait for those guys to leave, then we could…" I drag my thumb across my neck.

Gunnar lets out a bark of laughter, then schools his features quickly. "This isn't a joke," he chastises me.

"I know it's not a joke. She's killing off monsters, or Charmed ones, or whatever the hell you guys call us. We have to put a stop to it," I demand, still pumped up.

"We will, but we don't need these humans hearing you

threaten to kill her. It's inconvenient." Grim rests his hand on my shoulder.

"Fine, whatever." I cross my arms over my chest in a slight pout. "What are we supposed to do now? She knows we're on to her. We can't just let her go. She'll probably try to disappear."

"She can't just disappear, Dami," Calix corrects, urging me to walk even farther away from all the fire trucks and ambulances. There are still quite a few people from inside the club milling about too.

"She's going to try to cover her tracks," I warn them.

"She'll try. I have a few of my men watching her, and they'll report back to me if she does anything out of her norm." Gunnar has his arms crossed over his chest and his legs spread wide as he glares at the building we just left.

I scoff, "What good will that do? She's obviously been doing bad shit all along and nobody caught on."

Gunnar slowly turns his head and glowers at me.

"What?" I throw my hands in the air. "Tell me I'm wrong. Someone died in there tonight. I could feel it, who knows how long it's been going on." I'm sorry if the truth hurts his feelings, but putting a stop to Vanessa's killing is more important.

"Because now we know what we're looking for." Gunnar's shoulders puff up a little along with his chest. It's as if he takes a deep inhale and never lets the air go. I watch his mouth and jaw to see if his face will shift too.

"She's right. We need to make sure Vanessa doesn't hurt anyone else. She's already much more powerful than any other witch I've come across, and she can't be working alone," Grim adds.

"Let me handle this. It's my job," Gunnar growls past clenched teeth.

"This is bigger than just you, Berserker. I didn't even get called here to retrieve whoever they killed. That could mean they're finding a way to cannibalize the souls along with the magic," Grim informs him.

"We should just go back in there." I take a few steps in the direction of the club, but I feel a hand on my shoulder, stopping me.

"Look." Calix lifts his chin, and I watch as Vanessa and several others pile out of the club with the single focus to get to the cars waiting at the curb.

"We have to follow them." I dip my shoulder and dislodge Calix's hand.

"Wait, watch." Gunnar steps up to my side.

"What am I waiting to see?" I huff out a frustrated breath.

"Do you recognize him, the one holding the door open?" Gunnar lowers his voice so no one outside our small group could hear, even if they tried. "He's one of mine. Vanessa thinks he's a seeker."

I watch the man who interrupted us in Gunnar's office close the door behind Vanessa, and climb into another car along with two other men. "What good is he?" I shove Gunnar's chest as the all speed away. "Did he tell you Vanessa sacrificed someone in the club tonight?" I shove him again.

Gunnar takes my abuse, stepping back each time I push

him. “He wasn’t there, he was looking for the other witch you met, the man,” he answers.

“This is stupid, we should just kill her right now.” I spin and focus on the car, intending to put a stop to this right now.

“Don’t, we need to know who she’s working with. If not, killing her won’t stop the Charmed ones from dying,” Calix cajoles, sounding all reasonable and shit.

“Ugh!” I stomp my foot.

“Let’s go home. We can regroup and figure out a plan.” Calix wraps his fingers around mine, grounding me.

“Fine, let’s go. I need to talk to my friends and make sure everyone is okay.” I face Grim with expectation. I know he’ll be the one transporting me.

“WHAT DO you mean no one has seen Aeson?” My voice is shrill. Samson is crouched in the corner. He looks like a massive black dog, if you ignore the fact that he isn’t covered in fur but some sort of plates that resemble armor. He’s eyeing Gunnar and Calix as if he would like nothing more than to use their bones to pick his teeth.

Grim steps closer to the beast and Samson doesn’t even spare him a glance. *The Brownie hasn’t been seen. I was coming to learn when you last spoke with her.* Samson’s voice is almost regal as his words echo in my mind.

“Has anyone else gone missing?” Grim inquires, telling me he can hear Samson too.

A few, but none as formidable as she. Samson turns his head and acknowledges Grim with a slight bow of his head.

"Do you too know each other?" I furrow my brows.

"The Berserker has his army, I have mine," Grim answers. I look over Samson again, seeing him in a new light.

"Did you send him here to spy on me?" I'm incredulous.

The beast, Samson, makes a chuffing sound. *The angel has my allegiance, but you have my friendship.*

I click my tongue and close the gap between Samson and myself. "You're such a sweetie." I drop a little kiss on the tip of his warm nose, while giving him a scruff behind both ears.

"Uh, I don't think you should be doing that," Calix cautions.

Samson pushes his head a little harder to the left, telling me he wants a little more scratching on that side. I peer at Calix while Samson's massive head is still in my hands. "What?"

Calix lifts his hand and motions to Samson. "You do realize that's a Hellhound?"

Imbecile. Samson pushes into my thoughts. I chuckle a little as his mouth opens and his tongue lolls out the slightest bit. His behavior is at such odds with his thoughts.

"As you can see, Nemean, she has nothing to fear," Grim comments, sounding a little peeved.

"It's been a few days since I've seen Aeson." I think back to the last night she was here and I ran off without spending any real time with her. I step back from Samson as an icy thought fills my veins. "You don't think it was her at the club?" I reach for Grim's arm, half to hold myself up, and half because I *need* him to tell me no. That there is no way Aeson could have been the one murdered at Rumors today.

Grim pulls my hand and wraps his arm around me. "I don't know, Damiana. I wasn't called to collect the soul, but the magic didn't feel strong enough to be a Brownie." He searches my eyes before promising, "We'll find her."

I nod and cling to him, he's solid and strong. I peer over at Gunnar and Calix who are only a few feet away, neither of them looks bothered that I'm wrapped in Grim's arms. I already can't imagine what it would be like to lose one of them.

I push myself away from Grim, unable to meet his eyes. I can't let him or the others know just how much I've already come to enjoy having them around. I need to focus on Aeson and finding out where she is, not be worried about these three disappearing on me. "We need to find her. I don't think it's a coincidence that she's missing, and Vanessa's been siphoning Charmed powers." I turn my focus back on Samson. "Do you have any information that would help me find her? She's always been so secretive about where she spends her days and nights when she's not here."

The Brownie lives among her kind. One of her warriors reached out to see if we could contact you. They know of you, but not how to reach you.

"Shit," I curse, rolling my lips together.

"What's he saying, who's missing?" Gunnar demands, his voice rough.

"The Brownie assassin," Grim mutters. "We need to find her. If they get that kind of power…" He lets the sentence trail off.

I grab a hold of Grim's arm and squeeze. "If they hurt her, I will hang them with their own entrails after I shred their souls."

"She's perfect," Gunnar whispers softly.

"We will find her, Damiana," Grim promises again.

"Samson, tell her warriors, people, whatever… that we're going to find her. Make sure they know where I am. Please," I add as an afterthought. He doesn't deserve my irritation, but I know who does.

I release Grim's arm and stalk over to Gunnar. "I want to know where Vanessa is, Kitten, and I want to know right now." I pat my hand over his impressive chest, stroking over the muscles concealed under his shirt.

"I'll find out," Gunnar assures me quickly. "Give me an hour." He grabs the back of my head and fuses his mouth to mine. All my pent-up energy and anger coils out of me as I dig my fingernails into his heavy shoulders, and kiss him back with just as much aggression as he's offering.

Our teeth hit more than once, but I don't even care. When he pulls away, I bite his chin roughly for denying me, then shove his chest. Gunnar stumbles back, drawing his hand over his mouth and chin with a feral sneer on his face.

"Go, now!" I order, even more pissed because I let him distract me for those few precious seconds. In the next breath, he's gone, nothing but his lingering scent to tell me he was even here.

I face the others, daring them to say a word about the kiss. Grim has his head tilted to the side, while Calix has his hands shoved deeply into his front pockets. Their faces are smooth without any sign of censure to be seen.

I was expecting some kind of disapproval, instead, Calix asks, "Where should we look for her?" My thoughts go right back to Aeson. She's just so tough, I can't imagine her ever letting Vanessa, or someone from her coven, get close enough to be a threat.

I grab my hair and tug it backwards. "I don't know," I reluctantly admit, and suddenly feel guilty, because I don't know enough about her. "We talked all the time, but she always kept it vague. I know she has a penchant for leather and never has less than five men in her life at once, but I don't even know where she lived."

I'll get word to her band that she isn't here. Her disciples are already looking for her. The veterans are conducting business as usual so as not to draw attention to her absence. Samson steps forward on one huge, black paw, preparing to leave.

"Thank you, Samson, for coming to me," I tell him earnestly.

You're welcome, Dami. I will return if I hear anything. Try not to worry about the Brownie; I don't know many fiercer. Samson lumbers out of the living room to disappear the same way he arrived.

"I think I should check in with Rocky and the guys. I'm not sure if they'll know anything, but it couldn't hurt. Will you be able to stay with Damiana?" Calix looks to Grim for an answer.

"I don't need anyone to babysit me." My hackles rise at the implication that I would.

"I will not leave her unless one of you are present." Grim ignores my comment and answers Calix.

"Okay, I won't be long." Calix drags a small set of keys from his front pocket and tosses them on the counter, then tugs his t-shirt off.

I forget about my argument of not being treated like a baby and watch as he drapes the fabric over one of my chairs.

"Uh, not that I'm complaining, but what are you doing?" I question, when Calix reaches for the button of his pants.

"I can travel much quicker if I shift," he replies, not missing a beat as he drags the zipper down.

A whole lot of tawny skin is showing, enough that a girl can't take any blame as her thoughts scatter. Calix's chest is covered in a light smattering of short hair, it's a few shades darker than his light locks. His stomach is flat, and there's no clear definition of abdominal muscles, yet his body screams masculinity.

He shucks the pants off quickly, not bothered in the least with my staring. I watch his hand move to the waist of what can only be described as a pair of tighty-whities, but damn, I ain't ever seen a pair look so good. The material is tight enough that I can easily see his growing erection pushing against the fabric.

"Shifting, shifting." I find myself repeating the words, but I'm definitely not thinking about him shifting into a Nemean lion. Not at all. My eyes are glued to Calix's hands as he hooks his thumbs into the tight fabric and pushes it down enough that I can see where his body hair grows a little thicker, leading down to his dick.

"Don't hurry back, Nemean." At Grim's words, I startle a bit. I was so busy watching Calix, I didn't even think about Grim having to witness Calix getting naked.

I drag my eyes from Calix's lower body and meet his eyes. I can't help the grin covering my face. No wonder he doesn't have an issue with a little exhibitionism or an audience. "Are you sure you're not a horse shifter?" I tease.

Calix chuckles and stands in front of me, completely unabashed with his nakedness. "Try not to miss me too much." He winks and turns around, giving me a good look at his ass, then struts out of the room.

I shake my head, still smiling. "He's cheeky." I snort and look over at Grim. "Get it? Cheeky?" I'm such a dork.

Grim's lips are slightly parted, and the gray in his eyes are just tiny spheres around his dilated pupils. I lick my lips—he looks turned on. I don't know if that excites me or makes me a little jealous.

"You're aroused," Grim states.

"So are you." I wave my hand in his direction, checking to

see if I can see the evidence in his pants. "That was pretty hot."

"Was it? All he did was undress." Grim studies me.

"Yeah, but he's beautiful and looks like he was made for fucking." I watch Grim for his reaction to my words.

He surprises me by taking a step closer and reaching for the hem of his shirt. He drops it to the floor after removing it. Completely undaunted, he tilts his head to the side. "Am I?" He steps even closer, and I have to tip my head back to keep eye contact with him.

"Are you what?" I whisper, my throat going a little dry. Calix is masculine, but Grim is male perfection personified.

"Made for fucking?"

CHAPTER 22

I gulp, completely taken off guard by his question. He seems strangely sincere. I run my fingers from the outside of his shoulder over his collarbone to the center of his chest. I take in the lean lines of his physique and the sheer flawlessness of his face. It doesn't seem fair that he would be so damn, cruelly perfect. Even if he had a micro dick, he would still be a wet dream. But fortunately, I know from our little make-out session that he's not hurting in the package department either.

"I want to know what you feel like inside me, what you sound like when you come," I tell him with all honesty.

Grim exhales loudly enough that it could be considered a low groan. "I think I was made to fuck you." Heat flashes in Grim's eyes as a pool of warmth settles low in my belly.

"Aren't those just the sweetest words." I lean up on my toes and softly place my lips against Grim's. My hands immediately go to his shoulders so I can steady myself. There's something about him that makes me forget all reason, makes me want to just climb right inside him and curl up like a contented cat basking in the sun.

Grim grabs my wrist and glides it down his body. He sucks in a breath as my palm brushes over his nipple, only releasing it when I guide my fingers back up and gently flick it with my fingernail.

His grip tightens on my wrist and he drags my hand down over his obliques, I can feel his muscles shifting under my touch, jumping up to meet my fingers as if he can't wait for me to caress more of him.

We move my hand lower and it becomes clear pretty quickly that he can make these clothes disappear just as easily as the cloak. I gasp when I feel the little indent next to his hip. Grim slides his tongue, still tangling with mine, deeper into my mouth, and makes a masculine sound of need.

With a quick, jerky movement, Grim places my hand on his cock. I lick his lip with the tip of my tongue then retreat from the kiss so I can look down at him. His much larger hand is still locked around my wrist. I curl my fingers around his dick, and his knees bend slightly as he tips his head back on his shoulders. "Made for you," he murmurs, sighing as I move my hand up and down a few times, jacking him off.

While Grim's chest is bare, he has a thin line of dark hair

leading from his belly button down to his thick cock. He may not be as long as Calix, but fuck if he isn't just as perfect down here as the rest of him.

"Damn, I think you're right. How can you have such a pretty dick?" I lower myself to my knees, kissing my way down his belly as I do. Grim's breaths are coming in short, heavy pants. I look up to find him staring down at me, his chest heaving as if he's just run a mile. He releases my wrist then slams his hand against the wall, and I hear the plaster crack. "You'll be fixing that," I singsong, before taking him into the warm, wet heat of my mouth.

I let my eyes close, and a soft moan vibrates up my throat. Damn, he even tastes good. I never mind giving head—I like being the one to give pleasure—but giving Grim head is fucking magical. He smells like clean soap and tastes refreshing, like a cool glass of water on a hot day.

Grim's knees soften, and his thighs begin to tremble a little. You'd think he'd never had a blowy before. "Oh stars," he groans, while threading the fingers of his left hand into my hair. I'm not expecting the gentle way he cradles the side of my head, or the soft murmurs he's making. Keeping my hand fisted around his base, I pull my mouth all the way off him, but continue to slowly stroke Grim's dick.

"This changes nothing," I warn the both of us. I could grow addicted to the way he's making me feel right now.

Grim's eyes flash with that fiery heat. With deft movements, he reaches down and slides his hands under my arms, lifting me from the floor as if I weigh nothing. "Fuck you," he growls. "It changes everything."

I don't even have a chance to respond before my back hits the softness of my bed. I'm surrounded by my own pillows and blankets with Grim over me. In complete contrast to his harsh words, his lips dip down to mine softly. He nibbles and kisses me like he's begging for permission to deepen the kiss.

The power shift is swift, and not all that welcome. If I thought I could become addicted to him before, now I'm worried I already am. I open my lips, and he slides his tongue into my mouth, turning his head from left to right as his lips dance over mine.

I lift my knees to cradle Grim between my thighs. It seems my body hasn't received the message that I'm supposed to be resisting the temptation or, at the very least, I should be the one in control.

Instead, I find myself regretting the fact that I can't make my clothes disappear the way he can. My fingers travel over his back, and his skin is as smooth as silk. I can't feel even the smallest imperfection as I reach lower and grab hold of his ass. Grim hisses as I push him harder against me.

I turn my face away from him so I can catch my breath, but he continues kissing my jaw and neck. "Let me in, Damiana," he purrs into my ear. I know he's not referring to just my body. I bury my face in his neck. I wish I had the willpower to refuse him again, but I don't. I don't even want to try.

Grim slides his hand under my shirt, and my breath

catches as his warm palm skims up my ribs, his long fingers trailing up my side until he finally cups the underside of my breast. "I want inside you so fucking bad, my body aches."

Oh lord, don't tell me that Grim, my stoic gentleman, is a filthy talker. I don't think I've even heard him curse before the last ten minutes.

My back arches off the bed when he brushes his thumb over my nipple. "I want to know what you taste like when you scream, when you quiver. I want to know what you will smell like after I come inside you, watch your eyes when I'm buried deep. Will I be able to touch your soul again when you come for me?"

A soft whimper of need has me clenching damn near every muscle in my body. "Shut up and fuck me!" I demand, my voice harsh. I don't like that every word that crosses his lips makes me want him more.

"I will not just be fucking you, Damiana," Grim whispers into my ear, and bites the bottom of my earlobe.

I hold my breath and dig my fingernails into his ass. Is this it? Was he just trying to make me desperate for him to prove something?

"I'm going to worship you, and if you're a good girl…" Grim pinches my nipple between two fingers. My breath leaves my lungs with a heavy pant. "I'll let you have my soul."

Even with as turned on as I am, his words register, and I push Grim's shoulders back so I can see his face.

"Why would I want your soul?" I search his eyes. Does he think I want to feed off of him?

Grim's eyes are heavy-lidded as he gazes down at me. "Because it's already yours." Before I can ask him what he means, he kisses me again, all soft and sweet. He releases my breast and glides his fingers over my side until he reaches the waistband of my pants. He pauses there, asking for permission.

I lift my hips without breaking our kiss. I have no idea what he meant, but if he's offering his soul, I'll take it and hoard that shit like a dragon with treasure. I won't ever let him leave me. I shake that thought away, scared that it even came from me.

When I allow him to pull my pants down, Grim pulls back from the kiss, giving me a few open-mouthed pecks before kissing his way down my chin and throat. His hand shoves my shirt out of the way as he uses his nose to nuzzle between my breast. I feel his tongue make a swipe from left to right before he moves his focus over to my right nipple. I cradle the back of his head as his lips pucker around my peak, slightly tugging me into his mouth.

I look down as he kisses my tit as if it can kiss him back, his tongue sweeping from left to right, then up and down. Grim's eyes are glued to the spot he's kissing. I watch as his lips pull back in a snarl before he snaps his head forward and bites my nipple. I cry out, and my back and neck arch clear off the bed. The small amount of pressure he's supplying isn't enough to hurt, just enough to make my entire body sing.

He releases the bite and returns to soft, open-mouthed kisses. When the ache subsides and I collapse back against the bed, Grim murmurs, "That was too rough," against my skin, almost as if he's talking to himself.

I shake my head from left to right, but I can't come up with the right words to tell him just how fucking perfect he is. Both of his hands curl around my back and he lifts me slightly to meet his searching lips. His tongue swirls around my belly button before dipping in and out quickly. My pussy aches with an empty throb, almost like a sympathy pang.

Grim's fingers dig into my hips as he continues to move lower. "I can smell you." He buries his nose right above my fabric-clad pussy. His shoulders and chest swell with the deep inhale he drags into his lungs. His hand trembles as he draws his fingers over my lower stomach, pulling my pants off as he does. A slight burn tells me he's probably leaving the evidence of his excitement on my skin. Something inside me purrs with the thought of him leaving his mark on me.

I lift my hips again, and as he tugs the material down, my cute, black panties get tangled in with the fabric. Grim lifts himself off me and kneels between my legs. His eyes are locked on my body, furiously searching every inch of my exposed flesh. I wriggle a little, wondering if he's going to finish the job of removing my pants.

His eyes bolt up to mine. "I want to do things to you." Grim bites his bottom lip and his head shifts from left to right in a tiny movement.

He prowls forward on one hand and reaches for my pants

with the other. "What kind of things?" My voice has gone husky with need.

"I want to bite you right here." Grim gently strokes his fingers over the flare of my hip, while his lips peel back off of his teeth. "And here." His fingers dance to my inner thigh as he pulls my pants the rest of the way off. I swallow.

"I want every inch of my body to cover yours. I want you under me, around me. I want to be inside you so deeply, you won't know where you end and I begin." His words are spoken like a confession, as if he will be punished for his thoughts.

His eyes meet mine again, and his brow is furrowed. "Is that normal?"

I lean up on my elbows, his question catching me off guard. "What do you mean?"

"When you fuck, is it always like this?" Grim stares at me earnestly. Even now, his hand is flexing on my thigh, like he's restraining himself from acting on his words.

"Wait a minute: you're asking like you don't have any personal experience." I almost chuckle at how absurd that thought is. Grim doesn't respond, so I continue, "You do what feels right to you. If you hurt me or get a little too rough, I'll let you know. Are you a safe-word kind of guy during sex, or what?" I settle myself back against the bed.

"I don't think so, but I'll let you know after," he promises, all sincere like.

I let out a slight, nervous chuckle. "As long as you're not trying to hurt me, as long as it's just…" I stumble, looking for the right words. "If you want to cause me pain, or punish me, I'm not really into that. I mean, a spanking can be fun, but I don't get off on pain or torture."

Grim's face darkens as I talk. Something inside me thinks maybe I *would* let him hurt me if he really wanted to. If it would take the angry scowl off his face, I just might.

"Someone has hurt you?" Grim's eyes narrow as an eruption of fire dances in his gaze.

"Uh, no. I mean, not really. Like I said, I've never really gotten into that kink, but I'm not going to judge you if that's what you like." I marvel a little at why we're even having this conversation right now.

"Later, you can tell me their names and I will rip their souls from their bodies." Grim relaxes his grip on my leg.

"You say the sweetest things." I trace my finger down his nose.

"I'm going to taste you now," he tells me, and lowers his body back to the bed. His face goes right between my legs and he licks my labia.

"Okay," I sigh, and open my legs a little wider. There's no need to beat around the bush; I'm happy to oblige.

Grim grabs my hips and drags me a few inches closer to his mouth. "Oh stars, you're so soft."

I reach one arm up above my head and fist the sheet, the other I thread into his hair. "Stop talking," I demand, and lift my hips a little to meet his mouth.

Grim licks his way into me, using just the tip of his tongue. I don't know if he's teasing me, or if he thinks this is still part of our foreplay, but I need more, and I'm not willing to wait. I tighten my hold in his hair and push him harder against me. I'm about two seconds from flipping him over and sitting on his face.

He growls against me—I can feel it rumble past his lips. "You want my tongue here?" Grim opens me up with two fingers and blows a cool breath of air against my clit.

"Yes." I squirm a little.

Grim licks my opening from bottom to top, then pulls back. I groan. "What else?" he demands.

Fuck, is he going to make me tell him everything I want? "I want you to lick me, fuck me with your tongue until I come." I swivel my hips again, hoping that was enough of an answer.

"How will I know when you come? Are you going to tell me?" he purrs.

I foolishly thought I was going to be the one in control. I'd gladly let him spank me right now if it meant he would have his hands on me. I'm on the edge, and he's barely touched me.

"Yes, yes. I'll tell you," I agree easily. Grim doesn't make me wait any longer. He slips his tongue inside me and laps at me like he's eating the best ice cream he's ever had, and my clitoris is a sweet morsel of chocolate that he's trying to melt with the heat of his mouth alone.

I try closing my thighs when the sensation of him between my legs is too much, but he shoves my legs against the mattress and snarls, "Mine." He inches up higher, so his shoulders are bunched, and he's almost curled over me.

With a quick stab, he shoves his tongue inside me. My knees start to shake, and I let out a low moan of pleasure. Grim jerks me tighter against his mouth, with one hand on my lower belly and the other spread out under my ass. “I’m gonna come,” I pant, while my head is thrashing against the bed. My body is strung so tight, and the euphoria builds until I feel like I might break apart. With one more swirl of his tongue, I tip over the edge. I’m not quiet as the waves of pleasure spill over me, I can feel my inner muscles clenching over and over as he continues to lick me.

I eventually push him away and draw my legs together. Every time his tongue touched my clit, I would jerk with an echo of the orgasm.

“Did I hurt you?” Grim prowls up my body, pushing my legs to the side to accommodate his hips. Just the pressure of his body against mine has another moan leaving my throat.

“No,” I drawl. “But now I know why they call an orgasm la petite mort.” I grin and run my fingers through Grim’s hair.

“Little death?” His hips swivel as he gazes down at me. “Was that a little orgasm?” He licks his bottom lip, and his eyes close like he’s savoring my taste.

“Not at all, but maybe you should give me another so I can judge properly.”

Grim pushes away from me and crawls back down the bed, like he’s eager to try again. I chuckle and reach for him. “How about this time, you give me that pretty cock.” I slide my hand between our bodies and wrap my fingers around him. Grim sucks in a breath between his teeth. "Or would you like me to return the favor first?"

"What favor?" His forehead lands on my collarbone and he pushes himself deeper into my hand.

"Do you want me to lick you?" I purr into his ear, and nibble on his earlobe.

"I do want that, but I need inside you more. Maybe after." Grim pulls my hand off his dick and lifts it until it's above my head. The position sends a delicious wave of heat to my lower stomach, and my back arches. He pins me there and gazes down at me, his eyes molten. "I'm keeping you," he whispers, and places the sweetest little kiss on the tip of my nose.

"You're going to crave me." He bites his bottom lip. I feel him shift over me just as I begin to think he may be right, and maybe I should stop this before it goes any further, but then I feel the head of his cock as he brushes the velvet soft skin up and down my lower lips until I want to beg him to fuck me.

I roll my lips in and bite them to keep the words from forming. If he knows just how much I want him, he'll probably use it against me. "My touch, my scent, and just when you think you've had enough, I'll make you love me." My eyes dart up to his as Grim slides inside me.

He's staring right down at me without an ounce of remorse. Once he's so deep our hips meet, he pauses. "Oh stars. This is heaven." He pulls back out so slowly, I feel his every breath.

Even after his threat to make me love him, my eyes close as the pleasure of having him inside me takes over. This must be some sort of fucking magic, because I've never felt anything quite like this. I wrap my arms around his shoulders and bury my face in his neck. My heart is beating like I'm running a marathon. Every nerve ending in my body is alive and singing. He's right: I'll fucking crave him. He's still inside me, and I'm already thinking about the next time he touches me.

Grim retreats quicker this time and pushes back in, seeming to go even deeper. I pant out a little huff. Grim's shoulders tremble under my hands. "Are you okay, Omnia?" Grim's voice is again layered with many others.

I nod against him, not trusting myself to speak. If I do, I might say something I would regret later, like tell him how much I want him, or ask him who the fuck Omnia is.

I cling to his shoulders and curl my hips up to meet his. I'll be damned if this missionary, vanilla fucking doesn't feel more intimate than I'm used to. A sliver of panic hollows out my belly. I shouldn't be doing this—shouldn't be letting him in like this—but I can't make myself tell him to stop. If anything, I want to drag him closer, let him surround me.

Grim keeps his pace unbelievably slow as he pushes into me. Yet, the heat of his hands skimming my body seems to say he can't get enough of me, and the flex of his muscles is telling me he's working hard to maintain his leisurely tempo. I open my eyes to see him still staring down at me. I can't handle the intimacy of his maintained eye contact, so I let my heavy eyelids close and tilt my head back. Grim takes it as an invitation to run his lips up the column of my throat.

His hand slides under my ass, and he palms me, lifting me closer to him. I feel his forehead on my collarbone as he pushes himself up to his knees, my legs falling open as he kneels over me, his body curling around mine.

Grim's left hand pushes under the small of my back, and he lifts me from the mattress, until my shoulders are barely grazing the bed. He makes a sound that could be considered a growl as the angle shifts. I lift my arms above my head and gather the sheet in my hands as my toes skim the bed. Oh hell, I feel like I'm floating.

The hand on my ass curls over my hip until it's splayed over my belly. His palm is near my pubic bone, pushing just the right amount of pressure over my clitoris. Each time Grim grinds into me, I let out a breathy moan of surrender.

I swivel my hips as much as I can while being caught between his hands. I'm trapped in the best way possible. Grim slides his palm up my back, between my shoulder blades, and curls his fingers around my right shoulder, dragging me back up until I'm straddling his waist with our chests locked together.

He bites my chin roughly, and his breaths are heavy as he stills against me. I can feel his cock jerking inside me, but he's pinning me down against him so I can't move while he's frozen beneath me. I clench my inner muscles, begging him to move, to do anything, but he just pants, showing me his endless patience.

"Look at me," he orders, his voice echoing with many. I don't open my eyes, instead, I wrap my arms around his neck and nuzzle his ear and jaw. The hand he had on my stomach reaches around and pulls my ass forward, forcing me against him even more. My fingers trace over the smoothness of his back, eager to feel as much of him as I can. Yet, I can't bring myself to look at him, my heart wants to pretend he's just another body I'm using.

"Omnia." Grim individually releases each finger wrapped over my shoulder, only to retighten his grip. "Do you feel me inside you?" His cock jerks again, and my lips part as I nod. "Look at me," he demands again, and this time there's a roughness to his tone.

I want to deny him, but he snakes his hand up my back and tugs on the ends of my hair, forcing my neck back. I slit my eyes open and glare at him. Grim rolls his hips once, like it's some kind of fucking reward, and I'm silently cursing him, because it feels exactly like it is.

"Do you have any idea how long I've been waiting for this?" Grim lets his head fall back on his shoulders when I grip his dick with my pussy, but he's quick to snap his head back up, and he hits me with a glare of his own.

I lift one eyebrow and try for a nonchalant smirk. "I'd say a little over thirty years." My voice is husky with lust.

Grim rises from his kneeling position, and my weight shifts so I'm impaled on him even more while he's holding me in the air. "Try forever," he growls, jerking his hips back and driving forward, slapping his hips against mine. The hit is rough enough his skin smacks against my clitoris, but damn, it feels so good.

I climb up higher on him, so our faces are level, and wrap my ankles around his torso. I hear his words, but they're not really registering. "Then what are you waiting for?" I shift my hips back and roll them forward, working myself over him. I search his eyes, begging him with my body to give me more.

"That, right there," Grim whispers, his eyes locked on mine, and he returns to his slow-paced fucking. I don't know if I want to claw his back or beg him to go even slower. He lowers us to the bed, with my knees still high on his sides as he begins moving over me as if there's a sensual rhythm only he can hear.

My body goes completely lax beneath him, every time I think to close my eyes, he pauses, until I'm staring right back into his, and only then does he resume his punishingly slow rhythm.

"You're an asshole, but God, don't stop," I moan, reaching for his shoulders. Fuck if I don't feel like he's worshipping me. I can't even think past the pleasure to wonder if he's right there with me, blissed out.

"Do you want to come, Omnia?"

I reach up and grab Grim's jaw, snarling, "If you call me another woman's name again, I will flay you in my bed."

A slow grin lifts Grim's lips. He leans down close until his sinful mouth is near my ear, and whispers, "It's not another woman's name. I only see you…Omnia." He delivers the word with a hard grind, taunting me.

"What the fuck does it mean?" I grab a handful of Grim's

hair and fist it. A smile I could only call evil darkens his eyes as I jerk him back.

"Are you sure you want to know?" He licks his lips, unbothered by the grip I have on his hair. Sexy motherfucker.

I trace my fingernail over his collarbone, back and forth slowly, pretending to think about my answer. Then, when he relaxes a little from my seductive touch, I curl my finger and drag my nail over and his skin. Grim hisses, but doesn't make any other move to acknowledge the slice I just put along his upper chest. "Tell me," I command him, as a ball of ugly jealousy takes root in my chest.

My breath leaves me in a whoosh as he drops his weight against me. "It means my all, my everything, my universe." My body goes rigid, then I struggle to get him off of me. Panic hits, because I felt those words down to my soul. He's not fucking kidding. The part of me that can't sense if he's lying flares to life and I know his words are the truth, and he fucking means them.

"No, you don't." Grim pins me to the mattress and there's nothing I can do to get up, short of hurting him. "You asked, I answered." Grim slides his hands under my arms until he's leaning on his elbows, his face is next to mine. Thankfully, he's not making me look at him. My breaths are coming out choppy, and it has nothing to do with his fat dick still lodged inside me—well, maybe it has just a little to do with his fat dick. I hate lying to myself.

"The sooner you accept it, the sooner I can let you come. Do you want me to make you come?" His words are a softly spoken promise, at such odds with the rigidity of his body, which is still crushing mine.

I lick my lips. I knew I shouldn't have let him touch me. Stupid, greedy pussy. I could have grabbed Buzz and had some good one-on-one time with him.

Grim pulls almost all the way out of me and inches back in, as if he knows exactly what I'm thinking, and he's reminding me that my vibrator can't compare to his languid strokes. My head arches back on the pillow.

"Yes," slips past my lips. It seems it's not just my pussy that's a traitor: my mouth is, too.

"Yes what, Omnia?" There's that word again. It's like he's forcing it down my throat. "Yes, you want me to make you come? Yes, I was made to be inside you?"

I taste blood in my mouth from biting my tongue, but I still groan when he slides out of me and pushes back in.

"Yes to all of it, you motherfucker." I feel Grim smile against my neck. It's probably the kind of smile that would send children running for their parents and have fathers crossing the street. Yet, I feel another wave of heat blossoming in my lower stomach. Twisted bitch.

"I'm so glad you agree, Omnia. I've waited eons to feel this." Grim slowly rocks his body into mine, but with a new force. His arms circle around me like he's afraid to let go, and I melt against him, giving everything over to him. "I'll never go another day without being inside you." His words are muttered, almost like he's making a promise to himself.

I shut off my thoughts and focus only on the pleasure

spiraling low in my belly, at the heat and friction he's creating by pumping in and out of me.

"You can come now, Omnia," Grim growls harshly in my ear. My inner walls quake, but I fight not to follow his order.

"Fuck." I slam my hand against the mattress and fist the sheet, but there's nothing I can do to stop the torrent coming over me. A long, low moan steals its way up my throat and past my clenched teeth. My thighs are shaking uncontrollably as I let out a feral scream. My body bows off the bed, and I rake my nails down Grim's back, pushing his ass so he'll go even deeper, and I fucking come for him. The bastard.

His chest lifts as Grim throws his head back, letting out the sexiest fucking moan, calling my name as he does.

My body convulses, and so does my pussy when Grim nibbles my shoulder. "Asshole," I breathe with no heat. Here I thought I was going to be the one to pull him undone, yet he just fucking topped me, and I loved every second.

I look up when I feel Grim lift my leg up. "What are you doing?" My throat is dry from all the panting. He pushes himself against me while holding my ankle in the air. He's still hard inside of me. My brow furrows.

"I don't want to crush you," he offers, and slips my leg over him, then places it gently to the side with my other leg. Through the shifting, he slides out a little and grunts, shoving himself right back inside of me.

"Um…" I can't think of the right words to say as he leans forward and pushes me over to my side, still mostly inside my pussy with his semihard cock.

Grim lets out a sigh. "What are you doing?" I ask again, as he nuzzles his face on my neck and shoulder.

"Big spoon," he tells me, like it explains why he's nesting in my pussy like a fucking bird.

"I mean, what is your dick doing?" I glance over at the mirror above my vanity, and my body looks dwarfed by his. Should have been watching that while he was fucking me.

His head lifts. "What do you mean?"

"You got off, right?"

Grim leans on his elbow and scowls down at me. I literally feel his muscles contract. "I did not get off." He says it like getting off is a bad thing. He licks his lips and his eyes go down to my mouth. "I came inside you." I lick my lips too, like some fucking Pavlovian response.

"Right, okay. So why are you still...?" I point down to our still-joined bodies.

"Oh, I like it here." He settles himself behind me. "And I called big spoon."

I snort at the absurdity. "You do realize that calling big spoon does not mean you get to have your dick swaddled in my pussy, right?"

Grim slides his palm over my face and uses his fingertips to gently close my eyes, whispering a low, "Shush, rest."

"You want me to rest?" I chortle incredulously.

He responds by taking a deep breath and pulling my hips back into the crook of his body. This is foreign—I don't even do the whole cuddle thing after sex. "This is ridiculous," I scoff, not sure why it's bothering me so badly, but I also don't pull away from him either, so I must not hate it too much.

"Rest," he murmurs softly.

"I should be out looking for Aeson," I mumble dejectedly, yet I close my eyes.

"Let the Berserker and Nemean work, Omnia. We will find her."

CHAPTER 23

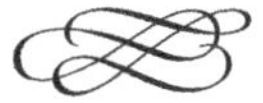

Falling asleep with a dick inside you isn't all that bad. Waking up after a short nap with a hard cock already raring to go and in position is even better.

I succumb to a second round with Grim. This time, there's no power play involved. I think he knows not to push me too much, but he must have a fucking PhD in tantra, because he still took his time making me come.

I hear the door to my room slam open while I'm rinsing my hair. I lean my head out of the stream of water. "Did you find out anything?" I don't have to ask to know who opened my door like that.

"Vanessa is at her home. She's gathering her coven, but I didn't hear anything about a Brownie." Gunnar pushes into the bathroom and leans against the doorframe, watching me through the clear shower walls without an ounce of remorse.

His eyes travel over my skin, and I find myself slowing my movements so he has a better view.

I lean back into the spray and let the warm water cascade over me. With my hair rinsed, I'm pretty much done, but I find I'm liking his attention. Gunnar licks his bottom lip and drags his teeth over it, pulling the skin around his scar and turning it white. I bend over a little and give my leg another good rinse. His eyes track my hand as I glide it from my calf to my thigh.

Gunnar's hand moves to his groin and he adjusts himself, but his fingers linger. I crack a smile, but I've already wasted too much time fucking around, plus, there's a small part of me that's worried I would be disappointing Grim.

That thought sends a cold wave over me, even though the water is still piping hot in the shower.

I twist the water off with a snap of my wrist and snatch the towel on the hook next to the shower. I'm irritated with myself for even allowing the thought.

"Vanessa," I spit. "Why aren't we going over there and demanding answers?" My question comes out accusatory.

Gunnar opens his arms and his lips flatten. "I'm being a team player. If that's our next move, then we can go right now."

"Is Calix back?" I wrap the towel around my body and grab another for my dripping hair.

"Right here." He comes into the bathroom and his eyes roam over me. "And seconds too late, I see," he mutters.

"Did you find out anything?" I tip my chin up to Calix while squeezing the water from my hair. I can't believe they're both just standing there, watching me like this is an everyday occurrence. I can't believe I'm letting them stand there like it's completely normal.

"Nothing, but I honestly didn't think I would. Brownie assassins usually stick to their own kind." Calix walks over slowly and pulls the towel from my hands. With a gentle palm on my shoulder, he pushes me down to sit in my chair. I tip my head back and look at him. He holds up the towel between his hands, asking for permission. I face forward and Calix places the towel over my hair.

My eyes jump up to Gunnar, but he's just watching us, his face almost calm. I keep quiet as Calix dries my hair, again struck by the intimacy of the moment, but too enamored with being taken care of to stop him.

When Calix's hands rest on my shoulders, signaling he's done, I mutter a soft, "Thank you," and look down at the floor. I feel strangely exposed in a way that Gunnar watching me shower didn't even create.

"I should get dressed." I pinch the towel around me and stand. "Is Grim still here?"

Calix hooks his thumb over his shoulder. "He's lying in your bed, where I'm sure you left him."

Grim fills the doorframe in the next second, naked as the day he was born, or created, whatever. I look at the other two guys. "Uh…" That's all I can say. No one is reacting to his state of undress. I decide to follow suit. "Should we go to Vanessa's?" I scratch the tip of my nose, trying not to look at Grim and his insanely perfect body. It's a losing battle, though.

I can't seem to not look. "Can you put some clothes on? I can't think!"

Grim swats the side of his dick, and it sways slowly. My eyes are drawn to it like a fucking pendulum. "This is hard again; I'm in need of you." I slap my hand over my eyes.

Calix lets out a heavy snort. "That's not quite how it works, my man."

"Are you sure?" Grim cuts his eyes to Calix.

I look up at the ceiling, "Ah, Grim?" I'm again at a loss for words. I've had the most ludicrous thought, and I don't even know how to ask the question without just asking the damn question. I clap my hands together slowly and bring them up to cover my mouth. "So, when you said you had been waiting forever for me…you actually meant…you'd never…?" I glance around, looking for someone to help me.

Gunnar turns to face Grim slowly. "No…just no. Tha-That's not a thing," Gunnar stutters incredulously.

Grim looks completely unperturbed by the entire conversation. He takes a step forward and his dick bobs with the movement. I find my head nodding to follow along. "I was waiting for you," Grim answers sincerely.

I pinch my temples between my fingers. "Can I have a second alone with Grim, please?" Calix snickers, then Gunnar's unmistakable retreating, heavy footfalls alerts me that the others are leaving.

I peek up at Grim from under my hand and whisper, "That was you as a fucking virgin?"

Grim's eyebrows draw in and I scrub my hands over my face. "Holy hellion balls."

"Only the first time," he tells me pragmatically.

I groan. "So, all that stamina?" I roll my lips in.

"It's been a long, few years." Grim plants his hands on his hips and it draws my eyes back to his dick.

"Well," I give him my most approving look, "from one masturbator to another, that was fucking amazing. Skills are on point." I'm actually a little in awe, and I'll be damned, but a lot turned on too.

The crest of Grim's cheeks flush with a slight tinge of red, before he peers at me from under his brow. "Wait until I have more practice," he promises. I fan my face and blow out a breath, and his dick bobs again while he watches me.

"Ahh, guys?" I call out to the others, or I might just take Grim up on his request to ease his hard-on.

Calix pokes his head around the door, I knew they wouldn't go far. "Did you get him worked over…out…" Calix frowns. "Are we all set?" he questions, finally settling on what to ask.

"Taking care of it now," I reply, and turn my focus back to Grim. I step a little closer, so he knows my words are just for him. "Listen, Loverboy, if I got to get down every time, I was horny, I'd probably never get out of bed."

Grim nods eagerly and hooks his hand over his shoulder. "I like your bed," he tells me, as if to say he's totally fine with that option.

"Death." Calix walks back into the bathroom with his arms

folded over his chest. "Look, man…" He starts, but he pauses too, like he can't find the right words.

"I'm guessing you never had the urge before Damiana, am I right?" Gunnar sidles up next to Calix.

Grim nods, and his dick does, too. I wave my hand over at Calix and motion for him to grab the dry towel still on the hook. Understanding my silent plea, he reaches for the cloth and tosses it to me. I nab it out of the air and shake it out, before snapping it open and slipping it behind Grim to wrap it around his waist. However, it brings me up close and personal to all that warm, perfect skin, and my mouth literally waters with the thought of licking my way up his chest. I pinch the fabric at his hip and step back a little.

I force my eyes down, but the sight of his dick tenting the front of the towel does absolutely nothing to curb my desire. I can even see the outline of his blunt head. Fucking hell, he's like some naughty calendar picture come to life.

"Bet being around her is torture." Gunnar's lips curl into a cruel smile, but it melts quickly. "It's rough on all of us, man. But just 'cause your dick gets hard, doesn't mean it needs servicing. You get me?"

My hand holding the towel slips a little, and I regather the fabric. I'm completely caught off guard by the sincerity in Gunnar's voice. He's not teasing or poking fun, he's actually trying to help in his own way.

Grim's eyes go unfocused and he nods. "It's worse now that I know what she tastes like, feels like—she's so soft and warm." The towel bobs up.

"Gonna ask you to keep that info to yourself. We don't want to hear about it," Calix interjects quickly, crossing his arms over his chest and tipping his chin up.

"Yeah, so…" I look around, still holding Grim's towel in place. "Now that that's handled, we should get dressed and go take care of Vanessa."

"It's noon. She's not going to be doing anything for the next few hours. We should rest," Gunnar suggests, sounding confident that she isn't going anywhere.

The lack of sleep is catching up to me. I already sapped the reserves for the hour nap I got with Grim. Sleep sounds really good actually.

I grab Grim's hand and place it over the towel where I'm holding it. "There." I pull my hand away and watch as he tightens the fabric over his groin.

"You like my body. Why do you keep trying to cover it up?"

I blow out a raspberry. "You're not the only one who gets horny, Loverboy. Now, all of you out, so I can get dressed in peace."

I hear a few low grumbles, but they all file out of the bathroom then through my bedroom door. "Dude, cover your chubby," Calix hisses, as Grim releases his grip on the towel, and I get another good look at his perfectly round ass before a pair of dark pants and a black shirt covers him in the next blink. The towel disappears from his hand and he saunters out the door—not a purposeful swag, just his natural gait.

I tip my head back and look up at the ceiling. "I don't

know if I'm blessed or fucking cursed," I mutter, wondering how the hell I ended up with all three of them somehow tied to me.

After sliding on a pair of silk sleep shorts and a cami, I peel back my covers and sigh when my overheated skin touches the cool sheets. I drag the comforter up to my chin and dip my head down. I can smell Grim. I let out a soft purr, liking the reminder.

A noise from downstairs has my eyes jerking open before I can fall asleep. I'm not used to visitors during the day, and they're loud. I thought we were supposed to rest. I nuzzle my head back into the pillow, then the floor outside my door creaks.

I know who it is, so I don't open my eyes. It's not as if a stranger could get in unnoticed with all three of them here.

The bed bounces and someone launches himself at me, landing half on my legs. I do sit up then and growl down at Gunnar.

"Big spoon!" he shouts, scooting up behind me in the same moment.

"You said no dibs." Grim enters the doorway with a frown on his face.

"Because you thought of it before me," Gunnar answers, unrepentant.

Grim's eyes travel over Gunnar as he lays his arm over my torso and pulls me back to the mattress. "I have things that I need to attend to," he mutters dejectedly.

"When will you be back?" My voice is soft, sleepy.

Gunnar is warm, and it's surprisingly easy to accept having him in my bed.

"Soon, Damiana, most likely before you wake." Grim comes over and sits on the side of the bed, and pushes my hair behind my ear.

I reach for his arm, suddenly more alert. "The last time you left, you said it was because of the Mimic. Did another monster die?" I search his eyes. Worry for Aeson eats at my stomach; should I really be resting right now?

Grim lays his hand over mine, and his eyes soften. "No, I would just rather check on the other side now than have to do it later when I could be here with you," Grim confesses easily.

"You'll tell me if you find out anything…" I can't bring myself to say the words.

Grim leans down and places a gentle kiss on my temple. "I will," he whispers. I feel the portal open up behind him. A wave of rage boils through, and it turns my stomach. Grim tilts his head as he pulls back. "When was the last time you fed?"

I gather my hand over my stomach, holding the blanket tighter. "A few nights ago." It feels like so much longer though.

"Are you hungry?" Grim assesses me.

I shake my head. "No, not in the least." I scrunch up my nose.

Grim makes a humming noise and brushes my hair back again. His eyes go above my shoulder. "I'll be back soon." The tone of his voice shifts, and I know he's talking to Gunnar.

"We'll wait for you," Gunnar tells him, and Grim nods his head quickly before standing and taking one large step backwards, his eyes on me the entire time.

I pat Gunnar's hand over my waist once the portal closes. "Look at my kitten, being all nice and shit."

"Your kitten?" I can hear the grin in Gunnar's words.

"Of course you're my kitten. Who else would you belong to?" I scoff, and resettle myself next to him.

"Considering I would probably kill anyone that dared call me a kitten, I would say no one."

"You know you love it when I call you Kitten, Kitten," I goad him, really enjoying the way Gunnar's body is relaxing behind mine.

"Only because you know I'm going to make you purr."

A low chuckle starts in my chest, and I feel Gunnar's body jerk. I twist and look over at him, his face is slightly red, and I burst out laughing. "That was so cheesy."

Gunnar chuckles dryly at himself. "Shut up and go to sleep," he orders, back to his bossy self.

I snicker a few more times but turn back around. "What's so funny?" Calix questions as he comes in. Using his toe on the heel of his boot, he steps out of them and yanks his shirt off next.

"Nothing." Gunnar pouts, which makes me laugh even harder.

When I open my eyes, Calix is grinning down at me and pulling back the covers. He's back in the tight, white undies that seem way too sinful for the childish moniker I dubbed them earlier. I lick my lips as something warm blooms in my lower stomach. All the humor dies, though, when he skootches his body closer to me.

Being between two men isn't new to me, but being between these two is, and having Grim only seemed to whet my appetite. I close my eyes and force my breathing to even out. Calix brushes against my nipple with his arm as he settles himself. I ignore the ache and focus on lowering my heart rate. Gunnar doesn't need to tell me he's not the kind of guy to share, it's in every fiber of his being. I know Calix likes an audience, but I somehow doubt Gunnar would be up for that either.

"Should we set an alarm?" It's such a mundane question coming from Calix. I want to punch the bed over the fact they can seem so completely unaffected.

"Go ahead." Gunnar's voice is lazy as he dips his face until his lips are hovering right over the spot where my neck and shoulder meet. I feel every heavy breath that passes his lips. I should have put on a turtleneck and leggings. Why am I letting them into my bed to begin with when I have plenty of other rooms?

I kick my legs back and forth a little. "I'm hot. Are you guys hot? I think I need a drink." I lean up on my elbows.

"Lie down and go to sleep," Gunnar orders. His eyes are closed, but he still manages to drag me back down to the mattress and tuck me right back where I was.

"Yeah, right," I mutter under my breath. I'll just wait for them to fall asleep and sneak out. Idea formed, I close my eyes and match my breathing to Calix's. He turns over and curls his ass tight up against the curve of my body. I'm forced to put my arm over his waist or let the blood flow between us get cut off.

Calix grabs my fingers and holds them to his chest. Leaning his head down, he kisses my knuckles and lets out a soft sigh. Instead of worrying about how sexy it is to be pinned between them, I think about the way Gunnar's body is softening behind me, and the little sigh of contentment that Calix just let out.

What was it like for them, knowing there was someone out there that was supposed to be their match, the one person that would make them feel whole? I'm not sure I believe in the fated thing, but they seem to believe it wholeheartedly. I mean, Grim never even slept with anyone else.

I think about how much I craved my parents' attention when I was younger, how I would have done just about anything if it meant they would acknowledge me, and tell me I wasn't crazy for seeing and talking to the monsters that visited me.

I think about how lonely I felt when no one would visit me for days on end. How isolated I became, because I felt so removed from everyone in the real world. Did they feel the same when only standing next to people? Alone in a crowd?

I think about Grim's visits and him feeding me, about how many times I found a new stone sitting in my bathroom, on my kitchen counter. My hand flexes over Calix's flat stomach. He said he stayed away so that he would never have to leave once he was able to be with me.

They were biding their time, waiting for something they didn't even know was going to happen. I've been adrift in a sea of loneliness that I never dared hope could change. Yet here I am, surrounded by them.

Which of us had it worse? Those thoughts and so many others circle around in my head until eventually, the darkness of sleep pulls me under.

CHAPTER 24

"Why did you let me sleep so late?" I growl. I'm not cheery when I first wake up. Add to that the fact that I went to bed with my hair still damp so I look like some 1980's video girl, and I am definitely not a happy camper.

All three guys pretend to be busy, or just outright ignore me. With jerky movements, I wrangle my hair back and snarl, "I'm not taking a shower," like it's an actual threat.

Out of the corner of my eye, I see Grim's lip curl up before he tamps it down. Too late—I already saw it. "What are you smiling at, Loverboy?" Grim looks down and doesn't fight the grin this time.

Calix's head lolls on his shoulder, and he looks over at me. "He's being cocky," he accuses.

I narrow my eyes. "How so?" I wrap a hair band around my high ponytail, and it tames the top of my hair, but, oh my, it's the opposite of sleek. I give up caring.

Grim peers up at me from under his brow and reaches down to adjust himself. "I'm still on your skin, shower or not." He licks his bottom lip. The sexy rat bastard. It's worse because he probably doesn't even know it.

"Anyone with any sense of power would know he was with you." Calix pushes his hands down his thighs as his knees start to bounce.

"Why are you so talkative today?" I ask Calix, as he tugs at his shirt collar.

"He's aroused," Grim supplies with a narrow-eyed glare at Calix. A little tit-for-tat this evening it seems, as Grim rats out Calix just as Calix did to him.

"Like that's news." Calix rolls his eyes, but his knees continue to bounce.

"Well, is something else bothering you then?" I lower myself onto my bed.

"No." Calix rolls his lips in and shakes his head.

I hold up my hands in surrender. I'm not going to force him to talk to me. He will if and when he wants to.

I turn away from him and look at Gunnar, who's been relatively quiet. "So, what's the plan for tonight?" I glance at the clock, noting that, even though I was complaining, it's still early. I bet Vanessa's not at the club yet, which is good. I'd rather catch her where we can't be interrupted again.

"I think we should just confront her with what we know now. Vanessa is cunning. If we give her too much time, she will cover her tracks if she is, in fact, involved with the deaths, which I think she is." Gunnar's jaw is set firm. I think admitting Vanessa was able to do some shady shit on his watch has put a dent in his pride.

"Sounds good to me. We can make her talk." I examine my fingernails, thinking about all the things Aeson taught me about interrogation. I feel a pang in my chest. I *need* to find her.

"Travel might be an issue," Grim muses, his voice back to cool and collected. "I'm not being called to her, and I don't know her residence."

"I have my bike here, so Dami can ride with me while you two take her car," Calix offers.

"Oh no, no, no." I shake my head before anyone can agree. "You guys don't know Betty, and she's a bit finicky." Plus, no one else has ever driven my car.

Gunnar lets out a long-suffering sigh. "Her car is only a two-seater anyway," he adds, and ignores my protests.

"Who is Betty?" Grim furrows his brow like he can't believe there's something about me he doesn't already know.

"Her car," Gunnar deadpans.

I glare at him. "I told you not to talk about her like that. She's a fucking beautiful machine."

"Still a car." He widens his eyes, daring me to prove him wrong.

I cross my arms over my chest. "One you won't be riding in."

"I'll ride Betty, Calix takes the bike, and you can meet us there, Berserker," Grim decrees.

"Ride *in* Betty." I don't know why I feel the need to clarify the distinction, but I do. I don't think I like Grim and riding associated with another woman's name, even if it's my car.

"Fine." Gunnar stands up in a huff. "That way I can keep an eye on her while it takes you guys forever to get there," he gibes, implying that us having to drive is such an inconvenience.

"I'm ready." I shrug. "Give us the address and we'll meet you there."

Calix drags his phone out of his pocket. One of his legs is still bouncing, but it seems having a plan has helped a little with whatever is bothering him. "Go." He nods his head at Gunnar with his thumbs poised over his phone.

"It's in Lakeview: 32059 Cheboygan Court."

I whistle. I know the area well—it's where I grew up after all. Well, before my parents shipped me away. "That's a long drive; we should have gone earlier. How are you going to keep her from going to the club?"

"I forbade her from opening the club until my investigation was complete," Gunnar tells me, assuming his word is law. I'm worried Vanessa might not feel the same.

"Do you still have people watching her though, just in case?" I slide my foot into my heavy boot.

"I do, but she won't push me—not on this, and not now."

I nod my head and grab my other boot, hoping he's right. "Who's ready for a road trip?" I come to my feet and look around. Calix stands and slides his phone back in his pocket, Grim follows suit.

"It says it will take an hour and seven minutes to get there," Calix offers.

I grin. "How fast is that bike of yours? I bet we can do it in under fifty minutes."

Calix sends me a smirk. "I already told you I can be as fast as needed." He walks out of my bedroom backwards, giving me a wink before spinning around and rushing down the stairs.

I dart my eyes to Grim. "Get us to my garage?"

He stalks over and wraps his arm around my waist, pulling me against him tightly. In a blink, I'm standing next to Betty.

"Sorry, sweetie, no time for introductions," I coo at my car. "Hop in, Loverboy." Betty purrs to life before Grim is even in the seat. He looks around the small cockpit-like interior with a keen eye. I hit the button for the garage as Calix's bike roars to life. With a mock salute, he hits the gas and peels out of my driveway.

I chuckle; this is going to be fun.

I trail Calix's taillight almost the entire drive to Lakeview. I couldn't push Betty the way I would have liked to. The most direct route was mostly freeway, which raises my chances of getting pulled over. However, we still beat the GPS prediction and made it to Vanessa's house in under an hour.

I slide out of Betty and glance up at the house. Another low whistle pushes past my lips. Nice digs. Even though I'm familiar with the area, I don't know this particular street. The few houses lined up are all large and illuminated, so everyone that passes by can't help but observe just how flashy they are. It's an in-your-face display of money. A calm lake shimmers with inky waves behind the houses, I can even see the tops of several large boats bobbing and shifting with the movement of the water.

Calix drags his helmet off and places it on his seat, then shakes his hair out, pushing it back from his forehead with his palm. His moves are purposeful and deliberate, not designed to entice. The fact that he's not trying to be alluring makes it even more appealing. Sexy motherfucker.

Grim sidles up next to me after he slinks out of my car, and I feel excitement bubbling up in my stomach. Not only do I get a thrill from being with them, but knowing I'll be there for Vanessa's downfall makes it even sweeter. Heaven help her if she has anything to do with Aeson's disappearance.

Gunnar steps forward from the shadows, joining our group, as we form a line and head up to the outrageously oversized front door. I mean, come on: unless she's entertaining trolls every night or guiding fucking marching bands through the door, does it really need to be this huge?

The massive entry opens before we reach the top step. One of the men I've come to assume works with Gunnar as security pulls it back and allows us entrance. Not a word is spoken between us as we enter a large foyer with ceilings so high, you can see the third-floor balcony up above.

I open my senses, and I'm not sure if I'm surprised at how *clean* the house feels or not. I know Vanessa is smart enough not to bring her business home, but I would think some of her witchy magic could be felt just because it's her house.

"She's not doing magic here," I mutter to Gunnar, who's on my left. He gives me a tiny head bob, letting me know he's heard me.

"Vanessa!" he bellows in the next second. "Stop fucking wasting my time and get down here!"

As I glance to the right, I watch as Grim sends a narrow-eyed scowl at another man, who's coming out of one of the halls splitting off the main foyer. I recognize him the moment his beefy face comes into view. He's one of the men I've come to associate as Vanessa's bodyguard. His other half comes from another hall, joining his companion to stand before us like a united front, much the same way we are.

I can't help myself. I step forward and give them a smile, but it's not a smile many people enjoy seeing. "Hiya, big boys." They stand stock-still in front of me, not even dipping their eyes in my direction. Instead, they keep their gaze on the men behind me. A small chuff of a laugh sneaks its way up my throat. I know the men behind me are deadly, I have no doubt about how this would play out if I allowed it, but I'm not patient, nor do I like the way they seemed to have dismissed me as a threat.

Without moving a muscle, and my sinister smile still in

place, I call the goon on the left's soul to me. He blinks several times. It's the first sign he knows something's wrong. He reaches up and drags a thin cord out from under his shirt, fisting something as his chest starts heaving. "Did you think that would protect you?" I almost want to laugh at the faith he put in the little trinket around his neck. It must be some sort of witch-created protection spell.

His cohort's eyes dart to him, but he stands firm. I'm sure he's wondering what's happening. I think it's time I show him. I release Lefty, not that I need to, and focus my attention on Righty. I reach for his soul, it's much darker than his friends. "Oh, you're a naughty boy," I whisper, while he makes a gasping sound. His sins have eaten away at his aura. He doesn't have the stink of magic, but his crimes against others are abundant. "You like little girls, huh?" I seethe.

Lefty's eyes are wide as he looks around, either for an escape or maybe an explanation for what's happening to them.

My mouth begins to water, and I feel my first desire to eat in days. Only I don't want his sins, I want his entire soul. One more quick draw and Righty crumples to the floor, his face as ashen as a corpse left in the snow.

"Sorry about your buddy." I lay a hand over my stomach as my shoulders pull back. "He was too tasty to pass up." I purposefully lick my lips.

Lefty takes a step backwards. His eyes jerking from the man on the floor and back up to me. He still doesn't understand what's happening.

I feel a hand land on my shoulder. Grim steps up to meet

me and he looks down, his eyes soft, without an ounce of censure. "Maybe you could let us talk to them before you consume their souls?" he suggests, like it's really a question, like if I decide just to devour them all, it would only be a slight inconvenience.

"Damnedest thing—I just couldn't help myself," I admit easily. This is a new development, but one I don't have time to worry about now.

I hear Vanessa's heels clicking on the floor before I see her. She saunters into the room and doesn't even acknowledge the corpse on the floor. "You called?" she asks glibly, cocking out her hip.

Gunnar takes a step forward. "Watch it, witch!" he rages, his shoulders already growing in size. "I want to know who you're working with."

Vanessa's lips part and she lets out a small hiss of air. She surprised, but hiding it well. I'm not sure yet if it's Gunnar's knowledge that she's working with someone else, or the fact that we don't know who it is, that has her alarmed.

"Why would I be working with anyone?" she blusters, but it's far too late. I would know she was being deceitful, even if I didn't sense the untruth.

"Cut the shit, witch." Calix shoulders his way up so he's in line with us again.

"You've never been one to work well with others, Berserker, but it seems you've found yourself some new friends." Vanessa's eyes linger on all of us, me the shortest.

"Powerful friends," she mutters, focusing back on Grim. I hate the way her eyes roam over him, greedy and hungry.

I ball up my fists. Before this evening is over, she'll be just as soulless as her bodyguard. There's *always* room for dessert. "Vanessa, you look like a snack," I purr the compliment, but the meaning behind it is so much more than she could possibly understand.

She looks down and assesses her dress. "Not all of us can pull off the trailer trash look quite as effectively as you, Deanna."

I snicker—not only do I sense her lie, but I know for certain that I can make jeans and a white t-shirt look damn good. I roll my eyes and let my head loll to the side to stare at Gunnar. She's reaching for straws if she's trying to insult me. "Can we get this show on the road?" I turn my gaze back to Vanessa. "I'm getting hungry again."

"What is this, Drott? Who are these people, and why are you here?" Vanessa feigns, acting like she doesn't know the reason for his presence.

"Listen, Vanessa, this can only go two ways. You either tell me what I want to know, and you might be able to walk away from this with just your title stripped—" I clear my throat, that's not happening "—or I get the information I need from you any way possible," he continues, not realizing she's going to die either way, but that's okay, he's not really lying since he doesn't know I'm going to kill her yet.

Vanessa clicks her tongue. Her demeanor shifts, and I hear several people I already knew were lingering start to come forward. None of them speak, they just line up around Vanessa in a silent show of support. A tremble works its way over Gunnar's shoulders.

Calix, who has been relatively quiet, lets out a weighty sigh. "Bad choice, witch." And all hell breaks loose.

CHAPTER 25

Gunnar lets out a roar that I think could rival Calix's when he is in his Nemean form. His shoulders grow bulkier, and his jaw and teeth transform even beyond what they did that day in his office. I watch him, transfixed; it's eerily beautiful. Now, he looks like one of my baddies.

I smirk and face the group of human-looking witches. A few hold their ground, while others are already looking for an escape. I want to take odds on the number that will flee at the first chance, but I know I won't be heard over Gunnar and the shouts that ensue soon after. He reaches out—his span is nearly double what it would be in his more human form—and grabs a male witch, palming his entire head before tossing him to the side like a ragdoll. The thud he makes when he splats into the wall makes me think he probably won't be getting up anytime soon.

The real screaming starts then. I tip my head back on my shoulders and let the fear consuming them wash over me. I lower my eyes and growl, "Let's not let him have all the fun."

Calix bounds forward and slams a man against the wall, he places his mouth next to the man's ear and whispers. The stench of piss hits my nose, and I scrunch up my face.

The woman from the club—the one who said she created the wards—is standing near Vanessa, with a furious look of concentration on her face as her lips move silently with a rushed fervor.

I stalk forward, not in the least worried about Gunnar or the others behind me. I have one objective in mind—her.

She doesn't even seem to notice me when I step right in front of her. Her eyes are open, but unseeing, as she continues to chant. I pull back my fist and put all my effort into punching her square in the nose. Her eyes widen as her head jerks back. Her hands fly up to cover her face just before a river of blood starts pouring over her lips. That felt fucking good.

I reach back again, but she ducks her head and cowers with her hands raised above her head. One punch—that's way too easy. I wanted to enjoy this more. "Tell me about the Charmed ones," I grate, pissed that she's giving up so easily.

"I… we…" She stammers, peeking up at me to see if I'm still going to hit her. "Antonio taught us the magic," she blurts, and looks over my shoulder.

I jerk my eyes in the same direction and see the back of Vanessa's head as she and a few others disappear deeper into the house. "Hey!" I shout, and all three of the guys' heads turn in my direction. Gunnar is holding yet another man by his shoulders, apparently shaking the life out of him, if the way the man's head is lolling around is any indication. Calix's fist is pulled back much like mine was moments ago, poised to strike, while Grim is just standing a few feet away from me with a circle of bodies all around his feet. Not a hair is ruffled on his head. I grin up at him, wishing I would walk over and kiss the hell out of him.

I look away, but my voice comes out a little husky as I say, "Vanessa is leaving." Who knew I liked carnage so much?

Gunnar drops the lifeless man in his arms, and steps over another near his feet, charging after the witch. Grim is quick to follow.

I put my attention back on the squealing rat in front of me. I sense Calix as he steps up to my back. "So, you were telling me about Antonio?" I question her, knowing Gunnar and Grim can handle Vanessa without a problem.

The woman looks around the room at what I'm assuming might be her friends—or at least her associates—littered on the floor or trying to sneak away unnoticed. "He taught us how to siphon the powers and not take the kickback, how to disperse it through the seekers," she confirms, solidifying what we'd already suspected.

I reach for her and she flinches, turning her face away from me as I lock my fingers around her throat. "Where is

Aeson?" My voice is nothing but a growl. Calix lays a hand on my shoulder when the witch's eyes begin to bulge.

I release the tips of my fingers, just slightly, and shake her in my hand. "The Brownie!" I demand.

"I..." She coughs violently. "I think she was next." She wheezes in another breath, tears filling her eyes. "Please, don't hurt me," she begs, and I tighten my hand again. She claws at my fingers and opens her mouth like a fish. "I'll take you to her," she croaks, beseeching.

I release her, and she falls to the floor. I crouch with her as she holds her neck, swallowing. "If she's hurt, I will scoop your eyes out with jagged spoons and cauterize the wounds. Then I will peel each piece of your flesh off and feed it to Theius." As I stand, I deliver a kick to her stomach that sends her sliding a few feet across the marble floor. I'm disgusted by her. Calix pulls me back, as if he knows I'm tempted to kick her again.

A scream from farther in the house has me looking in the direction that the others went. "Get up," I snarl at the woman. With jerky movements, she rises to her knees, using the wall for support.

"You don't have to do this," she offers.

I get right back in her face. "How many times have you heard that? How many times have you ignored it just to get a magic you have no right to?" The woman's face blanches, and she averts her gaze from me. She knows there will be no mercy for her. "The only thing you can hope for is a quick death," I snarl, and shove her forward.

She stumbles in front of us as we make our way to where I heard the screams. We have to step over bodies along the way. The hall leads to a solid wooden door. It looks expensive, but the way it's hanging half off the hinges shows me she should have chosen something stronger.

Grim is standing off to the side, his eyes already inspecting me as we walk into the room. Gunnar is facing off with Vanessa, her chin is tipped up in the air with a defiant set to her jaw.

"You should have just told me, Vanessa." Gunnar sounds disappointed in her.

"You would have killed me either way, but now he knows you're coming, and he'll be ready." Her eyes darken and thick, black veins start spilling over her skin, rushing up to her face. A sinister smile splits her lips and black goo drips from her mouth like sludge. A mirthless laugh bubbles up and her hand opens, dropping a small stone to the ground.

"I would never let you kill me," Vanessa sneers at Gunnar. "You don't deserve my life, or any other. We made you!" she screams, dropping to one knee, her eyes still locked on Gunnar, but then she turns her focus to me. "He's coming for you," she whispers, before crumpling face first onto the gleaming wooden floor.

Her stench of death and rot permeate the room far quicker than what should be possible. The last witch standing's shoulders are trembling as she heaves sobs into her hands. "How did you see this playing out?" I question the woman who promised to take me to Aeson. "Did you think you would just get away with killing people?"

"He said he'd been doing it forever," she snivels, as if it's an excuse.

"I can't even look at her." I turn around and storm out of the room. Grim is close on my heels. I trust Gunnar and Calix to bring the witch. I have every intention of finding Aeson tonight, but I need to get the hell out of this house.

"ARE you sure we should trust her alone in there? Couldn't she cast some sort of spell or some shit?" I glare through the car window at the witch locked inside. There was no way I was letting her contaminated ass in Betty. Calix left his bike at the Lakeview house and drove here with the witch in one of the cars that were at Vanessa's. It's not like she needs it now.

"That woman couldn't do a spell right now if her life depended on it." Gunnar balls up his fists. "As soon as I know she isn't lying about this being the location of the rituals, she'll be dead anyway," he adds.

"Just dying might be too easy for her. You wait until I find Aeson before you do anything," I demand, looking around at the empty alleyway.

We're at a crossroads, in the center of four dilapidated warehouses. All the buildings are tall and look abandoned for the most part. A few have overflowing dumpsters next to them, but I don't see any cars or activity to indicate anyone is using this place.

"Which one is it?"

"That one." Gunnar extends his hand and points to the farthest building on the right side. It looks the worst. The high windows are nothing but shards sticking up and out like crocodile teeth. There are even slats of wood missing high up on the building. Would they really use a place like this for something so important?

I step forward, but Grim braces his arm across my chest, stopping me. "Nemean, shift," he demands.

Calix doesn't argue, instead, he strips out of his shirt and tosses it onto the hood of the car the witch is sitting in. I storm over in his direction and get into his space, forcing him to take a step back. I don't stop until we're behind the car and he's out of the witch's sight.

Calix looks down at me, his brow furrowed. Then he looks at the car and a smile blooms on his lips, but he doesn't say anything. Instead, he inches a little closer and reaches for the fly of his pants. His nostrils flare as he drags in a deep breath.

He finishes stripping quickly and puts his jeans on the trunk of the car before giving me a wink. I stuff my hands under my arms and narrow my eyes at him. I don't like that I was just a possessive bitch, and he knew it.

Calix takes a few steps away from me, he's completely nude and looking pretty fucking good. He lowers his chin the slightest bit and it changes the features of his face, shifting from the hot motorcycle riding man, to something much more predatory, and fuck me if it doesn't make him even more appealing.

I watch Calix closely to witness his shift, curious if the process will be slow and subtle like it is when Gunnar hulks out or different. "You know I like an audience," he comments, while taking one more step backward. I nod my head, still waiting.

Calix's tawny skin seems to glow from within. I squint my eyes as a wave of golden light bellows out of him, and in its wake, I see a fully-formed, huge-ass lion with a golden mane, standing where Calix was. The small light show, which happened in a matter of microseconds, is the only evidence of his shift.

"Wow." I don't hide the awe in my voice as I take a step closer to him. My hand is already lifted, reaching out to touch him, not concerned in the least that he would hurt me.

"Wait." Gunnar steps forward. "His mane—stay away from his mane."

I let out a small snort. "I touch the baddies all the time, Kitten, I'm not worried." Calix steps back and turns to the side, as if he's presenting me with a safer option to touch. His flank is a golden bronze and looks smooth as silk.

Go ahead, Dami, I hear in my thoughts, and my eyes bounce up to meet Calix's.

"I am." I set my fingers into his fur and I'm surprised at how coarse it feels compared to how soft it looks.

You heard that? Calix's words filter through my mind.

"Yes, shush." I bring up my other hand and stroke over

Calix's side. "This is amazing." I hover my hand over his mane and let golden strands dance through my fingers.

"Okay, enough show and tell. Let's get this handled." Gunnar crosses his arms over his chest.

"Don't get pissy, Kitten. I like your freaky teeth, too." I step back and ball my hands up. He's right, though; I shouldn't have let myself get so distracted when I don't know what's happening to Aeson, or if she's even here.

I'll go ahead and see if there's anyone else around, Calix tells me, and I repeat his words to the others.

"I'm not really picking up anyone around here, but it could be the witches working wards. I never even realize they're there until I stumble into them. I might need to be closer to sense them," I admit, feeling a little useless.

"I'll meet you inside," Grim tells Calix, as I feel him open a portal. Before I have a chance to ask to go in with him, he's gone, leaving me alone with Gunnar and the witch in the car.

"Handy little trick you two have," I mutter dejectedly.

"Don't get pissy, Dami. I can think of several times your ability to kill someone without even touching them would be a nice trade-off."

I can't help but feel a little flattered, even though Gunnar is mocking me a bit. "I'm pretty badass," I agree with him.

Gunnar lets out a little chuckle, and he casts a sideways glance at me. "Do you really like my teeth?" He sounds unsure, like he thinks I might have been teasing.

"Hell yes, I do!" I turn to face him. "You don't know how many times I've wished that I could make my outside look like how I felt on the inside." Gunnar tilts his head and examines me. I feel like I've just given too much away, but I don't really regret it either.

Almost everyone I grew up around, the monsters I consider my friends, my family, all looked so different from me. All still beautiful, but they looked how I felt I should look: scary and unapproachable. Instead, I'm stuck in this human-looking body that doesn't always seem to fit right. I imagine it feels much like an adopted kid would feel when he looks at his family and can't find his red hair or any other markers that would make him feel like he belongs with them.

A loud roar splits the night air. "Think that's our sign?"

Gunnar reaches down and takes a hold of my hand. "There's no doubt that your beauty has edges, Damiana. One look is all it takes to be ensnared. Most are just too captivated to heed the warnings." He releases my hand and gives me a nod to walk ahead of him. "I'll stay with the witch, make sure she doesn't try to escape. Whatever's in there, you could handle alone, but holler if you need me."

Gunnar's words and his faith in me makes a funny feeling erupt just below my ribs in the center of my stomach. "I'll be right back," I whisper, then turn away to head toward the building, but stop and retreat back to his side. Without any warning, I lean up on my toes and wrap my arms around Gunnar's neck and hug him. It's a little foreign, but when his arms come around my back, I lean further into him and a calmness settles over me.

His chest expands once, and he tucks his head down until

his face is nestled in my hair. I step back without meeting his eyes, and mutter, "Be right back."

I jog over to the warehouse door with the feeling of Gunnar's eyes on my back. We must be at a rear entrance, because there's no handle: just a smooth, metal door. I pound my fist on it twice. I didn't even see how Calix got into the building.

I step back and look up, wondering if I could jump up to one of the windows, but the door opens seconds later, with one cloaked arm holding it ajar. "Thanks, Loverboy." I slide through the entrance, and I'm met with inky darkness. I blink several times, allowing my night vision to adjust.

I feel Grim as he comes up behind me and molds his front to my back. I don't miss the erection he's sporting, either. I snicker—he's like a randy teenager.

All humor evaporates when I hear Aeson's voice. "Come closer, and I'll wear your teeth for a necklace."

"Aeson!" I shout, and take a blind step forward.

"Shit! Get out of here, Dami. Hey you, kitty-bright! Yeah, you." Aeson is trying to draw Calix's attention.

"Why didn't you tell her we're here to help? Calix can't talk," I ask Grim, forging forward.

"I would have frightened her," Grim answers.

"Not if you lost the robe. I'm coming, Aeson. Where the hell are the lights?"

"She would know it was me even without the cloak, Damiana," he reasons.

I spin to face Grim. "Can you just get us there?" I'm even more eager now that I know she's here and okay.

Grim cups my cheek. "She's hurt, Damiana, and her pride won't allow her to ask for help." His lips whisper near my ear.

"Take me to her, she'll let me help." I swallow the lump in my throat.

The air shifts and I'm standing in an open room. A yellowish glow emitting from Calix's mane casts a slight radiance, but it's hard to make out anything that he's not near.

Aeson's tiny body is anchored to an altar-like table made of solid stone. Her tiny wrist and ankles are shackled with heavy iron chains. They must have been designed especially for her, unless it's some twisted magic that shapes them perfectly to the victim.

I choke on a sob but cover it up. "I know you're a kinky bitch, but come on, Aeson! Next time call a safe word, okay?" I find my way over to her side, and even my dark humor can't hide the fact that I'm near tears.

With my vision blurry, I grab hold of one of the shackles, and Aeson bows off the stone and lets out a hiss. "You shouldn't be here, Dami." She licks her dry, cracked lips.

I can't focus on anything other than her ripped shirt and the way she's half exposed. Please tell me that happened when she was fighting, not after they already had her tied up.

"How do I get these off," I inquire, sniffling and ignoring her.

Calix steps a little closer, and I see runes etched all over the table and the metal holding her down. "Is there anyone else here?" I pull the chain links with my hands, but they don't budge.

"It's empty." Grim takes his place at my side and gazes down at Aeson. Her eyes grow large for a brief second before she successfully hides her reaction.

"Do you know how to get these off, Loverboy?" My voice is soft, pleading.

"They won't come off, Dami, that's why no one is here guarding me," Aeson informs us.

"Calix, will you run out and get Kitten and the witch?" I wrench the chain in my hands as much as I can without hurting Aeson. "It's okay, honey, we'll get them off."

Aeson gives me a crooked smile. "I can't believe they got me, Dami. Three hundred years old, and I was lured by a witch." Her eyes close and I see her jaw tighten. "I'm going to lose my band. Who would want a leader that almost got sacrificed?" Her head lifts off the stone, and she pleads with her eyes for me to answer her question.

"Aeson," I put some heat in my tone, "suck it up! You fucked up—not even *your* gorgeous ass is perfect. Now shut up so we can get you off this table." I lean in closer with a steel set to my spine, and I whisper, "And I might even let you kill one of the bitches who trapped you here."

When I pull back, Aeson's lips thin into a flat line. I know —without her saying so—that she's ready. Just the promise of retribution is enough to get her to stop feeling sorry for herself and fight just a little while longer.

I hear Gunnar's heavy footfalls and the sound of him dragging the witch before I see them.

"This way," Calix urges them. He's shifted back to his human form.

"You better have clothes on," I growl.

"What happens if I don't? Do I get a spanking?" Calix jokes.

"Not one you'd like," I mumble.

Gunnar shoves the witch forward, and she stumbles but doesn't fall. Her eyes go to Aeson on the table, and they flash with greed and desire, before she looks to the left and her shoulders round in defeat.

"Unchain her," I demand.

The witch meets my eyes briefly. "I can't, not alone." The lie floats through the air and flutters against my skin.

"Liar," I accuse her, and take one menacing step toward her.

"Okay, okay." She looks around, like someone else might help her. "If I release her, will you let me live?" The witch's eyes dart all over the room.

I take a step back and raise my hands. "You have my word, I won't touch a hair on your head."

She bites her lip, as if she's considering her options. "You gave me your word," she confirms, while stepping closer to Aeson.

"I did." I nod in agreeance.

The witch moves even closer and blows out a heavy breath

of air. I don't trust her not to try something. I grab a hold of her wrist as she lifts her hands to place them over the altar.

"If you do anything, and I mean anything other than unlock those chains, I will keep you alive for years and feed off your screams. Do you hear me?"

The witch blinks and swallows heavily, before finally giving me a jerky nod. "Go ahead." I release her, and she rubs the spot I was just holding and stretches out her fingers.

CHAPTER 26

The witch closes her eyes, and I feel the oiliness of her coven's tainted magic bubbling up from her. The stench of rot permeates the room, and I cover my nose with the back of my hand.

Everything about this is wrong: it feels evil, tainted in a way none of my baddies are. I glance around the room, expecting some shadow creature to be clawing its way out of hell to witness this.

Whatever power she garnered from this magic isn't worth whatever it's doing to her soul, or to the souls of the unsuspecting seekers that they've been using as a filtration system. I step closer to Grim, and he tucks me to his side, while Calix closes in from the opposite edge.

The clink of the metal releasing is loud against the stone

table. Aeson sits up and bounds up the woman's still outstretched arm.

Before the witch can do anything—such as fling the Brownie off—Aeson is at her ear, and the whispering starts. I can't hear what she's saying—not that I would want to. See, Brownies aren't just deadly, skilled assassins. They're also able to infiltrate your thoughts and then implant an idea in your mind—like a maggot that eats away at anything and everything—until that thought is all you know.

The witch's eyes widen as she reaches up for her chest, but her face slackens while Aeson works deftly to untie a cord from around the witch's neck. A metallic ping resonates off the concrete floor as her protection charm hits the ground.

A scream tears through the air as the witch starts clawing at her arms. Aeson hops off the woman's neck and falls to one knee on the table, rising quickly to stand tall. I know the move cost her. I can see the raw bands on her wrist where she either tried to free herself from the shackles or the metal burned her skin with magic.

Small crinkles around her eyes tell me she's fighting to hide her pain, but I don't let on that I know.

Gunnar moves forward, and we all stand witness as the witch digs into the flesh of her arms, until she's covered in blood and gore. "I'm tired of her wretched screams, does anyone have a knife?"

I pull one of the tiny blades Aeson gave me from my belt. It's small in my hand but looks huge in hers as I hand it over to my friend. She looks down at the blade and tests the weight, hefting it in her hand a few times and tossing it up. When it lands in her open palm for the third time, Aeson fists the blade and lunges at the witch. Her scream gets cut off midway and a gurgle bubbles up as the knife is buried in the hollow of her throat.

Without further ado, the witch crumbles to the floor in a heap. The reek of rot comes swiftly again.

"You ready to get out of here?" I step closer to Aeson. I know her pride won't allow her to ask me to get her off the altar, so I pick her up and set her on the ground before she can object.

"What's with the army?" Aeson strolls across the warehouse as if she hasn't a care in the world, ignoring every ache and pain I know she's experiencing. I can't even imagine what other tortures she's had to deal with. Who knows what else the witches did to her?

"Oh, so, new development." I stop and the guys halt behind me. I turn and do a Vanna White reveal, waving my arms out wide. "These yummy morsels are my guardians."

"Fated guardians." Calix waggles his eyebrows.

"You're the bleeder." Aeson tilts her head to the side. "A Berserker, huh?" She eyes him openly with mistrust. Eventually, she moves on. "You must be the Nemean." She jerks her chin at Calix, but purposefully ignores Grim.

"In the flesh," Calix answers cheekily.

"Do you know what happens to Berserkers and Nemeans that cross Brownies?" Aeson stands tall, even though they have to look down to see her. Before anyone can answer, she does. "They die, just like anything else that gets on my bad side. You feel me?"

I click my tongue and smile. "Isn't she the best?" I grin at the guys, having gotten her meaning right away. She's threatening them for me.

Aeson sighs as a little weariness comes over her features. "I knew you guys couldn't stay away forever. Some of you never did." She cocks up one eyebrow at Grim.

"Mind your own business, Brownie," Grim mumbles, sulking.

"You sound like a two-year-old," Aeson points out.

Calix snorts but covers it with a cough. "Why don't we get out of here?" he suggests instead.

"I'm not up for a quick transport." Aeson lifts her hands.

"I have Betty. You can ride with me."

"I'll catch a ride with you, too." Calix tips his chin up. "I'm sure these two can manage to get home on their own," he adds.

"Is teleportation envy a real thing like dick envy is? I'm really feeling a bit left out at the moment." I pose my question to Aeson as we start walking back toward the entrance.

"No need to envy a dick, I have one ready to use," Grim pipes up, completely serious.

Aeson and I both stop and look at each other before I start cracking up. "He's a horny motherfucker." I giggle.

"Him?" Aeson looks back at Grim and starts shaking her head in disbelief. "He's like asexual or something, everyone knows that." Her eyes travel over Grim. "Such a damn waste too. Why do you think I've been trying to get you to fuck so many people? I knew he would show up soon enough, and your pussy would shrivel up and die."

I erupt in laughter again. "Maybe he was, but not anymore. I gave him a little of the good stuff." I scrunch up my nose and point down, not that anyone would be confused about what I'm talking about.

"Well, hot damn! That's a story I need to hear." Aeson resumes walking a little slower than her usual pace. I keep my strides unhurried as well. "What about the others?" She peers over her shoulder, assessing the guys. Calix and Gunnar each wear a sour expression.

"I'll tell you later; I haven't gotten to sample them yet." I snicker and push the heavy door open. Betty is parked right where I left her, under the single light angled down from one of the surrounding warehouses.

"What the hell are you waiting for?" Aeson moves around me and climbs into my car. I know better than to offer my help because she would see it as a sign of weakness, so I pretend to think about my answer, looking up at the sky.

"They wanted commitment-type shit. You know that gives me hives." I shudder. I don't even care that the guys are listening to every word I'm saying.

"Dami…" Aeson smiles over at me after climbing on the center consul. "That shit is happening whether you accept it or not. I say fuck them and enjoy every second." Her eyes close slowly as she lets out a heavy sigh.

"Yeah, I think I'll have a hard time ditching them at this

point. I mean, they know where I live." I'm only joking and, as fucked up as it is, I actually like having them around.

Calix slides into the passenger seat and Grim steps into the space between my open door and leans down. "Head straight home," he commands, to which I raise an eyebrow.

"We'll be waiting, unless you want me to follow you the entire way." Grim raises his brow, challenging me right back.

"I will, but only because I was anyway," I scoff.

"Good, see you soon." He stands and adjusts his dick in his pants and, because the car is so low, it's right in my face. Aeson lets out a tinkling laugh, and it brightens my soul.

I slam the door when he steps out of the way, shaking my head at him while rolling my eyes. "He needs to get that dick of his under control."

"Or you do," Aeson quips, chuckling.

"That works for me too." I snicker with her. "Let's head home."

"You have no idea." Aeson leans her head back and shuts her eyes as we pull away from the warehouses. Her head lands on my shoulder within the first five minutes of the drive. She lets out a soft snore, telling me how deeply she's sleeping. A sense of pride comes over me. To fall asleep like this, she must trust Calix and me to take care of her and not hurt her. Otherwise, she's been awake the entire time she's been missing and she's just too exhausted to fight it anymore.

On the drive back home, I don't speed as I usually would. I want her to have a little time to rest before I have to wake her up. But I also need to get word to her people that she's safe;

they deserve to know. And no matter what she said, I don't think anyone will abandon her for another band of assassins.

The house is lit up as we pull up the drive. I see several small shapes darting from the eaves when I cut Betty's engine off. Aeson sucks in a deep breath and her eyes bolt open. It takes her several seconds of looking around before her little body relaxes.

"There are people here for you. Do you want me to send them away?" I question, my voice soft. Aeson smooths her dark hair back, looks down at her mangled shirt, and curses. It's the first time she's even acknowledged that it's ripped.

"Want me to get you something else?" I offer, knowing I don't have anything that will fit her, but hell, I'll rip my shirt off and tie it around her if she wants me to.

"No, I'm good." Aeson's eyes harden a bit, and the line of her mouth thins to a slash. She rises up and brushes her hands down her curvy hips, straightening her back. "Out, Nemean, and stay out of my way," she orders briskly.

Calix, who's been quiet for most of the ride—I'm sure to let Aeson sleep—opens the door and slides out. He holds it open for her as she hops down into the seat then onto the ground. Her eyes scan the area as if she's expecting someone to jump out and attack.

I'm instantly on guard. I slam my door and look for whatever has her on edge. A few shadows slowly dislodge from the shelter of the house. They're small, so I know they're Brownies, but Aeson is acting like she thinks they might try something, like make a move against her.

I will kill them all where they stand, Charmed or not.

"Boss?" I hear a masculine voice call out, but it's tinged with worry.

"I'm here," Aeson answers. I don't know how, but those two words convey so much. Her little shoulders round down, and she's not worried anymore. I don't know if she expected someone else, or if she didn't know how they would respond to her, but a lump forms in my throat.

I look away so as not to encroach on the moment. Calix rounds my side of the car after shutting his door.

"Aeson?" the same man asks, but this time his voice is rough with emotion.

"I'm okay, Enzi." Numerous shadows shift until I can see several Brownies darting over from the house.

"We searched for you," another voice chimes in.

"I know. It was the witches—they had the building spelled," Aeson tells them. More rushed questions are asked, along with several 'are-you-sure-you're-okays,' before Aeson shuts them down a little harshly. "I said I'm fine."

"Got it, Boss." The men all fall silent.

I step around the car and see six Brownie males watching her. The one closest has a scowl on his face as he assesses every inch of Aeson.

"Did you want to come in?" I offer.

Aeson takes a deep breath and focuses on me. "I need to get back to the den, make sure I don't need to kill anyone who tried to take my place in my absence. I'll come back tomorrow at nightfall, and we can discuss the next move." I don't her doubt words, and I know she needs time to show her people she's okay, too.

"We'll be here, Aeson." I want to tell her if she needs anything to ask, but I don't. She would probably see it as a sign of weakness, especially now. "Come on, Calix, I can see Gunnar's big head peeking out the window. Hope he's not trying to be stealthy."

"Good thing he has brute force on his side, huh?" Calix adds, hopping up the stairs until he's at the door and holding the screen open for me.

Grim unlatches the door and steps to the side. It's a little unnerving having them here before me. The lights are all on, illuminating the large lion head stand at the entrance.

"Want me to park Betty?" Calix hooks his thumb over his shoulder. I peer out into the darkness. Aeson and her men are long gone.

I contemplate doing it myself, but the house is warm, and I've already started to kick my shoes off. Should I just leave her in the drive? "I guess," I mumble. I'm too lazy to do it myself, and she doesn't deserve to be left out.

Gunnar closes the door with Calix still standing on the porch. I blink over at him. "What?" He looks around. "It was letting the heat out."

I snort and shake my head. "You just closed the door right in his face." Gunnar just looks at me. "How did the Brownies know Aeson was here? I thought I would have to find a way to contact them." I change the subject. Clearly, I'm the only one that thinks it was rude.

"I sent word to Samson to let them know." Grim stays close on my heels as I head farther into the house. I hear Betty's motor purr to life and the garage door open seconds later.

I curl up in the corner of my sofa. Grim takes the seat next to me, grabbing my feet and placing them in his lap. Gunnar sits across from us.

"I'm guessing you didn't get much out of Vanessa before she did whatever she did that made her insides liquify?"

"Regretfully, I did not," Gunnar grates out.

"And I let Aeson kill the witch at the warehouse," I murmur, sighing and letting my head fall back.

"I still have a few men who were stationed with her who didn't get caught up in the skirmish at her house. Hopefully, one of them will have more answers, or at least be able to lead us to more witches who do have the answers." Gunnar squeezes the armrests.

"So that wasn't her entire coven?" I prop my head on my arm as Grim uses his thumbs to make tiny circles over the soles of my feet. My eyes want to fall closed, but I force them to stay open.

"No, thankfully. I'll have to go through the house, see who's left and find the next in command."

"When?" I ask, as Calix leans his frame against the doorway, having returned from parking Betty.

"Now. I just wanted to make sure you got here safe." Gunnar rises.

"I'll come with you." Grim pats my feet and I want to pout because my little massage is already over.

"That's not necessary." Gunnar crosses his arms over his chest.

"It's not, but that's what's going to happen. You need someone who can sense magic, and that's me. Damiana needs to rest." Grim stands, facing off with Gunnar.

Gunnar's scarred lips tighten as he glares at Grim. "Fine, but stay out of my way."

Grim dons his heavy black cloak, concealing that made-for-sin body beneath it, the edges lifting as if compelled by some unseen breeze. "I will ensure Damiana's safety," Grim responds briskly.

"And that is the only reason you're coming." Gunnar's chest heaves after he's finished speaking. It must be killing him to accept help. I have no doubt that he could handle the situation on his own, but Grim's right. Having someone with him who can sense the magic and the taint it leaves behind is smart.

"The testosterone is getting a little thick in here," I mutter.

"You stay here." Gunnar points his finger at Calix, who raises his hands in surrender. Gunnar's shoulders ease after he delivers the order and Calix agrees. I don't think he comes up against people that don't follow his directions very often, and having Grim around, who seems to make up the rules as he goes, isn't helping.

"Aeson will be here at nightfall." I yawn, it must be close to dawn.

"We'll be back by then." Gunnar moves to stand in front of me.

"Okay." I furrow my brow, wondering what he needs. His hands ball up at his sides. "What's up?" I peer up at him.

"Make them leave," he tells me, while tilting his head in Grim and Calix's direction.

"What, why?" I purse my lips. "I thought you were leaving with Grim."

"I would like a moment alone with you," Gunnar growls out through his teeth.

"Ah, okay, I guess." I shift to the side, and give Grim and Calix a questioning look. "Can you two give us a second?"

Grim reaches for my chin and plants his lips on mine. He slides his tongue across my bottom lip and lets out an appreciative hum, before pulling back just enough so his lips ghost over mine as he says, "I don't need to be alone with you to claim you." He releases my chin and steps away from me, not even bothering to look back, but my eyes trail after him the entire way.

Gunnar lets out an aggravated huff and looks over his shoulder to confirm both men have left. "He really likes pissing me off."

I think about Gunnar's words, but I don't find any truth to them. Grim seems closed off, but I don't think he's ever allowed himself to feel real emotions. "I don't think he does it on purpose, Kitten. I think he likes you and Calix." I reach for Gunnar's arm and pull until he's sitting next to me on the couch. "Just like I don't think you hate him as badly as you want to." I glance at him from under my lashes, watching him for a reaction.

His face sours, but then he looks away. "He's a useful ally," Gunnar admits. I want to smile, but I hold it in.

"What did you need?" I pat his thick-as-a-tree-trunk thigh —it's as hard as one, too.

Gunnar licks his lips and looks down at mine quickly. His hands ball up again. "Well…" He looks out at the empty room.

Oh goodness, he's acting as nervous as a whore in church. "Gunnar?" I prompt again.

"Well, he ruined it," he snaps, and jerks his hand toward the door through which Calix and Grim had gone.

"Ruined what?"

"He knew I was going to kiss you, and he did it first." Gunnar juts out his jaw and crosses his arms.

"I see, well..." I roll in my lips, thinking this is definitely the wrong time to laugh at him. "You could still kiss me, then you would have the last kiss instead of the first." I give him a slight shoulder shrug. It's no hardship for me.

Gunnar turns his head slowly to look at me, a rare smile blooming on his lips. "You're right," he acknowledges, and leans forward to place his lips tenderly against mine. He gives me several open-mouthed pecks, almost nibbling on my lips. It's the last kind of kiss I would expect from him. I figured he'd be rough and demanding, but he's the complete opposite. I curl my knee up to get a little closer to him on the couch. I can feel the scar across his lip as he presses his mouth against mine, and a shiver of desire has a shuddering breath leaving my lips.

This at-home sexy time is awesome. I don't have to worry about my clothes getting stained from grimy walls and hands. I can actually be comfortable. I lean in a little more and part my lips, inviting him to take the kiss a little deeper, and he obliges.

A throat clears just as I reach up and feel the stubble on his jaw under my palm. I don't break the kiss right away. I linger, giving him little pecks. When I do pull back, I stare up at Gunnar. I make a show of licking my lips. "See? Not so bad."

Gunnar's eyes are heavy-lidded as he returns my stare. "Point taken," he murmurs softly. Swallowing, he adds, "Stay out of trouble until I get back," in his normal rough, demanding tone.

I give him a mock salute, but say, "Not my boss, Kitten." Gunnar growls then stands up. He glances over his shoulder before walking out the door and past Calix—he must have been the throat clearer.

I wink at Gunnar and give him a goodbye wave.

"Take your time!" Calix calls down the hall.

"Shut up!" Gunnar barks. Calix and I both snicker.

CHAPTER 27

The television is on, but I'm not even pretending to watch it. My head has been on Calix's shoulder for the past five minutes. I've fallen asleep and woken up twice already.

I stretch out my legs and groan. "I'm going to bed."

Calix hurries to grab the remote and turn the TV off. "Finally," he mumbles, and pulls me up to stand.

"Why didn't you say anything if you wanted to go to sleep?" I question around another yawn.

"Who said anything about sleep? I was giving you time for a catnap." He tows me behind him, rushing until he reaches the bottom of the stairs. My steps are a little sluggish; I really am tired.

"If you're looking for more than a soft mattress," I tug my

hand back and cross my arms over my chest, "I'm going to need some motivation." I arch one eyebrow at him.

Calix wastes no time ripping his shirt off over his head and kicking his shoes off. His hands go right to the button on his jeans, and he pushes them and his underwear down his hips. His dick is already halfway hard, and it jerks up when I look at him, growing even harder as I stare.

"Impressive. I like your style." We both knew it wouldn't take much. "But I'm going to have to give you a low score on creativity."

Calix steps over to me after kicking his jeans off his feet—all confidence and warm skin. "Creativity is for guys who don't know how to use what they have." He steps up even closer and places his lips near my temple. His skin is hot, burning up. I lean in and I feel his hardness nestled between us.

"You've got a point," I concede, as I wrap my arms around his neck. In one swift move, Calix has his arms locked under my butt, and he hoists me up. I take advantage of the extra height, leaning down to kiss him roughly.

Calix makes his way over to the stairs and climbs them without putting me down. Once he steps foot in my room, he lowers me to the floor slowly. His dick ends up trapped between our bodies again. Reaching out, he plants his hand against the wall like he needs it to steady himself.

I step back as I reach down to take him in my hand. He's hard and heavy against my palm. I tug a bit and watch Calix's eyes close.

"Go over to the window," Calix orders, slitting his eyes open and watching me. A smile tugs at my lips.

"You mean this window?" I saunter over to the same window I attached my dildo to.

"Take your clothes off for me, Dami." It's not really a request; his words are spoken too gravelly for that.

I lift my top off and reach behind me to remove my bra. Calix's hand fists around his cock, and he gives it a few absentminded strokes.

I shimmy out of my jeans, bending all the way over so my ass is right up against the glass to remove the pants from my feet. When I stand, I have them in my hand, but drop them in a heap next to me.

"Beautiful," he mutters to himself.

"Want to know a secret?" I whisper.

"I want to know your every secret," Calix answers quickly.

I step to the side so Calix can see the window and run my hand over the frame. "The day I first saw you as a lion, Nemean," I amend, "was the day I met you at the club. That next morning, with the window, I was thinking about you. It was your cock I imagined I was riding."

Calix takes a heavy step forward, his nostrils flaring. "If I hadn't been so fucking mesmerized, I would have scaled the wall to get inside this room. Do you have any idea how much I wanted you?" It's not really a question.

I lift my arms. "Well, here I am. What are you waiting for?" Calix is on me in the next second. He spins me around roughly and fists the back of my hair. My back bows and the bottom of my ribs hit the wall in front of me. I grind my ass back against him.

The air in my lungs comes out in a whoosh as he flattens me against the wall. His shoulders are so big, they almost curl over mine as he surrounds me. Calix reaches down, grabs the inside of my thigh with his free hand, and lifts, so my leg is butterflied up against the wall.

I don't get any warning, any preparation, before he pushes himself inside me. I tip my forehead to the wall and lift up on my toes. Holy shit, he's big, but fuck if I don't like the rough friction of him sliding inside me. Once he reaches a certain point, he glides in smoothly, my body having already been prepared for his, merely needing a few seconds to catch up.

Calix releases my hair as he places his forearm on the back of my neck. "Is this what you imagined I'd feel like? Thick and hard, giving your hungry, wet pussy everything I have?" He punctuates his words with slow thrusts of his hips. I can barely breathe, let alone move, but my body is singing.

"Better," I pant. "This is so much better." Both of my hands are on the wall as I push back against him. Calix makes a rumbling sound and slaps his hips against my ass. I bet if I bent over, he'd go even deeper. My eyes roll back in my head at the mere thought. I don't know if I can handle more of him, but fuck, I'm going to enjoy trying.

"Years," Calix pants into my ear. "I've been waiting years to feel you around me. Damn near lost my mind thinking about what you would feel like wrapped around my dick. But this…" His words trail off and he starts bucking into me harder, faster. "Nothing could prepare me for this." He moves his forearm off the back of my neck and slowly releases my leg, until both of my feet are flat on the ground. Calix reaches for my wrists and tugs them behind me and out.

I lean back a little and steal a deep breath. My heart is pumping double time as he continues to crash his hips into me. Calix bites the side of my neck where my shoulder begins, hard, and a soft whimper falls from my lips as I squirm into his bite.

"Don't move." Calix's order comes out muffled. His teeth are still pinching into my shoulder. My body goes still at his command, as does his, and I start to pant. The hands on my wrists loosen as he gently trails his fingers up my arms, until he's cupping my breasts in his hands. The slight pain in my shoulder transforms as he rolls my nipples between his fingers and begins fucking me again, slowly this time.

Calix's teeth unlock from my shoulder and I feel his rough, wide tongue slide over the spot. "Hey, Chomper, a little warning next time," I mumble with a huff.

"Why?" Calix pumps into me hard. "Your body doesn't lie, Dami. Your pussy was about to break my cock off, you were squeezing me so tightly." Calix licks up the side of my neck and jerks me back. "Just like that." He chuckles darkly into my ear when I squeeze him again.

I pinch my lips closed and tighten my inner muscles. "You mean like that?" I swivel my hips and tilt my ass back toward him. Calix groans and his hands slide down to my hips. I may like to be fucked, but I like to do the fucking, too.

I push away from Calix and spin to face him. "I didn't say I didn't like it. I said to warn me first."

Calix licks his lips and bobs his head eagerly. "Okay." He reaches for me, his eyes wide and wild like he thinks I'm going to deny him now.

I let him come to me, let him slide his hand over the curve of my hip and draw me close. His lips go to the same shoulder he bit, and he kisses me gently, reverently. I walk us back-wards until the bed hits the back of my legs.

Calix climbs over me as I lie back on the bed. I keep my eyes on his as his gaze roams all over my body. When his eyes finally meet mine, he leans down and kisses me. I slide my hands into his hair and lean up to meet him stroke for stroke with my tongue and lips.

It's not too long before Calix is grinding against me. This time he doesn't rush; he waits until I grab the head of his dick and run it up and down my pussy.

His eyes squeeze shut, and he makes that rumbling sound again. "Okay, Chomper, you gonna be a good boy?" I croon into his ear, while still rubbing him over my clit.

"Fuck yes," he blows out.

I guide him back inside me, and we both groan in response. Calix places his forehead on mine, his eyes wide open, as he pushes deeper. Fuck, if it doesn't feel like he's peering at my soul with those hazel orbs of his. I'm tempted to close my eyes, but I don't. I let him look. Let him see all the dark places inside me, all the jagged edges formed over the years from rejection and loneliness.

I expect him to look away, to be the one to break the stare, but he doesn't. Instead, he tips his chin and places a soft kiss on my lips with his eyes still locked on mine.

My breathing starts to speed up even more as the desire to run from him fills me. I don't want to feel this; I don't want to get to the point of no return, the point where it will rip my heart out if he leaves.

"Damiana," Calix purrs, and cups my cheek. "Where'd you go?" His forehead lands on mine again, and his breaths mingle with my own. I'm fighting so hard not to let this mean anything, but it fucking feels like it does. Why does it feel like he's got his hand around my fucking heart instead of stroking my cheek?

I reach up and grab the back of Calix's hair in a fist. "If you're fucking with me…or waiting until you've seeped into my bones before you leave me, I'll make you beg for death. Do you hear me?"

One corner of Calix's lips tilts up, but it's not a real smile; it's doleful at best. "Dami, we're not going anywhere. I'm sorry we're part of the reason you don't trust us yet, but you will. I promise you will."

I release his hair with a flick of my fingers and click my tongue, angry that I even let him see how much he's already affecting me, and what's worse? He knows it's not just him, but all of them.

Calix averts his gaze from mine, but he glides his hands up my body, not letting me forget that he's inside me—in more ways than one. My stupid body caves to his touch the same way my stupid heart already has. I curl my hips up to meet his.

Calix takes that as a sign to start working his hips against mine again. I let the heady rush of pleasure help me forget about all the emotional bullshit, and give myself permission to just feel. I reach for his ass and dig my nails into him, urging him on. "Hold on," he mutters, and wraps his arms under my back. He rolls us until I'm the one on top, looking down at him.

Using my knees planted into the bed, I lift myself up and down, working myself over him slowly. The change in position is welcome, but my body still needs to adjust to the deeper invasion. I lean over his chest, and the shift puts some much-needed pressure on my clit. Calix's hands skim my back and ass as he lifts his hips from the bed, rocking into me.

My breath catches as the first tremble of an orgasm hits me…I'm on the precipice. My hips start to move faster, chasing that euphoria I know is right around the corner. "That's it, take it, Dami," Calix purrs, tilting his head back and exposing his throat.

His words spur me on, and I bounce against him. "Oh, fuck," he breathes, and the tendons in his neck go taut with tension as he clenches his jaw. Watching him under me—seeing how much I'm affecting him—pushes me past the edge until my orgasm crashes over me. I cry out and my hips move in a slow dance instead of frantic movements as I ride him, drawing out the pleasure.

Calix lurches upright into a sitting position and locks his

arms around my back. I feel him jerking inside me as my inner muscles milk him. I shudder when his fingers tickle down my back and he cups my ass, dragging me closer. His forehead is rocking against my collarbones as I gasp, trying to catch my breath.

He plants soft, sweet kisses across the tops of my breasts, only interrupted by his heavy breaths. I wrap my arms around his head and let my heart begin to slow, but it still feels like it's beating too hard. After several long moments, Calix lifts his head from my chest and peers at me. His eyes are soft, lazy, as he searches my face. I swallow, wondering what he might say.

He swats my ass with a loud crack, and I jump, slightly startled. "Amazing. Want some hot cocoa?"

I snort at his simple question, but I'm happy he isn't making a big deal about us having sex and isn't going to get all mushy on me. "Nah, that would take way too much effort." I start to lift off Calix, and his mouth drops open and a sigh escapes his lips.

"I'll make it," he offers, his voice all husky as I crawl off the bed to head to the bathroom.

"I have a feeling I'd be asleep before you even got back, so don't worry about me. If you want something, go get it," I tell him over my shoulder.

Calix lies back and knocks his head against my fluffy pillows. "I got everything I need right here." He lifts his head up again and watches me. "Or I will in a few minutes, anyway."

I tap my fingers against the door, closing it a little so I can clean up. For my sanity, I choose to ignore his comment.

Coming out of the bathroom, I move to my side of the bed. Calix is spread out naked, looking like some fuckable dream come true as his gaze stalks me to my bedside table where I flip off the single lamp.

I don't bother with jammies. Why should I when I have all that golden skin to keep me warm instead? The room is so silent that I can hear my breaths as I pull back the sheet Calix didn't bother to get under. I lick my lips. I'm going to sleep next to him: just he and I in my bed. Somehow, it feels as if allowing this goes even further to prove I'm making reckless choices when it comes to the guys.

But I'm too greedy to give it up. I want to know what it feels like to sleep next to him and the others. I want to know if waking up next to him, after a full day of slumber, will chase away some of the loneliness I inevitably rouse with every night.

"Why are you standing there, Damiana?" Calix's smooth voice whispers through the room.

I climb into bed, using that as my answer. Calix doesn't give me space; instead, he forces his legs under the sheet and slides his body right up against mine. I find myself holding my breath as he nuzzles his nose near my shoulder. I feel his tongue make a lazy lap over the place he bit me. It's still a little tender. I hold my body still, but my pussy tightens.

"Sleep, Dami," Calix murmurs, and I let out my pent-up breath.

It takes me several minutes, but as my breathing evens out, my body relaxes, and my eyes naturally fall shut.

"Oh, my fucking God! What are you doing?" I sit up and squint my eyes. I can see a sliver of light piercing the heavy curtains. A hand tightens over my lap, fingers digging into my thigh. I look over to see Calix, his lips slightly parted, and his eyes closed. How the hell is this racket not waking him up? I rip back the sheet and stomp out into the hall to find the source of the noise.

A few doors down from my room, I hear a grunt and the pounding start up again. I tilt my head to the side, and my mind fills with thoughts of what that rhythmic pounding added to the grunts could be, and I'm about ready to rip someone's dick off. Unless it's Grim and Gunnar. I bite my lip—shit, that might be hot. I shake away the thoughts and tiptoe down the hall. Gooseflesh pebbles the skin on my arms and thighs as my nipples tighten. Why the hell is it so cold out here?

More pounding, more grunts. I slap my hand against the door and shove it open. Gunnar spins around, flicking his hair and sweat off his brow as he does. I search the room, coming up empty, so my eyes go back to the man in front of me. His chest is heaving, all those delicious scars covering his naked torso glistening with sweat.

I bite my lip as I take in the rest of him. Loose black pants sit low on his hips. He has black tape banded across the tops of his feet, separating his big toes from the others. Something behind him finally catches my eye. A swaying, black, heavy bag is suspended from a short length of chain attached to a large, silver circle embedded in my ceiling.

"That's new." I give Gunnar a meaningful glare.

"I have…to take off…the edge," he pants, his eyes trailing over me. I'm as naked as I was when I went to bed, so he gets an eyeful.

I feel Grim's presence at my back. "You look lovely," he tells me from behind, like I'm decked out in a fancy dress.

I spin, always ready to accept a compliment. "Why, thank you, sir." I let my eyes travel over him too. He looks amazing, as usual, in jeans that fit just right, bare feet, and a loose black shirt. "You ain't so bad yourself."

I hear a thwomp behind me, so I turn back around. "You look delectable too, Kitten, but I have to say, I'm not happy you woke me up," I chastise him.

"You've been sleeping forever," he whines.

I peer over at Grim with a furrowed brow. "What time is it?"

"Three twenty-two," he rattles off without looking at a watch.

"That's oddly specific." I turn back to Gunnar. "However, that is not, in fact, forever." I cross my arms under my breasts, and it lifts them. Gunnar's eyes darken. "Have you slept at all?"

"No, that animal was in your room, stinking it up," he growls and hits the punching bag again.

I click my tongue at him. "Big boys share, Kitten." I wink and saunter out of the room, trailing my fingers across Grim's chest as I do. "I'm taking a shower," I announce loudly, as I walk down the hallway back to my bedroom.

Calix is still sleeping soundly, curled over on his side. A girl could get used to waking up to them being here with me—not the pissy-ness from Gunnar, although I do kind of like that, too. I like not being alone and ignored. I'm excited to get out of the shower and find out what Grim and Gunnar learned last night, even more so to see what today might bring.

As I step under the spray, the door pushes open slowly. "Damiana?" Grim calls softly.

"Hmm?" I lean my head back and let the hot water seep into my long hair.

"May I enter?" he asks just as softly.

"Yes. Why are you whispering?" I whisper back to him. The door closes with a soft click, and Grim materializes in front of me, naked.

"Whoa." I jump back and my foot slides against the tile. I reach out to stop myself from falling on my ass, and Grim grabs a hold of me, pulling me into his chest. His hard dick pokes into my tummy.

"Dude," I say in warning, "I'm not used to having someone pop up in the shower with me."

"I asked if I could come in." Grim looks down at me, clearly confused.

"I thought you meant the bathroom, I didn't… never mind." I shake my head, giving up on the explanation.

I glance down at the persistent nudge of the tip of his dick, then back up at him with a raised eyebrow. "Giving you a hard time, is it?" I try to keep a straight face at my pun.

It flies right over Grim's head, which makes me want to really laugh. "Stars, every time I see you or even think about you, it's throbbing for attention." Grim shakes his head, exasperated.

I can't hold in the laughter, it erupts from my closed lips and splutters across his chest. Reining it in quickly, I try for a sympathetic look. "Want to fuck around? Might as well put it to good use, am I right?" I lift my arms in a 'what can you do' gesture.

"Yes, please," Grim murmurs with relief.

I run my palm up Grim's thigh. "Now I know why you were whispering," I say quietly, letting my breath fan over his chest and my wet body slide against his.

He nods and swallows. I place a soft kiss against Grim's upper chest. He smells good, something altogether his own. My mouth dampens as I lick the beads of water off his skin. Grim lets out a breathy huff, and I grin. I continue to work my lips and mouth lower and lower, until I'm bending at the waist and letting my tongue slide up the matching lines that angle down to his groin.

Grim grabs my hair in a fist. He might be new to this, but his instincts work mighty fine. I lower myself to my knees and spread my legs a little, dropping my ass down to my calves. The tile is hard on my knees and shins, but worth every second as I watch his thighs tremble before I even touch him.

I blow a breath across him and his hips jerk in response. Wrapping my fist over him from the top, I lift his cock to point up, then flatten my tongue and lick him from his balls up to his tip, releasing each finger so he can feel my tongue on every inch. I linger on the underside of the tip, moving the end of my tongue up and down to bounce against him.

His fist tightens and he pushes forward, eager to be in my mouth. I lick a circle around the head. "Hey, Loverboy?" Grim's eyes drop to mine, wild. The fire is already burning across his gray irises. "Am I the only one who's ever tasted you?" I give him a long lick.

Grim lifts his head in a jerky nod. "Take me in, please." His eyes lower as he bites his bottom lip.

I already had every intention of doing just that, but since he asked so nicely, I'll make sure he's seeing stars before I'm done. Grim widens his legs and leans back ever so slightly as soon as I close my lips around him. Knowing he seems to love sustained pleasure, I hum deeply before doing anything else, just keeping him between my lips.

Grim groans, and I smile around him, then get to work. I relax my lips and mouth, making sure I can take him deeply, and tighten around him as I pull back. I deliver alternating pressure irregularly, so he doesn't get too used to anything. I listen to his every breath, his every groan, to gauge what takes him close to the end, then bring him right back.

After several long minutes, I increase the pressure and cup his balls gently. Grim bends his knees, and his thighs really start to shake. I know he's close, so this time I don't stop. I work my mouth over him harder until his hips jerk forward and he spills down the back of my throat. I don't swallow often, but for him, I will—any damn time.

I release him while he's still hard and wipe the edge of my mouth. Grim is staring down at me with his lips parted and a look of awe on his face.

I peer up at him a little shyly. I know I'm good, but that look on his face just cemented it. He said I was going to crave him; well, he's right, but he'll yearn for me, too.

Grim lowers his palm, offering to help me stand. I accept his hand and climb to my feet. "Feeling better?" I tease him a little.

Grim nods his head, answering wordlessly, while he continues staring at my mouth. Lifting his hand up, he brushes his thumb across my bottom lip. I nip the tip, and he drags in a deep breath. "I'm going to fill you up. I'm already inside you," he mutters, while still tracing my lips as if he's mesmerized by the sight.

I tug my head back. "I was kind of hoping you had a round two in you." I look down, noting that he's still thick and hard. "Looks like I was right." I step up close to Grim. He's throwing off almost as much heat as the shower and, with the door closed to the bedroom, it's like a sauna in here now.

Grim's eyes dart around as his hands land on my hips, drawing me closer. "The Nemean is still in our bed, I'll be right back."

"Wait," I chuckle, "we don't need the bed, and what were

you planning on doing with Calix? He's probably still sleeping."

"I would have dropped him somewhere else," he tells me pragmatically.

I pat Grim's chest. "You can't just go dropping people in unexpected places when you feel like it."

"Why not? I would have collected him when we were done. He's in our bed," he adds, like I'm the one not seeing reason.

I smirk and drag my finger over Grim's lips, shushing him. "We don't need the bed, Grim," I insist, then lean up on my toes and seal my lips over his.

CHAPTER 28

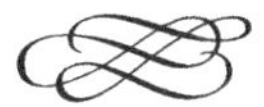

Gunnar is in the kitchen, slamming around plates and containers of food. "What did that chicken do to you?" I snark, knowing his attitude has nothing to do with the chicken. He narrows his eyes on me, and I glower right back at him.

Gunnar slams his hands onto the countertop and leans forward slightly. "You said share," he barks.

"I did," I agree.

"You're not sharing!" he shouts.

"If you mean allowing you to sleep with other people, that's your choice." I try for indifference and shrug my shoulders, when on the inside I really want to claw his eyes out for even suggesting it. Some part of me, no matter how deeply hidden that part of me is, understands that what I'm asking isn't right or fair, but a bigger part of me knows they're mine.

All of them are mine, and should be treated as such. I'm a fickle bitch—what can I say?

I cut my eyes to Gunnar to see what he's thinking. His chest is puffed out, his lips are screwed closed.

I try to hold my tongue, but I'm vibrating with anger on the inside. "You'd better hope I never find out though, Kitten." I lick my teeth. "'Cause if I ever so much as see you with someone else, I will kill you, cut your dick off, and mount it to my fucking mantel," I snarl.

Gunnar's face smooths out almost immediately at my threat, but it doesn't last long. Within seconds, he's back to scowling at me. "You. Said. Share." He pauses between each word.

"We just went over this." I enunciate each word slowly.

"I'm talking about sharing yourself." Gunnar pushes even closer to me. Only the counter is separating our lower bodies. "You've been with Death twice." Gunnar holds up two fingers as if it's some kind of evidence.

"What?" I scoff and snort at the same time.

"You heard me." Gunnar glares at me.

"Are we counting, seriously?"

"I've made her come five times." Grim pulls out the stool next to me, completely calm, as if he didn't just walk onto a landmine. Gunnar's nostrils flare, and his shoulders bunch up again. "We're good at sharing," Grim adds.

I roll my lips in and my eyes bug out. He did not just say that. "How often did you hang out with…" I circle my hand, encompassing me and Gunnar. “People, friends?” I scrunch up my face, not sure I chose the right words.

“I visited you all the time.” Grim turns to face me and takes a bite out of a huge red apple. I blink at him.

“Okay, anyone else?” I urge him.

“Well…” Grim squints and looks off into the distance. “There’s Samson, and all the others you call monsters.” He takes another bite.

“They are not your friends: they’re terrified of you—there’s a big difference,” Gunnar pipes up, just this side of belligerent.

Grim shrugs. “And?”

I plop my elbows on the table and circle my fingers over my temples. A little of the aggression Gunnar always seems to bring out in me evaporates. “I got you, Gunnar, and I’m sorry. I should balance things better. I’ll try.” I look up from the counter to find Gunnar watching me.

After a few short seconds, one side of his lips tips up in a tiny smile. “You said you’d kill me.”

I roll my eyes, of course that’s what he wants to talk about. “Don’t make me test the theory.”

I walk out of the kitchen then, head high, but heart heavy. Maybe this isn’t right. Maybe I should just choose one of them. It was easy to think I could have all of them, but I never really thought about how they would feel having to share me. I rub at the ache that forms over my chest. And that’s how Calix finds me, standing in the hallway massaging my own tit.

"Need a hand?" He holds up both of his and acts like he's honking squeezy horns.

I drop my hand and plant it on my hip. "Come on, Sir-Sleeps-A-Lot. We need to find out what happened last night."

I walk back into the kitchen, and it's like nothing even happened. Gunnar is digging into a big plate of roasted chicken, and Grim is still sitting on his stool, like he knew I was coming back.

"Stop being weird," I tell him defensively.

"How am I being weird?" Grim's brow pinches.

"I don't know; you just are." I drag my stool back and take the seat next to him, while Calix sits on the other side of me.

"So, how did it go last night?" Calix asks, reaching for a piece of chicken from Gunnar's plate. Gunnar swats at his hand before he can get there, but Calix pulls back before Gunnar can connect.

"Here." Gunnar holds up a piece to him instead. "Ask."

"Thanks." Calix tears into the chicken.

"We went through the house. Almost everyone was dead or close to it." Gunnar eyes Grim.

"I didn't know I wasn't supposed to kill them." Grim lifts his hands up in a 'what can you do' gesture. "Next time tell me, or mark them or something. One human is just like the other."

I look at Calix and shake my head. "We were able to locate two of my men," Gunnar continues, as if uninterrupted. "I have an idea on where to find this Antonio, but nothing concrete. He'll probably run as soon as he hears about

Vanessa and her coven, especially if he knows we're on to him."

"We should go back to the warehouse." I sit up straighter as the idea takes root. "We probably should have never left, one of them was bound to come back for Aeson." I look around to see if they agree.

"I have someone watching the warehouse," Grim confirms, "but it seems unlikely that anyone will return. I don't think someone who was able to do these types of rituals for years and not get caught is stupid enough to leave a Brownie completely unattended."

"What do you mean? Aeson was there alone. We saw her."

"Vanessa," Gunnar answers. "Whoever taught her the ritual probably didn't expect her to start picking off the Charmed on her own."

"That makes sense, it would explain why they got sloppy all the sudden," Calix reasons.

"Nothing else fits. It's the only thing we've come up with." Gunnar leans against the counter, the empty plate abandoned in front of him.

"Well, then, how the hell are we going to find this Antonio guy?" I look to them for an answer. This sleuthing shit is new to me.

"We follow the money." Gunnar nods his head. "Since this entire thing started to unfold, I've been examining everything I can to find out what involvement Vanessa had in this. Nothing seemed out of the norm until about two months ago." Gunnar pulls his phone out of his pocket and taps on the screen a few times, eventually turning it around so we can see an email account with only a few emails.

"What's that?" I scoot a little closer to get a better look.

"History of money transfers, set up to look like they were paid to vendors, but I know for a fact there hasn't been any new vendors at the club and she sure as shit didn't pay Vega Holdings to do any renovations." I cast my gaze over Gunnar. How deeply involved in the club and Vanessa's business is he?

"You sure seem to know an awful lot about someone that you were charged to monitor." I continue to watch him for a response. "I thought you hated her."

"I didn't always." Gunnar looks down at the ground before raising his head, but he doesn't meet my eyes.

"So, what? You were fucking her?" My question comes out bitterly.

"A long time ago." Gunnar glances over at Calix like he might be helpful, but Calix smartly keeps his mouth shut.

"How long ago?"

"Do we really need to get into this, Damiana? I mean, you had someone between your legs less than two months ago," Gunnar spews defensively.

"You're right, I did." I nod and agree with him. "But I didn't know about any of this shit, so your bringing it up now is a low blow, *Gunnar*." I spit his name, and he jerks his head back like I've slapped him.

"I—" He starts, but I lift my hand, cutting him off.

"It doesn't even matter right now." I shake my head. It's not like I didn't expect any of them to have a past, but something about knowing he was with Vanessa makes my blood boil.

"So how do we 'follow the money,'" I question, mocking his words.

"I have a Pixie looking deeper into her financials and trying to figure out where the money went to," Gunnar admits, sounding a little defeated.

"Fine, whatever. Aeson should be here soon." I scoot off the stool and head up to my bedroom, since that's always where Aeson pops up.

I'M SULKING. I didn't even know I sulked until I met these three. I don't like it.

The tiny tap of heels alerts me to her presence, and it's only because she wanted me to know she was coming that I do.

"Hey, Dami." Aeson saunters in looking none the worse for the wear, except her eyes—she can't hide the shadows in her eyes.

"Glad to see you showed up." I give her a little jab.

"What can I say? People needed killing." She hops up onto the edge of my bed after scaling my footboard. "A girl's got to do what a girl's got to do." She shrugs her small shoulders, not really giving an explanation why she was late.

"Everything okay?" I ask in a quiet voice. Aeson's not one

to tell me too much about what's going on in her life, but I want her to know she can. Especially now.

"Fine, thanks to you and those three downstairs." Aeson sits on my bed with her legs out in front of her, crossed at the ankles, and lets out a heavy sigh.

I give her a few minutes to relax. Eventually, Aeson draws in a heavy breath and turns to face me. "Thanks for coming for me, Damiana." When I go to tell her it's not a big deal, she cuts me off by lifting her hand. "Whatever you're about to say, don't. If it weren't for you guys…" She pinches in her lips. "I probably would have rotted on that table, Dami, no shit. No one would have found me. So, thank you. I owe you a debt."

"You don't owe me anything, Aeson, you're my friend, my family," I tell her with sincerity.

A moment passes between us, two women both so different, but not at all unsimilar. She comes here to escape, to not have to be the toughest or the bravest. I cling to our friendship because she doesn't treat me like I'm crazy, and because she's my escape—escape from the loneliness that eats away at me.

"Want to help us find the guy that taught Vanessa the ritual?" I offer when the conversation feels like it's getting too heavy.

"You have no idea how badly I want to." Aeson's dark eyes harden.

"We got this. As long as it takes," I promise and lift my knuckles to her. Aeson knocks her little fist into mine and agrees.

"As long as it takes."

CHAPTER 29

Aeson and I are giggling as we head back to the kitchen. This room is getting more use than it ever has.

"Brownie." Gunnar tips his chin at Aeson.

"Berserker," she responds coolly.

"Where's everyone else?" I swallow my pride and force my tone to be even. Being angry at him isn't helpful, especially right now. I don't know why his being with Vanessa feels like such a betrayal, but it does. Maybe it's because it was so easy to believe that he didn't like her; I truly believed he hated her. Perhaps that's just it: they say the line between love and hate is nonexistent, and I worry the line was blurred for him.

"Death and the Nemean are in the other room. Can I talk to

you for a minute?" Gunnar requests, pushing his hands into his pockets.

"For?" I plant my hands on my hips.

"I'll go find them, Dami." Aeson abandons me. Traitor.

Once Aeson clears the room, Gunnar steps a little closer to me, but I hold my ground. "I thought you might give me a chance to explain." He peers down at me, his face not giving away his emotions, so I can't read him.

"About you and Vanessa? It's pretty self-explanatory," I mutter glibly.

Gunnar huffs in frustration. "I'm trying to talk to you. Why are you making this so difficult?"

"Is that a real question? I didn't think so," I answer for him.

"I haven't so much as touched that witch since well before you were even born," Gunnar snaps.

I slash my eyes in his direction. "I hate her. I've hated her from the moment I laid eyes on her," I growl.

"Most people do. It's only the ones who want something from her who act like they like her," Gunnar replies smoothly.

"But you did," I accuse.

"I was part of misled minority who like her, the ones that don't see through her façade for what she really is until it's too late," Gunnar admits, as he reaches for my hand and tows me along with him, pulling out a stool for me to sit on.

"So, what, she used her magic on you?" I mock, while he sits then adjusts so his knees are on the outside of mine.

He snorts. "I wish I could say it was a spell, but it was just plain, fucking stupidity." Gunnar pushes his hands down his thighs.

I lick over my bottom lip. He's fighting to remain calm, and it helps ease my aggravation. That's, like, the third time I've noticed that when he gets all riled up, so do I. I file the information away for another day, another time.

I move over to the stove and start pulling out my pot and milk, hoping the normalcy of the routine will calm me. After a breath of silence, Gunnar continues, "I'm not the only one charged with watching the witches. There are a few Berserkers left, but not many." Gunnar lifts his heavy shoulders.

"We are shuffled around—you can only stay in one place so long—and I ended up with her territory. She was nice to look at and accepted me for what I was." I slam the pot down on the stove. "What we had was only physical, and it didn't last long."

I keep my back to him so he won't see how badly I want to kill her all over again. "But like I said, it ended a *long* time ago."

"Fine. Are you done? Got that off your chest? Feel better?" I resent the fact that I even had to know.

"Not if you're still pissed." Gunnar sighs. "I didn't know you, didn't know anything about you," he reasons, and my shoulders fall.

"You're not the only one who ever got lonely, Damiana." The low way he whispers the words tells me he's not trying to make a dig at me; he's just speaking his truth.

I pour the milk in the pan. "Do you want some?" My question comes out with a little sass, so I clear my throat and try again. "Some hot chocolate."

"If you're willing to sha—If you don't mind." Gunnar cuts off mid-word and changes what he was about to say.

I lift one shoulder casually. "There's enough. Will you grab the chocolate from the cupboard?"

Within seconds, I feel his presence beside me. "Want me to chop it up? I'm pretty good with a knife."

I set down the spoon and turn to face him. He gives me his undivided attention. I almost look away, but I force myself to hold his stare. "Hey, so, I'm not great with this stuff. Not that it's an excuse, but the jealousy, it's new, too. I never cared enough to be jealous before. What I'm trying to say is…I'm sorry. I probably overreacted." I wince.

Gunnar's shoulders ease. "I'll get the knife." He lets my lame apology slide. He's nicer than I am by a mile. I probably would have made him grovel. We work together making the hot cocoa. I make enough for all of us, even Aeson. It takes me a minute to find the thimble she usually uses.

Evidence that other people are staying here is all over the house: my plates are in different places, the dishwasher is always running, and even their scents are permeating and changing the house. I look around. Grim's apple core is sitting on the counter where he left it, and there's a pair of discarded socks balled up near the door. Instead of making me edgy, it gives me a sense of peace.

"Ready?" Gunnar asks, holding a flat tray with four mugs and Aeson's thimble.

"I am." I nod my head, thinking about more than just going to the living room to join the others. I'm ready to hope for more.

"Oh man, I smell chocolate," Calix comments. "That has to be good, right?" he mumbles, as we near the living room. I click my tongue. Nosy bugger. They must have known what we were talking about.

"We can hear you," I singsong acerbically, as I move into the room. Aeson is perched on the back of the sofa just a couple cushions down from Calix, while Grim is in one of the chairs. I glance around the room. It always seemed like I had too much furniture, but now it feels like I need more.

Calix pats the empty cushion next to him while he's angling his neck to look around me. His eyes light up a bit when he sees Gunnar holding the delicate tray in his hands. I watch his lips move as he counts the mugs.

I make my way over next to him and sit down gingerly so I don't dislodge Aeson from the back of the sofa, but she hoists herself up and moves over to the arm of the couch instead. Gunnar sets the tray on the coffee table, handing me the largest of the mugs, then looks down at the tiny thimble, then his hand. I know he's wondering how he's going to pick up the petite thing with his massive paw.

"Here, I got it." I give Aeson hers, while Gunnar takes one for himself before he claims the last remaining chair. "Thanks." I nod to him while blowing across the top of my cup and taking a sip. "Help yourselves," I tell the other two.

Gunnar takes a few minutes to bring Aeson up to speed on

the Antonio issue, and how he has the Pixies working to track the money.

Aeson sucks in a breath; it passes her lips like a whistle. "I bet that's not a cheap job. Pixies are known to gouge."

Gunnar shrugs. "They're the best with tech."

"Have you heard anything yet?" Aeson tilts her head.

"I told them to gather everything they could and give me a report by midnight." Gunnar glances over at the wall clock. "I'm not expecting a location tonight, but you never know; they've had all day."

"Mind if I stick around until you get word?" Aeson looks over at me.

I scoff, "You don't need to ask—you're always welcome." Aeson quickly scans the guys' faces, assessing if the sentiment holds true with them, too. It'd better.

Silence falls over us; this group dynamic is new, uncharted. I'm the bridge between them, so I feel like it's my job to span the gap—only I don't know how to do small talk. "How about that weather?" I chuckle dryly.

Grim tilts his head. "What weather?"

Calix repositions himself on the couch. "I worked with the Io band once." Aeson turns her head and focuses on him. "Ever met them?" Calix inquires.

"Sure, we've crossed paths a few times. How'd you end up working with them?" Aeson studies Calix.

"We had a rogue Thunderbird. He lost his mate, and…let's just say shit went bad real quick."

"I can imagine. What happened to the mate?" Aeson

smooths her hand down her thigh where I know she keeps a knife. It is not the first time I've seen her do this tonight.

"We're not really sure; it was several years ago. He felt her die and lost his shit. I'm not sure anyone ever found out." Calix looks off into the distance.

"Thunderbirds are pretty high on the predatory chain. I wonder what happened to her?"

"I know, that's why we called in Io. We needed to get him grounded to find out what happened to her and to get him to listen to reason." Calix pauses. "We wanted to take him down without hurting him, but none of us could do it."

Aeson sits forward a little, pulled in by the story. "How did Io manage it?"

"Shit, it took us a day to even make contact: Io is one cagey motherfucker." Aeson chuckles at Calix's response. "But, truthfully, I'm not even sure. I was there, and I have no idea how they got him to come down."

Aeson rolls her lips in. "How many were there? Brownies, I mean?"

"Had to be a dozen—maybe more."

Aeson nods her head like she has a better understanding now.

"Do *you* know how they did it?" Calix asks her.

"I could tell you, but then I'd have to kill you." She gives him an evil smirk, which causes Calix to chuckle.

I bet I have an idea. It's the same thing Aeson did to the witch at the warehouse, only on a much larger scale. Birds in general have acute hearing, as long as the frequency isn't too high. I bet with that many Brownies, they were able to whisper on the wind. I don't open my mouth to divulge my secret, though. I would never betray Aeson's trust like that.

"What happened to him?" I question.

Calix looks down, his face sobering. "He didn't make it. Even after they got him grounded, he ended up killing three bears. We had to put him down." Silence falls over the group. Calix's attempt at connecting with Aeson backfired.

"I collected them both." Grim strums his fingers on the arms of the chair.

"Do you know what happened to her?" I whisper urgently.

"I don't. She was far too upset for me to get any information from her spirit, but I have a suspicion now."

"Yeah, I bet that suspicion has everything to do with this bastard Antonio," I seethe.

"We'll find him, Damiana. He messed up, and we know what he's up to. It's only a matter of time now." Gunnar tilts his head left and right, I can hear his neck cracking and popping from here.

"I just hope no one else dies before we do."

Gunnar's phone rings at one minute to midnight. We've all been waiting for this call. He lets it ring once before placing it against his ear. "Speaker phone," I hiss.

Gunnar's lips tighten into a thin line, but he obliges me, setting the phone on the low table between all of us. "What have you got for me?"

"This line isn't secure," a male voice declares through the phone.

Gunnar looks around, his eyes lingering on Aeson before he responds, "I'm with my people," and leaves it at that.

"Okay, Antonius Wood, goes by Antonio. His birth certificate has his parents listed as Helena Wood with unknown as father. Born thirty-four years ago. But we've traced him back almost seventy; it's hard to find many records before that." He pauses, and I hear the sound of papers flipping.

"It took some digging, but he has at least seven shell corporations—one being the Vega Holdings. There could be more, but with the expedited time frame, that's what we've got so far on his businesses. We have several properties listed, most of them on the east coast. He's recently acquired a residential property within twenty miles from your current location."

"Twenty miles from here?" I interject "What city?" The line goes quiet.

"He won't answer you. You're not signing the check," Aeson supplies. Gunnar repeats my question and the man replies.

"Lakeview."

Curses fly from most of us. "He's probably gone for sure now." I throw my hands in the air. He had been right under our noses.

"Wait, let me think." Gunnar looks down at the ground. "We don't know that he's aware of Vanessa's death yet, or even if he was still in town. If she was siphoning magic without him, he might have already moved on."

"Or maybe she was just going behind his back like the two-faced bitch she was," I snap.

"Text me the address when we get done here, but what else?" Gunnar ignores my outburst.

"I'll send it over through the secure email we set up, along with all the other addresses we found. We've picked up little things here and there through the network, but we haven't had enough time for anything solid yet. Give us another twenty-four hours and I'll have something decent."

"You get anything concrete on his location, I want to know immediately," Gunnar orders.

"I have everyone on this. If he's within a hundred miles, we'll find him; just give me time."

"Send me those addresses." Gunnar smashes the end button on the phone.

I get to my feet. "We're going to check out the place, right?"

"Yes," Gunnar answers, then turns to Grim. "If you bring the Nemean and Damiana, I can manage the Brownie, she's small enough not to disrupt my rift. That's assuming you want to come," he addresses Aeson.

"Not even the devil himself could keep me away."

Gunnar nods, already suspecting the answer. "Meet us at the witches' house. We'll go from there." His phone vibrates. Gunnar looks down and taps a few times against the screen. "I got it."

"Come here, Omnia." Grim beckons me forward and I

wrap my arms around his torso. Calix doesn't need to be told to join us; I feel him grab on to me from behind.

Gunnar moves to stand in front of Aeson near the couch. Her hands are on her hips as she glares up at him. "I don't like this any more than you do, Brownie," he tells her. "You can always change your mind and not come."

"Just shut up," Aeson demands.

Gunnar lets out a low growl. "If it wasn't for you being Damiana's friend, I would crush you."

"You would try and fail," she deadpans.

"Knock it off, you two." I scowl. "Someone might think you're flirting."

"With the bleeder? *Puh-leeze*." Aeson scans him up and down.

"Shut up and stand still, or I'll leave without you," Gunnar grates through his teeth.

I blink as the smell of old blood and rot hits my nose. I'm standing in Vanessa's foyer. The bodies are all gone, but the scent of death still lingers.

Calix releases his hold on me and scans the area. Grim keeps one hand around my back as I take another look around.

"Don't get all high and mighty. If I'd had the time, I could have found a door. I let you bring me along. Don't forget it." Aeson's voice floats over to us. "Damiana!" she shouts.

"I'm right here," I call back.

"The bleeder is an asshole," she comments, while making her way into the foyer.

"You're no ray of fucking sunshine, either," Gunnar barks.

Aeson gazes around, seeing for the first time all the blood and gore we left behind. “Sorry I missed the party.” She grins up at me, her eyes as dark as the sneer on her lips.

“What’s the address?” I ask Gunnar, hoping the little, dick-measuring competition is over between him and Aeson for now.

“It’s on the other side of town, near your old place.” Gunnar looks up from his phone.

“Well, shit. Good thing it’s late—we wouldn’t want to chance a run-in with dear ole mummy and daddy.” I raise my voice to a proper woman’s tone just like I was taught, mocking them.

“You should have just said that in the first place. I could have been there like this.” Aeson snaps her fingers. It’s loud for her hand being so small.

“No, this is better. Who knows what kind of security they installed after they sent me away.” I turn to Calix. “Any vehicles left out there?”

“Yeah, the issue will be finding keys. I had to search the bodies for the ones I took yesterday.” He shrugs.

“We could always call a ride share?” I suggest.

“I can hotwire a car.” Aeson plants her hands on her hips like we’re insulting her for not assuming.

“I’m very familiar with where you grew up, I can take us there,” Grim volunteers.

“Not inside, right? You can get us out front or something?” I open and close my fists. I always said I would never go back to that place.

Grim pulls me in close again, and I feel Calix wrap his fingers over my shoulder when Aeson grumbles, "Ah, shit."

This time when I blink, I'm standing out front of my childhood home. Surprisingly, the lights are still on. When I look up, it doesn't seem nearly as tall or imposing as it did when I was a child.

It's still a garish white with matching tall columns that stretch across the entire front. It resembles the façade of the Pantheon far more than it pretends to be a home. I hate this place.

I speak past the lump forming in my throat. "Address?" I want away from this place and the memories it brings up.

"Two houses that way." Gunnar points to the left.

"That's…that's really close. Doesn't that seem weird?" I whisper, as I turn to follow the direction of Gunnar's arm. The wide driveway is lined with unfamiliar cars. No wonder the lights are still on; they must be having a party.

For just a moment, I wonder what they told people had happened to me. Did I die in some tragic accident? That would be my mother's style—she always loved attention. Maybe they told them I was studying abroad, found a husband in France, and they visit me twice a year. Maybe they just pretend I never existed, which would be the truest, most accurate of the three.

"Dami, are you coming?" Calix tugs my fingers.

I blink away the memories and look around, seeing the house for what it really was—a prison, complete with solitary confinement. A place designed to make me lose my mind. I think about how much I isolated myself over the years, how I continued to punish myself, just like they did.

I bend down and grab a large white rock in my palm, weighing it over and over. I release Calix's fingers and turn at the same time, throwing the rock as hard as I can through one of the long front windows.

Someone inside screams. Several other voices rise in question, asking what happened. The milky white curtains pull back to reveal my mother with her icy blonde hair, staring out at me. Her eyes round as her mouth drops open. I can't tell if the look is fear or horror.

Grim walks up to my side and my mother's eyes bounce to him then Calix. She swallows—definitely fear.

I turn my back on her and walk away, grabbing each of the guys' hands as I do. I'm mad at myself for even letting it get to me. I should have walked away the moment we got here. Some small piece of me feels like I let her win.

CHAPTER 30

I expect someone to rush to the door and demand we stay put until the police arrive, or for the cries of outrage to continue, but neither happens. I'm sure that had something to do with my mother.

The rage simmering under my skin boils hotter when I think of her. Grim and Calix guide me to the shadows of the house we came here to investigate. My breathing is ragged as I let my back fall against the short brick wall separating the homes.

"Would you like me to kill her?" Grim whispers near my temple. So damn seductive.

I want to laugh, but I just shake my head slowly. "She's not worth it." In truth, I want something worse for her. I want her to experience what it's like to always be left out, to always be alone. I don't know if that will ever happen, but if there's any justice in this world, it damn well should.

Gunnar's mouth is turned down in a heavy scowl. "I think we should paint the walls with their entrails."

I sigh. "I appreciate the sentiment, Kitten, but we have more important things to do than worry about two fucked-up people."

After a brief moment to collect myself, I nod my head and confirm, "I'm ready. Let's go find this witch."

Aeson scales the wall to one of the upper windows. People always assume windows on the second and third floors are too difficult to get to. We could have easily broken out a window, or even a door, but we want stealth on our side.

I send out my senses, but the house is a total blank to me. It doesn't feel like anyone has lived here in a long while.

We're all crowded around the back door, waiting for Aeson to unlock it, but my heart starts beating faster with every second that passes. She should be here by now—what's keeping her? I lean back and look up at the window she disappeared through.

"What's taking so long?" I hiss. Calix shakes his head, but doesn't have an answer. "Open that door," I order.

I stand back as Gunnar lifts his left leg and pulls back his arms, he delivers one hard-as-fuck kick to the edge of the door, right near the deadbolt and knob.

The door slams open and bangs against the wall behind it. I poke my head in as fingers wrap over my shoulder, holding me back. "Aeson!" I shout, completely giving up on subtlety.

"Fuck me, I'm up here. Motherfucker," she snarls.

I duck my shoulder, pulling away from Calix's hand, and step past the threshold. It's like stepping into a vat of quicksand—my breath is stolen from my lungs and I'm rooted to the floor. I turn my head in slow motion and warn, "Trap." I can feel the heaviness of a spell trying to coat my skin, but I imagine it sloughing off like water on a windshield until I'm able to draw a deep breath.

Gunnar's face would be comical if I were in any other situation. His mouth is contorted into a half scream, and his eyes look like they're about to bulge out of his head.

Time snaps forward, and I hear the tail end of Gunnar's shout to stop. "Well, fuck." My feet are still fixed to the ground, but I'm able to talk, able to breathe.

"You could have warned me!" I holler up to Aeson.

"I'm trapped. This motherfucker," she shouts.

"Calm your tits. I'll get out of this in a minute and come get you."

"You can't just go rushing into things," Gunnar chastises me from the other side of the door.

"No shit, Sherlock. I get that now. How about telling me how to get out of it and saving the lecture for another time?"

Gunnar's lips move, but no words come from him. "As soon as you get out of it, I'm going to take you home and lock you in your fucking bedroom!" he roars, leaning into my face.

I narrow my eyes at him and dare, "Try it."

"Okay, okay." Calix pushes his way between us, making sure not to pass the threshold with his feet.

"This is just a ward, Dami; it's not designed to keep people out, but keep them in." Calix meets my eyes and gives me a small nod when I focus on him.

"I've broken wards," I murmur.

"Yes, you have, baby. This one might be a little stronger, but it's not stronger than you."

"You're damn right it's not," I seethe. I think back to the club, the way it felt like I was trudging through water. I remember using my hands to move myself through it, physically.

"That's it," Calix purrs when my right foot slides a millimeter. "Keep going," he encourages.

A grin tugs at my lips. "Easy peasy, motherfucker." I keep shedding off the heavy feeling surrounding my ankles and feet, until it feels like if I just step out of my shoes, I'll be completely free. And that's exactly what I do.

My toe touches the tile floor on the other side of a circle I can feel right at the entrance. I crouch down and run my hand a few inches above the ground to familiarize myself with its energy.

I jump up and bounce on my toes a little. I'm not going to lie, breaking his ward has my blood singing in my veins. "I'm going to get Aeson."

"Wait!" Gunnar shouts, then takes a deep, calming breath when I do, in fact, freeze. "Getting yourself out and getting her out are two totally different things, Damiana."

"I'll have to do it." Grim appears next to me. "I don't want you in here alone anyway."

"How will you get her out?" I furrow my brow.

"I'll have to cross her."

"What?" I take a step backwards.

"You said we couldn't come to the other side, that we wouldn't come back." My voice is hushed, speaking words I don't want to say.

"We don't have any other choice, Damiana. We don't have a witch to help us. I doubt one would be powerful enough anyway, unless it was the caster, and I don't think he would remove the ward," Gunnar answers for Grim.

"What will happen to her?"

"She'll be bound, body and soul, until I untether her." Grim lowers his chin, staring right into my eyes.

"You act like that's a bad thing." I glance at Calix and Gunnar on the other side of the door.

"Omnia, there are times when death is a release. If she were to be captured and tortured, she would never die, no matter what they did to her. Do you understand?" I lick my lips. "I will give her the choice. I can cross her and bring her back, or…" Grim leaves the rest unsaid.

"Oh, she's coming back." I cross my arms over my chest defiantly. "If I have to reach into the other side and pull her out by her hair, she's coming back."

"Aeson is older than you know, Dami, let her make the decision," Calix tells me softly.

"Aeson!" I shout up the stairs. "We're coming." I stare into Grim's eyes. He's the only hope I have of keeping my best friend, and I just got her back. Please let her want to come back.

I take slow, measured steps behind Grim, since he insisted on leading. I don't mind. I'm too lost in my own head to really pay attention anyway. If I'd been paying more attention before, I wouldn't have stumbled into a ward or let Aeson fall into another trap.

Grim pushes open the door to the room I can hear Aeson cursing from. I cover my mouth to hold in my gasp, she's not just trapped with her feet on the ground. She must have landed in a crouch when she jumped down from the window. Even her hand is plastered to the floor.

"Hey, bitch." I straighten my back and try for an unaffected smile. She'll see right through it but appreciate the effort.

Aeson blows out a heavy breath, the air pushing her hair back from her forehead. "You're either my lucky charm, or the universe is trying to tell me something, Dami." Her voice is uncharacteristically serious.

"We all have bad weeks, Aeson. This one is definitely my fault; I'm the one who asked you to come along."

Grim skirts around me and forces Aeson to look at him. I've noticed the way she avoids him, but I just figured she, like the others who visit me, are a little frightened of him.

"Brownie." I swat Grim's arm and give him a mean-mug. "Aeson the Brownie," he says slowly, while watching me. I nod. He turns his attention back to her.

Aeson licks her lips. "I got no business with you, Reaper."

"Unfortunately, you do. I can offer you a choice." Grim spreads his hands and a small rift forms, one of his portals.

Aeson swallows. "What choice is that?"

"I can cross you and bring you back, but you will forever be changed," Grim states somberly.

"Or?" Aeson raises her chin as much as she can while being trapped against the floor.

"Or I just cross you, no coming back." He releases the portal, and it snaps closed.

"But what about..." Aeson's dark eyes lock on mine, asking me for help.

"I don't think I can break the ward, Aeson. I didn't break the one I was trapped in downstairs. I just slipped out of it." I shrug my shoulder, failing to come up with a better explanation and feeling like a failure that I can't save her.

Aeson looks away and swallows. "This motherfucker is really getting on my nerves," she growls. Her head falls forward, and she stays quiet so long, I almost start pleading with her to let Grim bring her back, but I keep my mouth shut.

"What kind of 'changed' are we talking about? Some zombie shit?" Aeson finally lifts up her head.

"No," Grim tells her, kneeling near her on the ground. He explains how he'll have to tether her soul, how she couldn't die until he collected her.

Aeson sucks in a breath. "No wonder your name is only whispered." She stares at him with a look of fear and wonder.

"Aeson," I call, then roll in my lips. I won't ask her to stay, but I'm sure my face is saying everything.

“I suppose I’ll need to stick around. I can’t have this asshole ruining my reputation.”

I let out a squeal and hop closer to her. In my excitement, I almost trip over Grim and land right next to Aeson in the stupid ward. Grim reaches back and bars his arms across my waist, his fingers biting into my hip.

“I only have so much patience, Omnia. If I have to watch you in another snare, I will probably lay waste to every witch I see, and that would grow tiresome.”

“Sorry,” I singsong. “He’s so sweet,” I whisper to Aeson.

“Oh yeah, he’s a fluffy ball of sugar,” she deadpans.

Grim stands and ushers me with his body to take a few steps back. “Wait here.” He plants his hands on my shoulders and squeezes.

“I will—I won’t move.” I make an X over my heart. Grim leans down and kisses me softly.

As he turns back to Aeson, I feel his portal open and the rage and anger boils out. I’m not tempted by it anymore, not even a slight twinge of hunger. Most likely it’s because I consumed a soul just a short time ago.

The portal opens wider and my hair blows back from my face. Grim steps closer to the ward and reaches for Aeson’s tiny hand that isn’t planted on the ground. “It’s your choice,” he reminds her when she hesitates.

Aeson squeezes her eyes closed and reaches her hand out. As soon as the tip of her finger touches Grim, her body crumples to the floor, her foot no longer rooted to the spot. Thankfully, the arm that reached for Grim is just past the circle. I lift my foot to go pull her free, then remember my promise.

I glance around the empty room, waiting for the portal that disappeared seconds after Grim gathered Aeson's soul to reappear, but nothing happens.

I lick my lips. "Grim?" I call him a few times, growing louder each time.

"What's wrong, Damiana?" Gunnar shouts from downstairs.

"Grim and Aeson. They're not back yet," I holler.

I can't take my eyes off Aeson. I feel a prick at my eyes. She's so still, so silent. I can't even see her face.

"Grim?" I call again, but this time it's a choked sob.

"I'm going in there," Gunnar warns.

"Fucking wait a minute, she's okay," Calix tells him. "Damiana, he'll be back. You know he'll be back."

"But what if she changed her mind?" I wring my hands together.

I feel the portal open again, only this time, it feels like it's pulling the air from the room. My feet start to slide, and I circle my arms trying to catch my balance. Some part of me knows I do not want to be pulled into that portal.

"Oh shit!" I look around for something to grab on to, but there's nothing. The bed makes a screeching sound as it drags a few inches closer to the forming rift.

"Oh shit what?" Gunnar barks. "What the fuck is happening up there?"

I see the tip of something silver pierce the tumultuous

gray fog from the other side. With a quick slash, Grim's scythe rips open the place the portal is forming, and he pushes his cloaked arm through. He steps out, his tall, lithe body rounded down, as if the weight of the world were on his shoulders.

The portal snaps closed as Grim jerks his scythe to the side. I take one step forward, watching Grim, but also looking for Aeson.

Grim pushes the hood back from his face with a slow hand and his eyes jerk up to mine. The fire that usually burns there is extinguished. He's left looking utterly exhausted and spent.

I take another step, my arms reaching out as if I would catch him if he were to fall. "Careful, Omnia," he cautions in his layered voice, but it's as low as a whisper.

"Pull the Brownie from the snare, but don't touch the circle," he instructs me. I move to take another step toward Grim, almost forgetting about Aeson. This cost him—I can see the toll.

"You must do it now," Grim orders, leaning against the shaft of his sickle.

I force myself to head toward Aeson's body. Bending down and being very careful, I tug on her tiny, cold hand, dragging her lifeless body across the floor until it clears the circle. I make a sound in the back of my throat that could be a whimper, but I don't acknowledge it.

"That's good." Grim drops to his knees next to me with no finesse—he just falls. He reaches out the same finger that he used to gather Aeson's soul and touches the side of her face.

Grim's eyes fall shut as his back bows and a silent scream forms on his lips.

Too afraid to touch him, I start to shake. I feel helpless as I watch his head finally slump forward onto his chest and his hand fall away from Aeson.

"Grim," I whisper. He doesn't make a move or respond. "Grim." This time it's more urgent, but he still doesn't answer me.

Aeson gasps on the floor, and her body spasms once. I should feel a swift sense of relief as she takes her first breath, but it's not there.

"Grim!" I shout his name this time, grabbing the cloak over his chest and shaking him. "You better get your ass up right fucking now, Loverboy. I mean right now!" His head lolls as I shake him.

Aeson stirs on the floor, coming to her feet slowly. "What the hell just happened?" She looks at Grim, whom I'm now holding up, then back at me.

I ignore her to wrap my arm around Grim's back and grunt as I hoist us both up. Thank fuck he didn't fall all the way to the floor. "Stay the hell away from any entry points and get back downstairs."

I drag Grim's body next to me, trailing behind Aeson. "You weigh a fucking ton," I grumble, after making it out of the room.

"Somebody better talk to me!" Gunnar insists.

"Keep your pants on, bleeder," Aeson grouses, as she makes her way downstairs. I stop at the top and lean against the wall. I don't know how I'm going to get us down without breaking both of our necks.

"Grim, please wake up," I beg him in a whisper. "I really want to go home. You can have big spoon, and I'll even let you fall asleep with your dick inside me. Please, just wake up." He doesn't stir, and I start to panic.

"I need help," I call down. "Please, help him." My eyes are leaking. I can feel the tears running down my cheeks, but I can't stop them. We're trapped in the fucking house alone and I'm not strong enough to carry him downstairs.

"Tell me what's happening, Damiana?" Calix asks, his voice calm.

"Um, Grim, he's…he's not waking up…and I can't get him down the stairs." I sniffle a few times.

"Don't cry, baby," Calix croons.

"I'm not crying!" I shout, sobbing.

"Okay, okay," Calix cajoles.

"I'm going to go in. I can see the bottom of the stairs. I'll be fine." Gunnar's voice is hard.

"And what if you're not?" Calix barks. "Listen, just give him a second. He's the Angel of Death, for Christ's sake; he'll snap out of it. He's too fucking stubborn not to." Then Calix calls to me, "Do you think he would let us have you without a better fight than this? You just popped his cherry." Calix tries to make light of the situation, but I can hear the tension in his voice.

"I'm scared," I whisper. I'm never scared.

"I'm going," Gunnar warns, and I hear Calix heave a sigh.

Gunnar appears at the bottom of the stairs, his eyes wildly scanning the place. “I’m in, I’m good...” His words trail off as he sees me holding up Grim against the wall.

Gunnar bounds up the stairs and grabs Grim, lifting him easily. As soon as his weight disappears, I want to crumple to the floor. Gunnar hoists Grim up over one shoulder, and Grim’s long arms dangle down Gunnar’s back, swaying too easily.

With his free hand, Gunnar reaches for mine. “We’re going down and getting out of here,” he tells me, staring into my eyes. I nod, because I want to believe him.

Gunnar goes ahead of me, but he’s half sideways because he doesn’t release my fingers. Once we reach the bottom of the stairs, he looks around the house for another exit. Calix is standing in the open doorframe with his hands braced on either side. He smiles when he sees me, but it’s doleful.

“Can you tell if he has all the entrances and windows warded?” Gunnar asks me, spinning around.

“I can check, but I’m pretty sure.” I nod and wipe my nose with my sleeve.

“Forget it. We’re going to make our own exit, and it’s going to be noisy.” Gunnar squats and uses his hands to brace Grim’s back as he sets him gently at my feet. “Stay here, I’ll be back for both of you.” Gunnar nods his head at me until I match his movement with my own. He’s remarkably calm. Aeson walks over from the bottom of the stairs to join us. I almost forgot about her. Damn good friend I am.

Gunnar moves to a wide expanse of wall, one far away

from windows and doors. He lifts his arms so his hands are up above his head. After one long yell, he pounds his fists and forearms into the wall. Plaster and dust start to fly almost as fast as his arms do.

Within just a few moments, I can see the darkness from outside winking through the hole he's creating. Seconds later, he kicks near the floor, making the hole large enough to walk right through.

He spins, his eyes on me, and between heaving breaths, says, "I should have done that twenty minutes ago. Come on, you two first." Gunnar beckons me and Aeson forward, rolling his arm. I look down at Grim and shake my head in denial. Gunnar lets out a sigh and stomps over. "Fine." He leans down low, hoists Grim right back over the same shoulder, and grabs my hand again. I look up in time to see Aeson use her hand like a springboard against a piece of wood and vault through the hole, landing in the same exact crouch she was trapped in. She bounces up quickly and hops to the side. I don't blame her for moving quickly. Being trapped, even for only a few minutes, sucked.

Calix reaches in through the hole and places his hands on my waist, lifting me from the debris on the ground, and making sure to set my bare feet on the soft grass. I hear the wailing siren of a police car off in the distance I somehow know is for us.

"We need to go, and quickly, if we want to avoid the cops." Calix looks around.

I lick my lips. "I know where to get a car."

CHAPTER 31

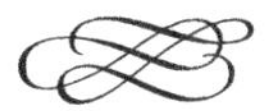

I have Grim's head in my lap. We're almost home, and he still hasn't woken up. I'm too afraid to check to see if he's breathing. In fact, I've been ignoring everyone and everything except my fingers stroking through his soft, dark hair since Gunnar silently placed him in the backseat with me.

Aeson tried to ask me what happened in the room while we broke into my parents' garage, but I just shook my head. I don't know if I can tell her if she doesn't remember, and I can't relive it right now anyway. She ducked off into the night, promising to find her own way home soon after.

Calix slows the car and turns onto my long, narrow drive. We're home. He pulls the car up near the front door and glides it to a stop.

Gunnar opens his door first, then comes to Grim's side. I

look up at him, wishing he would tell me everything is going to be okay, but I'm too afraid to ask. He sighs wearily and tugs on Grim's cloak, pulling him back over to the side so he can pick him up and carry him to the house.

"I'm going to ditch the car, Damiana," Calix informs me, as I shimmy across the seat, hurrying to get out the same door Gunnar just pulled Grim through.

I pause. "Okay, don't go too far. Be safe," I say, telling him words I'd never thought to say before.

"I'll be right back," he promises, meeting my eyes from the front seat.

Gunnar carries Grim all the way up to my bedroom without breaking a sweat. I, on the other hand, feel like I'm boiling. He drops Grim on the bed and a huff comes from Grim's lips. I rush over. "Did you hear that?" I dart my gaze to Gunnar, but I can't look away from Grim for long.

"He's breathing, Damiana." Gunnar lays his hand on my shoulder. It's the first time I've noticed that his knuckles are red and that he has chalky residue on his arms.

"He is?" I swallow the lump in my throat.

"Yes." Gunnar gives a soft chuckle. "I can't wait to tell him how many times I had to save and carry his fat ass."

I click my tongue. "He's not fat…but he's heavy as hell," I agree, watching Grim's chest to see if it moves.

"Do you mind if I shower?" Gunnar hooks his thumb over his shoulder.

"You remember where everything is?" I give him a weak grin, thinking about the first time he used my shower.

Gunnar leans down and whispers close to my lips, "I knew where everything was a long time before that day."

"Stalker." I push his chest, but he doesn't budge.

"I see it now," he whispers, searching my eyes.

"What?" I furrow my brow and gaze back at him.

"It's all of us," he mutters.

"All of us what?"

"He sees that you will love all of us," Grim answers, and drags in a deep breath.

I'm so shocked that he spoke, I don't even think about what he said. I drop down on the edge of the bed and grab Grim's hand. "Are you okay? Don't ever do that again!" I scold, as the water turns on in the bathroom and I realize Gunnar is gone.

"I'll be fine," Grim replies sleepily. He's out again in the next breath.

Feeling much better after hearing Grim speak, I walk toward the lamp on my bedside table and flip it off, before making my way to the bathroom. Gunnar's head jerks up with the snap of the door closing. He watches me as I lean my back against the door.

"Everything okay?" he inquires, his voice a little husky.

"I think it is." I nod.

"Did you need something?" His wide back is to me, so I let my eyes trail over all those beautifully brutal scars covering his body.

"Just you. I'll wait until you're done."

Gunnar licks his lips and turns. His body is bulky, broad,

and sturdy. Honed from hard work and dedication, and covered in the evidence of his will to survive. I take a step closer to the glass that separates us.

"Remember that first day I met you? You were a bloody mess and I still wanted you," I admit, placing my hand on the partition.

Gunnar swallows.

"I wanted to follow you into the bathroom and offer to wash your back." I smile at the reminder.

"You could have." Gunnar's voice is guttural.

"I was afraid of you." His eyes widen. "Not in the way you're thinking." I wave my hand, dismissing him.

"You scared me because I wanted to know you, not just sleep with you." I peer up at him from under my lashes. "Now, I know you. I know you're abrasive and tough. I know when you get upset, so do I. I know you would sacrifice yourself to make sure that I was okay. Them too," I state, whispering the last part, and Gunnar looks away.

I open the shower door and step in with him, fully clothed. "Want me to wash your back?" I grin.

Gunnar nods, biting his bottom lip so as not to let his smile show. I make a spinning motion with my hand, telling him to turn, then I grab the bar of soap from the shelf, lathering it between my hands.

I take my time running my soapy palms all over his back, paying special attention to each scar. I work the backs of his legs and even make him lift each foot to get the soles of his feet. Once that's done, I move to his front.

He looks down at my heaving chest. My shirt is soaked, clinging to me like a second skin. My heart is pounding frantically in my chest, but not from exertion. No, that's all Gunnar and his sexy body, but I make sure to take just as much time washing the rest of him.

After I direct him under the spray to rinse off, he watches me, even letting the shampoo he puts in his hair drip over his eyes, as if making sure I won't disappear.

I step out of the shower and start to pull my clothes off. Gunnar shuts the water off and follows. If I didn't hand him the towel, he probably wouldn't have bothered. He seems way too interested in watching me.

It was hard to ignore his erection in the shower, and it's almost impossible now. I wrap the towel around my body and place my finger over my lips in a shushing manner.

I flip the light off and crack the door open. Grim is still sprawled out on the bed, sleeping, resting, recovering, so I beckon Gunnar to follow me. Silently, we tiptoe out of my bedroom. I hear the sound of the television coming from downstairs. Calix must be home. I didn't turn it on.

A slight weight lifts from my shoulders. They're all here with me, and I'm keeping them that way.

I walk to the end of the hall and push open the door to one of the spare bedrooms. I don't bother with the lights, but I think this room would suit Gunnar. It's dark gray with deep maroon accents. The bed is a heavy dark metal that has an almost lacy filigree design. I drop the towel and reach for Gunnar's around his waist.

He steps up close to me and I tip my head back so I can see him. Gunnar takes it as an invitation to place his lips softly against mine. I sigh.

His hand reaches around me and slides over my back, moving down to the bottom of my ass. He tugs me forward until I'm fitted tightly against him. He doesn't tell me how badly he wants me, but he shows me.

Each caress, each kiss, is punctuated with so much more than just desire. I reach up and run my fingers through his hair and grab the back of his neck, pulling him even closer as our kisses turn more urgent.

Gunnar lifts me using only one hand, and walks us back to the bed. I smile against his lips. He knew right where it was, even in the dark. "You're a stalker, Kitten."

Gunnar makes a growling sound and places me down. Wasting no time, he climbs over me.

I pull him close, greedy for everything he has to offer. He's slow and sweet when he kisses me, but his hands are rough as he runs them over my body, pinching and squeezing like he can't help himself.

I break from the kiss and tip my head back. Gunnar moves down my neck, licking and kissing the column of my throat. I wrap my hands around his head as he moves a little farther down, kissing both of my nipples before focusing on my right. My hips start to lift from the bed, searching for the friction I know he can give me.

Instead of grinding down against me, Gunnar moves his lower body to the side and places his hand between my legs.

I'm already wet when he dips one long finger inside me. He makes a satisfied sound and sucks on my nipple, hard. My hips lift to meet his hand, and his palm connects with my clit. I pant a few times, freezing, because I don't want the feeling to stop. Gunnar slides his lower body closer to me while he's turned on his side. I lift my hips and angle my body until his cock is at my entrance. I let out a small huff when I feel his heat so close to me, and another when he pushes his hips forward, gliding right inside my pussy.

My head tilts back on the pillow as Gunnar lifts my leg in the air, holding my ankle while he pumps into me. I grab both of my breasts as he keeps up the perfect pace. Gunnar's hot breath is near my ear, I can hear every sound he makes, every groan that passes his lips, and it makes me fucking hot.

I grab his thigh and use it to rock harder against him. Gunnar drops my ankle and grabs my chin, roughly turning my face to kiss me. I melt under his touch and curl my leg so it's wrapped around his ass. When he releases my chin, his hand snakes down my center, and he slides his fingers between my legs, easily finding my swollen clit.

Gunnar's steady rhythm picks up, and I get lost in the feeling of him in and around me. It seems like his hands are everywhere at once.

"You thought I was a stalker before," Gunnar purrs in my ear. It's the first time he's spoken.

I chuckle and it ends on a moan when Gunnar circles my clit. "You don't know me very well if you think I mind."

Gunnar shifts on the bed, rising up on his elbow and lifting my leg in the air again. He uses the leverage to deliver deeper, more forceful penetration. I miss his fingers between my legs, so I suck my middle finger into my mouth then circle my clit just like he was.

He starts pumping even faster, harder. I move my fingers lower and feel him sliding in and out of me. Each slap of his hips against mine makes my palm connect with my clit, and I'm spiraling closer to the edge, about to fall over.

A low moan leaves my throat. My breaths are shallow pants, mingling with his. Another shift and Gunnar drops back to the pillow next to me, his face inches from my own, and slides the arm he was leaning on under my butt, rimming my asshole with the tip of his finger. I lift my hips in invitation. He pushes his finger in just a tiny bit, and I'm moaning out my release while he finger fucks my ass and drives his cock into my pussy.

Gunnar places his forehead on my shoulder and gives me several more, hard strokes before groaning through his own release.

I melt into the mattress, completely spent and sated. Gunnar removes his finger from my ass and curls his body over mine.

I wiggle a bit in his tight grip after a few minutes of relaxing. He doesn't let up; if anything, his grip tightens. "I need to use the bathroom to clean up." I nuzzle my head on the pillow anyway.

"Fine, but hurry up," Gunnar orders, right back to mister

bossy, but I know his secret—suspected as much all along. He really is a big sweetie when stroked.

"YOU KNOW what he does with all those marbles, right?" Grim asks, while sitting in the corner, eyeing Uncle. We're on our second hand of cards and I can tell he's a little nervous to be visiting while Grim's here. I glare at him and purse my lips. "He uses them to lure the children away from their parents. Once he has them all alone, he steps out of the shadows and—"

"Scares them!" Calix shouts, adding to the end of Grim's tale and making me jump. I throw a handful of marbles at him, and Uncle makes that dry, raspy sound I know is his laugh.

"Asshole," I mutter without any heat. Calix chuckles and plops down next to me.

"When is Aeson coming?" Gunnar is quick to follow Calix from the kitchen and stands near my chair.

"She should be here soon." I eye Grim. It's been a few days since we went to the witch's house. I still see the strain of what he did to save my friend around his eyes, but he promises he's okay.

"Is she bringing her *boyfriends* this time?" Calix singsongs.

I shrug. "That's up to her." She stopped by two nights ago, with Enzi and a few others by her side, and wanted to know what we were planning to do about the witch.

"No, I'm not," Aeson mocks Calix, and struts into the living room, looking around.

"Hey there, creepy." She lifts her chin to Uncle, and he nods back.

I place my cards down face up, so Uncle knows I'm done playing for now. He reaches over and scoops up all the marbles, even the ones he didn't win, and dips them into his chest. I know without him saying that he's leaving, but I also know that after tonight, he'll be back, and so will my other monsters.

I never thought I could have a life with someone—or three someones as it turned out—and keep the only family that ever stayed by me. "Tell Theius I miss him and to stop by. No one will bother him." I lift my eyes to focus on Uncle. He nods and pats his chest before slinking out into the hall.

"You know, I've never known him to spend time with anyone other than you." Grim studies me.

I shrug. "Maybe he was waiting for someone to give him an invitation."

Grim's head bobs. "Or maybe, he's just as drawn to you as the rest of us."

I scoff and pat the sofa. "Have a seat," I say to Aeson.

After taking her place, she looks around. "So, what are we going to do about the witch?" She gets right down to business.

"Oh, we'll kill him, and make sure that everyone he's ever taught that ritual is dead, too. He can't keep getting away with killing the Charmed and not paying the consequences," I tell her what I've been thinking about for days.

"Okay, so..." She's perceptive, as always. "Any new info from the Pixies?"

"Nothing. Everything that was linked to him has gone belly up in the last seventy-two hours," Gunnar interjects.

Aeson sits forward. "Tell me we have some other way to find him."

Grim raises his hand. "All my Reapers know I want to get notified of every Charmed death, no matter what the circumstances."

"So, we have to sit around and wait." Aeson drops back to the couch.

"What other options do we have? Vanessa's entire coven is gone—dead or scattered. No one knows who he is." The words taste like ash on my tongue, but I won't lie to her.

"That's fucking bullshit." She punches the sofa.

"Believe me, *I know*," I mutter, pissed off again. "But he's been doing this a long time. He won't be able to help himself. He'll do it again, and when he does...we'll catch his ass."

HAPPY HALLOWEEN

ALSO BY ALBANY WALKER

Completed Monsters Series

Friends With the Monsters

Some Kind of Monster

Completed series Havenfall Harbor

Havenfall Harbor Book One

Havenfall Harbor Book Two

Completed Series Infinity Chronicles

Infinity Chronicles Book One

Infinity Chronicles Book Two

Infinity Chronicles Book three

Infinity Chronicles Book Four

Magical Bureau of Investigation

Homecoming Homicide

Creeping it Real

Perfectly Wicked

Dollhouse World can be read as standalone novels

Amusement

Coming Soon Diversion

Standalone novels

Beautiful Deceit

Becoming His

Coming Soon

Stone Will Obsidian Angels MC Shared World MC Syndicates

ABOUT THE AUTHOR

Albany lives in Michigan where she's happily married to her high school sweetheart. She spends most of her time juggling her four children's extracurricular activities, with her nose stuck in a book. When not reading you can find her writing her very own book boyfriends. Albany's passion is writing romance with real characters that are far from perfect, but always seem to find their own happily ever afters.

For updates:

Readers Group Albany's Agents
Albanywalkerauthor@gmail.com
www.albanywalker.com

Made in the USA
Middletown, DE
05 April 2025